Bound to Bigfoot

Ellen Fritz

Bound to Bigfoot by Ellen Fritz
© 2018, Ellen Fritz
Tucson, AZ

Printed in the United States of America

Absence of evidence is not evidence of absence.

Carl Sagan

Chapter 1

Alone at an old picnic table, I glared around at the little kids running, screaming, laughing, seeming to have a wonderful time. Unlike me. I was aggravated by all the fake happiness surrounding me. It couldn't be real.

My thinking turned to Mom. I thought about her all the time, but especially during quiet times. Time to think had me sad about how much I missed her.

I don't know whose idea the camping trip was, but the whole thing was incredibly stupid. Sitting around all day in the woods with almost every foster child in the area hadn't sounded like fun when they told me about it, and I was right. It wasn't fun at all.

So why had I agreed to come? I guess because I'd only been in the 'foster system' for about four months and thought I had to. The others my age must have been smart enough to say, "No Way!" At seventeen, I was the oldest one here, and the closest to my age was a lame fourteen-year-old guy who kept trying to talk to me like he thought I was cute or something, and he had any chance with me.

I didn't like being a foster child and didn't need any reminders of the fact that I had no parents. Being around all these kids just kept reminding me that my mom was gone, and all I wanted was for her to still be alive.

Mr. and Mrs. Patton, my foster parents, were great as far as foster parents could be and were always nice, pretending to understand what I was going through, but they each still had both of their parents. My whole life was out of my control. How could they understand that?

Did our case workers figure this trip would give us some kind of togetherness? Some false sense of family? It wasn't working, not working at all. Surrounded by fifteen other foster kids that I barely knew and three social workers, I still felt as alone as always.

I knew very well that I had no family and never would again. I'd never known my father. Mom said his name was Curt Simmons, but he moved to California before I was born, so I certainly never missed him.

I had no brothers or sisters. My mom was an orphan, too, so I didn't have any aunts or uncles. Now that she was gone, I was an orphan, too. Since she died four months ago, I was alone. A camping trip wasn't going to change any of that.

The Pattons were really nice to me. The social workers were nice. Everyone was nice. But none of them were my family. None of them. Mom was my family and I missed her every minute of every day.

After we ate dinner, Mrs. Carson called us together for a game. We could choose not to play if we wanted, so I just stayed where I was. The other kids were all running over to her.

"Alison," Mr. Jones said as he headed toward the group. "Don't you want to play?"

"I'll just watch," I answered, trying to sound polite. Truth was, I just wanted to be left alone.

"Have you played kick-ball before? I'll show you if you want."

"I've played lots of times. Just don't like it much."

"Okay, but you have to root for my team."

"I will," I tried to smile through the lie. Why would I care who won?

I'd played kick-ball all the time when I was younger, and was pretty good at it. But I guess I'd outgrown it. Besides, I didn't want to play with all the stupid eight-year-olds.

Mr. Jones was my social worker and was keeping a close eye on me. I'm sure he thought I was depressed or something since my mom died, but I didn't have some huge mental defect or anything. I just really missed her.

If Mom was here, she'd be playing kick-ball with the whole group, and I'd love to play with her. We always had fun together and did all kinds of things when she didn't have to work. I couldn't see me playing games like that without her.

I sat and watched them for about an hour before it got too dark for them to see where the ball was going. Mr. Jones had left the game to start building a bonfire over by the tents. I figured I might as well join them there.

One of the social workers had brought a guitar and she strummed it while everyone sang silly songs. I'd never heard most of them before.

I'd claimed one of the smaller logs that formed a circle around the fire because I didn't want to share my seat with anyone else. I was fine alone, but I did join in to quietly sing Bingo when they started it. Mom and I used to sing that after I'd learned it in Girl Scouts.

Before long, though, the fire was burning low and the social workers were all scooting us off to bed. I shared a tent with Margaret, a twelve-year-old girl that said she'd been in foster homes since she was seven. Her parents didn't die. They'd gone to jail for something she wouldn't tell me about, but I didn't blame her. It would be pretty embarrassing to talk about why both your parents were in jail. Like it was sad to admit that my mom died slowly and painfully of cancer.

It felt like I'd been in my sleeping bag forever, but I wasn't anywhere near sleepy. Margaret had been breathing gently for a long time, so I knew for sure she was out for the night. I reached down to my feet for my backpack and pulled out my IPad.

No one knew I'd brought it with me, but I didn't go many places without it. Mom had saved for a long time to give it to me last Christmas. Then she died in January. It was the most important thing I owned.

Mrs. Albertson, my grief counselor, suggested I write letters to Mom to tell her how I was feeling, so I wrote on the IPad. Using the last gift she ever gave me made me feel closer to her as I began to type.

Dear Mom,

I miss you. I'm on the camping trip I told you about and I can't sleep. I wish you were here so we could have played kickball together and we could have sung together. I'd like to give you a hug and a kiss goodnight. Then I'd probably be able to sleep. I'd like to be out of this tent and home with you, but you know that. Goodnight, Mom. I love you more than anything.

Ali

I put the IPad away and crawled back into the sleeping bag, but still couldn't sleep. I don't know what kept me awake, the same thing that usually did, I supposed. I figured it was just not being tired. I wasn't thinking of anything in particular, or worrying about anything. I just wasn't going to fall asleep anytime soon.

It was against all the rules, and I usually followed rules, but I crawled out of the sleeping bag anyway. Peeking through the flap of the tent, I could see a little glow left from the bonfire, but no one was anywhere around. I figured the adults were all sound asleep since they'd been running around with the little kids all day. No one would see me.

Besides, I'd be an adult soon. There were only four months before my eighteenth birthday. Mom told me we were homeless, and she didn't start me in school when she should have because she wanted us to have a home first. She figured it was better than me having to change schools once I started, and having no home address to tell the school. She probably didn't want me to be embarrassed or teased by the kids, either.

Once I was eighteen, though, I'd be making my own decisions about my life, so I shouldn't have to follow the same bedtime rules as the little kids.

I crawled out and immediately went around the back of the tent. We'd set them up all around the bonfire and it reminded me of old movies when they'd circle the wagons every night as the pioneers moved across country. I didn't think that any wild Indians or bandits would be invading the park and attacking us tonight.

I sat behind the tent enjoying the solitude. I'd put on my jacket before coming out, and it felt comfy and warm with the cool air on my face. The stars were shining in the sky and I could see a full moon over the trees, so it really wasn't that dark. Looking toward the woods, I was surprised to realize that I could see pretty well.

I could pick out individual trees and the outhouses on the edge of the field. There were bushes and other undergrowth in the woods, but it was pretty thin on the edges, and I could see a lot of stuff as my eyes adjusted to the dark. I hadn't realized that a full moon could be so bright.

It felt like those trees were calling to me. Without a conscious decision, I got up to head toward the trees and was soon stepping between them. There was something very soothing about walking through the woods in the dim light. And it smelled good.

I could smell green, somehow, and dirt, dead leaves and living things. Thinking of living things made me stop for a second. I wasn't concerned with something hurting me, since there were very few big animals that could hurt someone as big as a teenage girl, but a lot of small things could bite, and I really didn't want to scare a skunk into spraying me. I'd need to pay attention.

At first it seemed quiet under the trees, but I soon realized that I could hear a lot of different noises if I simply listened. There was a subtle sound off to my right that I thought must be some small animal scurrying around. Probably a mouse or maybe something as big as a raccoon for all I knew. I heard crickets, the soft rustle of the new leaves on the trees as the gentle breeze blew through them, and then the sound of some bigger animal slowly crunching through the dead leaves off to my left.

A deer? I hoped so. Deer were all over the hills surrounding Cambridge, and you could see them every so often as you drove along out in the county. Too often, I'd see dead ones along the sides of roads, but, once in a while, they'd wander close to the Patton's house. I loved it when they did that and I could watch them. Mom used to love seeing them, too.

I crept as quietly as I could toward the sound and, through the trees, caught a glimpse of a brown butt with its white tail stuck up in the air. Behind it trotted a little dotted fawn. Both of them were moving quickly to escape me. I was the big, bad human invading their space and obviously not being as quiet as I'd thought.

I was sorry to see them go and sorry I'd scared them. I'd like to sit silently and watch them move around feeding. Maybe I'd even be able to watch the baby drinking its mother's milk. I'd love that.

Most of all, I'd love to pet one. Were they soft or coarse? What would the antlers of a big male feel like? I knew the antlers grew every fall for the mating season before falling off in the winter. As they grew, their antlers would be covered with soft-looking velvet, and I wondered if they were as soft as they looked.

I really wanted to see another one or catch up with that mom and baby, so I practically tip-toed along the path I was following. Mr. Patton told me that the woods were covered with deer trails, and I figured that's what I was following. Deer had small territories and created the paths just by always walking through the same areas. It made me feel like a pioneer or an Indian from one of the tribes that used to live in central Ohio as I traveled along that trail.

Going as quietly as I could, I kept my eyes and ears open for quite a while. It was darker under the trees, but I could still see the path well enough. Finally, I thought I heard a rustling again and stopped so I could listen more carefully and try to figure out where it was coming from.

A little way ahead, another narrow path crossed the one I was following. The sound was coming from my right. Something was moving along that path that would intersect mine. I'd be in a perfect position to see the deer, but would have to be practically silent if I stood any chance of not scaring it away.

Suddenly I realized something was running. It was coming toward me! I ducked behind a tree as fast as I could and peeked out to see a deer prancing and jumping down the trail. Not the same deer with the fawn. This one was bigger and darker.

The sound of something chasing it, though, was really loud and getting louder. It had to be huge to make that much noise, and the first thought that flashed through my mind was that it could be a bear.

I'd been feeling calm and peaceful under the trees, but, in an instant, my heart pounded in terror. I'd heard stories about bears in central Ohio, and it was making way too much noise for anything smaller.

Maybe it was another person? Another camper? A hunter? All these thoughts ran through my brain in a split second as the pounding of feet and the thrashing of tree limbs and bushes got closer to me.

The deer passed me and disappeared into the trees, but the thing chasing it stopped only a few yards from my hiding place near the crossed paths. This gigantic, dark thing stood on the path with its long, hairy arms hanging at its sides. Slightly bent over, its head stretched forward and moved back and forth as it sniffed the air.

The head stopped moving, facing me. I heard it take a big breath through its mouth and nose, and I heard a quiet growl. Its lips pulled back slightly, baring huge teeth, and it growled again. Still a quiet growl, but longer and deeper.

I was frozen to the spot, peeking out through the branches. Hugging the tree as if it was some kind of security, I was glued there. Petrified, fascinated, yet somehow numb. I couldn't think and wasn't even sure if I was still breathing. All I could do was stare out at the face just yards from me.

The full moon shown through the canopy like a spotlight on a stage, and I could see his dark features clearly. Wide mouth, flat nose. But it was the eyes that kept me motionless. They were huge, piercing, and a light color I couldn't quite make out, but they stared right at the tree that I hoped was hiding me.

Suddenly, the silence was broken by a deer that came crashing through the brush behind me and right onto the path in front of that monstrous thing. The deer had probably been hiding too, but let its fear turn to panic.

The monster sprang into action, took about three long strides, and caught the deer just a few steps away. It grabbed the deer by its hind legs and twisted it to the ground. Ignoring the poor thing's struggles and kicking legs, it leaned across the deer, reached up to it's head, and bent it way back until its ears were almost touching its back.

As I watched, it leaned down and took a huge bite out of the deer's neck. Blood spurted all over and the monster threw its head back with a mouth full of bloody, hairy meat. It swallowed and roared an ear shattering scream as if it was announcing its victory into the night. Besides being completely disgusted, my only thought was that I was glad it wasn't the fawn's mother.

What was I thinking? I was definitely glad it wasn't me!

A subtle spasm from my stomach made me realize that I might throw up watching this horrible sight. The monster leaned down and took another huge bite of the deer. Then a third. Blood flowed everywhere, and the sound of crunching and slavering as it ate that poor deer made my stomach clench again.

The creature was so strong. It easily tore a hind leg from the deer's body and took a bite of the meat still attached. Watching these details, I think my brain was slowing starting to work again.

Finally coming to my senses, it struck me that I was watching something that was not only horribly gross, but also potentially dangerous. I could be the next one that that thing decided to make a meal of.

I ran.

No longer following the path, I cut between trees and around bushes. I tripped over a log, but only stumbled and was able to keep on my feet. My arms were flailing as I swiped branches out of my way, and I had to duck under bigger ones. Leaves slapped me in the face and I knew my arms would have been all scratched up if I hadn't been wearing long sleeves, but I had to keep going.

That's when I realized that I didn't know where I was headed. I didn't care, though, because I felt like I was running for my life. Caught in that same kind of panic that caused the deer to run right into the monster's path, I plunged ahead without any clear thought except escape. I had to get away from that monster.

Luckily, I came to the edge of the trees and could see the circle of tents at the other end of the field. I was so thankful. Everyone else must have still been asleep, so I kept running across the grass, easily found tent number seven, and crawled inside.

I sat on my sleeping bag and was sure my breathing was going to wake up Margaret. The air rushed in and out of my lungs as my heart was thumping. That might wake her, too. I took a couple of deep, slow breaths to calm down.

The breathing eventually worked to calm me a little, but I was still terrified, confused, and full of a million crazy thoughts. No way could I think about stretching out between the layers of the sleeping bag to go to sleep.

What had I seen? It reminded me of a big, hairy ape. Really tall with long arms, long legs, hair all over. And it was fast, and strong enough to knock down the deer and kill it by biting out its throat. It ate it in huge gulps, all hairy and bloody. What the hell was that?

What if that thing followed me? What if it came after all of us sleeping soundly in these flimsy tents? The thought of it sneaking up on us and sinking its teeth into our throats terrified me. What could I do?

I crawled back out of the tent, dragging my sleeping bag behind. Instead of getting in, I unzipped it to sit on part while the rest wrapped around me. All I could do was sit there and watch to make sure nothing big and hairy came out of the woods surrounding us. I knew I wouldn't be able to defend us at all, but I could at least scream so everyone else woke up and had a chance to run for their lives.

Scanning the line of trees to make sure that beast didn't appear, I started to calm down enough to finally think about what I'd seen. I knew some people said they'd seen Bigfoot in central Ohio, but come on. They were nuts or liars, weren't they?

They'd seen other campers, hikers, or maybe a real bear. Some of them probably only saw bushes moving around in the wind. But ...

I think I saw Bigfoot.

I didn't want to actually think of it that way, because I didn't believe in Bigfoot and didn't know anyone else who believed in them, either. I mean, come on! Some kind of ape creature living in woods and forests all over the country and no one ever finding one? No one had ever gotten a really good picture or found a dead body. If they were real, wouldn't someone have taken a video? They couldn't be real.

I'd seen the shows on TV where people went out looking for one. They always acted like Bigfoot's existence was a fact, but just hadn't been proven. They heard sounds in the forest and said it was definitely Bigfoot. They saw blurred prints in mud and said, for sure, it was a Bigfoot print. I'd never even come close to believing any of it.

Now I'd seen one. At least, I thought I'd seen one. Maybe it was a hunter. Maybe some old, crazy guy that lived in a cabin out in the woods. But, that big? That strong? Taking huge bites out of a deer and eating it raw? Eating not only the meat, but the fur, blood, everything.

I could maybe believe a hunter was wearing a big furry coat if it was winter, but it was a nice, spring night, a little cool but not cool enough to wear fur. And I'd seen his face. It was covered with hair. Not like a chimpanzee that had bare, leathery skin on its face. It reminded me more of Chewbacca from Star Wars.

I really thought I'd seen a Bigfoot, but kinda' didn't believe myself. Could you trust your own eyes when you were scared to death and stuff was happening so fast? Maybe I was as bad as all those people who claimed they saw something that they hadn't seen at all.

Right then, I knew that I couldn't tell anyone. Ever.

I also couldn't just crawl back into the tent and go to sleep like nothing had happened. Everyone else was sound asleep and helpless, but I was determined to stay awake.

If something came out of the woods, I'd scream and wake Mr. Jones. Otherwise I'd keep the whole thing to myself. No one knew I'd gone out to walk in the woods and I'd never tell them. No one would ever know.

This was a secret I'd keep forever. People weren't going to laugh at me for imaging some creature in the woods. Inside, some part of me was starting to believe I'd really seen it, but I'd be the only one that ever knew that.

Chapter 2

"Ali?"

Someone was gently shaking my shoulder and calling my name.

"Hey, Mr. Brown," I answered when my eyes came into focus.

"What are you doing out here? Margaret snoring too loud?" he smiled down at me.

For a moment, I had no idea why I was sleeping on the ground outside the tent with my sleeping bag wrapped around me. Then I remembered.

"No, I ... I just wanted to sleep outside," I lied.

I'd sat up by then and was a little more alert. When had I gone to sleep? I must have fallen over onto my side or something. And I was going to be a guard for the night. Some good guard I was.

"Sleeping under the stars, huh? And I thought you didn't like camping," he smiled again. "Breakfast is about ready. Better get moving."

I shoved my sleeping bag back into the tent and noticed that Margaret was already gone. She probably told Mr. Jones I was outside the tent, but who cared?

The camp bathrooms were really outhouses and smelled just as bad as anyone would expect them to. It was gross, but what other choice did I have? If I'd been a guy, I'd have sneaked off into the woods to pee on a tree. Would have been much more pleasant.

The social workers always cooked us good stuff, but this was our last meal. We'd start packing up and loading the bus to go home right after breakfast, so they went all out.

Eggs, pancakes, bacon, sausage, muffins, fried potatoes, fresh strawberries, watermelon and lots of orange juice. It was great, and I stuffed myself.

Between bites, I noticed movement under the trees. A shiver of fear raced through my whole body, but it was just a couple of guys. The two big guys coming out of the woods were heading right for us. I knew they were just hikers, but something about them made my stomach flip-flop a little as I thought about what I expected to see coming through those trees the night before.

They definitely weren't Bigfoot or anything, but they were really tall with wide shoulders. They both wore jeans and those tan Carhartt jackets that farmers around here wear. I told myself to calm down, but couldn't help being a little tense.

The guys came into camp and started talking to Mrs. Carson and Mr. Jones, but I couldn't hear anything they said from where I was sitting. Good time to dump my trash because I had to go over there and try to hear something. I felt like I had to know what they were talking about. Maybe they'd seen me, and I had to know if they were telling Mr. Jones that I'd been out wandering in the woods in the middle of the night.

I tried to look nonchalant as I approached the trashcans, but still couldn't take my eyes off them. Dark hair, light eyes, the strong face of the older one smiled easily at our social workers as they talked. The other one was turned away from me, looking around the camp, but I could tell that he was much younger.

The young guy glanced over as I dumped my paper plates and plastic spoons and gave me a sexy smile with one side of his mouth tilting slightly higher than the other. He was seriously hot and stared right at me. I couldn't help but smile back, caught by those amazing pale brown eyes and long, dark lashes that swept down to his cheek as he blinked.

I immediately turned and headed for my tent. I wasn't used to hot guys smiling at me like that and was embarrassed that I'd smiled back. What bothered me the most, though, was that he somehow looked kind of familiar.

So much for trying to hear their conversation, but it was probably nothing. Probably just campers from another area being friendly. I was being ridiculous because I was still scared from the night before and letting my imagination run away with me. The best thing would be to forget about it.

We got on the bus after an hour of packing all our stuff and cleaning the campsite, and Mr. Jones sat next to me. He knew that I wasn't friends with any of the other kids and would sit alone in silence the whole way. He always tried to be extra nice to me, and, today, that could help me get some information.

"Who were those guys in camp this morning?" I tried to sound nonchalant, but didn't think I succeeded very well.

"Hikers. They live just outside the park and stopped to talk."

"Oh." If I could have gotten myself together enough to ask another question, I would have, but I just couldn't think of what else to ask.

"I saw you smile at the young one," he grinned. "He said he's seen you at school."

"He goes to my school?" So that's why he looked familiar.

"Yeah, said he's a senior."

"I've never seen him there." Not really a lie. I wasn't *sure* I'd seen him before.

"He's seen you. I think you have an admirer." Mr. Jones's grin turned into a huge smile.

"I don't want an admirer," I mumbled softly. How embarrassing. I wanted to crawl under the seat, but tried not to show Mr. Jones that.

"Seemed like a nice guy. I'm not talking about a boyfriend or anything, but you could use some friends, couldn't you?"

"I've got all the friends I need at my old school," I said defensively.

"You know none of us liked you having to change schools. We thought it was more important for you to be with a family that would be a good fit for you."

"I know, and the Pattons are great."

"Well, that guy's name is Jake, and that was his dad with him. If you see him at school, maybe you could say hi or something."

"Maybe. So, did they say anything else?"

I was afraid that they'd seen me the night before. Maybe while I was running back to the tent like a crazy woman. If they did, they'd tell Mr. Jones. He'd want to know why I was out there, and lecture me about being safe. I didn't want to answer a million questions about why I was out of the tent. Truthfully, I didn't know why I decided to walk in the woods.

"They thought we might be going hiking today and wanted to let us know we'd need to stick to the marked trails. There were some rough areas off to the west. I guess the last floods washed out some spots and some of them are hard to see."

"Oh." I was being paranoid thinking they'd seen me. They weren't out in the woods in the middle of the night, so how could they have seen me?

"So they just wanted us to know we needed to head in a different direction."

"That was nice."

"You have any plans for when we get home?" It would take us less than an hour to get back to the Children's Services office where all our foster parents would pick us up, so there'd be plenty of time to do something.

"A lot of times the Pattons go to Wal-Mart on Sunday afternoon."

"Now, that sounds exciting," Mr. Jones said sarcastically with a broad smile. I just smiled back at him.

I didn't tell him that I liked going to Wal-Mart because it was in town and I usually saw people from my old high school. It was nice to hang out with them for a little while, but not like it used to be.

Before Mom died, I had lots of friends and had a great time with them. As she got sicker, I spent my time with her and stopped hanging out with friends as much. Since then, I wasn't as interested in friends. On one hand, it was nice to see some of them again, but it kinda' felt like a waste of time. They couldn't do anything to make me miss Mom less, and certainly couldn't bring her back.

Mr. Jones said they didn't want to send me to another school, but I was actually relieved that they had. Strangers were easier to deal with. The kids in my new school didn't all know that Mom had just died. I could just go to classes without everyone looking at me and giving me sad faces. Only the teachers and counselors knew about Mom, so they were the only ones that asked how I was. I was fine. I just missed her every minute.

We were pretty quiet for the rest of the trip, only talking about my classes, grades, and such things. We always talked about that stuff, and I knew it was part of his job to keep tabs on me, but I got pretty tired of it a lot of times.

Actually, Mr. Jones was okay as a social worker. He was nice, listened to me, and didn't bug me a lot. I was glad I got him instead of Mrs. Carson or Mrs. West. They both seemed like the type that would pester their kids. I didn't like to be pestered.

We lived out in the country, and the school was in another part of the county. That's why I saw deer all the time on the roads we had to travel to get anywhere. And that's why I rarely saw anyone from school, but I was okay with that, too. It was just easier.

As we pulled into the Children's Services parking lot, I saw the Patton's car waiting for us. They both got out to help me with my stuff, and Mrs. Patton hugged me.

"Did you have a good time?" Mrs. Patton asked after the hug.

"Sure. It was fun," I answered. It wasn't really, but hardly anything was anymore.

We packed my stuff in the car to head home, and I told them everything we'd done on our overnight campout. We had to talk about something because they'd worry about me if I just sat there in silence like I wanted to. We didn't go to Wal-Mart, but I had other things on my mind, anyway.

I needed to start some research on Bigfoot. I wanted to find out everything I could. I'd heard that there'd been some sightings around Salt Fork, but didn't know much about them. A lot of people were in and out of a state park, and it seemed to me that there would be lots of sightings if Bigfoot was really there.

Besides, I was only about 80% convinced that I'd really seen one. The back of my mind kept saying that it could have been a bear. I'd have to research them, too. I didn't know if they killed deer or not. Whatever I'd seen, though, it sure did kill and eat that deer.

Mrs. Patton helped me wash my stuff and put everything away, and the three of us made some sandwiches for lunch. That was all fine, but I was anxious to be on my own to start my research.

Right after lunch, I headed up to my room and grabbed my IPad. Typing *bigfoot* into the search line, I was immediately surprised at how many different sites there were. Those creatures seemed to be all over the place. Still, I needed to know how many sightings were in Ohio, in Salt Fork State Park.

I searched *bigfoot salt fork state park ohio*. That did it. I found maps, eyewitness accounts, and even some YouTube videos. So I searched YouTube, and there were all kinds. Some were jokes, some were just shadows in the trees, but some looked like they might have been real. Or good fakes.

I knew that a lot of people liked to set up a hoax. They probably thought it was pretty funny to get other people all excited and convinced that Bigfoot was real. I didn't think it was funny. I wanted reliable reports.

Then I remembered that show I'd seen on TV where these people were out in the woods searching for Bigfoot. So I went to the TV Guide website and searched for them. The show was going to be on tonight! That was just what I needed.

At 10:00 that night, after a full day of trying to act normal in front of the Pattons, I was watching the TV show carefully. They weren't in Ohio, but I wanted to learn all I could. They belonged to an organization that specialized in looking for Bigfoot, so I grabbed my tablet and looked it up.

Not only was it a real organization, it looked like they were serious. On their website, I found all the sightings across the country, but was most interested in Ohio. There were so many listed, but only one county had more than Guernsey. All of the Guernsey County sightings were in Salt Fork. How many were there that no one had ever had the nerve to report?

My eyes got wide when I saw the link at the top of the page. They were going to have what they called a town meeting in Cambridge the next weekend. Everyone who had seen or heard a Bigfoot was invited to come tell the story. I had to go.

No way would I be telling my story, but I really wanted to listen to everyone else and know what they'd seen. There'd be some new stuff that hadn't been reported to the website, yet. Or stuff that people hadn't told before. Saturday at 10:00 am. I'd be there.

I wrote Mom almost every day, so I started to type before shutting down the tablet.

Dear Mom,

I miss you. If you're keeping an eye on me from heaven like Reverend Bigelow said at your funeral, then you saw the whole Bigfoot episode in the woods. Are they real? That thing really scared me, but I want to know the truth about them. I don't know why. Maybe because I haven't been interested in much for a long time. But you know that, don't you? I'll be careful. Goodnight, Mom. I love you more than anything. I miss you every minute.

Ali

After not sleeping much, or very comfortably, the night before, I was really tired. Still, I didn't go right to sleep because the upcoming meeting was too exciting. I'd be able to see and listen to other people who'd seen what I'd seen out in the woods. It took me a little while to stop thinking about it, but eventually I did get to sleep.

Chapter 3

The following week at school seemed like it lasted forever. Surprisingly, though, I kept seeing that guy Jake all week. After not being sure I'd ever seen him before, he was suddenly everywhere. Walking down the hall between most of my classes, leaning against a locker not far from mine, strolling through the cafeteria while I ate lunch. Everywhere.

Each time I caught sight of his eyes, it looked like they were just turning away. Was he watching me? Did he turn away because I'd caught him? I felt like he was following me, practically stalking me, but I kept telling myself that I was being pretty arrogant. Why would a hot guy like that be interested in following me?

He was standing just outside the door when I was leaving school Friday afternoon, and he smiled and started coming over to me. I didn't know what to do. Part of me wanted to run, but I really didn't know why. The only reason he seemed creepy to me was that he showed up the morning after my night in the woods. Besides, it had to be my imagination that he'd been watching me all week.

"You're Ali, right?" he asked. I felt awkward and a little embarrassed when I realized that Mr. Jones must have told him my name.

"Yeah ... Alison Adams. You're Jake?"

"Right," he said smiling. He seemed to like it that I knew his name. "Jake Shepherd. When I saw you at the campgrounds, I thought you were pretty cute, even with your hair all sleeping bag crazy." His smile was warm and sweet. Was he flirting with me?

"I ... uh ... hadn't combed it yet," I stammered. I must have looked like crap that day, and this guy was seriously cute.

"I know how it is. Dad and I camp a lot. You wanna' do something? Nothing big, just go to McDonald's or something?"

I knew there wasn't a McDonald's within miles. All the way to Cambridge in fact. "I can't. I've gotta' get the bus and go right home today."

"I've got my truck. I'll take you home."

"No, I can't today," I shook my head. I couldn't face being alone with this guy.

"Maybe some other time, then?"

"Okay," I stammered, looking down at my feet.

"Then I'll see you next week. We'll work something out," he said with another gorgeous smile.

"Okay." And he was gone.

Shit! Had I just agreed to go out with him sometime? Why was he asking me out? I hadn't had anything like a boyfriend since right before Mom died. I think as things got intense when she was dying, Tommy couldn't take it. I knew I couldn't pay attention to anything except Mom. Tommy and I just floated apart, and he never called again. Not that we were a big item or anything. He was a decent guy and we went out once in a while. No big thing.

But Jake was something else. A big, cute guy that looked like he could have his pick of any girl in school. He was really hot and just looked more like a grown man than a high school guy. I wasn't ready for anything serious, and he looked way too serious for me.

I'd have to come up with some excuses, because I didn't think I could face going out with him. Besides, I reminded myself, he'd probably forget about it by next week. Someone like him would move on to another girl without any problem. Some girl with a lot more experience than me.

That night, I forced myself to forget about Jake and told the Pattons I wanted to go to a tennis match at school Saturday morning.

They let me take their car. They probably assumed I'd be meeting friends there and were glad I was doing something besides hanging around.

Of course, I really drove right to North Salem, just outside Cambridge, and found the community center where the Bigfoot meeting was being held. I was excited as I walked in and surprised to see so many people there. All these people had some kind of experience with Bigfoot? I could hardly believe it. Mostly because I wasn't sure if I believed my own story.

They talked and talked. Some people heard sounds in the woods, some saw a figure disappearing into the trees, some saw something far off, and some had pictures of footprints. It all seemed vague, though. No one had seen anything like what I'd seen.

Part of me wanted to tell them they were all lame. I'd seen the monster right in front of me. I looked right into his eyes. He chased down a deer and killed it. It was all within a few feet of me, for God's sake. Hadn't anyone seen anything close to a sighting as good as mine?

By the time it was over, I was disappointed and a little angry. I hadn't heard anything that would really help me get good, solid facts about Bigfoot. No one here seemed to *know* anything. Well, I knew what I'd seen. At least I think I knew what I'd seen.

"Hey, girl, what are you doing here?" I heard as I stepped into the parking lot.

I spun around to see Jake right behind me. "Where ... Were you at that meeting?" I stammered. I hadn't seen him in the audience, but that didn't mean anything. There were a lot of people there and I'd avoided looking around very much.

"Yeah. I saw you sitting a little way in front of me. Have you seen one?"

"No. No, I haven't seen anything. I was just curious."

"That's why I showed up. I figured it'd be a few laughs, but no one there was laughing. They all seemed really serious."

"Yeah. And scared."

"So, wanna' hit McDonald's now?"

"Oh, I can't. I have to get the car back home."

"I could follow you and take you home after."

"Thanks, but I can't." My mind was working furiously, but I couldn't come up with any good excuse.

"You know, I'm gonna' keep asking ya'," he said, leaning his head toward me and smiling.

"You are?" That was a stupid thing to say, but it just came out of my mouth.

"Yeah. You're cute. A lot cuter than the rest of the girls in that school." That sexy smile was cutting through my resolve.

"Well, maybe if we arranged something ahead ..." I was stammering again.

"I've got a family thing tonight, but what about tomorrow afternoon? Maybe a movie?"

I could have made up another lie, but part of me really didn't want to. It was the part that kept noticing his gorgeous face and muscular body. He said that he was going to keep asking, so I might as well get it over with. Besides, Mr. Jones wanted me to make more friends and he seemed to think Jake was probably a good guy. A Sunday afternoon movie was no big deal.

"Okay," I nodded.

"Good, I'll pick you up about noon."

"Okay," and I started to turn toward my car.

"Wait." he called out, still flashing that smile at me. "I don't know where you live."

Of course he didn't know where I lived, but I was having a hard time thinking clearly. He gazed down into my eyes and I couldn't help looking down at my feet. I pulled myself together as best as I could, and told him the address and a couple landmarks to look for. We were way out in the country and it wasn't like following the streets in a town.

"You're practically in Salt Fork, but I'll put it in GPS if I can't find it. Give me your phone number in case I get really lost." He pulled out his phone and entered my number as I recited it.

Then he gave me another smile that almost made me gasp, said goodbye, and walked away. I thought his regular smile was good, but the full thing was amazing. His pale brown, almost caramel eyes sparkled when the corners of those full lips lifted and caused the lines around his mouth to deepen. I suddenly noticed how high his cheekbones were and the hard lines of his jaw that had a little whisker stubble growing along it.

I realized that I was standing there staring after him, and quickly turned away before I got even more embarrassed. There was something about Jake that I hadn't felt from any other guy. It scared me a little when I realized that I was attracted to him. Seriously attracted.

* * *

"How was the meeting?" Jake's dad, Doug, asked when Jake walked into the cabin.

"Same old stuff from everyone. But Ali was there."

"Did she tell what she saw?" Doug asked, looking a little alarmed.

"Nope," he shook his head. "She didn't say anything."

"Then she's not sure," Doug speculated.

"Or doesn't want to be laughed at," Jake answered. "She's really quiet, shy. I don't see her standing up in that group. I'm taking her to a movie tomorrow afternoon."

"You're going out with her?" Doug's surprise showed on his face and in his voice.

"You want me to keep an eye on her, don't you?"

"Because you're in the same school every day. I don't want you getting involved. You know better than that."

Jake laughed. "I didn't propose. We don't know for sure what she saw, so I'm trying to get her to tell me, and what she might do about it. Her being at that meeting was perfect. I just need to get her to trust me."

"Yeah, well, keep your hands to yourself. A quiet girl like that? She could fall hard when a guy like you pays some attention to her."

"Don't worry, I'm not touching her. I'll stay *so* far away, I'll have her thinking I'm gay."

"Don't make light of this." Doug stared seriously at his son. "Be careful. We don't need the complication of someone who doesn't belong to the family."

"Dad!" Jake was surprised that his dad looked so concerned. "I'm not interested in her. Really. Not interested," he said emphasizing each word.

"Okay, but I'm serious. You remember the mess with Max and that girl a few years ago? We're not going through that again."

"I was 14 and not paying much attention," Jake smiled.

His dad wasn't smiling. "You know what happened. Keep this girl at a distance, and be careful. We don't need another dead girl."

"Dad!" Jake protested. "I would *never* put her in danger."

His dad raised his eyebrows.

"You know what I mean." He sighed. "I wouldn't put anyone in danger."

"Jake, you know how easily it can happen. We can't take the chance with a human. We *can't* take that chance. And you sound like you're already attracted."

"I'm not," Jake insisted. "I'm doing what you told me to do."

"I didn't tell you to ask her out. I told you to keep an eye on her. Just make sure you're careful. Don't touch her, and for God's sake, don't kiss her."

"Dad, you know I've always followed the rules. Half the girls in that school flirt with me and want me to ask them out. Hell, some of them are pretty obvious that they just want to hook up. I've stayed away from all of them, and you know it. You know I haven't been with anyone out of the family. Ali's cute, but I'm not about to mess things up for her. She's too shy, too innocent. I doubt if she's ever been with any guy."

"She sounds dangerous."

"I think she saw me pretty clearly, and she's scared."

"And you caught her scent," his dad said, his anxiety clear in his voice. "You should have turned away from a human, but you didn't. If that deer hadn't run, you'd have gone after Ali."

"I was just curious, you know that." Jake stared at his dad, ready to let his anger out. Instead, he shook it off. "I need to convince her she's wrong, but I can't do that until she admits what she saw. The only way she's dangerous is if she convinces anyone else what she saw was real."

His dad looked at him thoughtfully. He knew Jake wouldn't lie to him, but he acted as if Jake was lying to himself. "You think she could convince anyone?" he asked.

"She might." Jake shrugged. "If she believes it, but enough about her. I need to hunt tonight. You going with me or is Uncle Max?"

"There're a lot of humans around. I'm thinking both of us."

"Okay. I'm gonna' chill for a while. See you later."

"Yeah, see you in a few hours."

Doug sat at his desk and worried while Jake went to rest. He'd need the rest before tonight, but so would Doug and Max to keep up with him. He was still so young. Extra strong, extra fast, and still slightly unpredictable.

It took years of hunting to get the control they all needed, but Doug knew that Jake wasn't a kid anymore. If he hadn't had good control, he might have gone after Ali immediately. Thank God that deer bolted when it did, because Ali's scent was drawing Jake in, tempting him. That could have been a disaster.

Ali's sighting was the closest they'd come to being caught in decades. If she'd had a camera, it might have been all over. But she didn't. So it would be her word, and no one would believe her.

Doug had been Jake's sentinel last Saturday, and felt guilty about letting him be seen. But it really wasn't anyone's fault. In the middle of a chase, a sentinel couldn't very well be everywhere at once. Just dumb luck that Ali happened to be right there when he was closing in on the deer.

Worst case scenario, they'd have to move their group out of the Salt Fork area, but that wouldn't be easy. Everyone was happy here, the couples, the singles, the kids. They hadn't had any problems since the incident with Max and the human woman, but Max couldn't help that, either.

He'd met her in town, and the chemical bond had grabbed them with a vengeance. The issue was that she couldn't accept the truth. She was afraid of him, afraid of all of them. Hell, she was even afraid of the other women in their group.

And she ran. Ran into the woods while a young visitor was hunting. The young one didn't know her, didn't have enough control, and had outrun his sentinel. It was the worst recipe for disaster.

Doug could hardly bear to think of it, and he knew Max had never been the same, and never would be, again. It'd probably be best if they all had two sentinels from now on. At least for awhile. Maybe through the summer, while all the humans were around.

Shaking the worry out of his head, he walked over to Max's cabin to make sure he'd be ready for tonight. If not, he'd get one of the other guys. Being a sentinel was still hard for Max, and Doug rarely asked him to do it alone. He'd lose it if anything went wrong or got dangerous.

"Hey," Doug said as he walked in.

Max was cooking something that smelled pretty good. Without a wife he was usually on his own. At least Doug had Jake to share the work while Jake's mom was gone.

"What's up?" Max asked.

"Jake's hunting tonight, and I thought we should both sentinel him. You willing?"

"Sure," Max nodded slightly. "But why? Jake's pretty straight these days, isn't he?"

"Yeah, he is," Doug smiled. He was proud of his practically grown son. "But that girl that saw him last week has me spooked a little. I'm thinking we should all have two sentinels until next fall when most of the humans are out of the park."

"Not a bad idea. I'll chase with you."

"Thanks."

"I think I should hunt tomorrow. You guys chase me?" Max asked even though he knew what the answer would be.

"No problem. Jake doesn't even have school Monday."

"Good," he nodded. "You want some of this?" Max asked indicating the pan on the stove. "Squirrel stew. Potatoes, onion, garlic, carrot. I don't remember what else I put in."

Doug smiled. "Smells damn good."

"Oh, yea," Max smiled back, "and Tabasco, chili powder, some other stuff."

"I'm in," Doug chuckled. "Jake can catch his own tonight."

"So tell me about the girl who saw him last week?" Max asked as he spooned stew into two big bowls for them. He tried to sound nonchalant, but Doug could sense the underlying tension in his voice.

"Jake's watching her at school and he saw her at the meeting this morning."

"Did she tell?"

"Nope. Never said a word. He thinks seeing her there, though, was a lucky break. It'll give him a reason to ask her if she's seen anything. You know, try to get her to talk to him."

"He was drawn to her scent. Is she someone he might be interested in?" Max spoke quietly, but his anxiety was obvious.

"No," Doug shook his head emphatically. "She's not his type at all."

"He needs to be warned. Attraction to a human can really sneak up on you."

Doug knew Max was uncomfortable even hinting at his own experience that ended in tragedy, and there was no way he was going to tell Max that Jake was taking Ali to a movie the next afternoon. "I warned him. He knows how to handle this."

"I hope so."

"Max, I know how much you hurt, but some humans have been brought in. Some can handle it."

"Yeah? I thought Lucy could handle it, but she couldn't. How are we supposed to know? How can we know the woman we love can accept our lives?"

"We can't. But do I need to remind you that our grandmother was human?"

"No," Max shook his head. "She was a strong woman."

"Should we live in fear of every human woman we might touch or even talk to? It was easier in the old days. Women weren't so forward, didn't come after guys. It's not right that Jake has to fight off every girl in that stupid school, but he does, and he hasn't been involved with any of them. He sticks to our own girls like he's supposed to."

"I can't stand the thought of something bad happening to him."

"I know. But, hell, I don't know why we're worried. It's not like we bond with humans very often. It's rare. Jake just needs to get information from this girl."

"Eat your stew, damn it," Max said, intentionally changing the subject. "It's getting cold."

Doug smiled and lifted a big spoonful to his mouth. He felt horrible for Max. Lucy was the one to be his mate, but she couldn't handle the truth about them. If they'd had more time, maybe they could have convinced her that they weren't monsters. At least not most of the time.

The odds were incredibly slim that Max would ever bond with another woman that could be his wife, and, without a wife, he had a hundred years of being alone to look forward to. No one deserved that.

He started to think about Jake's mother. Nina would be back this week after two weeks in Europe, and Doug had almost gone crazy waiting for her. International law had sounded good until they realized she'd need to travel so often.

Their women were the ones with the educations, because the guys couldn't hide who they really were long enough to do college and something like grad school. But the worst would be over after this trip. She'd be starting a new job with different duties, and she'd be home full time with him where she belonged.

She needed to talk to Jake. She'd make him understand how strong a chemical bond could be. First, though, she needed to spend some quality time with her husband. Thinking about her made him miss her more. More importantly, though, her absence meant he didn't have his usual control. That worried him, but he knew he'd get back to normal once she was home.

* * *

I spent all Saturday afternoon with research on the net. The Pattons used to try to get me involved in stuff, but they'd pretty much given up on most of that. They were cool, and took me a lot of places, but somehow knew I wanted to be alone when I was home. Maybe because they were pretty young. Still in their late twenties, I figured they remembered what it was like being a teenager better than a lot of older foster parents.

Right now, Bigfoot research was the only thing on my mind. I read every website I could find and watched parts of episodes from the TV show. Getting to a place where I thought I'd found everything I could, I sat on my bed and thought.

There were questions I had to find the answers to. How come I got so close to the Bigfoot when no one else had? How could I get that close again? Could I get a picture of one of them?

I'd been quietly following the deer, not making any noise, and moving slowly between the trees. The whole time I was in the woods, I was trying to kind of melt in and be part of the forest. Was that the secret?

Maybe the guys on TV were wrong. They were making loud calls and banging on trees. Maybe that just warned the Bigfoot that they were being watched. Listening to the people at the meeting and reading things online, it seemed that everyone saw them accidentally, not while trying to attract them.

One thing they'd said on TV that made a lot of sense to me was that sticking to one area where Bigfoot had been seen before would probably get the best results. *Yeah,* I thought, *that could be the answer.*

I'd go back to the same place and stay just as quiet as I'd been that night. I'd wait. Wait for anything to come to me. Maybe I'd see a Bigfoot again without one of them seeing or hearing me.

At least I sure hoped one of them didn't see me. That's when I started to realize, again, how dangerous all this could be. Would one of them chase me down and kill me like he did the deer? Shit!

"Okay, get a grip," I said out loud. I'd have my phone ready for pictures, so I could easily call 911 as soon as I realized he'd spotted me. Then I'd run. I'd gotten away before because that Bigfoot was kinda' busy with the deer. What if I couldn't get away this time?

Okay. If the worst happened, and I was killed by that big, hairy monster, I had to find a way to let someone know what happened to me. I'd start by emailing the first picture I took to myself. And I'd leave a note in the car. If I got back to the car safely, I'd destroy the note.

It was kind of sick to be planning something that could get me killed, and I didn't really know why I was doing this. Somehow, for some strange reason that I couldn't identify, I had to find out if I'd really seen Bigfoot, or if I was just another nut case. I was pretty sure I had seen it, but there were still doubts. If I could see it again and get some pictures, I'd know.

Did I plan on ever doing anything with those pictures? No. Part of me thought, if there were some hairy monsters hiding in the woods, they deserved to keep hidden. Didn't they deserve our protection instead of exposure? Were they any different from any other endangered species? Of course, the other part of me didn't want to sound crazy if I started telling people.

But I didn't need to decide what I'd do until later. I needed to make plans for now, for tomorrow night when I'd be in the woods. Later could wait for later.

The campground wasn't far from my house. We'd had to take the bus into Cambridge to meet foster parents at the Children's Services building, but it would have been a lot closer for the Pattons if they'd been allowed to pick me up at the campsite.

I could easily get back there myself. It would be easy to sneak out and take Mrs. Patton's bike. It'd only be about a twenty minute ride. No, I'd need a car. I'd be too scared to ride through those dark woods on a bike. Besides, sneaking out on the Pattons didn't seem fair. They always trusted me, and I didn't want to give anyone an excuse to move me somewhere else. Things could be much, much worse than living with the Pattons.

Clara. I could say I was spending the night with Clara, the only friend I'd made since starting at the new school. We weren't really close friends, but the Pattons would believe I'd stay overnight at her house, and they'd probably let me take one of their cars. Much less scary than riding a bike along those dark roads in the middle of the night.

Since there was no school Monday because of Memorial Day, Sunday night would be perfect. It made sense that Clara would ask me to stay with no school the next day. This could work.

"Hi, Clara, this is Ali." Clara had answered on the first ring. She must have had her phone right next to her.

"Hi, Ali," Clara said.

"Hey, I have a favor to ask you."

"Sure," Clara answered with some hesitation. I'd never asked her for any kind of favor and, as a matter of fact, I'd only called her once before.

"Well," I hesitated now that I really had to ask and realized I hadn't planned on how much to tell Clara. Not the truth, but I had to tell her something. "I just need to be out really late tomorrow night, and I thought I could tell the Pattons that I was staying at your house."

"Where are you going?" Clara's voice brightened. Man, she thought I was up to something and sounded like she was looking forward to hearing about it.

"I can't really tell you. I just need someplace to go real early in the morning. Maybe four or five o'clock."

Clara giggled. "Who's the guy? Do I know him?"

"It's not a guy."

"Come on, Ali," Clara teased. "Why else would you need to be out most of the night? Tell me. You going to a hotel? I've never been to a hotel with a guy."

Clara was so sure I was sneaking out with some guy. Well, that worked better than any other story I could think of. "It's someone from my old school. Someone you don't know."

"How hot is he?"

For some reason, my mind flashed to Jake. "He's pretty hot," I said and realized I sounded embarrassed.

"If I let you sneak in my house in the middle of the night, do I get to meet him?"

"No. I think the Pattons will let me take their car, so he won't be with me."

"Damn! I want to see this guy." She almost sighed thinking that I was going to hook up with some strange hottie.

"Maybe someday. So, will you do it?"

"Sure. My parents go to bed at 10:00 almost every night. I'll tell them you're coming over after a movie or something. But, once you get here, you better be ready to tell all."

"Well, that's the thing," I said while my mind frantically searched for a reasonable answer for her. "I might end up not coming to your place at all."

"No fair! If I have to cover for you, I should hear all the details."

"I'll make it up to you. Promise."

"This guy must be pretty good ... or pretty bad. Is he one of those guys that you're not supposed to see?"

"Nothing like that. Will you do it?" I was getting tired of the lies. And starting to feel guilty that I was using Clara like that.

"Sure, I'll do it. Text me when you get here, and I'll meet you at the back door."

"Thanks, Clara."

"See you tomorrow night. Or at school. Either way, I want details."

I really didn't like my plan with Clara, but I knew I couldn't just forget the whole Bigfoot thing and do nothing. I had to go out and watch for them, and there was no other way out of the house. I knew it was dangerous, but I couldn't make myself care. For some reason, I had to do this. It was like I was obsessed with that Bigfoot and had to get all the information I could.

That's when it dawned on me that one night would never be enough. I'd have to be out there for dozens of nights to see one again. There was a lot of luck involved in actually finding a Bigfoot, let alone being close enough to get a picture.

I suddenly felt really stupid. Like I could stroll on out to the woods and *poof,* find Bigfoot ready to pose for my camera. If it was that easy, there'd be a million good pictures everywhere. It wasn't even that easy to find a deer and there were thousands of them all over the place. The smartest thing would be to cancel the whole thing.

I couldn't. I was sure, at least pretty sure, that I'd seen Bigfoot just yards away from me, and had to find out. Was my mind playing with me while I was under all those dark trees, or had I really seen something that most people thought was just a myth?

I'd always thought that people who believed in Bigfoot were kinda' nuts. Or they'd seen something in the dark they couldn't identify and let their imaginations run away with them. I might be one of the second group, but I knew I wasn't nuts.

So I'd do it. I'd give it one night, see if I could find anything, and then decide what I wanted to do. What did I have to lose? The trust the Pattons had in me, my placement in a home that I liked, maybe my life. But still, I had to do it.

I reached for my IPad to write a letter to Mom like I did almost every night. I typed *Dear Mom* and stopped. What was I going to say to her? That I was lying, sneaking out of the house, and planning to sit alone in the middle of the night in the dark woods? That I was setting myself up to get killed? I couldn't.

If she were here, and I told her what I was doing, she'd be ashamed of me. She'd say, "Allison. You know better than that." And I did know better. I knew the whole idea was stupid, but something kept convincing me that I had to do it.

Something was drawing me back under those trees. Something I really didn't understand, but had to follow. I was obsessed with the idea of seeing that Bigfoot again. Reluctant to admit it and a little ashamed of myself, I was determined to go out there. I wouldn't tell Mom because I knew she wouldn't approve, but I had to at least give myself one chance to see him again. A chance to prove to myself what I'd seen.

Chapter 4

Jake was picking me up any minute, and my mind was spinning. What did he expect from a simple Sunday afternoon movie? Hell, what did I expect?

I'd finally admitted to myself that Jake was amazing. One big, tall, handsome, sexy guy. When I pictured him, I could see those incredible smiling lips that I really wanted to kiss. I wanted to feel those long, strong arms around me as his caramel eyes stared into mine.

Would he put his arm around me in the movie? Would he kiss me? Would he try to do more than that? I didn't have much experience with more than that, but Jake made me want to start getting some of that experience.

Or was he just interested in being a friend? Had Mr. Jones said something to him at the campground? Had he told Jake that I needed friends and some kind of social life? Maybe Jake was just being nice to a sad little girl who needed a way to get her mind off her mother's death. God, I hoped Mr. Jones hadn't said anything to him.

I heard the doorbell ring and froze in front of the bathroom mirror.

"Ali, Jake's here," Mrs. Patton called from the hall outside the bathroom. "You ready?"

"Yeah. I'll just be a second." I think my voice sounded normal, but couldn't help admitting to myself that I was scared to death.

"Okay, get a grip," I whispered into the mirror. He'd never given me any hint that he was after me. He acted like a nice guy, like a friend. Yeah, well, a lot of stuff could start with being friends.

Besides, he was nineteen and looked twenty-two. A guy like him had to have a lot more experience than me. Why would he be interested in being friends with a seventeen year old?

The Pattons were happy I was going out when I told them, but now that they'd met Jake, maybe they wouldn't be so pleased. They'd see how much he looked like a grown man and wonder if they could trust him with me. Or trust me with him.

Well, I couldn't back out now. I took a deep breath and headed for the living room where I found the Pattons comfortably talking and smiling with Jake. "Oh," I heard myself quietly sigh. He looked every bit as good as I remembered.

"Hey, Ali," he smiled. "Cute outfit."

"Thanks," I smiled back. It was just jeans with a multi-colored top and a black shrug sweater, but I'd brooded over what to wear forever. I'd had on three different outfits before picking this one.

"We just found out we met Jake's dad when we were looking at cars last week. He owns the Ford dealership," Mr. Patton was saying, but I was hardly listening.

"Oh, yeah?" I mumbled like an idiot.

"You ready to go?" Jake asked.

"Sure."

"Have a nice time, you two," Mrs. Patton said.

"Thanks," I answered.

"We won't be late," Jake said.

"That's fine," Mr. Patton nodded.

We walked out to his gigantic Ford truck in the driveway without touching. He opened the door for me and took my arm right under the elbow to give me a little boost up. Just a gentle grip, but I could feel the strength in his hand. I could also feel a little tingle of warmth spread through me from his hand. I wanted him to touch me again.

"Did you have any trouble finding the place?" I asked as we started down the road. Lame question, but I had to think of something to say.

"Nah, it was easy, being so close to the park. I know my way around the park."

"Oh." I couldn't think of anything else to add. Silence is horrible in that kind of situation, but my mind was blank.

"The Pattons seem nice. They're your foster parents?" Jake said.

"Yeah," I nodded.

"What happened to your parents? If you don't mind telling me." He sounded like he might not have asked if he'd thought about it first.

I didn't like to talk about it, but facts were facts. After all, I *was* in foster care. Kinda' obvious that something had happened to my parents.

"I never had a dad, and Mom died of cancer. No other relatives, really." It always made me sad to talk about Mom so I didn't look at him when I answered. Hopefully he didn't notice.

"I'm sorry," he said quietly, sounding like he really meant it. "How long's it been?"

"Mom died in January. Right after Christmas."

"Just this past January?" He sounded surprised. But there was some pity in his voice, too. That's why I didn't like to talk about it. I hated the pity.

"Yeah. Four months ago."

"Oh, man." He hesitated before asking, "Is that why you changed schools?"

"They couldn't find a good foster home for me at my old school. At least not one that was willing to take a teenager."

"Damn. I wanna' say I'm sorry again, but that sounds like it's just not enough. I can't imagine not having my parents."

"You live with your mom and dad?" Maybe we could get the topic of conversation off me.

"Yeah."

"I don't know what that would be like." Why had I said that? I certainly did know it would be much better than living with no parents at all.

"Sometimes they drive me crazy and I wish they'd leave me alone, but most of the time it's good."

"I think it's better than good," I grinned, hearing in his voice how he felt about his parents. "You just don't want to make me feel bad about it."

He glanced away from the road and looked at me sideways. "You're right," he nodded, smiling. "My parents are great."

I grinned again. "It doesn't make me sad to see someone else happy. I'm glad you're happy."

He made some soft sound like he didn't know how to respond to that. "I wish you could be happy, too," he said with a shrug.

"I'm not sad all the time, even though I miss her a lot."

"My mom's been in Europe for work the last couple weeks, and I miss her every day. Hell, I don't know how I'd react if she wasn't coming back."

"Sometimes you just have to deal with things. You don't have a choice, you know?"

"Yeah, I do know." His voice sounded so serious, but, after all, we'd been having a serious talk. Still, I couldn't shake the feeling that there was something Jake had to deal with, too. I wondered what it could be.

About that time we were pulling into the parking lot at the movie. There were like ten movies showing, but we hadn't even talked about which one to see. We got out of the truck, letting the subject of parents drop, and started walking toward the entrance.

"What'd you want to see?" Jake asked.

"It doesn't really matter," I answered.

"I'm thinking we might need a comedy," he grinned, gazing right at me. Our eyes locked for a few seconds, and I glanced away. There was something special in the look he gave me, and I was embarrassed to see it. A look that said he was really interested in me.

I smiled back while staring at my feet. "Sounds good."

We settled on one of those silly, animated movies mainly because it was starting in about ten minutes. But it really didn't matter to me what we saw because I realized I was happy to be doing something besides sitting around the Patton's house. Strange because sitting around was usually the very thing I wanted to do.

Surprisingly, I was more than happy to be with Jake. The more I was around him, the hotter he seemed, and that was scaring me a little. I'd had the chance to look into his face and felt myself ready to melt. I'd never felt anything like that before.

While he was driving, I'd also had the chance to glance at the rest of him. The muscles in his arms flexed as he drove, and the short-sleeved tee-shirt he wore didn't hide a thing. I could see his chest with those strong pecs and flexing abs. His long thighs bulged against his jeans when his foot moved between the brake and the gas pedals.

That was as far as I let my gaze travel around his body. I was just too embarrassed to check him out anymore. I was getting way too attracted to him, and everything about him made my heart beat a little faster. Even his voice was deep and sexy, and I couldn't stop listening to it.

We'd talked about some serious stuff, and I'd meant everything I'd said, but I would have been happier to just listen to him. He could have told me anything and I'd have been melting, enjoying the sound.

I looked at posters of the other movies while Jake got our tickets and I found myself sighing with relief that we'd be watching animation. What if he'd wanted to see one of those sexy, love story movies? I'd have died of embarrassment. Not because of what they might be doing on the screen, but because I was starting to realize that I'd want to do those same things with Jake.

"Get a grip," I whispered to myself as he started walking toward me from the ticket booth.

I knew this was just a friendly afternoon out of the house. Sunday afternoon isn't exactly the prime time for a hot date, and he hadn't shown much indication that he was feeling the same stuff I was. Just that look in his eyes that, to be honest, I might have misread. I mean, he was so incredibly sexy and I wasn't. He'd said I was cute, and I could accept that, but not hot or sexy.

The movie was good and we both laughed out loud at a couple parts. While his smile was sexy, his laugh was warm and friendly. He didn't make any move on me or put his arm around me, or anything.

He did lean his shoulder against mine to half-whisper something about the movie. I could feel his warm breath against my cheek and I liked that a lot, but he didn't mean anything by it. He did seem to hesitate and lean against me longer than he would have needed to, though. No, maybe I imagined it. He was just making a funny comment about one of the characters.

We walked out talking about the silly movie, and I was honestly feeling happier than I had in a while. Maybe getting out of the house and doing something with someone my own age was a good idea.

But something about him had changed during the movie. There was a lot of space between us as we walked toward the car, and Jake had a funny look on his face. Kind of a worried look with his eyebrows drawn slightly together. I wondered what was bothering him.

"You hungry? We could stop at Wendy's," Jake said as he started the truck.

"That sounds good." Wendy's was right down the street and we didn't say much on the way.

We talked about the movie and how good the double burgers and fries tasted. The whole time we ate, though, I couldn't help noticing how all the girls in the place kept looking at Jake. He was just too hot for any girl not to look. Waitresses, customers, and even some older ladies couldn't keep their eyes off him. He was way out of my league.

"Hey, I wanted to ask you about the meeting yesterday," Jake said while we ate.

"What about it?" I didn't really want to talk about the whole Bigfoot thing and was prepared to deny everything. I wasn't about to tell anyone why I was really there.

"So, you haven't seen one?"

"Me? No!" I tried to sound as honest as I could, but wasn't sure he believed me. "I was just curious, like I said. I mean you always hear about sightings near the park, and I guess I just wanted to hear what people said."

"That's why I went, too," he said as he took a big gulp of his Coke. "There's a lot of stuff on the internet, though."

"That's where I saw a posting about the meeting," I admitted.

"You were searching stuff about Bigfoot?" He smiled like it was a joke.

"No. I was looking at stuff about the park, but saw a link to Bigfoot, so I just thought I'd check it out."

"Do you think they're real?" His expression said that I could let him in on the secret.

"I don't really think anything about them. Like I said, I was just curious."

"I know what you mean," he nodded.

"Do you think they're real?" I turned his question back to him, because I was starting to get the idea that maybe he knew more about them than he was admitting.

"No," he shook his head. "I know a guy who says he saw one when he was like ten years old, but I don't think he knows what he saw. It was probably a bush, or something."

"Probably."

"So, you have any plans tonight?"

Was he going to ask me out again tonight? A little bit of my brain wanted to skip the whole plan of looking for Bigfoot, but most of me knew I had to go through with it. Besides, spending the evening with him might just be too much.

"I'm going over to Clara Miles' house. I'm spending the night."

"Sounds like fun. I have a family thing again."

Okay, he was just making conversation. Not planning on asking me out at all. Why was part of me disappointed?

"Your family must be pretty close."

"Yeah, we are. And ... well ... we live in a really close community, too." He hesitated and looked down at his hands for a second like he was thinking about what he should say. "In fact, I didn't tell anyone that I was seeing you this afternoon. We're kinda' not supposed to hang out with anyone that's not part of our group."

Okay, that's why he looked worried. "Is it your church, or something?"

"Not a church. It's hard to explain."

He looked uncomfortable, like he didn't want me to press him for an explanation. I knew there were all kinds of weird groups that lived in compounds around the country, especially out in rural areas. Was his family part of one of those? It might embarrass him, but I wanted to know more.

"Do you all like, live together?" I asked.

"Not together, but close to each other. And a lot of us are related." He hesitated as he spoke, and I could tell he was having a hard time. "But the point is ... I'd like to ask you out again, but I don't think I can. I'm just ... it'd just be against the rules."

"I get it. Kinda' like you're Amish, only I don't think you're Amish," I smiled.

"No, I'm not Amish," he laughed. "I just want you to know that I like you, but I'm not allowed to get involved with someone like you."

He liked me? Wow, I liked him, too. "Maybe we could just be friends at school, you know? Maybe eat lunch together sometimes. Just to keep in touch."

"I'd like that."

"Good." Yeah, I'd like that, too.

"I'm sorry," he sighed.

"You don't have any reason to be sorry."

"I shouldn't have asked you out. I feel like I kinda' started something that I shouldn't have."

"It's not wrong to make a new friend," I smiled.

He stayed quiet for a minute, like he was deciding what he wanted to say. "I think we'd better head home." I guess he didn't want to say anything else about his family and the group they lived with, but I understood that. Sometimes stuff is just private.

The ride home was pretty silent, but it didn't feel as weird now as it did on the way. I liked him a lot, and he obviously liked me, too. But I'd settle for being his friend because I didn't think I was ready for more than that, anyway.

As we stopped in the Patton's driveway, he turned to look at me. I should have started to get out of the car, but couldn't make myself move. His hand slid across the seat toward me, but it never reached my hand that rested next to my thigh. I had this overwhelming feeling that he wanted to touch me.

He looked right into my eyes, and I saw a longing there. "I want to kiss you. But I can't."

"I understand," I said as I looked down into my lap. I wanted him to kiss me.

"I guess we should say goodbye."

"Yeah. But I'll see you at school Tuesday," I said smiling up at him. That might have been a mistake. His incredible eyes locked onto mine and I could see more than longing there. Something that looked almost like hunger.

That scared me. I was really attracted to him, but his eyes were saying so much more than attraction. Like he wanted to possess me, own me. No one would ever own me.

I pulled myself together and turned away from him to get out of the truck. "Thanks, Jake," I said as my feet hit the ground. He just nodded.

As I got to the front door, I couldn't help turning around to wave goodbye. Those eyes were still locked on me and Jake hadn't moved an inch. I watched from the front window as he sat there like he was frozen. It took him almost a minute to shake his head and start backing out of the driveway.

I didn't know what to think of that. It was a little creepy, but I figured he had a lot on his mind. What kind of a group could his family be part of?

* * *

Jake went straight to his father when he got back to their cabin. "You have a minute?" he asked.

Doug could hear the tension in Jake's voice. Something was wrong. "Sure, son. I was just getting a sandwich and warming some soup. You want some?"

"No, I ate."

Jake sat in the kitchen with his elbows on the table and the heels of his hands pressing against his eyes. His dad could feel Jake's stress radiating around the room.

"What happened?" Doug asked with a tone in his voice that was close to fear

"You were right. I could barely tear myself away from her," Jake didn't look at his dad. He just sat there hiding his face in his hands.

"Did you kiss her?"

Jake's head flew up to look at his dad. "No! Hell, no!" Jake shook his head. His voice was full of emotion as he continued. "I didn't dare, Dad. I touched her elbow helping her into the truck. That's all. But it was sitting next to her in that movie. I could smell her, hear her little giggles and sighs at the movie. I could feel her there … deep inside me."

Doug let the silence build between them, giving Jake a chance to get his thoughts together and tell him the rest. Jake dropped his head to let his forehead thump into the table. "I wanted to grab her and hold her against me. I wanted so bad to kiss her. I could feel the bond starting between us, Dad. What do I do?"

"Did you say anything to her?"

Jake sat up and leaned back against the chair. "I told her the story about the closed community. Said I wanted to ask her out again, but couldn't. And I told her I wanted to kiss her."

"What did she say?"

"She seemed okay with the whole thing," Jake shrugged. "Said we could be friends at school." Jake shook his head. "I don't want to be her friend."

"No. I can see what you want. You're sweating, your skin is flushed. Your eyes are almost sparkling. You want her to be your mate."

"What am I gonna' do?" Jake shouted. "A human! A shy, defenseless human girl! How could I bond with her? She'd never be able to accept us!" Jake's voice got quieter. "Never."

"Stay away from her."

"She wants us to eat lunch together at school and keep in touch," Jake said with pain in his voice. "She has no idea what she's asking of me."

"You have two weeks before graduation. You can stay away from her for two weeks." His dad was trying to stay calm and be understanding for him, but Jake could tell that the thought of him bonded to a Human tore at his dad's heart. "I'll have to," Jake admitted.

"Or you can quit. There aren't many of us that make it through public high school, you know that."

"But I've worked so hard," Jake sighed. "I missed a whole year when I started changing, but I went back. I'm a year older than all those kids, and I've stayed away from everyone! I want my diploma, damn it!"

"Okay. How about if you go Tuesday. If you can't resist her, we'll claim an injury, an accident or something. Maybe the school will let you bring work home to finish."

"I had no idea bonding felt like this." Jake rubbed his face and shook his head.

"It's strong, but it's never one-sided, son. You must have sensed that she wanted you, too."

"So, it's hopeless?" his voice was rising again. "I think she wanted me to kiss her. Does that mean we have no choice?"

"No! You haven't given in to the feeling. Haven't kissed or touched her. It means that you have to stay away from each other so the bond doesn't get any stronger. Then it'll probably pass with time."

"Probably? And if it doesn't? I'll be alone my whole life like Uncle Max?" Now Jake's pain was clear.

"The only other choice is to pursue her and tell her the truth."

"Tell her we're shifters? She couldn't handle that." Jake hesitated for a few seconds before continuing in a voice that sounded almost like a whine. "She's so damn sweet and vulnerable. Shy. Hell, some of our own women have trouble with all our shit."

"Then you have no choice but to stay away from her. But you hunted last night and didn't change until 5:00 this morning. Part of this could be leftover hormones from your shift. Besides, your mom's been gone for two weeks, and we're both missing her strength."

"I sure do miss Mom," he shook his head.

"It'll work out. We'll do whatever we have to so you can get through this."

"Thanks, Dad," Jake said, but they both knew that this situation might not work out. Jake might never be able to bond with one of their own women.

Silence hung in the room for a few seconds. The whole point of Jake talking to her was finding out what she knew, so his dad asked, "Did she say anything about seeing you last weekend?"

"She denied seeing anything, but I could tell she was lying," Jake shook his head. "I know she saw me, but wouldn't admit it."

"Then we'll just have to let that go," Doug shrugged. "No one will believe her anyway."

"I'm going to get some sleep before we chase Uncle Max to-night," Jake sighed as he stood up and stretched his shoulders and neck.

"I can chase him alone if you'd rather."

"No, I think it'll help me work out some of this. I'm on edge and could use a good run."

"Okay. I'll call you when it's time."

"And, Dad, I'm not going to mention any of this to Uncle Max. It'll worry him too much."

"Good idea."

Doug lost his appetite and threw his ham and cheese sandwich into the trash. His son. Bonding with a human female. A very young female. It could hardly get worse than that.

He wanted Jake to bond with one of their own women in the next few years. The women helped keep them stable and safe. They gave them an emotional and physical outlet for all the hormones that surged through their bodies.

Being alone, Max had to shift several times a week. Sometimes more than that. Nina made it possible for Doug to hold it together for at least a week at a time. He could hold a human job and function normally in human society. All because of Nina.

That's what he wanted for Jake. Could a human woman give him that? Jake's great-grandmother had been human, but she was an unusual woman. Incredibly strong both physically and emotion-ally. And determined. Raising two shifter sons, she'd never backed down from any of them. This Alison girl didn't sound like that at all.

"Nina," he whispered into the empty room, "we need you." But she wouldn't be home until Wednesday. They just needed to hang on until Wednesday, and she'd be able to give Jake some of her strength so he could resist this girl. He nodded to himself. Yeah, Nina would be able to help her son.

They still had time. Jake and Ali weren't bonded, yet. The chemistry was just starting to stir them. If they stayed away from each other, nothing would happen. They wouldn't be drawn into the emotional, physical bond that would leave them helpless, barely able to function normally without each other.

Like Max. Doug would not let Jake end up like Max who couldn't even hold a job, was dependent on his brother and cousins to keep him alive, and felt the pain of Lucy's death every day. No. That would *not* happen to Jake.

Chapter 5

I hated lying to the Pattons. They'd been really good to me, and I'd never lied to Mom. At least not since I was about seven and lied about who broke one of her good vases. She hadn't believed me, and I never figured out if I wasn't good enough at lying or if she just knew me so well she could read the truth on my face.

With the Pattons, I'd just gotten away with a big lie. They'd let me use their car so I could go over to Clara's and spend the night. They thought I'd pick her up so we could go shopping before heading for her house. I was set but still felt guilty about it.

I shoved my sleeping bag into the backseat of the car, telling the Patton's we'd probably sleep on the floor in her family room so we could watch movies half the night. I made sure my phone was fully charged, but had to think about what else I might need.

I'd be sitting out in the woods doing nothing but waiting and listening. A heavy sweatshirt and maybe some water bottles and some snacks. But, quiet snacks. I didn't need to be crinkling a potato chip bag. I grabbed a protein bar out of the cupboard and four bottles of water out of the fridge. That would do.

Pulling out of the driveway, my fear started to come back. I really had no idea what I was doing, and wished I had some kind of gun. Of course, I would have to know how to use a gun for that to help. If it came right down to it, though, I'd never be able to shoot something. Even if it was attacking me, I didn't know if I could actually shoot it.

This whole thing could be the stupidest idea I'd ever had. I could turn around, tell the Pattons that I got a call from Clara, and she had to cancel. I almost did it. I slowed down to turn into a neighbor's drive so I could go back, but changed my mind again and kept going. I had to find out.

I couldn't figure out why I was so obsessed about seeing that hairy monster again, but couldn't give up just because I was afraid. It was as if it was calling me back to those woods, and I had to go, had to find out if I'd really seen Bigfoot or had just imagined it. I had to know.

It was Memorial Day weekend, so I expected that there'd be a lot of people at the park. Lucky for me, though, it had gotten cold for the end of May, and threatened rain. That should keep some of the campers away.

I got to the campgrounds right before dark because I wanted to be able to see clearly where I was going until I found a spot to hide. So I grabbed my backpack and rolled-up sleeping bag, locked the car, and headed off into the woods. As I hoped, there weren't many camps set up, at least not within my sight.

The night we were camping, I'd walked into the woods for about a half hour before I saw Bigfoot, or whatever I'd seen, so I tried to follow a deer trail about the same distance. Trouble was, I wasn't sure exactly where I'd entered the woods, but knew I was close. I just couldn't be sure. It was dark that last time, and I wasn't really paying attention. I might be following the same trail, but I didn't remember it sloping up and down hill so much. At least I was sure I was close.

Needing a place to sit and hide before it was completely dark, I had to make do with the area I was in rather than worrying about it being the exact same spot. Besides, I didn't really think the *exact* spot mattered. They must be able to cover quite a distance as fast as they could move.

I found a big pine tree, one of those with the branches sloping down to the ground. If I could see through the branches, it might be a good place to hide and hopefully be out of the rain that felt like it would be starting any minute.

Crawling in, I found the ground under the tree was flat, dry and covered with old pine needles. Looking up, the branches covered me completely. I couldn't see anything above me, and it was still pretty light.

The lowest branches weren't so thick, so it would be easy to peek right through them. I leaned my backpack against the trunk and crawled out. Looking back, I couldn't see my backpack at all from the path. I had to get really close and look right in to where I knew it was. This would be perfect.

I crawled back in, unrolled my sleeping bag and spread it on the ground. Then I decided I'd better unfold it completely in case I needed to pull some of it around me to keep warm. I checked my cell phone connection, and got out a bottle of water. Then I sat and waited.

The thought of the note I'd left in the car still kind of bothered me. I wrote that I was searching for Bigfoot and had sent a picture to my email. It included my email address and password and ended by saying that, if someone found the note, I'd been killed. Killed by Bigfoot.

Writing it had given me the creeps. No one would ever see it if things went well. But, if things went wrong, it would probably become famous. It'd be all over the news with my picture of Bigfoot. That's not what I wanted. I wanted to know that I hadn't been imagining things the last time. Then I'd destroy all the evidence and keep it to myself.

But, if I was killed, I had to let someone know what had happened to me. I couldn't let some hiker find my partially eaten body out in the woods so everyone could wonder what I was doing out there and what had killed me.

That Bigfoot had somehow latched on to me. I couldn't let thoughts of him go, couldn't put him behind me. I wanted to chalk it up to an amazing event that I could take with me and always remember, but that wasn't enough. I had to know.

Maybe it was because I was finally interested in something. Maybe thinking about that Bigfoot helped me think about Mom less. Maybe I was half nuts to believe I'd seen something that probably didn't exist. I only knew I had to see him again, but feared I might not survive the experience.

Chasing the thoughts of my impending death out of my mind, I waited, trying to enjoy the smell of the pine needles that surrounded me. As it got darker, much darker than the previous weekend because there'd been a full moon that night, the woods changed. Again, I heard gentle rustling around me, but it was made by small creatures. What I thought were frogs kept calling through the night. There must be a pond nearby, because they were loud.

Then the rain started. It was just a gentle patter on the leaves and pine needles overhead, so I stayed dry under the tree. It'd been a good idea to hide there. After an hour or so, the rain stopped again.

It seemed so quiet without the sound of the rain. I felt like I was alone in the woods and all the little animals were gone somewhere. Even the frogs were silent. I'd been there for hours, comfortably enjoying the peaceful woods, but the silence felt ominous. Why was it so quiet?

A strange smell started wafting toward me and mixed with the pine smell. Something musty, yet warm. I thought of the way a wet dog smells, but that wasn't it because wet dogs smell terrible. This wasn't an unpleasant smell, but it was very wild.

At first I thought it was part of the trees themselves, but then realized it smelled alive. It had to be some kind of animal. It wasn't the smell of the trees and plants. Not like the dead leaves or pine needles on the ground, either.

Could it be? Could it be a Bigfoot that had gotten wet in the rain? I didn't remember any smell from the last time, but it hadn't been raining.

I'd been comfortable sitting under my tree, but now I shivered as the fear moved through me. The silence, the smell. This was it. I knew it was close. I got out my cell phone and checked the time. It was almost midnight, about the same time that I'd seen the other one. Is this when they usually chased deer through the woods?

Sitting without moving a muscle, I gazed warily out between the branches of my tree. I kept the cell phone in my hand so I was ready to capture a picture of anything that got within sight. Moving only my eyes and head, I waited.

It seemed like forever and there still weren't any noises, so I just kept watching. My legs were starting to get stiff from sitting cross-legged for so long, so I stretched them out as silently as I could. I'd need to be ready to get up and run if something happened.

Then the rustling started. It was something bigger than the raccoons, or whatever I'd heard before, and it was moving slowly along the deer path. Probably a deer again, but maybe a Bigfoot was following it.

There was movement on the path and coming from my left. Big, dark. My God, it was. I stared into the dark and froze, waiting for it to get right in front of me so I could get a picture.

But it didn't come any farther in my direction. It turned and walked into the trees on the other side of the path. It was getting away, but just walking, not chasing anything. I couldn't follow it without being heard. No way was I giving it a chance to see me.

But, even without a picture, I now knew. I knew it was real. I knew what I'd seen before was really a Bigfoot, and here was another one. Or maybe the same one. It seemed a little smaller than before and maybe a lighter color, but it was so hard to tell in the dark. I didn't know how, but it just seemed different.

Then I heard more rustling. Something was moving behind me, off to the right. Another one? Shit! Another sound across the path like a third one was following the first. What had I gotten myself into? Was this a whole pack of them?

The one behind me was getting closer. I thought I was holding absolutely still, but realized I wasn't. I was shaking all over. What if it found me? I never considered that there might be more than one. Did they travel in packs? Did they socialize at all, or live alone like bears?

I wanted to close my eyes and cower against the tree, but I had to see it. I had to. I turned my head slowly to my right so nothing would accidentally see me move. I stared out into the dark and saw a big, booted foot step next to the tree.

It was wearing jeans and I could see the sleeve of one of those Carhartt jackets. It was a guy. I wanted to warn him. Tell him that Bigfoot was right in front of him. Maybe two of them. Tell him to run.

Then he turned a little to his left to look down the path, and I could see his face in the dim light. A face I knew.

Jake was walking across the deer path and heading right at the Bigfoot that had passed into the trees, but then he stopped just off the path. Another guy joined him. It was his dad, I was sure. The same guy I'd seen come strolling into camp with him last weekend.

They talked too quietly for me to hear what they were saying, but didn't seem excited or nervous. I had the feeling they'd done this a lot. Maybe they knew Bigfoot wouldn't hurt them if they left it alone. Maybe they'd seen all kinds of them.

I realized it all made sense. Jake questioned me twice about Bigfoot and why I'd gone to that meeting. He was trying to find out what I knew because he knew more. I started to think that he and his dad probably did this all the time and were some kind of Bigfoot researchers.

The family thing that he'd had two nights in a row. Maybe it was the family business of hunting for Bigfoot. But then, they didn't need to hunt because they'd found them. Jake and his dad followed that one like they knew what to expect. They were way ahead of me.

They walked off into the woods and away from my hiding place. I waited about twenty minutes with all kinds of thoughts about what they might have seen going through my mind before I felt like it was safe for me to crawl out and head for the car. I still moved as silently as possible and as quickly as possible, because, more than anything, I wanted out of there.

My original intent was to go to Clara's, but I couldn't face it. She'd be all over me with questions about this hot guy I was supposedly with and my mind couldn't come up with anything to tell her.

I'd just sleep in the car somewhere and face all the questions at school on Tuesday. By then I'd have had time to think of something. Right now, I had to think about what I'd seen.

I drove into Cambridge and parked in the hospital parking lot where I'd been so many times visiting Mom. I thought I'd be safe and no one would notice the car. I stretched out on the back seat, but didn't think I'd fall asleep anytime soon. I was excited and had way too much to think about to sleep.

* * *

Jake and Doug followed Max into the cave that was well hidden behind a thick growth of trees and bushes. The family had used this cave for almost a century and it still hid them well. If it was ever discovered, they'd have to find somewhere else, but weren't worried about that happening any time soon.

Just outside the park, it was on their own private land where they'd built their cabins, their homes. Their land was clearly posted with no hunting and no trespassing signs, so odds were good that they'd be able to use it for generations to come. Besides, the cave could only be approached from its side and could be difficult to find even if someone knew it was there.

Max sat on the dirt floor leaning against the wall and grunted softly as they approached. Jake rubbed the back of his hand across Max's cheek in greeting while looking into his eyes. He'd change soon.

He could see the blood left on Max's lips and chest from the fawn he'd caught a few miles away from the cave. Max needed to hunt often, but didn't need to eat much during each hunt, so a fawn was plenty.

Doug, Jake, and their cousins had wives and mothers to calm their instincts, so they hunted much less often and needed bigger animals to feed themselves. Full-grown deer were the best choice for them.

"Good hunt," Jake said in a voice Ali would have hardly recognized. It was deep, course, and barely human. But that was what Max would understand.

Max, and all of the males, could understand basic words when shifted, but couldn't talk at all. Still, there were other ways to communicate.

Doug leaned over to greet Max with a face rub. Cheek to cheek, the brothers were as close as any siblings and not hesitant to express their concern for each other. Hunting was always somewhat dangerous and a successful hunt was to be celebrated.

When Doug pulled away from Max, they both barred their teeth and gently growled their congratulations on a successful and safe hunt. There was no threat, no anger. They both knew what was being communicated. Jake couldn't help himself, and joined them in the growl.

Max's expression altered into one of mild pain as his change started. He bent forward and growled louder toward the floor. His muscles started to pulse and seemed to stretch. In actuality, they were shrinking down – back to human size.

The air around Max seemed to vibrate as his body was losing the features of the creature that hunted through the night. He was becoming his human self. Still tall, still muscular, but changing back to his human proportions. Within minutes, the hair that once covered his body was gone.

He sat in the same place, but he leaned over his knees with his face in his hands. Physically, he was again human. Chemically, the hormones that flowed through his body weren't quite back to human levels. He continued to growl, roll his eyes and periodically snap his jaws.

His brain was somewhere between human and beast. The beast didn't understand what was happening to him, but the human knew. Completely naked, slimy from the thick fluid that oozed from every pore as he shifted, Max was nearly back to his human self. Slowly, the human side took over, his breathing slowed, and he looked up at his brother and nephew.

"Thank you, brother," he said as he gazed into Doug's eyes. "Jake," he nodded.

"No problems tonight," Doug said. "A clean hunt."

Clean hunt meant one thing. He had caught and consumed his prey, left the carcass for other predators, and moved calmly and directly to the cave. All without any humans getting anywhere near. Otherwise, Doug would have told him of any problems, just like Jake had been told about Ali after his hunt the previous weekend.

Max stood while Doug poured the buckets of clean water over his head to rinse away the shifting fluid. That would get him clean enough to get back to a real shower in his cabin. After handing Max a towel, Jake took the buckets to the nearby stream and refilled them for the next time they were needed.

Once Max was dressed they began walking to their cabins a couple miles away, talking quietly about nothing important. His dad told stories about events at the Ford dealership, and Jake talked some about school.

By the time Jake got to bed, he was dead tired. Hunting last night and chasing tonight had worn him out. He and his dad wouldn't need to hunt again until next weekend, but they'd go out with Uncle Max again in a couple days. Acting as sentinel for close relatives was the most important job of all.

There were four groups scattered across their land, each with their own cluster of cabins. All related by birth or by marriage, they included eight hunting, adult males, five females, two children, and one couple expecting their first child. Max was the only one who didn't have a wife or mother to help control him. But he was too old for his mother to help him, anyway.

Jake and his cousin Pete would be the next ones to marry, and Jake knew that Pete had almost completed his own cabin near his parents and married brother. Jake looked forward to starting his cabin this summer.

Completing a cabin meant that he would be ready to bring in a woman to share his life as his wife. According to tradition that would mean that Jake and his dad would travel in the fall or winter to another group where Jake could look for a mate. A young woman who would bond with him and be part of him for the rest of their lives.

As Jake stared at the ceiling unable to sleep, he couldn't help thinking that he'd already found his mate. The woman he wanted to bring to his cabin. The woman who would bear his children and keep him calm and controlled. The woman he would always love.

No one in their group had bonded with a human since his great grandfather, Peter, had brought Ester into the group. She had successfully learned their ways, and lived a happy life with them. She gave her husband the control he needed and their bond had given her a very long life.

Could Ali do the same for Jake? Did she have the determination to turn away from her human life and join him in the woods? She was so quiet and shy, how could she stand up to the anger and strength of a shifter when it was necessary for her to control him?

And physically? She seemed so delicate. Would he hurt her when he wanted nothing more than to make love to her? The strength and power of a shifter was not something every woman would want to take into her bed. They may live in human form most of the time, but the creature was still inside, and that creature crept closer to the surface when lost in making love to his bonded mate.

Another problem, though, was that Ali was so young. Seventeen, with a year of high school left. How could Jake wait for her? Once a couple bonded, there was no stalling the inevitable. He would want her with him always, and wouldn't be happy for her to live with strangers. The Pattons were nice people, but they were strangers.

Jake was already feeling anger at all the jerks that walked the halls of that high school with Ali. They had to have noticed her. Her dark hair waving gently onto her shoulders, the bright green eyes that sparkled when she smiled. At about 5'9", she was tall, but thin and delicate. Not skinny. He could see her curves under her jeans and colorful shirts and wanted to touch every inch of her. That thought made him want to hurt any other guy who even thought of touching her.

How could he ask her to turn away from everything human to be part of his life? How would he be able to turn away from her? He had to. He had to never see her again and look for another woman of his own kind to bond with.

Just thinking of Ali made Jake more aware of the creature inside him. That wild, other side of him wanted Ali, too. His dad had been wrong. He couldn't see her Tuesday at school and hope to walk away from her. Hope that the bond wouldn't grow.

If Jake saw her again, he knew that mysterious, chemical bond would be set and he'd be lost. He'd have to tell her everything or walk away to live his life alone like Uncle Max. If the bond took hold, he'd never find another woman to take Ali's place.

To top it all off, something in those woods tonight smelled like Ali. While calmly following Uncle Max, her scent had come back to his mind as if she was right there again. He'd almost started to look for her, but forced himself to turn away and join his dad.

Jake knew there was only one answer. He wouldn't be able to stand being around her at school. His only choice was to make sure he never saw Ali again.

Chapter 6

Monday was okay. I got home from my pretend sleepover with Clara about 9:00 because I thought it would look suspicious if I got home too early, and that was the latest I could bear to sit in that car anymore.

I hadn't slept much, but had time to think through everything and was now sure that Jake and his dad were Bigfoot hunters. Very successful Bigfoot hunters. I figured if they wanted the world to know what they'd found, I would have heard about it by now.

They obviously wanted to protect Bigfoot like I wanted to. They didn't want the world stomping through the woods disturbing them and shooting them. A lot of people would see them as dangerous and a threat. I didn't think they were, and didn't think Jake thought so either.

I'd never heard any story that even hinted at them being dangerous to humans. They were hiding and minding their own business. They were killing and eating deer, but humans did that too.

I was sure Jake and his dad were trying to help Bigfoot, and I wanted to help them do it. They should be able to live in peace like the mountain gorillas, only Bigfoot would have to stay a secret. I wanted to help them keep that secret.

I couldn't wait to see Jake at school on Tuesday. I really wanted to call him, but didn't have his number. While I looked through the phone book and searched online, I kept wondering why I hadn't thought to ask for his number when I gave him mine. There was nothing to do but wait, and Tuesday couldn't come soon enough.

Meanwhile the Pattons had some people in for a Memorial Day picnic. It was nice, but there really wasn't much for me to do. There were no kids my age, which was fine because I didn't like to be thrown together with strange people that someone thought I should be friends with just because we were both teenagers.

The food was good, and we played some volleyball on the lawn. It was fun, but I kept wondering what those other couples would think if I told them I'd seen Bigfoot – twice.

Tuesday morning, I kept looking for Jake at school. I'd seen him around all the time before, but now that I actually wanted to see him there was no hint of him at all. Finally, it was time for lunch and I sat alone watching for him. I checked every guy that came down the hall to the cafeteria, but never saw Jake. Wasn't he in school? Maybe he was sick. How could I find out?

I didn't know anyone who knew him. Maybe I could figure a way to get his schedule. That's when Clara spotted me and practically ran over to me with a tell-me-all look on her face.

"Okay, so you spent the whole night with him. Tell me..." she said as she sat down.

"I never met him," I confessed. But I still needed to pretend like there was someone I planned on meeting.

"What? Didn't he show up?" She seemed so disappointed.

"No ... I mean ... he called me," I hesitated, creating the lie as I went. "His parents wouldn't let him go anywhere."

"Why?"

"He did something ... they grounded him."

"You're kidding. Couldn't he sneak out?"

"I guess not."

"Damn. Well, there'll be another time. I'll cover for you again if you need me to. Then maybe you could cover for me sometime," she grinned.

What the hell have I started? "Yea, we'll see how things work out."

I didn't know what else to say to her. The last thing I wanted was to be involved in sneaking around so she could have sex with some guy. Besides, I really didn't like the idea she thought that's what I was doing.

I might need her again, though. I couldn't very well tell the Pattons that I was spending the night in the woods looking for Bigfoot. Or that I was spending the night in the woods with Jake and his dad. They wouldn't go for that at all.

Thankfully, the bell rang and we had to get to class. I'd figure something out. I needed a new plan instead of saying I was staying with Clara. I couldn't let her keep thinking that I was screwing some guy in secret. Once I talked to Jake, we'd figure something out together.

Sitting in class, I forgot about Clara and starting trying to figure out how to get in touch with Jake. I didn't want to make a big deal of looking for him by going to the office to ask about him, so all I could do was wait one more day. He'd surely be in school tomorrow, and I'd get a chance to tell him what I'd seen. I'd tell him how much I wanted to help and I'd never, ever tell anyone else. It was only one more day.

* * *

Monday morning, Jake had sat down with his dad at the kitchen table and poured himself a cup of coffee.

"What are you doing up so early when you don't have to go to school?" Doug laughed. "I thought you'd sleep 'till noon after hunting and chasing the last two nights."

"I'm afraid to go to school tomorrow," Jake said quietly while staring at the cup on the table.

Doug took a good look at him and could see that he'd hardly slept at all. "What's wrong, Jake?" Doug said hesitantly. He so hoped it was something else besides that human.

"It's Ali. I can't stop thinking about her. If I see her, I know we'll bond ... I won't be able to help it. Last night I even imagined I smelled her in the woods and I felt my beast wanting to go look for her. I couldn't say anything in front of Max, but I had to force myself to stay with the two of you."

Jake kept his head down, staring at the table. He'd blurted it all out as fast as he could. It was so embarrassing to have to tell his dad he was afraid to see Ali again.

"I'll call school first thing in the morning." Doug sat across from Jake.

"I want to start on my cabin, so we can go look for someone this summer. I have to bond with someone else to get her out of my mind."

"The cabin won't get done this summer." Doug was trying to keep his voice casual to spare Jake further embarrassment and turmoil. Inside, though, Doug wanted to scream. Jake was right. He wouldn't forget about Ali until he bonded with someone else. The real problem was that Jake might not find anyone else. Maybe he'd already bonded with Ali.

"Yeah, it will. I'll work on it constantly. I'll get it done and it'll be ready for me to bring a wife back."

"Look, Jake ... it was just yesterday you went to that movie with her. Her scent's still in your head. This will get easier when you've been away from her for a while. Finding a mate can wait. You've got time."

"I don't think I do." Jake finally looked up at his dad with eyes filled with worry and pain.

"Have you already bonded?" There was a little shock and a lot of concern in Doug's voice.

"There's no way. We haven't been together that much. You can't bond that fast, can you? I mean ... I barely touched her."

"No, you shouldn't bond that fast. But I don't want you finding a mate because you're desperate to forget someone else. You'll never find someone under those circumstances. Let's plan on visiting in the fall, okay?

"We'll see. Once I'm out of school, I think it'll stop bothering me so much. I just can't stand the thought of walking around that school, terrified of running into her. You'll call tomorrow morning?"

"I'll call. Don't worry ... I'll take care of it."

"Thanks, Dad." Jake almost smiled at his father as he got up to hug him.

"It's okay, son. Everything will be okay," Doug said as he held Jake. He wished he was as sure as his voice sounded.

* * *

Wednesday came, then Thursday and Friday. No Jake. He must be seriously sick.

How can I find out what's wrong with him? How can I get his phone number?

I'd tried everything I could think of short of walking the halls shouting, "Does anybody know Jake Shepherd?"

Finally, I thought of my counselor. She'd called me in to see her a lot when I first started school here, but had backed off recently. I guess she thought I was getting along okay. This time, though, I'd go see her.

"Hi, Ali, it's good to see you," Mrs. Brookings smiled.

"Good to see you, too," I smiled back. "I have something to ask you."

"Sure, come on in."

We both sat down in her office. It was set up so we faced each other if she swiveled her chair away from her desk, which she did whenever we talked. I felt her gaze and all her attention turned toward me and wasn't sure how to start.

"Well, I met this guy a while ago ... and ... well, I can't find him."

"Can't find him? Does he go to school here?"

"He's a senior, but he hasn't been in school all week and I need to get in touch with him. He has my phone number, but I don't have his."

Mrs. Brookings got a look on her face that led me to believe she was thinking I was interested in some guy that wasn't interested in me. She probably thought he was purposely avoiding me.

"So ... how can I help?" She may not really mean that she'd help, but she'd break that to me gently.

"We're not involved or anything," I said. "We're friends, and he hasn't been in school all week. I'm kinda' worried he's really sick or something."

"What's his name?"

"Jake ... Jake Shepherd."

"Huh," she said obviously thinking. "Seems to me I did hear something about him. You said he's a senior?"

"Yeah."

"Hold on while I ask the senior counselor. He might know something."

Mrs. Brookings left me for a few minutes while she walked over to the next office. It was far enough that I could hear their voices quietly, but couldn't understand anything they were saying.

"Yeah, Ali, there is a situation with Jake," Mrs. Brookings said as she walked back into her office. "Mr. Summerville says he's been hurt and won't be back to school this year. I guess his dad came in to arrange for the teachers to put work together so he can still graduate."

"He won't be back? He's hurt?" My mind was whirling! What could keep him out of school for the rest of the year? It was only another week, but still, it was the end of his senior year. "Can you give me his phone number?"

"No, I'm sorry, but I can't. His dad said he didn't want people calling to disturb him. But I think it would be nice if you wrote him a note. His dad will be picking up his work this afternoon, and we could send the note for you."

"Good idea. I'll write him a note," I said while thinking about poor Jake hurt and all alone. "How did he get hurt?"

"Some kind of an accident while hunting ... although I don't know what he'd have been hunting this time of year," she smiled. "I guess he fell off some kind of ledge. He'll be fine, but it's so close to the end of the year."

My mind was spinning because I knew what he'd been hunting. "When did it happen?"

"I guess Sunday evening."

No, I saw him Sunday night, really late Sunday night, and he'd been fine. Did something happen as they walked away from me? Could the Bigfoot have attacked him? That was a scary thought.

"I'll write him a note," I said trying to keep my fear out of my voice.

I pulled out some paper from my binder, but couldn't think for a minute. I couldn't put in writing what I really wanted to say to Jake.

Jake,

I'm really sorry to hear that you're hurt and hope you feel better soon. They say no one's supposed to call you, so please call me. I really want to talk to you and sure wouldn't mind visiting if that's possible. Take care. Call me.

Ali

What else could I say? My heart was flip-flopping between wanting to tell him I knew about Bigfoot and worrying about how hurt he was. Hearing that he was injured enough to miss the end of his senior year and graduation made me realize that he was important to me. Dismissing the whole Bigfoot thing and him being hurt, I realized how much I just wanted to see him again.

The whole business about him living in some kind of closed community didn't sound like a situation where his dad would welcome me visiting, though. I got the idea that he'd be in trouble if they even knew that we'd gone to the movie and hoped my note just sounded like a friend.

My heart, though, was feeling like he could be more than that. After all, he'd said he wanted to kiss me, and I could tell from the look in his eyes that it was true. I knew that I wanted to kiss him, too.

I gave the note to Mrs. Brookings so she could put it with the stuff his dad would pick up. All I could do was wait for him to call. I'd been waiting all week to see him, now I had to wait again. I hated waiting.

That night I finally wrote another letter to Mom. I'd been feeling guilty all week, but knew I couldn't keep this from her any longer. I told her everything. All the sneaking around, all the lying, and my obsession with Bigfoot. I even told her how attracted I was to Jake, and felt much better once I was done. It was the longest letter I'd ever written to her, but getting it all off my chest let me fall asleep quickly.

Chapter 7

Jake had been felling trees and scraping bark for three days. He was sore and dead tired, yet determined to keep going.

He hooked the last log of the day to the small backhoe that The Family had bought several years ago and dragged it to the home site. Thank God they'd decided to buy it. Before they had the tractor, every man in The Family lugged the logs by hand. This way Jake didn't need to wait for anyone else to help him, and it gave him a lot of satisfaction to do it himself.

Dad had gone into the local big-box hardware store to get all the nails, plumbing, electrical and roofing materials. Cement blocks for the foundation and roofing shingles would be delivered in the next week. Soon, all the basic materials would be neatly stored around the area Jake would dig for the basement. The interior finishes would wait until they were needed. They may live in log cabins in the woods, but they still had modern amenities.

Max was the plumbing and septic tank expert, Uncle Nathan and his son Glen would take care of the electrical, heating and air conditioning, but the rest would be Jake and his Dad. Jake would work on every step, though, even the final furnishing.

Jake had to think that his dad had been right when he said the cabin wouldn't be done this summer, but he would finish it as soon as possible. He couldn't wait to begin laying the log walls that would shelter his wife and children in the years ahead. Those walls would protect them from any danger, any storm, anything that might threaten them. He felt great pride thinking of that.

But his mind still went to Ali. His hard work helped keep him from thinking about her too often, but she was still there. The only thing that would get her out of his mind was to find his true mate, and that couldn't happen until he had a home to give her. So he kept working even though his muscles felt like they might explode. He'd even been too tired from the work to help his dad chase Uncle Max.

But the thing that helped the most was the return of his mother on Wednesday afternoon. She soothed him and helped settle the soul of the creature inside him. After hearing his story of meeting Ali and the beginnings of the bonding process, she knew what he needed.

"My poor boy," she sighed as she touched his cheek. "Go on down to the basement. I'll be there in a few minutes."

"Thanks, Mom," he whispered gazing into her loving eyes and reaching out to give her a hug.

Doug smiled and squeezed Jake's shoulder. He, too, knew that Nina would take care of their son.

As Jake headed toward the basement, Nina walked across the kitchen to Doug's arms. "I've missed you," she sighed as she wrapped her arms around his broad shoulders and their lips met.

Doug breathed her scent deeply. They'd been happily married for thirty years, but he still felt the chemistry of their bond coursing through his body. His deep breaths pulled her scent through him. The sweet, musky scent that was only Nina.

"Jake's not the only one that needs you," he whispered as his mouth moved to her neck.

He buried his face below her jaw, breathing deeply, growling quietly. His teeth grazed her skin making her sigh. That made him growl louder. He never wanted to let go of her again.

She pulled away, taking his face in her hands to gaze into his eyes. "I love you," she murmured.

Doug bared his teeth with another subtle growl. It made him look like he was ready to devour her. That is what the creature inside wanted, but the human in her arms would never harm her.

He would wait until she'd soothed Jake before he took his turn in the basement to feel the calming of her arms. Later, they'd lie together in their huge bed. They would make love passionately, and both human and creature would be satisfied and soothed.

She let go of him. "Do you think they've bonded?" Nina asked Doug once the creature subsided and Nina knew Doug could think clearly again.

"I'm not sure, but I'm afraid they have. From what he says, I don't think this girl will be able to accept us."

"Well," she sighed, "there's not much we can do about it, is there?"

"Nothing except hope he finds someone else at the gathering."

"I'd better go to him," she sighed.

"I'll wait for my turn," he grinned. Nina stroked his face and kissed him once more.

She walked into the basement and smiled at the huge beast standing against the wall. So different from the gentle son that had just left the kitchen, but still her child.

Reaching for his hand, she led him to the overstuffed couch and took him in her arms. This is what he needed. The nurturing of a female he loved. She stroked his hair and held him as they sat together, letting her calmness, her serenity seep into his soul.

The creature inside a male was always ready to force itself out. Always ready to assert itself to run through the forest hunting, killing, and devouring prey. The creature wasn't happy to rest quietly and wait until the male couldn't resist it any longer.

Once a male reached puberty and began to change, it was his mother that soothed him and helped him control the beast. But a mother's love would only soothe him for so long. As he grew older and became an adult male, he would need the love of a mate. It was her emotional love that would replace his mother and keep him in control, but he'd also need her physical love.

The creature inside would need a mate to hold him as his mother had through his life, but his human side also needed to claim and possess his mate's body. It was this physical domination and shared pleasure that helped hold the beast at bay.

It was as if the beast equated the possession of his wife's body with the creature's possession of his prey. His wife, though, was prey that possessed him as well. Male and female, together they kept the male in control and able to function in human society.

The beast held his mother as she stroked his head and whispered soothing words. He understood little, so it really didn't matter what she said. It was the tone of her voice that calmed him. The same tone she'd used since he was born, even before his first change forced itself upon him.

Yet, though her love strengthened him, her influence wasn't what it used to be. He knew that his mother wouldn't be enough for long. His mother felt it, too. He would need to find a mate soon.

Jake grunted softly and whimpered as his mother spoke to him. With his eyes closed, he rested his head on her shoulder and became totally relaxed. Not until the beast was controlled and seemed to be almost asleep, would she move away from him to leave. But the beast never really slept. Only humans relaxed enough for that.

She looked at her son's hairy face and closed eyes as she held that huge body. She could barely get her arms around him. Could a human girl do this? Could she hold this creature and give him love and acceptance like a woman of The Family? How could they ask any human to understand their males enough to give them what they needed?

"Upstairs," she said quietly. He knew that word, and he'd go back to the kitchen once he shifted back to his human self, showered, and got dressed.

"How long since you hunted?" Nina asked as Jake finally came up from the basement and sat again at the kitchen table. He'd barely dried his hair and left his shoes off, but he couldn't wait to join his parents. She'd served the dinner that Doug had gotten out of the oven, and they were ready to eat together.

Jake was noticeably calmer, more relaxed, somehow, more human since his other side had rested in his mother's arms.

"Last Saturday," Jake sighed.

"Not since you've seen Ali?"

"No ... I saw her Sunday."

"I think you should go out tonight," she whispered.

"It's only Wednesday," Jake said with surprise. "I've been okay for a week at least."

"I know. But I think you need the hunt to help rid you of the need for Ali. It may erase the beginning of the bond. It might help you forget her."

"That's a good idea," Doug said. "We hadn't thought of that."

"Of course not," Nina smiled at both of her men. "You guys don't understand your creatures like we women do."

It was true. It was the females who recognized the male's needs and how to overcome them. The females didn't have the ability to shift or the physical strength to hunt with the men, but they had the emotional strength to understand them.

"I know it's early, but I really do think it would help," she continued. "It'll give you an important outlet for your needs."

"Max and I can chase you tonight," Doug added. "Max hunted last night, so he'll be good."

"Okay. If you think it'll help, Mom."

"Can't hurt, can it?" she smiled, reaching out to stroke his cheek. She let her hand rest against his cheek while saying, "Tell me why you think this girl wouldn't be able to handle the truth about us."

"She's just so shy and quiet. So ... innocent, and so young. She lost her mom in January, and I don't think she's over that, yet."

"Of course she's not over losing her mother," Nina said with concern. "But was she attracted to you? Do you think the bond was mutual?"

"I don't know. But the way she looked at me ... I think maybe it was."

"How old is she?"

"I think seventeen."

"She's young. But you're only nineteen. You could wait for her."

"Mom ... I'm so afraid she wouldn't be able to handle it and I'd end up like Uncle Max. I couldn't face that. You and dad would have to always take care of me. I need to find someone from The Family."

"The thing that went wrong with Max and Lucy was that she ran in the middle of the night while someone very young was hunting. It was only his second hunt, and he couldn't resist her running through the trees. Max should have told her in the morning when it had time to sink in."

"You think it was Max's fault?" Jake had never heard any hint of that before.

"No! Not his fault, but ... he was so in love with her, he never considered that she may not be able to accept us right away. The whole thing was so horrible, but it might not have happened if she'd had time to think. Time to remember how much she loved Max. If she hadn't been killed that night, she might have come back to him. Mating with a human can work, but the male has to be very careful."

"You think I should see Ali?" The surprise and shock in Jake's voice was obvious.

"No. You're right, she's too young. But I'm afraid that, to spare Ali, you'll pick a female that isn't a true bond. That can be a horrible life. She won't be able to help you as she should. Just make sure it's a true bond, someone you *can't* live without."

"I get it," Jake nodded.

"Good. Then let's finish dinner and you can hunt tonight. You'll feel better."

"Thanks, Mom." He reached over to give her a half-hug and kissed her cheek.

Chapter 8

After dinner Wednesday night, Jake slept for a few hours before he and Doug headed over to Max's cabin. He'd been working so hard on his new cabin and not sleeping well. After being soothed by his mother, though, sleep finally came easily. It was fully dark by the time Jake woke from his nap, and the woods were quiet that night.

"I think we should head away from the park," Max said as they turned toward the cave. "I hunted last night and the deer may be a little skittish if we hit the same area."

"Good idea," Doug said. "Let's go a little north."

"Sounds good to me," Jake answered.

The cave was pitch black, but Doug lit the torches on the walls that gave them just enough illumination to keep track of the process. They could have used flashlights or any battery-operated light, but the old ways felt more comfortable to them. Jake began to remove his clothes as soon as he could see what he was doing, and Max folded and stacked them on a flat rock against the wall.

Jake stood naked in the center of the dirt floor, and Max could see the change beginning in his eyes. Max watched as Jake began to stare blankly, and as he squinted through the pain that began the process. That subtle but all-encompassing pain that they all knew so well.

Without another word, Jake sat on the bench they'd built about five years before to replace the one that had been used for decades. Jake closed those bright, pain-filled eyes. His breathing became deep as his heart started beating faster. His whole body began to quiver.

The first time Doug brought Jake to the cave, when he was fourteen, his change was out of control. It was going to happen whether Jake was ready or not, which could be a very dangerous time.

Every Bigfoot father watched his young son carefully for the signs in temperament and behavior that indicated his first change was imminent. They watched his growth, breathing, and reaction to others.

If a young man changed without his family near, it could be a disaster. While his father could detect the physical signs of impending change, a young man's mother also watched and waited. She could sense his emotions. She knew when his desire for prey was growing into the need to act.

Jake and Doug had camped for three days at the cave, waiting for the first uncontrollable need to run, to hunt, to devour whatever he could catch. Jake's first time had been a raccoon and a rabbit. Small prey, but enough to quench his first craving for raw, wild meat and blood.

After that night, Jake had learned to feel his need to hunt and had learned to reach deep into himself to initiate the change instead of waiting for it to happen without any restraint. He also learned to change and wait in the basement for his mother when he needed her to soothe him. Doug was proud that he'd learned quickly and gained the control he needed within a few months. That was what every father hoped for his son.

After almost five years, Jake had the control of a grown man. He could start his change or delay it for a better time. Not for very long, though. None of them could delay for long, but Jake had the control he needed to live and hunt safely, surrounded by the many humans that lived within the area.

It was the presence of Nina in their lives that made it possible for the two of them to wait a week or sometimes more between hunts. Every adult male with a loving mate and every young man with a nurturing mother could delay that long.

Max was the one that still hunted as if his beast were new. Without a mate to help him maintain control, he had to submit to the needs of his body.

Jake's mother's calm nurturing wouldn't help for much longer. Maybe a couple years, but no more. Jake was a grown man, and Doug knew that finding his mate was critical to Jake maintaining control.

The actual change happened quickly. Within seconds, Jake was covered with the shine of the viscous liquid that erupted like sweat across his whole body. He grew taller, broader, and more muscular as the dark, course hair sprouted from every pore.

The transformation was complete.

With a deep sniff of the air, a threatening snarl and deep growl, Jake stomped out of the cave paying no attention at all to his dad and uncle. Doug and Max followed as Jake turned to the north and crept silently through the trees.

Jake remembered the decision to head north, away from the park, because his human mind wasn't completely lost to the beast. A small part of Jake remained as he hunted. He knew he had to avoid humans, stay hidden, and move away from any populated areas.

But most of him was under the control of the creature that took over and demanded he hunt. He couldn't speak, couldn't reason like a human, and couldn't understand more than basic commands. Since he functioned from almost pure instincts, what he did best was hunt.

Doug and Max watched him to make sure there were no unexpected problems. They spread out to make sure no humans got close enough to interfere, or close enough to attract Jake's attention. They'd find a way to lead humans away if necessary.

Control over the beast wasn't absolute, and the human part that remained wasn't strong enough to keep them from approaching a human if tempted enough. No traditional prey in the area and the presence of helpless humans, especially running, could lead them to approach the human. It was just luck that Jake had strong control and he was already devouring a deer when Ali started to run that night.

Additionally, the beast had an inborn curiosity about humans. Even after feeding, they sometimes couldn't resist watching humans, moving close enough to hear them, smell them. That's when problems could start very quickly, and that's when the sentinel would need to step in to solve that problem.

It was a very dangerous life they led, but they had no choice. They were born to shift into the beast humans called Bigfoot, and could only hide and live isolated lives away from the human community.

Bigfoot, Sasquatch, Yeti, Wildman, Hairy Man, Skookum in the Pacific Northwest, and Yowie in Australia. Just a few of the names attributed to them over the years and in different parts of the world. There were so many others.

But they knew themselves to be The Family. In so many different areas of the world and so many different languages, they'd never had another name. Populations had grown and diminished as humans moved into The Family's territories, but still they'd remained.

Remained hidden.

There were a lot of people who'd seen them over the years, but no one could prove their existence. Within the last century, it was becoming harder to stay hidden, but they managed. The last fifty years were especially tough, since so many were out looking for them, but they'd do whatever was necessary to hide their secret. The Internet was the worst thing that ever happened to Bigfoot, but there were still enough isolated areas of the world to hide them.

For now.

Jake moved quickly to find the scent of deer, his favorite prey. Most of The Family hunted deer, at least in the United States. Once in a while a calf or colt would be taken, but that drew the attention of farmers, and could cause problems.

It didn't take Jake long. Within an hour, he'd chased down the deer, killed it easily and devoured most of the carcass. Doug and Max watched from a distance as Jake finished and stood, throwing his head back to howl into the dark sky above him.

The howl of conquest echoed through the trees, and Doug and Max couldn't resist their own deep growls in response. Then Jake started to wander. This was the most dangerous time. Jake's beast wasn't ready to give up its existence, even though he was done hunting.

It was the wandering that usually resulted in sightings and near sightings that were reported time and again through organizations that hunted them. While roaming aimlessly through the woods, they were too easily seen or heard. This was the time when a trusted sentinel was most important.

Before long, though, Jake started to head back to the cave. His hunt was over for the night, and he was ready to change back to his human self. Not much longer, and they'd all be safely walking back to their cabins.

Doug thought about how thankful he was that he'd be walking back to Nina. Back to her arms, to their bed, where he could show her his love and how much he'd missed her. She would strengthen his control. It had been so long. He needed her desperately, but Jake needed him first.

For days after the hunt, Jake felt better and could work on his cabin without constant thoughts of Ali. But she wasn't gone. As the week went on, he could see her again in his mind, smell her soft, feminine scent, and hear her gentle voice.

He'd already hunted twice that week, but was starting to feel the beast inside wanting to hunt again. It wanted the release of chasing, overpowering, and consuming its prey. Was it already starting? Was he getting like Uncle Max?

What if Ali could become part of The Family? Could she accept his two-natured existence and love him? If she ran like Lucy had, Jake would be lost. The best thing, if that happened, would be to move in with Uncle Max so they could keep a close eye on each other.

Jake knew Dad gave up much of his freedom to take care of Max's needs. How could he ask his dad to do the same for him? How could he ask his dad to chase him and Max every few nights? It would be too much. Maybe he and Max could help each other. Meanwhile, he knew he'd need to hunt again in the next couple days.

* * *

I'd been waiting for two weeks for Jake to call or at least send me a note back. But nothing. Was he that sick or had his dad not even given him the note? School was out for the summer. Graduation had already happened, and I had no way to send another note.

Most likely, his dad had thrown the note away before Jake saw it. The whole business of Jake saying he lived in a closed community kept nagging away at my mind. Jake's dad probably thought Jake and I were involved and decided to put an end to it.

Jake probably didn't even know I'd sent the note and was trying to get in touch with him. He might even think that I'd forgotten all about him. Even without the whole Bigfoot situation, I was realizing I wouldn't soon forget Jake.

I could pretend we were simply friends, but couldn't forget his voice or the look on his face when he said he wanted to kiss me. Feeling him near me in the movie, and the touch of his shoulder as he leaned over to whisper something were things I'd never forget. His touch, his breath against my cheek, the warm scent of him . . . I remembered them so well.

I had to find him, and there was only one way I could think of to do that. His dad owned the Ford dealership, so he must be there during the day. I'd go into Cambridge and talk to his dad. His dad might kick me out, but I had to take that chance.

I borrowed the car, pretending to want to do some shopping, and went straight to the Ford dealership. I'd never been in a new car showroom before and had a good time looking around at the shining paint and chrome. Then I noticed the prices. No wonder Mom never bought a brand new car.

"Want to test drive this one?" a voice asked behind me. It took me a second, but I soon realized that it was a salesman.

"N-no," I stammered. "I'd like to talk to Mr. Shepherd."

"He's on vacation this week, but I could show you anything you'd like to see. Are you looking for a used model?" I guessed he noticed how young and obviously poor I was.

"I just wanted to talk to him," I said. "Do you know when he'll be back?"

"Not till next week."

"Oh," I said. Now what could I do? "Could you give me his phone number?"

"We're not allowed to give out his cell number. But he might call in ... could I give him a message?" The salesman had a questioning look on his face. What did he think? That I had something nasty going with a guy as old as Mr. Shepherd?

"No. No, that's okay," I said as I started to turn away from him.

"Is something wrong?" the guy asked. I must have let the worry about what I was going to do show on my face.

"No," I said trying to smile. "Um ... do you know how his son is doing?"

"Oh, so that's it," he smiled back. "I hear he's doing fine."

"Good," I couldn't help sighing in relief. "Thanks."

Then I did leave – quickly. I think the guy thought I was just a girl who had the hots for Mr. Shepherd's teenage son. It may be true that I thought he was a gorgeous guy, but I had more important things to talk to him about.

So now what? The only solution I could come up with after failing at the car place was to find him out in the woods because there was no way I could wait for Mr. Shepherd to come back from vacation. I'd been waiting for weeks and couldn't stand to wait anymore.

Jake might not be hunting for Bigfoot with his injuries, but his dad probably would be. If I could just talk to his dad, just explain why I wanted to see Jake, I knew things would work out. Otherwise, I may never see Jake again.

Getting out of the house in the middle of the night, though, was the hard part. No way would I use Clara again. She'd already wanted me to cover for her last weekend and I'd had to make up an excuse about going somewhere with the Pattons. It was just too complicated involving Clara. I think she had things going on in her life that I didn't want to be a part of.

My original idea from weeks ago was what I'd have to go with. I'd sneak out tonight, take Mrs. Patton's bike, and hide in the woods again. I knew I'd been incredibly lucky before. Seeing a Bigfoot both times I'd been out there alone, was beyond lucky. And I knew it would probably take several times to find Jake's dad hunting again.

Part of the problem, though, had been solved beautifully. Searching Salt Fork Park's website last weekend, I noticed that they were hiring summer help, applied immediately, and been offered a job. It might be things like dumping trash, giving directions to tourists, and helping at the lodge, but that would work just fine.

The Pattons and Mr. Jones all thought it was a great idea for me to get a summer job, and I should be able to come up with excuses to stay late at the park so I could continue hunting. At least I hoped I could. Maybe I'd even get a job on the night shift.

That job didn't start until next weekend and I couldn't stand to wait any longer. I had to go out on my own to look for Jake's dad. Besides, I might not be able to find a good reason to stay at the park into the wee hours of the morning. Sneaking out was the only way, and I just had to hope the Pattons slept soundly and wouldn't catch me.

Saturday night, a little after midnight, I grabbed my backpack, tiptoed along the upstairs hall, silently crept down the stairs, and went out the kitchen door that led to the garage. I eased the bike out the small back door of the garage so the noise of the big door wouldn't radiate into the house, and I was on my way.

About a half hour later, I pulled into the camping area of the closed park and hid the bike in the trees next to the parking lot. The nearly full moon was shining brightly like that night of the camping trip, which had given me a lot of comfort as I rode along those deserted country roads.

There were a lot of campers, but they were all in the designated areas which I easily avoided. I found a spot that I thought was close to where I hid the last time, and crawled under the same kind of tree. Now all I needed to do was wait and keep my eyes and ears open.

It wasn't nearly as quiet as the last time. In fact, the woods seemed to be filled with life. Gentle rustlings, the hoot of an owl, even the flutter of a bat's wings sounded near my hiding place.

It was strange how comfortable and safe I felt sitting under that tree. Almost like the world was moving around me and I was just a spectator. Yet, at the same time, I felt like I was the center of the world. Like I was part of the forest, or maybe the forest was part of me.

I saw a deer wander past, and smiled. They were so cute, so gentle. But I couldn't help thinking about how I'd seen that Bigfoot kill and start to eat that one a month ago. I didn't like the idea, but that was the way nature worked. Survival of the fittest, and all that.

A little while later, I heard the sound of something bigger moving through the trees. Not running, just moving slowly and deliberately. Maybe more than one big thing. *This is it*, I thought as I gazed through the branches. *It's got to be.*

I could hardly believe it. Three times out in the woods, and I'd seen Bigfoot every time. It was almost like they were attracted to me as much as I was attracted to them. Really strange, but I had to smile to myself thinking about how lucky I was.

The big, hairy creature came out of the trees on my right, and started to follow the deer path in front of me. He wasn't chasing the deer, though, just walking, almost strolling, along the path. My eyes were wide as I watched it, and I could feel my heart beating faster.

The plan was that it would pass by my tree like the last time, and I would see Jake's dad following behind as it moved along its way.

That's not what happened.

The Bigfoot stopped next to my tree, raised its chin and seemed to sniff the air. *Is that how they find deer?* I wondered. *Do they smell them?*

Then it bared its teeth and let out a subtle growl. It must have detected something. It'd start striding away toward that deer any minute. *Poor deer*, I couldn't help thinking.

But it didn't go anywhere. It just moved its head from side to side, sniffing the air, like it was trying to zero in on something. Then it pivoted to its left, sniffed deeply again, and I could see its wide, pale brown eyes reflecting the dim light from the moon. Its eyes were almost caramel, like Jake's.

Oh, God! I thought, as the realization hit me.

He's looking right at me!

He sneered and growled again before taking a step toward my hiding place. I got to my feet as fast as I could, crashed through branches at the side of the tree, and ran. Ran for my life.

The Bigfoot screamed as I started running away from him, and quickly started to follow. I was running as fast as I could, pushing branches out of my way, stumbling over clumps of weeds and sticks on the forest floor. But I kept hearing it getting closer. It continued to make half growling, half screaming noises.

In all the accounts I'd read on the internet and listened to at that meeting, I'd never heard of a Bigfoot actually chasing someone. This one was definitely chasing me, and it was catching up.

I thought I was getting close to the end of the trees, but wasn't really sure what direction I was going. What good would that do me, anyway? If I only had the car, I could lock myself inside. A bike wouldn't do much good. I'd just have to jump on as quickly as possible and ride like the wind. If I could get to it in time.

Its footsteps, grunts, and growls kept getting louder. I zigzagged my way through the trees to try to lose him. I ducked through bushes and behind trees, trying anything I could think of to get away, but nothing was working.

Without me realizing the Bigfoot was so close, it suddenly grabbed me from behind and pulled me back against its body. I squealed, then screamed as loud as I could as those long, hairy arms wrapped themselves around me – one across my chest, and one across my hips. My arms were plastered against my body, and I was being held so tightly, I could hardly move.

I kept struggling. Kept screaming. Its head was on my shoulder as its mouth pressed against my neck right under my ear. It stood up to its full height, lifting me off my feet as I kicked and squirmed with every bit of strength I could find. I couldn't hit him--and for some reason I was sure it was a male--with my arms pinned tightly to my body, but I kicked his legs as hard as I could. I didn't know if it was hard enough for him to even notice.

Somehow my brain registered that he was smelling me. Over and over, I heard the sounds of sniffing, punctuated with soft cries, grunts, and whimpers. So far, he wasn't biting me. He wasn't trying to bite my throat and devour me like he'd done to the deer. I was thankful for that, but what did he want?

Maybe he wasn't used to the scent of humans instead of deer. Maybe, once he figured out I was perfectly edible, he'd be willing to make a meal out of me. How long would the sniffing and grunting go on before he decided to take a big bite?

I realized he was lowering me as he dropped to his knees and gently rolled onto his side. Never changing his grip, he'd laid us down on the leaves and pine needles like lovers spooning. He continued sniffing my neck and my hair, while his quiet cries grew louder. Somehow, I had the crazy feeling he was making happy sounds.

The sounds I was making were not happy. They reflected my terror. Grunts from my efforts to break away, fearful moaning, and screaming, "Stop! Let me go!"

Stretched out on the ground, pressed hard against his big, hairy body, I couldn't figure anything to do. I kept squirming, yelling, and trying to twist away from him, but was getting nowhere. He was just too big and too strong.

Then he bit my shoulder.

My terrorized screaming ramped up louder and became frantic. I screamed loud and long because I thought the next bite would be him killing me. He threw his head back and actually screamed with me. I could turn my head enough to see the red mark of his teeth on my shoulder, but he hadn't broken the skin. No blood, but it hurt like hell.

When his scream stopped, he continued with the sniffing and gentler bites up my neck and across the top of my back. Then I felt his teeth on either side of the back of my neck. I could feel his whole mouth and tongue on me and figured this was the end. He was going to bite through my spine, and I'd be dead.

With another high-pitched shriek, I started to fight and kick harder. I fought him with all my strength, but nothing I did could get him off me, and his mouth still held on to my neck, making it hard for me to move much at all.

"No! Bad! Bad!" came a shout from behind us. A human voice.

"Help!" I screamed. "Help me!"

Suddenly, a man's face was in front of me, staring directly into the Bigfoot's eyes. He touched that big, hairy face and spoke quietly, but forcefully. "No! Bad!"

The Bigfoot moved his mouth from my neck and let out a whimper that sounded sad. He grunted and shook his head, but didn't let go of me.

"Stop!" another voice said forcefully. The other man hunched down next to the first man and also touched the Bigfoot's face. It was Jake's father.

The Bigfoot whimpered again, even sadder this time, and rolled away from me. His arms just relaxed and I was free, but still too shocked to move.

Jake's dad stepped over me to approach the Bigfoot.

The strange man leaned farther down to look into my face and asked me if I was alright.

"I don't know," I stammered. I thought I was alright, but I was so pumped up from fear and trying to get away I couldn't really feel much. "He bit my shoulder, but I don't think it's bleeding."

The man pushed the neck of my shirt to the side and looked at the shoulder I indicated, and nodded. "You'll have a hell of a bruise," he said quietly and somehow apologetically.

He looked over me as I lay almost frozen on the ground. "Doug?" he said.

"He's better, now," Doug answered. "I'll start walking him back. Bring her along, but at a little distance."

"Do you want me to tell her anything?"

"No. I need to think. Just bring her to the cave."

As they talked, I felt my stomach roll. I got to my knees, turned to the side and threw up into the leaves. The man touched my head as my stomach emptied and sweat beaded on my forehead.

"That's the adrenalin," he said quietly. "You'll be okay."

"Did he say a cave?" I mumbled, wiping my mouth and somehow feeling embarrassed that he'd just watched me hurl.

"It'll be okay," the strange man nodded.

"But ... I need to go home!" I wasn't thinking clearly. My heart was still thumping in my chest and I felt exhausted as the adrenalin drained away, and I needed time to think.

"Not yet. We'll get you home in a little while."

"No, I'm going now." I got to my feet, but the guy took my arm and started leading me toward where Doug had taken the Bigfoot. "Let me go!" I snapped at him.

"Look, I can't let you go until we've had the chance to tell you what's going on here, and we have to make sure he's safe," he said, tilting his head, to indicate the Bigfoot that walked next to Doug through the trees. "So walk with me, or I'll have to carry you."

"Carry me?" Then he gave me a look that let me know he wasn't kidding in the slightest. I started walking with him. After being grabbed by that Bigfoot, I really didn't want to get man-handled by this guy.

I'd been terrified when that Bigfoot had his arms around me, but was almost as scared of this strange man leading me through the trees. He was with Jake's dad, so would he really be that dangerous? I couldn't see Jake's dad hurting me, but what did I really know about him? Nothing.

"By the way, my name's Max," he said without ever letting go of my arm.

"I'm Ali," I answered automatically.

"That's what I figured," he mumbled.

I gave him a questioning look, but he just ignored it and kept walking. What had he meant by that? How would he have any hint what my name was?

We walked in silence most of the way. I tried to tell him why I was out here and what I wanted, but he just kept shushing me. "We need to be quiet. No talking," he whispered.

Okay. I couldn't figure why. Obviously Doug and the Bigfoot that I could see walking next to him in the distance knew we were there. But this Max guy wouldn't let me say another word.

Suddenly we stopped, but all I could see was dense bushes at the foot of a small cliff. The stones rose above us, but I didn't see any kind of a cave like Jake's dad had mentioned.

"Where are we?" I whispered taking a chance. Maybe I'd be allowed to talk now.

"Near the cave," Max answered quietly. "We need to wait."

I heard grunting, groaning, and some whimpering from behind the bushes. The cave must be hidden back there.

Then it dawned on me. "Is Jake's dad in there with the Bigfoot?"

"He'll come out to get us soon."

He stood there next to me, still holding my arm. I had this strange feeling that he didn't want to look at me. He just stared off toward the cave while we waited. What were we waiting for?

"Is he safe in there? The Bigfoot won't hurt him or anything, will it?"

"He's safe," Max answered with a crooked, little smile. Why was he smiling?

About ten minutes later, Jake's dad came out from behind the bush and sighed as he looked at me. "We're going to take you in there," he said to me. "But ... it's going to be quite a shock for you. You just need to stay calm long enough to hear us out, okay?"

I knew my eyes were huge. I must have looked like a scared rabbit or something, but he was letting me in on some Bigfoot secrets. A big part of me was scared to death, but I was also excited. I wanted to know Bigfoot secrets. They probably had him in a cage or something. Maybe they'd even drugged him. Whatever it was, they were including me.

Max held back the bushes and Doug led me in. Standing in the middle of the dirt floor was Jake. His hair was wet, his eyes were gleaming, and he was smiling his sexy smile, but with unmistakable worry in his eyes.

Chapter 9

"Jake!" I smiled and took a step toward him, only to see him take a step back.

"Hey, Ali," he said, breathing hard.

"I thought you were hurt ... didn't think you'd be out here. Are you better, now?"

Jake looked at his dad before answering. "I'm great."

"I'm glad. I was worried about you."

Jake made an odd face and looked back at his dad again.

"Might as well start telling her, son," his dad said quietly.

Jake looked back at me. "Can I kiss her first?" he asked quietly. Talking to his dad, but staring at my eyes.

That surprised me, but before I could say anything, I heard Max sigh like he was in pain.

"I'm sorry, Uncle Max," Jake said, looking at him with worry in his eyes. "Do you need to leave?"

"Yeah, I think I do. Good luck, boy."

"What is going on here?" I asked as I watched Max head out of the cave. Everyone was acting so strange.

"Can I kiss you, Ali?" Jake asked so sweetly, but I was embarrassed.

"Jake ... your dad ..."

"It's okay," Jake answered quietly as he took a step toward me. "He understands."

The next thing I knew Jake had his arms around me and was staring deeply into my eyes. "Just ... just one little kiss, okay?" he whispered.

Then his lips were on mine. I'd kissed several boys before, but this was something else. Besides his warm, velvety lips, I felt something move through me.

A warmth radiated from his body to mine. I could feel his muscles pressing against me, but I could also feel some kind of a mental, emotional connection that I'd never felt before. It was amazing. I groaned softly as his lips moved on mine.

Then, as his lips pressed harder, I got a little scared. This was strange. Almost like I could feel some kind of connection being forged between us. It swirled from him to me, and, somehow, from me to him. I pulled back to break the kiss.

He gazed into my eyes with a look of wonder. "I knew it," he sighed.

"Jake," his dad said calmly. "You need to talk to her."

Jake stepped back from me and looked almost scared. "Where do I start?" he asked his Dad.

"Hey, guys," I said before either of them could continue with whatever bizarre business they were talking about. I was still recovering from that remarkable kiss, but had to tell them what I knew. "You don't need to tell me as much as you think. I came out here to find your dad so I could tell you both that I know Bigfoot is real. I've seen one twice ... before tonight ... and I saw both of you chasing one. What happened to that Bigfoot tonight? Is there another part of the cave somewhere? How did you get him off me?"

I began to look around to see if there was another passage or something. The two of them looked kind of shocked.

"Ali," Doug said, "We've got a lot to tell you, but ... when did you see us chasing a Bigfoot?"

"That Sunday night that Jake was hurt. Did the Bigfoot attack him or something?"

"I told you I smelled her," Jake said to his dad with a smile.

"Smelled me?" *What the hell was that about?*

"I think we need to sit down," Doug said.

He put his hands on the back of my shoulders to lead me to a bench at the back of the cave. Jake sat beside me and Doug sat on the floor in front of us.

"Well, Jake," Doug said. "You're the one that has to do it. Start with tonight."

"Yeah," Jake answered, nodding. He turned towards me, hesitating and looking apprehensive. "Ali, the Bigfoot you saw tonight was ..." he began, then glanced at his dad before continuing, "was me."

A little laugh burst out of my throat. "What? Is this a hoax?" I'd laughed when he first said it, but then, my voice got more serious. In fact I was getting a little mad. "Have you guys been playing Bigfoot, or something?"

Had they been fooling me all along? Was I just like those other idiots who thought they saw something that wasn't real at all? Why would they do that?

"No! We haven't been *playing* Bigfoot. We *are* Bigfoot."

"What are you talking about? You're sitting here right in front of me. We were in school together. You're not looking much like Bigfoot right now." I was back to practically laughing as I said it. *What kind of a joke is this?*

"Okay," Jake said. I looked down at his dad who was watching me with a serious look on his face. "Bigfoot is real," Jake continued. "Only Bigfoot is a shifter. No one catches us or ever finds a dead body because we're usually in our human form. Every so often, though, we have to shift so we can hunt. Being two-natured is what we are. We can't help it."

"A shifter?" Was I hearing him correctly? I didn't know what to think and wasn't quite sure I knew what he meant by shifter. "You mean ... like a werewolf or something?"

"I don't know about werewolves, but ... yeah ... we're shifters like werewolves," he shrugged. "Only the full moon doesn't have anything to do with it."

"You've got to be kidding me. That Bigfoot tonight. You're saying it was *you*? Only you shifted into a Bigfoot? You grabbed me, and sniffed me ... and bit me!" My voice got angry toward the end of that little speech. I'd moved right through confused disbelief into anger.

"I couldn't help it. We ... you and I, have bonded. That's why I couldn't come back to school and take the chance of seeing you again. We're bonded mates. You felt it when we kissed. Didn't you?"

"Mates? Were you planning on ... raping me?" I suddenly knew that the sniffing and nibbling weren't the aggression of a Bigfoot that wanted to kill me. It was the passion of a Bigfoot that *wanted* me.

"No! Oh, God no! I'd never do that! It was my human side wanting to show you how much I love you, but my Bigfoot side couldn't express it any other way. We don't have anything to do with our females when we're hunting. Bigfoot doesn't have sex. All he knows is hunting and feeding. But I would never hurt you. Would never hurt any female."

"But that wasn't *really* you. I mean ... if I believe this, it was you inside, but you attacked me and you hurt me. You bit me, hard!" I couldn't get my mind around what he was saying, trying to explain to me. But I could still feel the pain of that bite on my shoulder.

"I'm sorry. But I didn't draw blood. I was trying to show you how much I love you. When I had your neck in my jaws ... I wanted to bond with you, but my human part knew we weren't ready for that, yet. I just couldn't stop on my own."

"How much you love me? You hardly know me." *Even if I believed the whole shifting business, how could I believe he loved me?*

"With us it's a chemical bond. We know."

"Maybe you do, but ... *I* hardly know *you.*"

"Didn't you feel it? When we kissed. Couldn't you feel the bond connecting us? I felt it."

"I felt something, but ... I don't know what it was."

"It was our bond." He got such a miserable look on his face. "Ali, I need you. We have to be together."

"Excuse me? Are you saying that now I have to sleep with you because of some chemical bond that I'm not sure even exists? Not happening," I said as I leaned back away from him. This business of us having to be together was just too much. I was mad as hell.

"Ali, I ... I ..."

He was a mess by this time. He looked like his emotions were all out of whack and I was afraid he was going to start to cry or something. Did he really think I'd be ready to fall into his bed just because he said we were bonded and meant to be mates? Was he crazy?

"Jake," Doug said calmly. "Let me explain."

Jake just nodded while he took several deep breaths and look devastated. What was wrong with him?

"Ali, Jake is not making things clear for you. His emotions are out of control right now. It's just that it's so important to him that you understand."

"Then explain." I sounded snippy and angry, but I didn't care.

"You see, the females of our species don't shift. They give us the control we need to function in human society. They give us the strength we need to only shift once a week or so. That's why I'm able to own a car dealership and not have any problems.

"When young, our males depend on the closeness with their mothers to find that control. That's why Jake's been able to go to school. Most of us can't finish high school, but he and his mother are both very strong. Once we reach adulthood, though, we have to bond with a mate.

"When Jake met you, he knew the two of you would bond, but, truthfully, didn't want that to happen with you because you're human. We normally don't bond with humans, but it does happen sometimes. My grandmother was human.

"But, if the human woman can't accept us, a male will never find another. He'll never have enough control to live as a human. That's what happened to my brother, Max. That's why he had to leave.

"So, while Jake feels the permanence of your bond, you both need time to get to know each other and make plans. It doesn't mean that you'll start a sexual relationship, but it does mean that Jake will need to spend a lot of time with you."

"Yeah, Ali," Jake interrupted. "I'll need to be near you, and touch you. We have time to sort things out."

"The main thing, Ali," Doug said, "is for you to decide if you can accept us. It's your choice. You need to decide if you can eventually live with us and be the strength that Jake needs."

"Live with you? As Jake's mate? His wife?"

"Eventually," Doug said carefully.

Meanwhile I looked at Jake. He was a mess. I think he wanted me to say right then and there that I'd mate with him and live with him forever. He looked like he might lose it if I said no.

How was I supposed to say anything now? I'd listened carefully while Jake's dad spoke to me, but wasn't even sure I understood half of what he'd said. While I liked Jake and was really attracted to him, I couldn't commit to a lifetime together. I hardly knew him. And the whole Bigfoot, shifting thing?

"I-I don't know what to say," I stammered.

"Just say that you'll spend time with Jake. You'll date, get to know each other," Doug said in his smooth, calm voice.

"Please, Ali?" Jake asked. His face was so sad. Just looking at him, made my heart ache.

"Yeah, we can spend some time together. But I can't promise that it'll be forever. I don't know if I want that. I don't know what I want."

Jake looked devastated. "Please, don't leave."

"Jake," Doug said quietly. "Listen to her. She said she'd spend time with you. She didn't say no."

"Yeah," Jake said and smiled a little. "Can I see you tomorrow?"

Tomorrow? I didn't know if I'd be able to get my mind around all this by tomorrow. "I guess," I mumbled.

"Can I pick you up in the morning? We'll go for a long walk ... maybe see a movie again."

"Okay," I said hesitantly. "About 11:00." It just came out of my mouth, but then, I had no idea what else I could say. I guess I should have said goodbye and gone away, but I couldn't.

Then he gave me one of his killer smiles. "We'll get to know each other," he sighed and reached out to take my hand.

"I think I need to go home." By this time, I was completely overwhelmed. I needed to be out of that cave and alone where I could think.

"I'll take you," Jake said as he popped up off the bench. He was ready to go right that minute.

"Jake, I'd like you to go check on Uncle Max," Doug said. "I'll take her home in her car and you can follow later to pick me up."

Jake looked at his dad like he didn't like that idea at all. "I think she needs some time. You gave her quite a scare tonight."

"Please don't be afraid of me," Jake said staring into my eyes. "I would never, ever hurt you."

I stared back into those dreamy, brown eyes. "No, I don't think you'd hurt me. When you were holding me, I couldn't do a thing to get away. You could have done anything to me, but you didn't. I didn't appreciate the bite, but it'll be okay."

Jake smiled again and kept staring at me. It was like he couldn't take his eyes off me.

"Let's go get your car," Doug said.

"I rode a bike," I said, finally looking away from Jake's eyes. "It's hidden in the trees next to the parking lot."

"A bike? Brave little thing, aren't you?" Doug smiled.

"I try," I smiled back.

"Jake, go get the truck and meet us at the parking lot."

"You rode a bike all the way out here in the middle of the night?" Jake's expression had changed, but I didn't really know what it was. He looked scared, worried, angry, and determined all at the same time.

"I snuck out, but I couldn't take a car without being heard."

"You snuck out? Alone?" Now the anger was showing in his voice and I didn't like it.

"Yes, I did. I can take care of myself," I answered with a little bit of anger in my own voice.

"You can't do that. It's too dangerous. I can't allow you to be roaming around the countryside all by yourself in the middle of the night!" He was actually yelling at me.

I yelled back. "Allow me? Who do you think you are? You can't tell me what to do just because you think we have some kind of bond thing going on. Even if we were married, you'd have no right to tell me what to do!"

Jake growled and stared at me. It was really close to the same growl I'd heard from Bigfoot, but this one was angry.

"Jake!" Doug said firmly, but calmly. "You're getting a little intense here."

"But she could have been hurt!" He spoke to his dad but kept staring at me.

"But she wasn't. You think I don't worry about your mother when she's gone on business trips? I know it's hard, but you have to back off."

Jake rubbed both his hands over his face. After a minute, he quietly said, "Okay. I'll back off." But I could see the anger was still there.

"Good. Now go get the truck. Go."

Jake started toward the cave entrance. Before he left he turned to look at me one more time. The anger was gone, but the longing in his eyes was unmistakable.

Doug and I walked back toward the parking lot where I'd half hidden the bike. I could see Jake jogging through the trees the other way. Toward what, I had no idea. We walked in silence for awhile, but then questions started popping into my head.

Part of me wanted to talk about the whole control freak thing Jake was pulling back there, but a bigger part of me didn't. In a way, he was right that it was dangerous, but he still didn't have the right to tell me what to do. That's one I'd have to talk to Jake about.

"Where do you guys live?" I asked, settling on an easier topic.

"We have quite a bit of land alongside the park. We each have a cabin and several families live fairly close to each other."

"Jake told me he lived in a closed community."

"We own the land, so no humans live anywhere near us."

"What about the cave?"

"It's part of our land. It's where we shift when hunting. Keeps things private."

"I kinda don't know what to think about all this."

"I know," he nodded, seeming to understand.

"Jake seemed so intense." I hadn't planned on talking about it, but there it was.

"Part of that was your influence. Just being close to you, and your scent."

"Was he serious? Does he really think we're bonded forever?" We'd been talking very calmly, but getting back to the subject of Jake spiked my emotions again.

"Very serious. I hope you'll eventually feel the bond with him, and come live with us."

"I just don't know how I feel about all that." Except scared, confused, disbelieving, and still a little angry about him biting me and trying to order me around.

"It's really hard for a human to understand and accept us. I know it'll take time, but Jake ... he's just kind of lost in the chemistry of the bond. He'd just shifted back to human form, and it takes us a while to be fully human again."

"Fully human," I murmured. "That sounds strange."

"I know it does. But we're actually more human than Family. That's what we call ourselves – The Family. Humans gave us the name Bigfoot."

"And a lot of other names. Are you all one thing? I mean ... all the different creatures people say they've seen. Are they all you?"

"Yeah, we're all Family. Different parts of the world, different languages, variations, but we're all pretty much the same. Like you're different from an Asian, but still the same."

"Amazing." We were quiet after that. I don't know what Doug was thinking, but I had all kinds of thoughts and emotions swirling through me.

"How did you get this way … you know … shifters?"

"No one really knows. Evolution, I guess," he shrugged. "Some say we might have descended from Neandcrthals, others that we already existed when they did. Most seem to think that there were once three of us, Homo Sapiens, Neanderthals, and Family. It was the Neanderthals that didn't make it."

We were soon at the parking lot without saying much more, and could see Jake sitting in the truck waiting. I thought we'd have to wait for him, but the truck must have been close to the cave.

"How far did he go to get the truck?" I asked.

"Not very far, really. But he's pretty fast when he wants to be."

"I guess so," I said quietly, mostly to myself.

"Sure I can't ride along?" Jake asked as he jumped out of the truck.

"No, I really do want you to check on Max. You'll see Ali soon enough."

Jake was smiling and seemed more back to his old self. "Yeah. I'll see you tomorrow at 11:00."

"See you tomorrow." I smiled back.

Jake lifted the bike into the back of the truck and watched Doug and me drive away. I watched him watching us. My mate? I sure was attracted to him, especially after that kiss, but committing to him for life? How could I do that?

I had no answer. At least not right then. My mind was in a whirl and my emotions were even worse. I didn't know what I thought about all this.

Sometimes my mother would tell me to be careful about what I wanted. Now I understood what she meant. I wanted to know about

Bigfoot. I wanted to kiss Jake and get to know him better. I'd gotten all that, but did I want everything else that went along with it? What had I gotten myself into?

Doug parked down the street from the Pattons and we walked my bike to the back door of the garage together. He lifted it up on the hooks in the wall for me.

"I hope you don't let Jake's behavior tonight influence you too much. It takes us a little while for our hormones to readjust to human form, and he didn't have much time. A lot of what you saw tonight was still the influence of Bigfoot."

"He was really different at the movie. Did you know we went to a movie together?"

"He told me."

"Did you give him the note that I sent with his school work?"

"He thought he didn't dare contact you. And he was right. You know what one sniff of you did to him tonight."

"It's all so hard to believe."

"I know, but it's true. I'd like you to meet Jake's mother, Nina. I think you'll be able to see how normal we are most of the time."

"She doesn't change or anything?"

"No, our females don't shift. But it's hard to put into words how important they are to us. They keep us centered. Keep us human. Without them, we have very little control."

"She must be something special."

Doug just smiled as he thought of his wife for a moment. "Try to treat Jake the way you did before you knew. Just a guy you're dating. You do like him, don't you?"

"Yeah, I like him. But I don't know if that's love. I don't have much experience with love."

"Neither does Jake. Maybe the two of you can learn what it is together."

I tried to make myself smile. "He's just so sure."

"I know. And the whole thing tonight was pretty intense, but ... don't let that scare you off. Just give him a chance, okay?"

"I will. Doug, tell him ... I don't know." I shook my head slightly and looked down at my feet. "Tell him I'm not completely freaked out or anything. I'll just need some time."

"I'll tell him," Doug smiled. "Goodnight, Ali."

"Goodnight."

He walked back toward the truck while I snuck in the kitchen door. The Pattons were still asleep, but why not. One glance at the clock told me it was 4:00 in the morning.

I fell on my bed fully clothed and stared at the ceiling. I had so much to think about, but my mind was mysteriously blank. It was just too much. What the hell had I gotten myself into?

Chapter 10

After very little sleep because everything was screwing with my head, I was surprisingly wide awake by the time the Pattons were getting ready for work. I'd been on the internet again searching for anything that would give me a hint that what Doug and Jake told me was true. There was nothing. Nothing about Bigfoot actually being human guys that shifted into the creatures running through the woods.

I eventually gave up and went down to breakfast to tell the Pattons that I was going out with Jake again. They were thrilled. Why was everyone so sure I needed friends, or a boyfriend? I wasn't sure at all that I did, or that I even wanted someone else in my life.

I'd told Doug the night before that I wasn't freaked out, but, honestly, now that the light of day made everything clearer, I was terrified. Jake had been so intense, and so insistent that we were meant to be together. Bonded mates. What did that even mean?

There was no doubt that I'd felt something when he kissed me, but so what? He was a gorgeous guy that I was really attracted to and he was kissing me. Kissing me so sweetly, so gently, so lovingly.

I'd never been kissed the way he kissed me – like a man that was holding the woman he loved. But no one had ever loved me before. Kissing Tommy wasn't like kissing Jake, but I knew Tommy hadn't really loved me. I certainly didn't love him.

Was I in love with Jake? No. I couldn't be in love with someone after knowing them such a short time. Could I see myself falling in love with him? I didn't know. I just didn't know how I might feel in the future. What was love anyway?

Did Jake love me? He said he did with such conviction, and his kiss sure felt like he did. He said that the beast inside him was trying to show me how much he loved me, but couldn't express it any other way.

The beast inside him. Now that was another problem. A huge, change-your-life type problem. In the light of day, the whole thing seemed like it'd happened so long ago, and I didn't even know if I believed the bizarre Bigfoot story they'd told me. Could they both be insane? Both be delusional?

They could be. There was a group of people I'd read about that lived in a compound and thought their leader was an alien and they were all prepared for other aliens to come get them. They'd all poisoned themselves, sure that they wouldn't really die. They thought the aliens would take them away to another planet.

That was a whole group of people who lived together and all shared the same insanity. Could Jake and Doug be part of the same kind of group? I'd seen and felt the beast that held me down, sniffing and biting, but was it real?

What if they put on really good Bigfoot suits and ran around in the woods thinking they shifted into the creatures? Maybe drugs were involved somehow. The whole thing could be a great big, group hallucination.

My mind was whirling with these thoughts. I'd considered those same things the night before, and letting them turn over and over in my mind again could be caused by all the anxiety and worry in my own head. It could be because I was a reasonable, logical person who wouldn't just believe whatever bizarre story I was told. Mom had always told me to think before acting, not to just jump into something on a whim.

Going out with Jake could be one of those crazy whims Mom was talking about, but he was going to be showing up any time to take me to another movie. Did I really want to go out with him? Should I just refuse to go?

Sure the Bigfoot shifter thing was scary, but when I thought about Jake he made my head spin. The way he held me and kissed me. I had felt something between us, but I still didn't know what it was.

Here was this hot, older guy kissing me in a way that said he wanted me, wanted to have sex with me. I still felt like a young girl some of the time, and had never had those feelings for anyone. There were a couple of times when Tommy was tempting, but not like Jake. So not like Jake.

I'd never felt anything like my reaction to Jake, but was that love or just my hormones? I'd seen a very different Jake from the guy I thought I was interested in. Not the nice, normal guy that took me to movies and dinner, the guy I thought I might want to get serious with, might want to be the first guy I slept with. He was so much more than what I thought he was.

Mom had never said anything, but I always got the impression that she didn't love my dad, and he didn't love her. I think I was one of those mistakes that people make. I had no doubt that Mom loved me, so I was probably a mistake that she didn't regret very much, but I know she would have been happier if my father was someone that loved us and was in our lives.

Even though Jake said he loved me and wanted us together for-ever, the reality was that I didn't have any experience with people that really loved each other. I guess the Pattons probably did, but I'd only known them a few months. How did you know that you loved someone enough to commit to a lifetime together?

All this was still going through my head when I heard the door-bell ring and knew that it was Jake. Part of me wanted him to go away. But that was the scared, young girl part, not the maturing young woman. I realized that part was more scared of him saying he loved me than she was of him changing into some big, hairy creature. That young girl part was scared because he wanted me to love him, and that would mean growing up forever. There would be no going back to the innocence of childhood once I'd committed to loving a man, as a woman, especially not if I made a commitment for the rest of my life.

But I wasn't a little girl, no matter how young I sometimes felt, and I'd told him we'd go out today and I'd give us a chance. So I took a deep breath, glanced once more in the mirror, and went down the stairs.

He was standing there talking to Mr. Patton and gave me a smile that I couldn't resist giving him back. All my fears seemed to be long gone when I looked into those shining eyes and saw his gorgeous smile. I knew right then that I'd have to keep control or I'd be falling into his arms very soon.

"So ..." Mr. Patton was saying, "... you two haven't gone out for a while."

"No ... uh ... I was in an accident and couldn't drive," Jake answered.

"A car accident?" I don't think Mr. Patton would be very confident in Jake's driving if he'd just had an accident.

"No," Jake shook his head. "Just clumsiness out in the woods hunting with my dad. I stumbled over a rock ledge." He shrugged and kinda' laughed at himself.

Mr. Patton kinda' laughed, too. "I'm glad you're back on your feet. You two have a nice time. And drive carefully."

"Thanks," Jake said as he put his hand on the small of my back to lead me toward the door.

"Bye, Mr. Patton," was all I could say. Jake's hand on my back was way too distracting to think of anything else.

Jake opened the truck's passenger door for me again and took my elbow to help me climb in, but didn't say a word as we backed out of the driveway and turned onto the lane. As soon as he got out of sight of the house, though, he pulled over to the side of the road, put the truck in park, and turned to face me.

"I have to apologize for last night," he said, looking very serious and a little worried. "I couldn't help jumping you like that, but it still shouldn't have happened. I'm really sorry I scared you so bad and for ... well, for everything."

"I shouldn't have been out there looking for you guys," I kind of mumbled because I couldn't think of anything else to say.

"No, don't try to make it sound like it was your fault, 'cause it wasn't. I think we're not being as careful as we should be. We need to be more careful. But, I can't say I'm sorry ..." he paused and looked away for a second. "No." He shook his head. "I promised Dad I wouldn't push you."

Jake kept looking like he was unsure of what he was saying. I got the idea that there were a million things going around in his head and he didn't know where to start. I understood that completely. I had a million things in my head, too.

"Look, Jake," I said, "we can't do anything about last night. It happened. How about if we just ignore it for right now. We'll just talk about something else and go from there."

"Okay," he grinned, obviously relieved. "That sounds good. Wanna' go to a movie?"

"Yeah. Whatever you want to see." He gave me a look that said he was more relaxed, flashed a big smile, and pulled back onto the road.

When he smiled, I again noticed his gorgeous eyes and remembered those same eyes gazing at me when I hid under the tree. "Your eyes don't change," I muttered almost to myself. So much for not talking about it.

"What?" he asked, probably not entirely sure I was talking to him.

"When you shift," I said, looking toward him. "Your eyes don't change at all."

"No," he half laughed. "Everything else does."

"If I had any doubts, I guess your eyes would convince me that was really you."

"You have doubts?" he asked glancing away from the road and giving me a look that said he'd be really hurt if I doubted him. "You think we lied to you?"

"No," I said thoughtfully, almost hesitantly. "No. I don't think that at all," I repeated with the surety in my voice that I was really feeling. "But, you've got to admit, the whole thing's pretty wild. Wouldn't anyone be a little skeptical before they'd had a chance to really think about it?"

"Have you thought about it?" I got the impression he might not want to know the answer to that question.

My turn to half-laugh. "Oh, yeah. I think I only slept about an hour. The only conclusions I could come to were that you were telling the truth or it was some mass insanity. Of course that would mean that I was insane, too." I shrugged.

"It's all true, Ali," he said quietly.

"I know. But still mind-boggling. And ... a little scary." I answered just as quietly.

"Yeah. I know," he said as he reached over and took my hand as we drove in silence the rest of the way.

Once again we picked a movie based on the fact that it was starting soon. It was some kind of horrible alien thing with people and ugly creatures being blown up every other minute. Not my favorite kind of movie.

I don't know for sure how Jake felt because he kept glancing over at me. After about ten minutes and half a tub of popcorn, he reached his arm across my shoulders.

"Is that okay?" he asked with a voice that sounded like he was begging a little.

"Yeah," I nodded.

He pulled his arm back. "I can feel you tensing up. It's okay. I don't have to touch you."

"No. I didn't tense up because *you* were putting your arm around me. Hell, I'd do that with any guy. I'm just not used to it. I liked you putting your arm around me."

"Yeah?" he smiled so sweetly. "You sure?"

"I'm sure," I almost giggled. He was being so careful, so protective of my feelings. His dad must have really laid down the law. "Put your arm around me," I said quietly.

He stretched his arm back across my shoulders and gently clasped my arm right above my elbow without stretching at all. I realized he had a really long reach. He was smiling at me again.

"It makes me calmer to touch you," he whispered, then shook his head looking away from me. "I'm sorry ... I shouldn't have said that."

"Jake," I sighed. "Look at me." He turned his head back, but looked worried now. At least he hadn't pulled his arm away. "If we're going to get to know each other, we have to be honest. I might not understand how touching me calms you down, but ... you're allowed to say it."

There was that look in his eyes again. The one that said he loved me. "Okay, but you have to tell me stuff, too."

"I will."

Then we started watching the movie again. At least we both pretended to watch the movie again.

I was thinking about how I could feel the muscles of his arm on my neck and across my back. How his hand held onto my arm while his thumb gently stroked the skin inside my elbow. How good he felt next to me.

I don't know what he was thinking, but the little smile on his lips as the aliens blew up another hundred humans made me think his mind wasn't on the movie either. I think – no, I hoped – he was thinking about me.

I had to admit that I did really like him, and sitting in that movie with his arm around me made me forget about the Bigfoot thing. Without planning it, my head tilted over onto his shoulder. I heard him sigh. Did my touch, my closeness, really affect him that much? Did he really love me?

We hardly said a word the rest of the movie, but that was okay. I think we were somehow just enjoying being together. The movie ended, and we drove away without saying much to each other.

Jake suddenly said, "Hey, how about we go for a walk?"

"Sure. Where?"

"Well, you know I like the woods," he shrugged and smiled.

"Yeah," I laughed lightly. "I don't mind the woods."

"I know a place not far from your house. I think you'll like it."

"Okay," I said.

At this point, beyond seeing movies we didn't really want to see, I had no idea what things we should do or might do together. If he had some suggestions, that would be fine.

"Not planning on grabbing me again, are you?" I said with a little smile and a sideways look at him.

"Oh, God, Ali. No! I wouldn't do that!" He looked devastated.

"Jake, I was kidding! I know you wouldn't do that. I'm sorry. I guess I was just trying to ... I don't know." I was shaking my head. I felt like such an idiot.

"No, I'm sorry. You were trying to make me feel better about it, but I just hate that I scared you so much."

"I know," I nodded.

Then he smiled. "I'm not saying that I won't want to hold you, but I won't attack you."

I just smiled back. What could I say to that? Yeah, I want you to hold me and kiss me again like you did in the cave? I couldn't say that.

He pulled over a couple miles from the Patton's house and took my hand as we crossed the road.

"There's a deer trail that's used by hikers and hunters. It goes over the hill and we can cut back down near the road to come back to the truck. It's pretty up there."

"Good," I answered. "Mr. Patton told me about all the deer trails. That's what I was following when I saw you." We'd already plunged into the trees and were following one of the well-trodden paths.

"The first night? When you were camping?"

"And the second time when I saw you and your dad following Bigfoot."

"Dad was following me the first time, and he figured you saw me. The second time, it was Uncle Max."

"And the third time, was you, again." I turned to face him. He had that worried look on his face, and I wanted him to stop feeling so bad about it.

"Yeah," he said. Then he smiled. "And I knew you lied to me when you said you hadn't seen Bigfoot."

"Jake," I said as I pulled him to a stop. "You need to believe that I went out there again to be sure of what I'd seen, but I planned on not ever telling anyone. I figured Bigfoot had a right to stay hidden. I didn't want anyone to find him and hurt him."

"You decided that before you knew the truth?"

"Yeah, they ... I mean, you ... well, you deserve to be protected."

"That means a lot." He gave me a devastating look, and I think I sighed a little.

I started walking up the hill again, and Jake followed. When he caught up, he grabbed my hand. We got to the top of the hill, and he led me between some trees. He put both his hands on my shoulders and turned me around facing away from him, so I was looking down on the most beautiful valley with gently rolling hills continuing into the distance.

"It's gorgeous! You can see some of these hills while driving on the freeway, but this is so much better. It's like there's no one else in the world."

"I'm glad you like it." He moved his hands from my shoulders and clasped them in front of me at my waist.

I was held against him again, my back to his front, but it was nothing like that creature confining me. This was nice. Not clutched tightly against him with his face plunged into my neck.

We were barely touching, but his arms were around me. I knew his head was looking out over mine, and could feel the warmth of his body. I put my hands over his and held them. It felt so nice.

We stood there for several minutes just gazing into the distant hills before he said quietly, "Ali, can I kiss you again?"

I thought for about half a second before I turned around in his arms. I didn't need to say a thing. He leaned down and kissed me just like he'd done the night before. This time, though, I was ready to kiss him back.

After several blissful moments we pulled our lips away from each other. Jake tilted his forehead against mine and quietly said, "Thank you."

Something about the way he said it irritated me. "What's that mean?" I asked.

"Just ... thank you," he said with confusion in his eyes. "Thank you for calming me."

With that, I felt my anger flare and stepped away. I couldn't help glaring at him.

"You ..." I stuttered for a second and let out a deep breath. Then I let him have it. "You JERK!" I yelled while punching him in the arm.

"What'd I do?" I'd never seen him so surprised.

"Holding hands, hugging, kissing ..." I didn't know how to say what I was feeling. I was so frustrated and didn't know how to get the words out. "Damn it!" I finally spat out and turned away from him to stare into the distance. This time I didn't even see that beautiful view.

"Ali. I'm sorry." Now it was his turn to not know what to say, but he came toward me and put his hands back on my shoulders.

"Don't touch me!" I jerked my shoulders away from him and took another step.

"Tell me what I did," he practically begged.

"You ..." My brain was finally starting to put some words to what I felt. I spun back around to tell him to his face. "You say you love me, but everything is about *you*. About your damn calm and control. I didn't kiss you to help that stupid beast!"

By the time I threw those last words at him, I was yelling. I saw his face melt into something, but I didn't look long enough to recognize it. Instead I turned away and started down the path back toward the car. I was seriously mad, but also hurt. He didn't get it.

"Ali ... wait!" he called as he followed me. He caught me without a problem and turned me back around to face him.

"Why did you kiss me?"

"Why do you think? Because I wanted to. Because I like you." I didn't know what else to say. "Leave me alone."

"No! Tell me."

I took a deep breath. I'd told him we'd go with the truth, but I barely knew the truth myself. "I ... you ..." I sighed and stood there for a second thinking. "I don't think that kissing someone you say you love is supposed to make you feel calm and in control." I felt tears start to pool in my eyes.

"I haven't kissed many guys, but I know kissing you doesn't feel like it did with them. You say you love me, but ..." I ran my hand through my hair and stamped my foot. I was so frustrated with trying to explain this. "Damn it, Jake. I don't know how to love someone. I don't even know what love is, but I don't think it's supposed to feel like this." I felt a tear run down my cheek.

"You think I don't ... want you?" He stood there staring at me.

"I don't know what I think," I said as I dropped my head so I didn't have to look into his eyes anymore.

"This isn't just about sex ..."

"I didn't say I want to have sex with you." Now I was embarrassed and starting to get mad again.

"I know, but that's where this could get to if we let it ... because I do want you. I want you more than I want to keep breathing. And I think you want me, too."

I had no idea what I should say to that so I just kept looking at the ground.

"Look, I've had sex with a few girls, girls from The Family. But that was just sex, just for fun. That's not what I want from you."

That hurt me a little. He didn't want to have sex with me, but he said we were meant to be married and live together the rest of our lives? "Then what do you want from me?" I looked back up at him as I said that, and I think he could see the hurt in my eyes.

"I want us bonded. And don't get me wrong, bonded mates have sex a lot. But there's more to it than that."

"What else is there?" I think that scared me a little.

He looked like he was debating whether to tell me or not. "I was going to wait to tell you some of this, but ..." He shook his head and then looked right into my eyes. "My great-grandmother was human, but because of her bond with my great-grandfather, she lived to be 193 years old."

"What? How could that be?"

"Remember when I had my mouth on your neck? I could have bitten you. I *wanted* to bite you. But even my Bigfoot side knew that it wasn't time. We had to wait because bonding is your choice, not mine. But when we ... *if* we ... bond, I will bite you and we'll be one for the rest of our lives. And we'll live our lives together, and probably die together."

"The Bigfoot will bite me?"

"Yeah. At our bonding ceremony." He looked so worried while he told me. He was so worried I'd run. I'm sure I looked like I might. I felt like I should. "But it'll be *me* and you'll control me. You'll tell me to shift and when to shift back to human form. I won't do anything you don't tell me to do."

He stopped talking and I just continued to look at him. "I don't know what to say," I practically whispered. It was the truth. My mind felt like I couldn't put together a coherent thought.

"We're not human, Ali. There are things about us that are different. Other stuff besides the shifting. When I bite you to bond us, my saliva will change you. You'll age much more slowly, and I won't be able to live without you. When you die, I die, too. Say you understand."

"I think I understand, but it scares me." My voice was so quiet, so hesitant. I'd told him it scared me, but the truth was that it completely terrified me.

"That's why I wanted to wait to tell you. When we're ready to bond, we'll know. You won't be scared."

We stood there with me staring down at the ground for what seemed like a long time, but it was probably only moments. Without thinking, I finally said, "I think I want you to hold me."

He stretched out his arms and I walked toward him. We wrapped our arms around each other and I buried my head in his chest. I was so confused.

"I think I need some time to know how I feel about all this," I finally said into his chest.

"I know that. You're seventeen with a year of high school left. I know I can't expect you to quit school or something. We have plenty of time, and we'll wait."

"Until after I graduate?" That surprised me and I tilted my head back to look up at him. I thought he was talking about maybe waiting a couple months for me to make up my mind.

"As long as it takes. Spending the rest of my life with you will be worth it." He said that gazing into my eyes and looked so serious.

Once again, I didn't know what to say. I squeezed him tighter, buried my face again in his chest and wiped a stray tear on his shirt.

"Maybe I'd better get you home," he whispered into my ear. Before we moved apart, he kissed me on the top of my head.

"Yeah," I said quietly. I should have known there'd be more to it than what I'd been told the night before, but his saliva changing me and making me live long past a normal human lifespan. How did I deal with that?

We held hands all the way down the hill, and he opened my door and helped me climb up into the truck. We were silent most of the way home, but it was okay because we'd both said a lot and had so much to think about.

He said he'd wait for me, and that's exactly what he'd need to do. Until I was eighteen, Mr. Jones had the legal right to make decisions for me, and I was sure he wouldn't be giving me permission to get married before I graduated.

Besides, I wasn't ready to get married anytime soon. I knew I still had some growing up to do and still didn't know for sure how I felt about Jake. Could I marry him, let him bite me, just because he was so sure we were meant to be together? No. I needed to be sure, too.

When he parked in the Patton's driveway, he turned toward me and took my hand. "Ali, you need to know that I don't touch you just because you help me control my other side. My mom still helps me a lot with that. I touch you because I want to. And I love it that you want to touch me. We just need to go slow ... for both of us."

"Yeah. I wanna go slow, too. Will I see you tomorrow?"

He shook his head. "We have to go to Pennsylvania for a few days for our summer gathering with other Family groups. I won't be back until Saturday."

"Others like you? You have meetings?"

"Sure," he smiled at my surprise. "It helps us solve any problems and gives young ones a chance to meet each other and look for the one they're meant to bond with."

"Will you be looking?" I asked and realized my voice sounded almost shy. Maybe a little jealous.

"No," he shook his head. "I would have been, but I've found my mate," he smiled. He looked almost embarrassed to say it.

I decided to avoid responding to that statement. "I start work at the park on Saturday. Maybe we could go out Saturday night?"

A big smile crossed his so-sexy lips. "I'll call you Friday night."

"Okay."

Without asking, he leaned over and kissed me gently. "I'll miss you. See you Saturday."

I got out of the truck and walked into the house after turning to wave at him. The Pattons weren't home, but I found a note that said they'd gone to get groceries and would be home in plenty of time for dinner. "Good," I said out loud.

I needed time alone to think.

Chapter 11

School was out and work didn't start until the weekend, so I had nothing to do that week except hang around. The Pattons were at work the first day Jake was gone, so I did some cleaning around the house because I figured I owed at least that much to them. After all, they treated me really well and left me alone when I needed it.

Besides, cleaning gave me something to do with my mind instead of thinking about Jake the whole time. Too bad their house wasn't really dirty or messy. Cleaning an already clean home didn't give me nearly enough to keep my mind off Jake. I spent half the day thinking about what else I could do and finally came up with my own project.

"Have you guys ever thought about putting in a garden?" I asked hesitantly while we were eating dinner.

"Not really," Mrs. Patton answered hesitantly, "but maybe we could."

"I'd do it for you," I offered. "Mom and I always had a garden. Just onions, green peppers, some tomatoes. Nothing fancy."

"Really?" she said.

"It'd give me something to work on, and fresh tomatoes are great." I think they knew I needed something to do now that school was out for the summer.

"What about your job? You start in a few days," Mr. Patton asked. He was always the practical one.

"I can get it planted this week and then just have to weed and water it. I'd have plenty of time."

"We don't know much about gardening, but ..."

"I could teach you. It's fun once you get into it," I interrupted him, trying to be convincing.

"What would we need to get?" Mrs. Patton asked. I think she was convinced, but Mr. Patton was still questioning the whole thing.

"Just the plants, maybe some fertilizer. It'd be a small garden, so not much at all."

"I think it's a good idea," she said giving her husband a look. I think it was a look that said I needed to do it. She was probably thinking it would help me because it was something I did with Mom, but I just needed something to keep me busy so I wasn't just hanging around thinking about Jake all week.

"I guess we could go to the garden store and see what we can get." He'd given in.

"We'll go after dinner," Mrs. Patton added. "You can start on it tomorrow if you want."

I smiled at both of them and dug back into my dinner.

We bought tomatoes, onion sets, green peppers, cucumbers, tomato stakes, fertilizer, and a hoe to eventually weed around the plants. The people at the garden store kept trying to talk them into other stuff, but that was all I really needed.

The Pattons had everything else – a hose to water, big, flat shovel to get rid of all the grass, and a garden rake to smooth out the dirt. I couldn't resist talking them into a couple herbs. Just sage, basil, and chives because I knew they were easy to grow and tasted really good.

The next day, I went out right after they left for work, used some spray paint I found in the garage to mark off a square in a good, sunny spot, and started to dig out the grass. That was the hard part. I'd only done that once before with Mom, but it didn't take a lot of knowledge, just a lot of physical work. Physical work was just what I needed.

Once the grass was gone, I had to dig in and turn over all the soil. The deeper I dug, the more room all the plants would have for their roots and they'd be healthier. After that, I sprinkled in some fertilizer, raked out all the clumps, and smoothed the soil. I'd put all the tufts of grass I'd scraped off into a trash bag that I had to drag over to the trash cans. It was much heavier than I expected and figured I'd probably left too much dirt attached to the grass, but I got it lifted into the can.

By the time I was finished with all that, the spot was ready, and I was bushed. Sweaty, sore muscles, blisters on my hands from the shovel. I needed a break. It felt good, though, to accomplish something useful, and I'd hardly had time to think about Jake at all.

I resisted the temptation to jump in the shower since I'd keep going after lunch to get the plants in. I scrubbed my hands and face, put a Band-Aid over the worst blister, made a quick sandwich, grabbed a Pepsi, and took them out to the plastic patio furniture. I didn't want to sit on Mrs. Patton's kitchen chairs with my filthy jeans.

When the Pattons got home from work, they found me sticking in the last of the onion sets, which I'd saved 'till the end because they were the easiest and quickest. I was even dirtier and sweatier, but they both hugged me for all the hard work I'd done.

"How did you get all this done so fast?" Mrs. Patton asked as she looked down at the droopy little plants.

"I know it doesn't look so good right now," I said, "but it'll look better once the plants get established and start to grow."

"No, it looks great," Mr. Patton said. "How long before we get tomatoes?" he grinned.

I laughed. "Not for a while, but we'll be able to cut some herbs pretty soon. They'll keep growing after they're cut."

"Ali, it's amazing you got all this done in one day!" Mrs. Patton said. "But you look like you're exhausted."

"Not really. I just need a shower big time."

"You go shower while Jane starts dinner. I'll put your shovel and hose away for you," Mr. Patton said.

"Leave the hose hooked up. I have to water it in the morning," I said as he started picking up the tools.

"Mike," Mrs. Patton said as we all stood there, "with a gardener in the house, maybe we could get those flowers along the front walk that we talked about."

"I could do that for you," I smiled.

"Or we could do it together, so Jane and I know how," Mr. Patton answered. "I could dig out the grass while you two go pick out flowers. I think I know how to use a shovel," he teased.

They were both laughing and seemed excited about the new flower project. It made me feel good to do something for them. They'd been doing a lot for me.

We had a great dinner, but anything would have tasted wonderful to me because I was starving. Working that hard all day hyped up my appetite like I couldn't believe. I was all clean and warm from the shower, Mrs. Patton gave me a couple Tylenol for the achy muscles, and I slept that night better than I'd ever slept before. At least better than I had since Mom was first diagnosed.

The next day, after watering the garden, I hung around again watching TV, playing computer games, and searching the internet some more for Bigfoot. I would have gone out to start digging along the front walk for the flowers, but I knew Mr. Patton wanted to do it. Beside, I was still kinda' sore.

So I was left again with thoughts of Jake. The main thought I kept having was that I missed him. It had only been a couple days, but I wanted to see him. I wanted to hold him. I wanted to kiss him.

Was I falling in love with Jake, or was it just the whole thing about someone saying he loved me? I had to admit that the idea of being with him for the rest of my life was sounding pretty good. Actually, the idea of being with anyone sounded pretty good.

The only person I'd ever really had was Mom. The Pattons were great to me, but they weren't mine. They belonged to each other and let me in that life for a little while. Once I was eighteen, I'd be on my own.

Being on my own seriously scared me when I took time to think about it. What would I do? The plan in the back of my head had been about going somewhere for college, but I'd still be alone. Who would I go home to for Christmas break and summers? Who would come visit me? Who could I call when I was upset or lonely?

The answer could be right in front of me because I could have Jake. All I needed to do was say yes. He'd be there for me, and his whole family would welcome me. Not just family, but The Family. I'd belong to all of them.

It was tempting. If I told Jake I loved him we could start planning a wedding. Not until I graduated, because I knew Mr. Brown would never give me permission to get married until then. Of course, I'd be eighteen this August, and starting my senior year.

Once I was eighteen, I'd be able to make my own decisions and could marry Jake whether Mr. Brown approved or not. But Jake said he'd wait for me to finish school. In fact, he was pretty definite about that. He wanted me to graduate.

Was marrying Jake just an easy way out? Could I honestly say I loved him, or was it just a way to belong to someone rather than being alone?

I was definitely attracted to him, and I did like him a lot, but was that love? Would I feel the same way in a few years? Or in a hundred years? He said we'd both live over a hundred years, but that sounded crazy to me. He was so sure, so sure we were meant to be together, but I just couldn't be sure that what I felt was a love that would last forever.

Then there was the whole Family thing. I would have to spend my life supporting a guy that needed a lot of support. Watching him change into a monster and giving him the emotional support he needed to control it. What he'd told me so far sounded like it was all about him, but what about me?

I needed support, too. I needed someone who would think about me once in a while. Would my whole life be about being there for him? Who would be there for me? I still cried myself to sleep many nights thinking about Mom. Would he understand that? Sometimes I just didn't want to talk to anyone. Would he get that and leave me alone?

If I said no, I got the idea that he wouldn't find someone else. Doug said that losing the woman he was destined to bond with had meant that Uncle Max would always be alone. I didn't want Jake to be alone, but I couldn't pretend I loved him just to make him happy. I needed to know for sure, because he wasn't asking for a normal human marriage. He was asking a lot more than that.

Stop it! I mentally yelled at myself. We'd really only been out once since I knew the whole story. We needed a lot more time to know what was what.

I had to stop thinking like I needed to make a decision right away. It only made sense that I didn't know if I loved him or not. I'd only known him at all for a little while, and I needed to meet his mother and the rest of The Family, didn't I?

How was I to know I loved him and could join his bizarre life when I really hadn't seen it, yet? I needed to tuck everything into the back of my mind and wait to see how the summer went. By the time school started in the fall, I'd have a better idea what I wanted.

I needed to chill until then, date him like any other guy, and worry about making up my mind later.

I turned on the TV, grabbed my tablet, and played solitaire on it while watching re-runs of Pawn Stars on the History Channel. It helped a little, but my mind still kept slipping into thinking about Jake.

When the Pattons finally got home from work, we did just what we planned. I showed Mr. Patton how to scrape away the grass before digging deep into the soil, Mrs. Patton and I went out to get flowers, and we got back home to find the edges along the front walk all ready for planting. By the time it was getting dark, we had pink petunias planted all along the front with a nice dark mulch around them. Then we ordered a really big pizza with everything on it for dinner.

The next day was Friday, and I woke up thinking about Jake calling me that night. I couldn't wait. At least I had two gardens to water, laundry to do, and a nagging worry about starting my first job the next day. I still thought about Jake a lot, though.

Finally, about 6:00, he called.

"Hey, Ali," his deep voice said when I answered.

"Jake. How are you?" I knew he could hear the smile in my voice and I couldn't help it.

"Good, but I missed you."

"I missed you, too. When will you be back?"

"Early tomorrow afternoon. Can I come over to get you? We can go out to eat or something."

"I work from 11:00 to 4:00. It's my first day."

"Oh, man, I'm sorry. I forgot about that. How about if I pick you up at work?"

"I'd love that. I'm getting kinda' nervous about starting a job and all that."

"Then it's a deal, and you can tell me all about it. At the lodge?"

"Yeah. Mr. Patton is taking me, but it'll be so nice if you pick me up. You can park on that upper level, and I'll dash out as soon as I can."

"Can I come in to see you working?" I thought he was teasing, but wasn't sure.

"Well, it's my first day, so I don't know for sure where I'll be. Once I figure things out, I'd love it if you came in some time."

"Okay."

"So, how did your meetings go?"

"Good. No problems. Uh, I told them about you."

"About me? What about me?" Did that make me mad? Not really, but I was a little shocked that he was talking about me with the whole Bigfoot group – with The Family.

"We have to report any sightings, and I needed to tell them that I'm bonding with a human. I'm sorry."

"No, I guess it's okay. I think the idea of them knowing about me scares me a little."

Jake gave me one of those explosive little laughs that says, *Yeah, well*. "It scared me to tell them. I was afraid I might pass out if I had to stand there any longer."

I laughed a little at that.

"So," Jake said, obviously changing the subject, "how'd your week go?"

I told him all about my gardening and how much the Pattons liked it. He acted like he was proud of me doing all that myself. I was proud of myself, too, for getting it done, but some little part of me thought he liked it because being able to garden would make me better wife material, like I would be able to take care of him. That was a nasty thought, but I couldn't help that it popped into my head.

"Hey, Ali, I'm sorry, but I have to go. They're calling a final gathering. Dad would be really pissed if I didn't show up."

"That's okay. I'll see you tomorrow, though, right?"

"4:00, at the lodge. I'll be there."

"Goodnight."

"I can't wait to see you. Goodnight."

He told them about me, and I couldn't get that out of my head. Scary, but it also made me kinda' feel good that he was serious enough that he told them.

I mean, wouldn't he keep me a secret if he wasn't sure, or at least pretty sure? But couldn't he have waited until I was sure? Until *we* were sure? It was all rolling around in my head again.

I wanted to talk to Mom. I could always talk to her and could tell her anything. We talked a lot about guys, but I think that was because she didn't want me to make the kind of mistake she'd made.

I couldn't talk to her about this, but I sure could write to her. I hadn't written as much lately because I didn't know what to tell her, but I couldn't keep it to myself anymore.

Dear Mom,

I miss you.

I met this great guy who says he loves me, but there's a big problem. He changes into Bigfoot at night and runs out to kill and eat deer. Sounds crazy doesn't it? It's true, though, he really does. All the guys in his family shift into Bigfoot, but the women don't. They somehow keep the men calm so they don't have to shift all the time.

He says he loves me. Says we've bonded and are meant to be together. I don't know if I love him or not. I like him a lot, and he's so good to me. How do I know if I love him? Don't worry, we haven't had sex. He says that can wait until I'm sure. I don't know how I feel, or what to do.

It would be so easy if I married him. I wouldn't be alone. I feel so alone since you've been gone. There's no one I can really talk to. No one who really knows me and understands me. I wish you were here. I wish I could tell you all this and you could meet him and see what a great guy he is. Would I want him so much if I still had you?

I stopped typing on my IPad. For the first time, I felt like writing all these letters to my dead mother was ridiculous. She'd never see them. I had all kinds of questions and she wouldn't be able to answer any of them. I needed someone to tell me what to do, and Mom couldn't do that.

I deleted the letter and shut down. Writing about all my problems wouldn't solve them, and writing those letters wasn't really telling Mom. I had to decide what I was going to do myself, because there was no one I could tell. Telling the Pattons or Mr. Jones that a big, hairy, mythical creature was in love with me would get me committed into a psych ward. Besides, I felt like the whole thing was making me crazy.

I had to stop thinking about Jake, so I made myself start thinking about my first job which would start the next day. I got out the uniform the Pattons had to buy me and tried to think about anything else I'd need. That didn't calm me down much, but at least it was a different worry rolling through my head.

Chapter 12

Mr. Patton knew I was nervous as he was driving me to the lodge at Salt Fork the next morning. He kept talking about unimportant things like the garden. Then he moved on to the less than vital topic of the warm, early-summer weather.

I kept looking at the hills and trees around us as we traveled south on the park's Rt. 1. All those trees off to the east, and I knew what ran through them. What hunted by night. Right now, though, all those creatures were driving along the freeway, returning from Pennsylvania. I couldn't help but think that Jake was traveling along in a car just like I was and wondering whether he was thinking about me.

"So, you ready for this?" Mr. Patton asked as he pulled into the parking lot.

"I guess so," I answered. I so wasn't sure I was ready at all.

"Jake will be here to pick you up, right?"

"He'll be here," I smiled.

I wanted a job. I needed some extra money, and I needed to start saving for college. But I really didn't know what would be expected of me and wasn't sure I'd be able to handle whatever it was. The one thing I did know was that I would use my first paycheck to take Jake out to dinner. That would be fun.

I walked into the lodge and up to the check-in counter. Taking a deep breath, I told the girl standing there who I was. She had me wait for a minute until an older guy named Joe Rich came out to meet me and start my training.

"Hi, Ali. Nice to meet you," he said.

"Hi. Nice to meet you, too."

"I see you got your uniform."

"Yeah," I answered. It was simple. A black pair of slacks, black shoes, and a deep wine-colored, button-down shirt. Mr. Rich handed me a name tag, and I pinned it to the left side of my shirt like I noticed on the girl I first talked to.

"We're going to have you working the front desk. Before we start there, though, I want to show you around."

We started walking. Through the gift shop, past the restaurant, meeting rooms, guest rooms, and lounge areas. The gift shop had Bigfoot t-shirts, key chains, and such things in the back corner since sightings at Salt Fork were legendary, and I had a little trouble concentrating on the rest of the tour after I saw that. Everyone treated Bigfoot like a joke, but I knew better. Then we got back to the check-in counter and Mr. Rich got busy teaching me everything that needed to be done while working there.

There were so many things to learn. Mr. Rich said he wanted me to learn the computer system first, and that was complicated enough. I couldn't help noticing all the stuff the other girls were doing while I stood over to the side struggling to remember everything he was telling me.

People kept coming to the counter and asking questions – room numbers, directions, stuff for their kids, rules for camping, restaurant hours, when the pool was open, and so many other things. I didn't think I'd ever be able to learn it all and answer quickly and accurately like those girls.

Finally, after a pretty frustrating day, it was almost 4:00.

"You've done a good job, Ali," Mr. Rich said with a smile. I had trouble believing him.

"Thank you ... I hope I remember everything."

"Oh, you will," he said completely dismissing my fears. "The first day's pretty overwhelming, but it'll all make sense. Why don't you get your purse and get ready to go home. I'll see you at 11:00 tomorrow, right?"

"I'll be here."

I'd spent my lunch break staring into space and thinking that he wouldn't want me back, not able to eat a thing. Like my first day might be my last day. I felt like such a dunce with most of the stuff he'd been showing me. Maybe it hadn't been so bad because he seemed pretty sincere when he said I'd done well. But he also seemed like a nice guy who would probably say nice things to me no matter how stupid I'd been.

He was right, the whole thing was pretty overwhelming, so I started concentrating on Jake. I couldn't wait to see him, and I was sure he'd be waiting out in the parking lot. As I headed through the entryway, I kept looking for his truck.

"Ali?" a male voice said from behind me.

I turned and saw it was Robert, a guy I half knew from my old school. As usual, his friend Danny was right at his side. I didn't know if I'd ever seen one of them without the other.

Robert was tall with light hair and actually not bad looking. Danny, however, was short, heavy, and kind of funny looking. His jaw was much wider than his forehead, and he had beady little eyes.

"Hi, guys," I said waving over my shoulder and planning to keep walking without talking to them.

"Wait up!" Robert added, and I felt like I needed to stop just to be reasonably polite. "Are you working here?"

"Yeah. I just started today."

"Cool! We're going to be around here a lot this summer. We'll see you all the time."

"Are you guys working here?" I was so hoping the answer was no.

"Nah," Robert shook his head. "We're camping most of the summer." He said that with a silly grin toward Danny, and I wondered what they were up to.

Robert and Danny had been kind of legends at my old school. They were always on the edge of trouble and somehow involved in almost everything that happened. Most of their stuff was bizarre and just a little crazy. I know they were heavy drinkers and probably smoked a lot of weed. I didn't trust them and couldn't see how anyone would.

I'd kept walking while we talked and finally got through the door, spotting Jake's truck near the back of the lot. The lodge was busy, and he'd probably had to park way out there to find any spot at all.

"So, you two like camping?" I had to say something since the two of them were tagging along with me.

"Not really," Danny half laughed.

"We're going to be hunting for Bigfoot." Robert looked so proud as he said that.

Holy shit! I thought. *What if they find one?* "You guys believe in Bigfoot?" I asked like I was really shocked to hear it. Truthfully, I *was* really shocked, but for a different reason than they would think.

"Sure!" Danny said.

"And we're going to get proof," Robert added. "We'll get pictures or video and everyone will know they're real."

"You want to come hunting with us?" Danny asked with a strange expression on his face. "We'll let you share out tent." Then I realized what the strange expression was all about.

"No. That won't be happening."

"Ah, Ali," Robert added. "The three of us could have some fun. We don't have to look for Bigfoot *all* night."

As he said that, he reached out to take ahold of my arm. I didn't want him to touch me at all – the two of them were just creepy. I was starting to pull away from them when I felt a strong arm around my shoulders, and Jake leaned down to kiss my cheek.

"Hi, babe," he said. "These guys a problem?" As he said that last part, he glared at Robert and Danny with a distinctive threat in his eyes. All of a sudden I could feel that huge creature I knew he could become.

"Jake, these are guys from my old school, Robert and Danny," I said, indicating each of them. "Guys, this is Jake ... my boyfriend."

Jake looked down at me and smiled. "Time to go home, right?"

"Yeah. Time to go," I said as Jake and I started walking away.

"We'll be seeing you around, Ali," Robert called after us. I thought I heard a little laugh in his voice. I definitely heard Danny giggle softly.

Jake stopped in his tracks and turned back to face them. "I wouldn't suggest it," he practically growled. "And remember, camping can be dangerous. I wouldn't want you two guys to get hurt out there in the middle of the night."

There was no way to misunderstand the threat in his voice or in his eyes. Was he serious? Would he really go out and hurt those two idiots? Besides the whole Bigfoot thing, I was sure he could give them a serious smack-down in human form.

"Jake, stop it," I whispered.

He didn't answer, but just squeezed me tighter around the shoulders. I kept staring at him as we neared his truck and could feel my anger growing. His homecoming wouldn't be what I'd looked forward to with both of us mad as hell, but I knew the shouting would start as soon as we got in the truck. I was going to start it.

"What was that?" I half-yelled as soon as the doors were closed.

"What?" Jake actually looked like I was asking a stupid question.

"Threatening them! You were acting like some overprotective caveman."

"You think I should let two assholes make passes at you ... and touch you?" Now he was yelling back.

"I think you should let me handle it," I said with a grim look and determination.

"Let you ... Do you know what they were suggesting? Saying the three of you could have fun out there camping all night?"

"Duh, no," I said with a stupid look on my face. "Camp songs and ghost stories? Of course I knew what they meant! Do you think they're the first idiots that have made a pass at me?"

"Other guys? Shit!" Jake shook his head and looked away. "Yeah. You're gorgeous. I know guys have made passes at you, but I couldn't just stand there and watch it. I had to. Ah, Ali, I've missed you so much and the first thing I see is two other guys after you." He looked back at me with so much feeling in his big, dreamy eyes. "I couldn't stand it."

"I think you overreacted," I said quietly. "Don't you trust me?"

"Of course I trust you! I sure as hell don't trust them, though."

I gave him a little smile. "I don't trust them, either. They've always been idiots, but I really don't think they're dangerous. They just don't know how to avoid saying something stupid."

He sighed. "Can we not fight anymore?"

"I don't want to fight with you, but you have to understand that I can take care of myself. I know how to give guys like that the brush-off."

"I know you do. I just felt like I had to protect you." He sounded like he was begging me to understand.

"Part of the bonding thing?"

"Yeah, but because I missed you so much, too. Can we start over? Pretend like we just saw each other and those two guys weren't even there?"

"I think we could do that," I smiled.

"How about a hello kiss?" There was that sexy grin that I had so much trouble resisting.

I smiled and scooted across the bench seat toward him. He opened his arms and wrapped them around me – one across my back, and one hand on my waist. My arms went around his neck.

His kiss was fantastic as usual. I could never believe how I felt when his lips touched mine. Was this love, lust, or something else having to do with us being bonded? While his lips were on mine, I didn't care. I just enjoyed it.

His tongue lightly stroked my lower lip, but he didn't plunge it in like Tommy had done. Jake just stroked gently, sending a pleasant chill down my spine as I opened my lips so my tongue could play with his. When he pulled away, he stared into my eyes.

"I missed you so much," he sighed as he pulled me against him and my head rested on his chest.

"I thought about you almost every minute. I put in that vegetable garden for the Pattons so I could get you off my mind. It didn't work."

I pulled my arms down to rest them on his chest next to my head, and he squeezed me tighter. I could have stayed there in his arms for hours. The muscle I was feeling under my hands was amazing. Yeah, he could easily beat the crap out of Robert and Danny.

He took a deep breath and I could feel his exhale on my cheek. "I figure you've got to be hungry after working all day, and I'm starving. How about Theo's downtown?"

"Sounds great." I sat back up after he gave me one more squeeze and scooted over to put on my seatbelt. "I'll let the Pattons know,"

I said as I pulled out my cell. They were both still at work, so I texted. Not easy when I could hardly take my eyes off his gorgeous face.

As we drove along, I started to giggle.

"What?" Jake asked with a big smile. I think my giggle got him ready to laugh even though he had no idea what I thought was funny.

"I was just thinking. We've had two fights already, but we're still okay with each other. Maybe we're gonna' be one of those couples who like to yell."

"Nay," he grinned. "We can handle the arguments, but we like kissing a lot better."

I smiled and reached over to stroke his hair right above his ear. His eyes opened a little wider and I saw his nostrils flare as he took a deep breath. I didn't know what that was about, but I think he liked it. I know I did, but I got the feeling it meant more to him than it did to me.

"Shouldn't I have done that?" I asked hesitantly.

"No, no, it's okay. Just that, well, it's how our females usually soothe us. Stroking our hair. Hair's a big deal, I guess."

"Oh, I didn't know. Just stroking your head like I just did? I figured it was more about sex."

Jake laughed. "Well, sex between bonded mates is kinda the ultimate, but Bigfoot hasn't got much to do with that. Our women hold us and stroke our hair."

"I'll hold you and stroke your hair," I smiled. As I said it, I realized I'd like that very much.

"No, that wouldn't be a good idea. It's, once we're old enough to change, our mom's do it when we've shifted." He paused and added very quietly, "I think I'd want more from you."

"Oh." What could I say to that?

"Yeah," he answered with a slight frown.

"So I can't see you shifted until we decide we're meant to be together?"

"You want to, to see me shifted?"

"I think I'd like to watch you shift," I said with a lot of hesitation in my voice. Did I really want to watch that? Maybe I thought I needed to watch it before I could be sure of anything.

He looked surprised. "Mom doesn't watch," he said.

"Why not?"

"Well, for her, I think it's mainly because I'm naked. But it's pretty messy, too."

That embarrassed me. Naked. A Bigfoot obviously didn't wear clothes, but I never thought about Jake being naked before he changed. I tried to put the vision of him naked out of my mind and concentrate on the mess.

"How is it messy?"

"Our bodies secrete a thick fluid, a lot of it, to moisturize our skin and help the hair grow. We have to wash it off when we shift back to human."

"I guess there's more to it than I realized." I was feeling a little stupid or naive. Seemed like every time I started a conversation about Bigfoot, there was something else I didn't know.

"Maybe you could watch sometime. I'll ask Mom and Dad. Maybe later on."

By that time we'd gotten to Theo's. It was an old, established place where everyone in Cambridge ate, but nothing fancy. They just had great food.

My burger was huge, and I could only eat half of it. Jake ate the part I couldn't finish, all of his burger, his fries, and most of my fries. Then he added a big piece of pie for desert, insisting that I have a bite.

"Don't you want some more?" he asked. "It's great!"

"I'm stuffed. How come you're so hungry today?"

"No lunch, and I need to hunt tonight." He looked almost embarrassed when he said that.

"Oh." Something else I hadn't thought of.

"We get really hungry. I'm thinking about getting another burger to go," he smiled.

I laughed. As he continued smiling through the last big mouthful of pie, I realized that I was getting more comfortable with all this. I didn't cringe anymore every time he mentioned some Bigfoot thing. I used to cringe, so maybe things weren't sounding as weird as they used to.

"Not that I want to talk about those two idiots, but Robert and Danny said they're camping in the park to hunt for Bigfoot," I said with some hesitation.

"Are they kidding?"

"They said they're going to get pictures and video."

"That's been tried before." Jake grinned. "Don't worry about it. And we don't go into the park very often. We'll just make sure we stay on our own land."

"I found you in the park," I said quietly.

"But there weren't many humans around yet. Now that it's really summer, we'll stay away."

"Good. If they see one of you, they'll tell anyone that will listen. So tell me how your meetings went," I said while we sat there finishing our Cokes.

"Our gathering? It was good," he nodded sounding pretty noncommittal. "I got to hang out with some friends and that was pretty cool. Nothing special, though."

"I didn't think about you having friends there. Was that fun?"

"Sure. Actually kinda' different this time, but it was cool," he nodded again.

"Why was it different?"

"Well, I guess I might as well tell you." He looked unsure, but plunged ahead. "Usually those of us who are about the same age and unmated hang out together and hook up, you know?"

"Oh. With the girls?"

"Yeah. Although there are a couple guys that I know are gay." He smiled. "And I don't know what they'll do about being soothed by a mate. I haven't asked." He shook his head, grinning again. "But I skipped the whole thing this year. I hung out with Mom and Dad."

I just looked at him. Should I say thank you for not cheating on me? Would it have been cheating when I hadn't been able to commit to him?

"I wasn't interested in any of them or any casual sex," he continued.

"Because of me?" I practically whispered.

"Yeah," he nodded his head. "You're the one I want, Ali, and I don't mean just a hook up. I know we'll work out."

"I'm sorry," I said. "I wish I could be sure like you are, but I just can't. I'm not sure of anything."

"I know. I told you I'd wait for you, as long as it takes."

"Thank you for not pushing me," I said very quietly. He was waiting for me and not having sex with girls at the gathering like he normally would. The whole thing just embarrassed me. He probably realized that because I was having trouble looking at him.

"We need to get home so I can hunt," he kind of mumbled, changing the subject. "God, it's good to spend time with you again. I thought the gathering would never end, and I think I drove Mom and Dad nuts."

He paid the bill, and we strolled down the street toward the truck, holding hands. He was right. It was so nice to spend time with him after so many days apart.

"How's Uncle Max?" I said as he pulled into the street. "Doesn't he need to hunt tonight?" I thought about Uncle Max a lot because I knew his problems were because his human woman had said no. A part of me felt guilty that I may cause Jake to end up like that.

"He hunted there. We usually don't go out at gatherings, there're just too many of us in a small area, but he had to. He'll go again tomorrow and Dad'll wait 'till Monday."

"You guys have to keep it all organized, don't you?"

"Yeah, especially in the summer when a lot of humans are around. It's more fun, though, when we can go out together in the winter."

"Don't you have other relatives that live close?"

"Yeah, but we stick to our own areas unless the deer have moved for some reason. We rarely run into each other."

"You don't fight do you?"

"No," he laughed. "In fact, the only danger is that we start playing and chasing each other which makes it easier for humans to see or hear us." He looked over at me. "Sometimes the females join us in the deep snow when we're sure we're alone."

"What? You go out and play in the snow?"

"Sometimes."

"Sounds like fun."

By that time, we were close to the Patton's, but Jake pulled over on the side of the road instead of going on to the driveway.

"Something wrong?"

"Nope," he said as he unfastened his seatbelt and scooted toward me. "I just wanted to kiss you again without the chance of the Pattons seeing it."

I giggled and leaned toward him without hesitating. We kissed for several minutes and I loved every second of it. As we started to move apart, I reached up and ran my fingers through his hair, again. I figured, *What the hell?*

"I really do like it when you do that," he sighed.

"Good. I like it, too."

He actually growled a little before he scooted back and put the truck in gear. A few seconds later, we pulled into the driveway and, what do you know, the Pattons were sitting on the porch.

"How did you know they'd be there?" I practically gasped.

"I swear I didn't know," he laughed. "Just wasn't willing to take the chance."

I leaned over and gave him a quick little kiss on the lips which I think surprised him. But I figured the Pattons had to know we were doing more than talking. They weren't stupid.

"Wait," he said as I reached for the door. "How about if I take you to work tomorrow ... and pick you up after."

"Sounds good to me." I think my smile was a mile wide.

I jumped out and practically skipped along the sidewalk as I joined the Pattons on the porch. Our petunias had perked up in the sun and were looking good. They looked as happy as I felt.

Chapter 13

Jake's hunt went well, but then he started wandering. Doug and Max followed him as he moved through the trees and undergrowth, but they'd only let him go so far. He didn't need to be wandering through the park with so many humans around. Two humans had already gotten closer than expected, but Doug had led them away, so they couldn't take any more chances.

Then Jake stopped in his tracks, sniffed the air, and leaned over to sniff the ground. He rose up with a deep, threatening growl. He looked around with his teeth bared, snarling, seeming to warn some menace to stay away.

"What?" Doug asked as he moved into Jake's line of vision.

Then Doug took a deep breath and knew what Jake was reacting to. A stranger. A shifter that they didn't know. Someone had been hunting in their territory without permission.

"It's okay, Jake. He's gone. Gone."

Jake growled again into the night.

"Cave ... back to the cave."

Doug gently took his son's arm and turned him toward their cave. He'd be ready to shift back to human soon unless he felt the need to follow the trail of the stranger. They needed to get him away from the scent and back home. There'd be time to track down that shifter later.

"Cave, Jake. Good," Max was saying as he took a couple steps ahead of them. "Cave. Come."

Jake followed Max as Doug continued to sniff the trail of the stranger in their territory. A stranger would stop to ask permission before hunting on their land. One who didn't could be a loner. A shifter without a family. Without others to watch and protect him while he hunted. A loner could be very dangerous. On the other hand, he might have tried to ask permission, but they'd all been in Pennsylvania at the gathering. He could have been passing through and be long gone by now.

Some loners wandered constantly. Spending days as a human with no connections, just traveling and hunting when the need hit. Those were the ones that wandered into human campsites, got spotted crossing roads, and sometimes even shifted during the day and got spotted. Sometimes they became obsessed by human scent and couldn't stay away from them.

They'd search during the day and follow the trail that shifter left, because they needed to know who that stranger was. The most important thing at that moment, though, was to get Jake back to the cave. He had to be safe before they could do anything about the stranger in their territory.

* * *

Jake picked me up Sunday morning right on time. Even though I'd seen him just the day before, it was great to see his huge smile and shining eyes as I jumped into the truck.

He grabbed my hand as soon as I got in and pulled me close to give me a soft kiss on the lips.

"Good morning," he grinned.

"Hi," I smiled. I couldn't help it. Just seeing him made me feel good, happy, at peace with the world.

"Let's go. I have to tell you something." He looked serious.

"Did something happen?" His tone of voice let me know it was not something good.

He pulled onto the road and turned quickly to glance at me. "Dad saw two guys while I was hunting last night. I think it might have been your friends Robert and Danny."

"They're not my friends!" My voice was sharper than I intended. "But did they see you?" I realized that was the important point here.

"We don't know. Dad doesn't think so, but they were pretty close."

"Were you chasing a deer?"

"I just finished and was starting to wander. Dad made noise behind them to attract their attention and led them away from me. But we don't know. They might have seen me before Dad and Max noticed them."

"How close were they?"

"Well," he sighed before continuing. "I kept smelling humans and was following them. We get curious after a hunt, and I think I got pretty close."

I shrugged slightly. "I guess I'll just have to ask them if I see them today."

"I don't want you talking to them," he said with a frown on his face. "I don't trust them, and you shouldn't trust them. Besides, why would they tell you?"

"First of all, I told you I don't trust them. But they'll tell me because they like to brag. They thought they were hot stuff yesterday, saying they were going to find Bigfoot. If they actually saw you? They'll tell me."

"I don't like it, but Dad thought you should ask, too," he shook his head. "You be careful, okay? Don't be alone with them."

"If they did see you, what're you going to do?"

"Hunt them down and eat them," he said with a snarl.

"What?" My eyes must have been as big as saucers.

Jake laughed and kept taking his eyes off the road to look at me. "I'm kidding! We don't eat humans. They'd taste horrible!" Then he started laughing again.

"I was serious! What will you do?"

He still had a huge smile and crinkly eyes from laughing. "Probably nothing, but if anything comes of it, Dad can say he was out tracking deer. Maybe say he saw a bear. He'll say something that'll throw them off."

"You wouldn't really hurt them would you?"

"No! Ali, you've got to know we would never hurt a human. At least not on purpose." He got a funny look on his face when he said that. "It's happened accidentally over the years, but we wouldn't. Besides, we *are* human ... most of the time."

"So you consider yourself human?"

"Not really" he shook his head slightly. "We're two-natured shifters. Science doesn't acknowledge us, but that's what we are."

I let that hang there between us. Jake was sitting next to me and looking like an ordinary human. No. An incredible human. Thinking about him changing into Bigfoot was always at the back of my mind, but, while I thought about *him* a lot, I didn't think much about the whole shifting thing. Maybe I needed to think about it more.

"There was something else," Jake said like he wasn't sure he wanted to tell me. "We smelled a stranger."

"What do you mean, a stranger?"

"Another shifter that we don't know."

"So you know each other by smell?"

"Yeah, but none of us had ever smelled this guy before. We think he just passed through while we were at the gathering."

"So I guess I don't get the problem."

"We're pretty territorial. If someone needs to hunt in our area, they'd normally come to us first and ask. This guy didn't. Could be he's long gone, but I don't want you out in the woods until we know."

"I'm not planning on going out there, but is this you being protective of me, or could he be dangerous?"

"He could be dangerous," Jake said very seriously. "Once in a while one of us becomes a loner. They live and hunt alone and have no one to soothe them. If they run into humans, it can go badly."

"You're trying hard not to say that they could kill a human.

"If he's a loner, it's hard to tell what could happen. He was probably just passing through and needed to hunt. But you don't need to worry about it. We'll keep our eyes open and figure it out."

"Was he in the park?"

"He was on our land. I think the people in the park are safe."

"You *think* ..." I said quietly, trying hard not to look worried, but I was, and Jake probably knew it. "You know," I finally said, changing the subject. "Robert and Danny were probably drunk and didn't see anything."

Jake grinned. "I hope you're right. But they were pretty far from any park campsites. They were outside the park, too."

"But that's good. They're too lazy to walk very far, so they must have been drunk and lost. I bet they didn't see anything. Don't worry, I'll find out."

By that time, we were pulling into the parking lot. Jake unhooked his seatbelt and scooted over against me again. Every kiss was amazing. I felt it down to my toes as the warmth and connection we shared spread though me.

When our lips parted, I couldn't help but sigh deeply. I wanted to stay there in his arms and kiss him forever. I had to shake my head to get rid of the feeling, though, so I could go to work.

The thought that this working business wasn't such a good idea flitted through my head. On the other hand, it was an excellent idea, because I'd be spending every minute of every day with Jake if I didn't have to stand behind that registration desk and smile at customers. I had the feeling we'd be moving way too fast if I was with him any more than I already was.

"I'll pick you up at 4:00," Jake said quietly as we held on to each other. My head was resting on his chest and I could hear his heart beating.

"If I'm talking to Robert and Danny, just stay in the truck."

"I can't come out and beat on them a little?" he smiled, pulling away enough to look down at my face.

"They deserve it, but let me handle it this time."

"Be careful," he said as he gave me another quick kiss. As the feel of his lips radiated through me, all I could think was that it was Jake I would have to start being careful with. Dealing with Robert and Danny was much easier.

The day actually went very quickly. I was trying to remember everything I'd learned the day before while Mr. Rich was explaining new stuff. I'd forgotten about Robert and Danny until it was almost 4:00, when I saw them leave the gift shop and come marching right at me. Luckily, there weren't any other customers around.

"You can get ready to go, Ali. Good job today," Mr. Rich said while Danny and Robert stood about ten feet away and stared at me. I just gave them a tight, little smile.

"Thanks," I said to Mr. Rich. Then I went to the employee room in the back to get my purse, but had the feeling Robert and Danny would be waiting.

There they were. Sitting on the couch in front of the big fireplace and watching for me to come out from behind the counter.

"Hey, Ali," Robert said as they both jumped up to follow me toward the door.

"Hey, guys. What's up?"

"We gotta' tell you somethin' in private."

"Yeah, outside," Danny added.

"What are you guys up to?" I pretended ignorance but was afraid they were going to tell me about seeing a Bigfoot. Seeing Jake.

We got out to the covered walkway that led to the entrance and they both stopped. It was almost like a bridge with a little man-made waterfall underneath. Maybe they thought the sound of the water would cover whatever we'd be saying.

"That boyfriend of yours around?" Robert asked, looking a little tense.

"I imagine he's waiting in his truck."

"He better not try ..."

"Tell her!" Danny interrupted with a back-hand swipe to Robert's shoulder.

Robert gave him an irritated look. "We got a picture," he practically whispered. "We knew you'd want to know about it. We're taking it to the paper."

As he talked, my eyes opened wider and wider while my mouth fell open. My God, had they actually gotten a picture of Jake?

"A picture of what?" I made myself ask.

"Bigfoot! Whadya' think?"

"You're saying you camped *one* night and got a picture of Bigfoot? How many six-packs did you guys have?"

"We weren't drinking, at least not until after," Danny practically guffawed as he threw an elbow into Robert's side.

"Cut it out!" Robert shouted at Danny before turning to me. "We've been camping in that stinking tent for over a week. Last night, we really got a picture. We're gonna' ask them to put it in the paper. A lot of people have tried to get one, but we really did!"

"What was he doing? The Bigfoot I mean."

I was trying really hard to make my voice and face say I didn't believe them. I was acting on the outside like the whole thing was a stupid joke, but inside I was ready to scream.

"Strolling along. Those big arms swinging. I mean we really got a good look."

"How's the picture?" I barely knew what to think by this time.

"Here, look." Robert pulled out his phone and showed me a dark picture of something, something that really couldn't be identified. Maybe that was wishful thinking on my part.

"I don't know guys," I said shaking my head. "Looks like a blob to me."

"Are you kidding? See his back sticking out from behind that tree? And his foot there."

"I don't know," I sighed.

"You'll know when we get that million bucks," Danny said with a grin.

"Million bucks?" I asked. "What million bucks?"

"Danny!" Robert sighed as if it was something Danny shouldn't tell.

"What? It's on their website, everyone knows," he said to Robert before turning back to me. "The Olympia beer company is giving a million dollars to anyone who gets proof that Bigfoot is real. That's why we're doing this."

"Well, that picture's not proof," I said shaking my head.

"Yeah, well, we'll get it." Danny sounded very determined.

Robert gazed over my shoulder causing me to turn around. There was Jake. He'd pulled the truck up close to the entryway and was sitting there staring at us. He didn't look happy, but at least he didn't look as dangerous as he had the day before.

"I've gotta' go, guys. Good luck with that," I said, pointing at the phone.

I jogged over to the truck and jumped in. He was still scowling, and I knew that scowl would get much bigger once I started telling him what the guys had seen and gotten a picture of.

"I'll tell Dad and Mom tonight," Jake said once I'd been through the whole story.

"Shouldn't you call him or something? God, thcy got a picture!"

"You said it looked like nothing."

"Yeah, but you know how the papers are. They'll probably print it."

"And no one'll believe them. One look at those guys and everyone will think it's a hoax."

"Well I guess you're right about that."

"Dad'll know what to do, but we usually don't do anything," he shrugged.

"I guess that makes sense. Even the clear pictures I've seen on the internet look like they were faked."

"Exactly. Let's go eat somewhere and I'll need to get you home. I'm chasing Uncle Max alone tonight 'cause Dad's at some regional meeting for work."

"Alone?" Why did the thought of that send a little wave of fear through me?

"It's no big deal," he grinned. "I've chased him and Dad before."

He sounded like it really wasn't a big thing, so I let it go. "Then where do you want to eat?"

We ended up just hitting McDonald's and going for another walk in the woods. Somehow it was really comfortable holding hands under the trees with Jake. Obviously he was at home there and always knew where he was going.

He led me up another hill that had a grassy, open area at the top. Again, we looked down onto the hills and valleys of the park.

"Let's sit down and catch some sun," Jake smiled.

I smiled and found a comfy spot on the grass. He moved behind me and stretched out his legs around mine. His arms wrapped around my waist and I couldn't help but lean back against his muscular chest.

"I love wrapping my arms around you," he sighed. "And that's the human side talking."

I smiled and twisted a little to look at him. "The Bigfoot side doesn't like it?"

He laughed and kissed me gently. "The Bigfoot side is really happy right now."

I turned back to lean against him again and put my hands on his. "Well, this human is very happy, too," I whispered.

Jake rested his chin on my shoulder and we sat there just staring out at the scenery as the sun was setting over the hills. Mostly, we were simply enjoying being together. After a while, I realized I was playing with his fingers. Bending them, squeezing them, stroking them. I loved the feel of his sun-warmed skin.

He squeezed me tighter and kissed my neck. "We have to go," he sighed. "After hunting last night, I have to get some sleep before chasing Uncle Max tonight."

I turned onto my left hip to put my arms around his neck and kissed him. I heard that same little growl that I'd heard that night in the woods, but this time it was quieter. It was human.

He took my face in both of his hands. "Do you know how much I want you?"

"I think so," I sighed.

"And I don't just mean sex, although ... damn. I mean I want you in my life, in my house, in my bed. I want you to give me my children. I want us to grow old together. I want you to be mine ... and I want to be yours."

"I don't know what to say," I whispered. He'd told me he loved me, but had never said anything before about children and all that. I was still in high school. How could I think about having children?

"That's okay." He moved his hands and started to get up off the grass.

"Jake, look at me," I said as I pulled him back down. "I think maybe I'm falling hard for you, but ... forever? I'm not ready to say forever to anyone. I don't know how to explain it."

He smiled. "Falling hard, huh?"

I hit him lightly on the shoulder.

"I know what you're saying," Jake nodded, looking more serious. "Time, remember? I'll give you all you need."

I hugged him and held on tight. "Let's go," he finally said quietly.

I was starting to think that I might love him, but how could I know? How did anyone know?

"Pick you up for work tomorrow?" Jake asked as we drove along.

"No. I don't think so," I shook my head. He gave me a hurt look like I didn't want to see him. "I'm off tomorrow," I smiled.

"Oh!" A big smile crossed his face. "Wanna' come out to meet my mom?"

My turn to say, "Oh!" It would be great to meet her. One of their females, and the one who'd been calming Jake for years. Why was I feeling so apprehensive about it? "Yea, that would be nice."

"Don't be scared," he smiled and almost laughed. "There's nothing scary about Mom unless you're on the other side when she's negotiating a contract or something."

"No, I'm not scared. I just didn't expect it."

"She's been wanting to meet you," he said with a voice that almost sounded like he was pleading. "About noon. We'll have lunch."

"Sounds great." I finally smiled.

Chapter 14

I'd been expecting the Pattons to start worrying about all the time Jake and I were seeing each other. Almost overnight, we'd gone from practically nothing, to wanting to be together constantly. They had to notice that. The worry exposed itself that night when I got home.

"You've been seeing a lot of Jake lately," Mr. Patton said, trying to sound very casual. The TV was on, but none of us were very interested in whatever we were watching.

"Not really," I said kind of apologetically. "I mean, I see him every day, but only for a little while. We don't really have that much time together."

"Well, Ali," Mrs. Patton took over and I could tell she was choosing her words carefully. "He's older than you, and I hope he's not pressuring you into something you're not ready for."

"You can say it," I told them, trying not to look embarrassed by the conversation I knew was coming. "You mean sex."

Mr. Patton cleared his throat. He wasn't comfortable with this conversation, either, but Mrs. Patton plunged ahead. "It's easy to get all caught up in a guy like Jake. I mean, he's a really good look-ing guy, and paying a lot of attention to you. A girl could get carried away."

I laughed a little. "He's not like that. In fact, he's pretty old fashioned. He's not pressuring me at all."

"That's good. I'm glad to hear it," she said before hesitating a moment. "But, Ali, I think you probably feel pretty alone right now." I suddenly realized what was coming next and didn't like it one bit. "I'd hate to see you thinking Jake was a way not to be alone.

It's just not a good idea to get too close to anyone so fast. You understand?"

Yeah, I understood. They'd been talking to Mr. Jones and figured I was using my closeness to Jake to substitute for missing my mother. No one could ever take Mom's place. No one.

"You think this is about my mother." I accused her with anger in my voice, but I didn't care. Being with Jake was *not* about missing Mom. "It has nothing to do with her. Jake and I hug and kiss. That's all. He's not pushing me into anything." Yeah, anything except marriage and a life out in the woods with Bigfoot for a husband.

"Jake's the first person you've been close to since you lost your mother. We don't want you to be hurt." I could tell by her face that they did care about me, but still. Bringing Mom into all this with Jake just wasn't right.

"I don't want to talk about Mom. Jake has nothing to do with her." I was starting to feel like I'd be crying soon if they didn't shut up. Of course I missed Mom, but talking about it just made it worse. I'd talked about it enough with my counselor. I tried to keep with the anger. Anger was a lot better than crying.

"Ali," Mr. Patton said, "we just think things may be going too fast. Why don't you just see him a few times a week?"

Because I wanted to see him every day. All day. "I'm going to have lunch at his place tomorrow with his parents," I said, trying to get all the emotion out of my voice. I didn't want the anger to make me start yelling at them.

"Where do they live?" he asked.

"They have land outside the park. They live in a cabin."

"Have you met them?"

"His dad. His mom just got back from some business trip. She's a lawyer."

"In Cambridge?"

"No, some international thing." I was getting tired of this whole discussion. "This sounds like you're trying to figure out if he's good enough to marry me or something. It's not like that. It's not like I'm in love with him, or anything."

"Okay," Mrs. Patton took over again. "Just be careful and take things slow. You're just seventeen, and we don't want to see you get too involved."

"I'll be eighteen in August."

"We know," she said. I think that worried them.

While the law said that Children's Services had custody of me until I was eighteen, an exception was often made for teens, like me, who were still in high school. I'd already been told that the Pattons would let me live with them, the state would still support me, and Mr. Jones would continue as my social worker. At least until graduation.

At eighteen, though, I could walk away, and none of them could stop me. I had no intention of doing that, but they all knew they'd have to be careful not to push me too far.

"I'm going to bed. Goodnight." I got up off the couch and started toward the stairs.

"Ali," Mrs. Patton called me back. I turned and looked at her. "I want you to know we're not going to turn our backs on you once you graduate. Anytime you need us, we'll be here."

Her voice was so tender and serious. She meant it, she really did, and that made tears come to my eyes. "Thanks," I said quietly, before turning again for my room.

They thought I was in love with Jake and things were moving too fast. Was I in love with Jake? I still had no idea, but it made me mad that they were poking their noses into it. I was sure they'd talked to Mr. Jones, and that made me even madder.

But the thing that made my blood boil was the idea that Jake could take Mom's place. Being with Jake would mean I wouldn't be alone anymore, but he could never replace Mom.

Yet they really did care about me, and they knew how alone I'd be once I was out of high school and heading for college. Legally, there'd be no one to care about what happened to me, and the Pattons understood that. That was really touching because they certainly didn't have to do that.

And things weren't moving too fast with Jake. We hadn't gone beyond kissing, and I didn't think we would go beyond that anytime soon. Jake wasn't about to start anything. But did I want him to start something? Maybe.

Maybe I'd know if I loved him if we made love. Why was he so insistent on giving me time? Oh, yeah, the age thing. He'd said practically the same stuff the Pattons said – I'm only seventeen. He wanted to go slow and give me time. The Pattons said they wanted me to go slow and take my time.

Everyone was so sure how I should handle my love life except me. Well, that was something to keep me awake that night.

The next morning, my phone woke me up about 8:00. The Pattons had already left for work, and I was sleeping later than usual because I was up half the night thinking. Too bad I didn't come to any conclusions.

"Hey, Ali," Jake said when I answered. "Did I wake you up?"

"That's okay. I'm usually up by now." He had to hear the sleepiness in my voice, even though I tried to wake up quickly.

"How about if I get you about 11:30? Mom's excited to meet you."

"That sounds great ... I'll be ready."

"Wait. You want me to get you earlier? We could spend some time together."

It made me smile that he wanted to have the extra time with me. "Yeah," I whispered into the phone, "make it 10:00."

"Are you still in bed? I mean, will that give you enough time?" I could hear it in his voice. He wasn't worried about me having time. He was picturing me in bed.

"Yeah, I'm still in bed," I whispered. I wanted him to picture me.

"Okay. Uh, I'll see you at 10:00." And he hung up. I could hear in his voice that he wanted me, and I knew right then and there that I wanted him, too.

I jumped out of bed to get in the shower. I wanted to look nice to meet his mother, so it'd take some time to decide what to wear, do my hair, and put on a little make-up.

I also wanted to look nice for Jake, so getting ready wasn't a quick process.

He was right on time, and I ran out of the house as soon as I saw his truck pulling up the lane. I opened the passenger door and jumped in before he had a chance to get out and help me up into his giant truck.

"Hey," he said as I scooted over to him.

I was in his arms and kissing him before saying a word. I was glad to see him and I wanted him to know it.

He pulled away from the kiss first. "Good morning," he practically sighed.

"Hi," I sighed back.

"What do you want to do this morning?"

"I don't know. Do you know any other places in the woods where we could go?"

He smiled. "I know thousands of them."

"Okay," I smiled.

"There's a place on our land that I'd like to show you."

"Sounds good."

I wasn't much for words right then, but I think he was okay with that. He just smiled, scooted me back to the passenger side of the truck, and reached over me to grab the seatbelt and click it into place.

"So, you slept in this morning," he said after we drove in silence a little while.

"Yeah, I was up late."

"Anything wrong?" Had my voice given away the fact that I'd been upset the night before?

"No, just not sleepy."

We talked about little unimportant stuff as we drove. I wasn't going to tell him about what the Pattons said. They were wrong, so there was no point talking about it with Jake.

He finally pulled over and we started to climb another hill. It wasn't very long before we got to a spot that looked out onto the woods, but it didn't have the same wide view of hills and valleys that the other places had.

These were more gently rolling hills with a few clear meadows showing in different places. I could smell the pine trees and hear the birds singing. There were pretty clouds spotting the deep blue sky, and it just felt really comfortable. Maybe it was being with Jake that was comfortable.

"We've been on our land for the last several miles. Come sit down."

He led me close to the edge of some kind of cliff and we sat with our legs stretched out towards the steep plunge to the trees below. He put his arm around me as we sat down.

"This is your land?" I asked.

"Yeah. We're on the cliff right above the cave. I wasn't sure I should bring you here. Does it bother you? I mean to remember that night."

"No," I shook my head. "I think I like remembering that night."

He smiled and leaned down to kiss me. We were next to each other and I felt like I couldn't get my arms around him enough. I needed to be closer to him.

I got to my knees, twisted around and straddled his lap. Now I could get my arms around his neck while his arms wrapped around my waist. I started to play with his hair and stroke it gently. I heard the quiet growl that let me know how much he liked that.

Without planning anything, I started to move my lips along his jaw and onto his neck. Then my hands started to unbutton his shirt. I wanted to touch more of him. I just wanted more, and knew he wouldn't volunteer to give it to me.

"Ali," he breathed out heavily. "Stop, Ali." He took my shoulders and carefully moved me away from him. My back was to the drop-off. If he pushed, I could plummet down.

I gazed into his beautiful, caramel eyes, looked down at his muscular chest, and back up to his eyes. "Make love to me, Jake," I whispered without really planning what I was saying, letting my hands lightly stroke his chest. Maybe I had planned it. I knew he wouldn't move things forward, so I'd have to.

"That's not a good idea."

"I want you to," I sighed leaning in to kiss his neck again. "I need to know."

"Need to know?" he said, sounding a little surprised. "You know I love you."

I moved my head back to look into his eyes. "But I don't know if I love you. If we make love, I'll know." I think I sounded desperate. I would rather have sounded sexy, but didn't know how to do that.

"No, babe, that's not how it works."

"It has to be! I want to be in love with you, Jake. I really do. But I don't know what love is. I've never loved anyone." I was almost whining at him. Not a good way to get a guy to make love to you.

"Yes, you have." He looked at me so sincerely, so honestly. "You loved your mother."

"Don't!" I shouted and felt the tears start to roll down my face.

"Come here," he said quietly and pulled me into a hug, scooting back, away from the cliff. I cried against his chest.

"I know you don't want to talk about it, but I think we have to." I just sobbed some more. Talking about Mom always broke my heart. "I think that *you* think loving me will mean you love your mom less. I could never take her place in your heart. No one could. I think you're afraid loving me will push her away, but there'll always be a place inside you that's just for her. It'll always be *her* in that place. But I know there's room in there for me, too."

"I miss her," I sobbed. Why was he doing this? Talking about Mom always made me cry. It would be so much easier to just have sex and lose all these thoughts.

"Of course you do," he said while brushing my hair back and gently kissing my forehead. "But I want more than just sex from you, Ali. I want us to be bonded. I want you forever, and I can't make love to you, no matter how much I want you, until I know that's what you want, too."

I just continued to sob while Jake continued talking. "When you're ready to let me into your heart ... with your mom, not instead of her ... then we'll bond. And I'll make love to you for the rest of our lives."

I cried and cried as I buried my head against his chest. He stroked my back and started to slowly rock us back and forth. I felt like no one understood. No one except Jake. I couldn't stand the idea of loving anyone as much as I loved Mom. Somehow, he got that.

And I think he was right. It did feel like letting Jake in meant pushing Mom out. Could I find a way to give them both room? He'd give me time, but how long would it take?

After what seemed like I'd been crying forever, I was finally ready to stop. "What made you so smart?" I asked as I wiped some tears off my cheek.

"My mom," he whispered.

"You talked to her about me?" I finally looked up at him. My eyes were probably all red and swollen and I probably looked like hell, but I looked anyway.

"Yeah. No one understands how people feel better than she does."

"Oh," I said.

"I'm sorry. Does it bother you that I talked to her?"

"It's just embarrassing. I haven't even met her and... Oh, hell! I'm on my way to meet her and I must look like crap!"

"You look beautiful," he whispered and hugged me a little tighter.

"Yeah, well, to you. I need a mirror."

"Let's go back to the truck. It has that nice big rearview you can use." He smiled.

I felt good enough to smile back. "I'm sorry," I sighed. "I'm sorry I started all this."

"I'm not. Remember when you said we needed to be honest with each other? This was maybe the most honest we've ever been," he paused for a few seconds. "And I love that you want to have sex with me," he grinned.

I let out a little breath and looked away. The whole thing was really embarrassing, but I was still smiling. I looked down at his chest again and buttoned him up because I couldn't think of anything to say.

Jake planted a quick kiss on my temple and stood up to head back to the truck. Walking in silence, hand in hand, I had never felt so close to anyone ... except Mom.

We pulled off the park's highway #1 onto a smaller road. After a few miles, we turned onto a dirt road. It was so shaded, there was still some mud from the rain the other night. The trees grew right on the edges and arched over the road creating all that shade, even though the sun was shining brightly. There were spots where it looked like we were going through a tunnel.

We kept going as the road got narrower, and I told Jake I understood why he had this huge, 4x4 truck. We curved around and went up and down a few hills, until we started climbing again. At least the trees weren't as thick, so the sun had gotten in and dried up all the mud.

At the top of a hill, the road ended between two cabins. The forest was groomed here, with grassy areas, flowers blooming along the walls of the cabins, and a couple smaller outbuildings. It looked like the lower branches of the surrounding trees were trimmed off so everyone could move around easily. There was plenty of space between the trees so the sun shone in brightly. It was really pretty.

Jake parked on a cement pad along the side of one cabin. Another truck was already there. Someone looked out the window of the cabin across an expanse of grass, and Jake waved at him. "Uncle Max," he told me quietly. "I don't think he's comfortable seeing you again."

"I think he's worried about you," I answered, trying to sound understanding.

"Probably," Jake shrugged. "But he's just not comfortable around human women."

I didn't know what to say to that, but didn't have a chance anyway because Jake's mom came out of the other cabin to greet us. She gave me a huge smile and I couldn't help but notice her deep blue eyes. She was a little shorter than me, had dark-blond, shoulder length hair, and a great figure. She was dressed simply in jeans, ankle boots, and a turquoise, button-down shirt that made her eyes sparkle.

She was so self-assured. One look at her made me feel like I was meeting a queen. No wonder she was strong enough to keep Jake and his dad calm and controlled so they could live their daily, human lives. She was beautiful and looked way too young to be Jake's mother. How was I expected to live up to her?

She took both my hands in hers and gave me a warm smile that made me remember how she'd understood about Mom and how she'd explained it to Jake. I thought I'd be embarrassed to meet her since she knew so much about me, but I wasn't. I felt welcomed.

"It's so good to meet you, Ali," she said as she gently squeezed my hands.

"It's good to meet you, too, Mrs. Shepherd."

"Please call me Nina. Mrs. Shepherd is my professional name." Then she laughed slightly as she said, "I'm not a lawyer here." I just nodded.

She reached up to touch Jake's shoulder as she gave him a light kiss on the cheek. "Come into the house, you two," she said as Jake smiled down at her.

The house was beautiful in a simple, but obviously expensive way. It was a mix of modern and rustic that somehow worked to be very pleasant and relaxing. The earth-tone colors created a warm, woodsy feeling. The log walls were different from anything I'd ever seen, but I liked them.

Nina had made us a delicious lunch of a big salad with mixed greens, pecans, cranberries and blue cheese with a raspberry dressing, and chicken salad sandwiches.

While we ate, I was glad to talk about something besides me and my screwy emotions. But we didn't talk about shifting, women calming their men, or anything else remotely serious. At least not until I laughed at Jake for eating two of those huge sandwiches.

"You'll find that our men have big appetites," Mrs. Shepherd smiled. "The two-natured use a lot of energy."

Jake and I sometimes avoided talking about his Bigfoot side, but I liked the way she casually slipped it into the conversation. Maybe I was getting more comfortable with the whole thing. Or maybe she was really good at making me comfortable.

As we sat at the table after eating, she asked me if I had any questions. I had a big question, but didn't know if I should bring it up or not. Jake acted funny when I mentioned it to him. It was so easy for her to talk about Bigfoot, though, I decided to plunge in.

"Uh, I told Jake I'd like to see him again after he shifted. He wasn't sure about that."

"His Bigfoot side," she said very matter-of-factly. "Why did you think that wouldn't be a good idea, Jake?"

"I didn't want to scare her," Jake answered, but then glanced over at me. "I think you were really scared that first night."

"Yeah, but I thought you were going to kill me, and I didn't know it was *you*. I know you'd never hurt me."

Jake looked at his mom with a question in his eyes.

"It gets a little complicated." She sighed, looking at me. "If we were sure you were going to mate, then you could comfort him and start to take over from me. He's sure you're the one he's meant to be with, so you'd be able to soothe him. But, if you decided not to bond, it would be devastating for him."

"Oh, I didn't think of it that way," I said, quietly glancing between Jake and his mom.

"I'll be able to help him for awhile yet, but after he's found his mate ..." she shook her head. "Once that happens, a mother's influence won't help anymore."

I gazed at Jake. "I don't mean to make things hard for you. I just ..." I stopped talking and looked down at the floor.

"I know," he said quietly.

"You're really sure, aren't you?" I asked, looking back into his eyes. "I mean, if I was sure, too, we'd be mated already, wouldn't we?"

Now it was Jake's turn to look down at the floor.

"Ali," Mrs. Shepherd said softly. "If you were Family, you probably would be mated. But we know that humans don't recognize the bonding chemistry like we do. You need time to realize it's there. We can't blame you for that."

"So, you'll keep taking care of him?" I think my voice sounded like I was pleading with her.

"Of course I will. But I don't think you should see his Bigfoot side until you're sure."

"Okay." Part of me wasn't sure I wanted to say what was on my mind, but I had to. "But I'd still like to. Does that mean I'm starting to feel it?"

"It might," she looked at me like she was thinking something over very carefully. "But I think the real issue is chemical."

"Chemical? What do you mean?"

"Women born in The Family have the same chemical bonding ability that the men have. We feel the bond almost immediately, like they do," she explained. "You're different because you're human. For you, love usually takes time. Even when it's love-at-first-sight, humans often have trouble acknowledging it."

"If we're chemically different, how can I ever help Jake the way I should?"

"Have you told her about bonding?" she asked Jake.

"I told her I'd bite her," he said, looking embarrassed.

"Just like a man," she smiled. "He told you the scary part, but not the positive part. The bite will break the skin, and his saliva will enter your system. That's what gives us the ability to comfort our men. Without that physical, chemical bond, our influence isn't as strong."

I looked over at Jake and saw the love and longing in his eyes. I didn't know what to say for a few minutes, but my thoughts finally came together. I looked back at Mrs. Shepherd. "But he says being close to me, kissing me, helps him."

"That's because you're meant for each other and I still soothe him. Once you bond, I won't be able to calm him anymore."

"I'm sorry, Jake, but I just can't be sure, yet," I said quietly.

"And there's still the issue of you finishing school," Mrs. Shepherd said like that uncomfortable moment hadn't happened.

"Another year," I sighed.

"I'll wait, Ali," Jake said, looking into my eyes. "You know I will."

"Yeah, I know." His eyes were full of his love for me. I wished I could be sure I felt the same love for him.

"School's important, Ali," Mrs. Shepard said, "especially to females. We're the ones who can function in human society. Our males give us our homes and keep us safe and secure. But they can't make it through school to get professional jobs. It's just not in them to spend that much time around humans."

"I'll still be able to go to college?" I had to ask.

"Of course. Unless that's not what you want to do."

"Waiting for me to finish college seems such a long time," I sighed.

Mrs. Shepherd gave me a gentle laugh. "Married women go to college all the time. I didn't finish law school until Doug and I'd been married for ten years."

"I didn't think of that," I smiled.

"Enough of these serious discussions," Mrs. Shepherd said as she stood and started collecting dirty dishes from the table. Jake immediately got up to join her, so I carried my plate over to the sink, too.

"The dishes can wait," Mrs. Shepherd said, turning away from the dishwasher. "Why don't we go see the work Jake's done on his cabin?"

"His cabin?" He'd never mentioned anything to me about a cabin. "Are you building a cabin?"

"Yeah, but I didn't want to pressure you or anything."

"How would that pressure me?"

Mrs. Shepherd grinned when I asked that. "Jake, you should tell her," she said as she turned away from us to put the leftovers in the refrigerator.

I looked at him with my eyebrows raised.

"Young males build a home for their future mates. I've been working on it since ... well, since I missed the last couple weeks of school."

I took a deep breath. "You're building it for *me*?"

"I hope so." Jake gazed into my eyes and I could see that it meant a lot to him.

What did I say to that? My God, he was building me a house. A place for the two of us. A home. I hadn't realized how much I missed having a place that belonged to me, where I belonged. My eyes got misty as I thought about it and I was afraid I would cry if I said anything. I'm sure Jake could see the sparkle of those tears in my eyes.

Mrs. Shepherd came over and stroked Jake's shoulder. I could see him relax a little. "Let's go see it," she said quietly.

We walked a little way into the trees before I could see stacks of logs around a clearing. I couldn't believe how many logs there were. As we got closer, I noticed a big hole in the ground with stacks of cement blocks on the cement floor. Along one side, many of them were already set in place. It was obviously the beginnings of a basement.

"You're doing this?" I asked. I was so surprised. Amazed that he could actually build a house on his own.

"Yeah," Jake smiled. "But I'll get help on the stuff I don't know how to do. You know, electrical, plumbing, that kind of stuff."

"Where'd you get all the logs?"

"I cut them," Jake answered like it was no big deal.

"You mean you cut down the trees and took off the bark all yourself? How did you learn to do all this?"

"We all learn and help each other. Some of the younger males that live nearby come help me so they'll learn. Each of us has to have a place to bring our bonded mate. She has to have a home."

I was so touched. I just wrapped my arms around him and whispered, "It's beautiful."

"Not yet," he whispered back. "But it will be."

I realized that Mrs. Shepherd was gone. She walked quietly away and left us alone. Jake and I held on to each other for a few minutes. When I stepped back from him I turned slowly to look around at the view.

It was surrounded by trees, without another cabin in sight, but I knew Jake's parents were just through the undergrowth in their own cabin. From here, though, you could feel like you were the only people in the world.

"I'll clear out the underbrush when it's done so we'll be part of Dad's and Uncle Max's yards. Dad wanted me to put it closer, but I wanted this spot. Come here," he said taking my hand.

We walked around the basement foundation and through a couple trees. "I'm going to cut and trim some of these trees so we have a view of the hills out there," he said quietly, pointing into the distance which we hadn't been able to see at all just a few steps back. "I'll use them to put a balcony off the bedroom, but I don't think anyone will be able to see the cabin from below. It'll still be hidden, but we'll have a great view."

We'll have a great view. He was putting in things I'd like. Actually that we'd both like. My heart fluttered. "I love it," I whispered.

I wished I could say so easily that I loved him.

Chapter 15

"Will you finish the friggin' beer?" Robert yelled at Danny. "We'd never get outta' here if it was up to you."

"Then go without me!" Danny shouted back, even though he knew Robert wouldn't.

"Yeah, and leave you cryin' like a little girl."

"Shut up!" Danny yelled. He started to walk away, before turning back and saying, "Well? Are we goin', or not?"

Neither of them were as anxious to start hunting the dark woods for Bigfoot as they had been on previous nights. Actually seeing one had terrified them both, even though neither of them was ready to admit it.

What they saw had been huge, incredibly dangerous looking, and moved like it was looking for something to kill. Robert knew he really didn't want to see another one, but wanted the million dollars more than he wanted to get out of the woods. Admitting they were scared was something neither of them was willing to confess to the other.

"Look, we've gotta' be careful tonight," Robert said as they left the tent and started moving along a marked hiking trail. "That last one must've heard us. We've gotta' get a better picture."

"Yeah, I know, I know," Danny waved his arm like he was dismissing whatever Robert was saying. "And I say we hafta stay on the deer trails until we see something. He won't hear us there."

"Right!" Robert agreed. Once they were out of sight of other campers, they moved from the human path through the trees, looking for a clear deer trail. They switched on their flashlights to watch where they were stepping. Even though the stars were bright, they didn't help light the area under the trees.

"That damn paper," Robert said after a few minutes. "Wouldn't even let us tell our story!"

"The hell with the paper! I want that million bucks! Can you believe it? Us with a million bucks?"

"How much beer would that buy?" Robert added. They both laughed and punched each other as they started down a surprisingly wide trail.

They'd walked around for over an hour without seeing or hearing anything. Finally, they came to a small stream that cut across the path they were following.

"Can we jump it, ya think?" Danny asked.

"And get where? Climb that hill on the other side? Hell, I'm taking a break. Gimme a beer." Robert sat down on a log next to the path and reached out his hand. He stared at Danny, waiting for a can of cold beer to appear in his hand.

Danny sat on the log with Robert and pulled off the cooler/backpack he was carrying. "The friggin' things are too damn heavy. Oughta' just drink 'em so we don't have to carry 'em."

"Sounds good to me," Robert answered as he pulled the tab on the can.

Danny half chuckled. "Shouldn't we be drinkin' Olympia?"

"Let 'em give me a million ... then I'll drink their beer." They both laughed.

After about ten minutes, they were both on their second cans. "We should check that stream for prints," Robert mumbled and acted like he was about to get up off the log.

"Go check it," Danny answered making it obvious that he wasn't ready to move very soon. "I'm finishing this here." He raised his can like he had to show Robert what he was going to finish and took a long drink.

"You're not coming?"

Danny shook his head as he swallowed. "I'll be here."

"Fine. I'll do it myself." Robert stood, drained his can before throwing it under a tree, and marched off toward the stream.

Danny watched him gazing down at the edge of the steep bank before moving off into the darkness to the left. "Asshole," he mumbled as Robert disappeared into the trees. Danny said from the start that the picture wasn't good enough to take to the paper, but Robert couldn't wait.

They'd been laughed out of the paper's office, but Robert was still sure they'd get proof right away. In the back of his mind, Danny figured they'd have to capture or kill one to win the million, but hadn't mentioned it to Robert, yet. Robert was stubborn as hell and wouldn't listen to Danny's arguments, so Danny'd just wait for him to figure it out for himself.

It felt like Robert had been gone quite a while when Danny finally heard him moving back through the trees. But the rustling sounded like it was coming from behind, and Danny figured he was going to try to sneak up on him. Too bad he sounded like an elephant moving through the brush. Danny just sat there and let Robert approach.

But it wasn't Robert.

Suddenly, something rammed Danny from behind sending his third beer flying out of his hand and skidding across the ground. He heard the growls and felt the warm breath of the creature against his neck as incredibly strong, hairy arms wrapped around his chest. It all happened so fast, Danny hadn't even had time to think.

Squeezed so hard he couldn't get a breath, Danny wasn't able to scream, even though that was what his brain kept telling him to do.

Instead, he kicked, squirmed and tried to break away from that vice-like grip. But it held his arms tight against his sides, and Danny could barely move.

The monster started to swing him back and forth, sending his legs sailing from side to side like they were playing some childish game. He lifted him higher by standing straight and leaning back. Then Danny heard a loud growl and felt himself falling, crashing to the ground. He felt like he'd fallen from the top of a tree. The hairy beast was on him again before he could move to get to his feet, but he finally got a good breath and screamed out as loud as he could.

Danny was grabbed by giant hands around the waist and lifted high over the monster's head. He had to be ten to twelve feet in the air and really didn't want to be dropped again. The creature lifted him like anyone else would lift a two-year-old and stared into Danny's face.

He could see the cold, green eyes and the huge teeth sneering at him. The hands held him so tight, he thought he might throw up and had the ridiculous thought that he would make the monster really mad if he threw up in its face. While those thoughts flew through his head, he kept screaming.

But he didn't have to stare down at the monster for long. It growled really loud right in Danny's face and dropped him again. Actually, it threw him to the side. Danny's screams got louder and more desperate as he flew through the air, feeling like he was a spiked football when his back hit the ground. All the air whooshed out of his lungs and, again, he had to struggle to breath.

The monster stared down at Danny who started to stammer, "P-p-please stop. L-l-let me ga-ga-go." He was crying, slobbering and trying to crab-crawl away. Now that he could get short, gasping breaths, all he could think was that he didn't want to die. He didn't want to be some bloody body left for the buzzards to find.

But some part of Danny's brain must have still been functioning normally, because he caught sight of movement behind the monster. Robert was sneaking up on him. For a second, he felt the relief of knowing he was saved, but then realized that Robert would just end up as another body out here to be food for any scavenger that came along.

The Bigfoot suddenly spun his body to his right swinging his arm out to catch Robert and send him flying. The creature's reach was unbelievable. Robert's feet came completely off the ground from the force of the blow and he sailed about ten feet away. He landed with a loud crash in the bushes, and Danny saw him lie there like he was dead.

"Robert!" Danny cried out, but then saw him move, trying to get up.

The monster glared at him, and looked over at Robert. Then he threw his head back and growled long and loud into the night. Danny had to cover his ears, as the growl changed into a terrifying scream. It was so loud and intimidating. *This is it*, he thought. *It's going to kill us now.*

But the Bigfoot just took a breath like it was calming itself down. His nostrils flared as he sniffed the air around them, and he turned to stroll off through the trees. Before Danny knew it, the creature was gone and he and Robert were still sprawled out on the ground where they'd been thrown.

* * *

Doug, Jake, and Max had spent two days searching for the stranger that they'd detected on their land. His trail was all over, crossing many times and extending into the park. It wasn't someone just passing through. Someone seemed to like hunting their land.

"I'll need to call Adam today," Doug said. Max had joined him and Nina for breakfast before work. Jake was still sound asleep. "He'll bring his sons, and that should be enough of us to find him."

"The trails are heading over to his area, too," Max said. "I wonder if they've picked up his scent, yet."

"Probably not. They usually hunt farther east. This guy seems to head south once he gets near their territory."

"So he's staying closer to the park?" Nina asked.

"Yeah. Mostly on the north and east sides of it," Doug answered. "Pisses me off, too. Damn loner causing problems."

Max got a painful look on his face, but didn't say anything.

"What?" Doug asked, looking at Max.

"It's just, I kinda' feel for the guy, you know?"

"For a loner? They're a curse," Doug said dismissing what Max said.

Max looked at Nina and knew she got it, but Doug obviously didn't. "Doug, I think Max is trying to say he could have ended up being a loner."

"No, Max. You wouldn't do that."

"Not now. But if it wasn't for you, I might have." The look on his face easily showed how much he appreciated Doug and all the help he'd given him over the years.

"Max, you'll always have family. Not just us and Jake, but Adam and his boys, too. We'd all do anything for you."

"I know it. But, if things had been different."

"They aren't different. You're part of us. That's just fact."

"I appreciate that," Max said looking in Doug's eyes. They both nodded, communicating all they needed to.

"Oh! I have to get to work," Nina said as she glanced at the clock and jumped up, grabbing her plate and coffee cup.

Doug checked the clock, too. "I didn't know it was so late. I'll get the dishes. You go, sweetheart."

"Hey," Max added. "You both go, and I'll get the dishes."

"You don't have to do that," Nina said.

"I don't mind. Here or at home, what's the difference? So go!"

"I'll owe you," Doug said with a slap to his back.

"You already gave me a free breakfast." He grinned. "Get out of here."

"Thanks, Max," Nina said, as she kissed his cheek. "But, if Jake wakes up, don't you dare cook him breakfast. He can do that himself."

"You kidding? At his age, he'll sleep for hours. I'll be long gone."

"See you tonight!" Doug called as he and Nina left for work.

Max started loading the dishwasher and cleaning up the pans from the bacon and eggs. He stopped long enough to turn on the radio before dumping the coffee grounds into the trash. Then he heard the news that made him freeze in his tracks.

"Doug," he gasped as soon as Doug answered his cell.

"What's up, man, I'm still on our lane."

"Turn on the radio. Two kids were attacked in the park last night."

"Attacked?"

"They're saying Bigfoot."

"Okay. Wake up Jake. I'll be right back."

"Jake," Max yelled as he headed for the bedroom. "Jake! Wake up, man!" Jake was flat on his stomach with his head buried into the pillows and covers. He jumped up onto his knees as he woke.

"What? Uncle Max, what happened?" Max could tell he wasn't fully awake, but they didn't have time to fool around.

"Two kids attacked in the park last night. They're saying Bigfoot."

"Ah, shit! The loner?" Now Jake was awake, jumping out of bed, and starting towards the bathroom, leaving the door open. "Dad at work?" he shouted to Max.

"He was on his way, but I called him. He's coming back."

Max heard the toilet flush and water run before Jake came out grabbing clothes. "Are we headed out?"

"I imagine. You know, they might just be lying."

"Yeah, that's happened before."

"Yeah."

They heard the front door slam as Doug yelled, "Max! Jake!"

"We're ready," Max said as they hurried into the living room with Jake still pulling his shirt over his head.

"There's liable to be cops around the area. We'll need to be careful and stay cool."

"Did they say anything about these guys?" Jake asked with a confused look on his face. "Who were they?"

"They said the names ..." Max answered while thinking. "One of them was Robert Dugan, the other Danny something."

"Shit! I knew it," Jake shook his head and looked mad as hell. "That's those two guys who know Ali. The ones that said they got a picture."

"So now they're saying they were attacked? What's with them?" Doug asked.

"Ali says they're idiots."

"We'll have to check it out," Doug said. "If they really did run into one of us, it had to have been the loner."

"Shit!" Jake was shaking his head. "We should have kept after him. We should have caught him before he ran into humans."

"Jake, we tried," his dad said calmly. "We tried, son."

"I know." Jake shook his head.

It didn't take them long to find the general area, which wasn't far from where their own land started. All they had to do was follow the scent of the loner. Once they smelled the slight trace of human blood and sweat, they knew they'd found the right spot. It was off any of the main hiking trails, but near a stream.

"Let's circle around the area," Doug said. "See if we can find out which way he was traveling."

Jake and Max just nodded. They spread out so they were within easy sight of each other, but could still cover a wider area. It didn't take them long. They found the scent heading out of their land and right toward the scene of the attack.

"This is fresh," Doug said.

"Yeah," Jake answered. "And he's come through here several times. I can still pick up the older scents from days ago."

"Let's head back," Doug said shrugging his shoulders. "Nothing else for us to find here."

"What're we gonna' do?" Jake sighed.

"I'll call June," Doug said.

June had been on the police force for about ten years, and had been steadily climbing the ranks. Within a few years she'd probably make detective. Most importantly, though, she was Doug and Max's sister. Bonded with Nathan, and the mother of two teenagers, they'd settled to the south side of the park near Nathan's parents. Having Family on the force was a benefit they were all thankful for.

"She must be saying something," Jake said as he and Max watched Doug sitting in the truck with his cell to his ear.

"Maybe she's telling Doug what they don't know," Max answered.

"It doesn't matter what she says." Jake was pacing and shaking his head. "We still have to find that damn loner. We have to kill him before he steps up to really hurting someone."

"I know. We will."

"Okay," Doug said once he'd called Jake and Max back to the truck. "Neither guy was hurt bad, but scared to death. They had scrapes, bruises, but no bites. She figures the loner was playing with them. The cops found empty beer cans and a backpack with a couple more still inside, so they figure they got drunk and beat on each other."

"That's good, then. They won't be investigating," Jake said.

"There's more," Doug added. "I guess the paper's all over it. They've sent reporters to talk to the two of them."

"Ah, shit!" Jake growled.

"Does June think the paper's taking them seriously?" Max added.

"The area's hot for Bigfoot stories. She says it's just something to get people to buy the paper, and it'll probably be in today."

"Ah, shit!" Jake growled again.

"You know any other words?" Doug asked.

"None that fit."

Doug shook his head. "She said Nathan can't help us right now. He's watching their boy, Glen. He'll be shifting for the first time really soon."

"I forgot Glen's that old," Max said. "Nathan hasn't had any sign of the loner in their area?"

"Not yet," Doug shook his head. "I'll get Adam and his sons. All six of us will head out tonight, and we'll get him. You need to hunt tonight, right, Max?"

"No, I'll wait."

"We can take you north right after dark," Doug offered.

"We need to be out here from dusk 'till dawn. I'll wait."

"Then I'm going to work. There's nothing we can do until to-night," Doug said.

"Yeah. Nothing we can do now," Max agreed.

"Ah, shit!" Jake growled one more time.

"What now?" Doug blurted out.

"They've been bragging to Ali about what they're doing. Those assholes might have called her."

"Maybe *you'd* better call her and find out," Doug said.

"I wanna' check online first. Sometimes the paper puts stuff there before the print version comes out."

"Good idea," Doug said as Jake used his phone to access the paper's site.

"Here it is," Jake said. "Ah, shit, that picture they took is in."

"Lemme see," Doug said as he reached for Jake's phone. "Okay, that looks like nothing."

"Yeah, but it's my ass sticking out from behind that tree."

Max couldn't help but laugh. "Call Ali before she hears it some-where else."

"Yeah," Jake said. "I'm calling her right now."

"Jake!" Ali sounded surprised and pleased as she answered. "I thought I wouldn't hear from you until tonight."

"Hi, sweetheart," Jake hesitated. "Something happened."

"Oh God, what?" She thought her heart skipped a beat wonder-ing what it could be.

"Your two guys are saying they were attacked by Bigfoot last night."

"Oh, Jake," she said, sounding confused and worried. "What happened?"

"They were beaten up some, but not hurt bad." He sounded almost like he was apologizing. Ali had a sudden terrible thought that Jake did it. But, no. He wouldn't have done that. "The cops think they beat each other, but it's in the paper. They're telling the whole story."

"It was him." Not a question. It had taken a total of two seconds for her to realize the real story.

"Yeah. But I can't say a lot on the phone. Okay if I come on over?"

"Sure, the Pattons are at work."

"Then I'll see you as soon as I can get there."

"I'll call Robert ... see what he's willing to tell me."

"You have Robert's number?" He sounded more than a little jealous. Ali shook her head, even though she knew he couldn't see it.

"Don't be like that," she said, scolding him. "The two of them went around school putting their numbers in every girl's phone. We all left them so we'd know who it was if they called us."

"Yeah, well, that makes sense. I'll see you soon."

"Jake?" Ali called right before he hung up.

"Yeah?"

"Hurry. Okay?"

"Okay, babe, I'll hurry."

Chapter 16

By the time Jake got to me, I was really upset. Not the crying, hurt kind of upset, but the mad and worried kind. How could those two have actually run into a Bigfoot? Again. Just walking around, drinking beer, and being oblivious targets out in the dark woods, they'd been attacked.

I remembered the night Jake attacked me out there. I was so terrified, but he hadn't hurt me. He loved me.

Robert sounded almost crazy when I talked to him. He kept saying the cops didn't believe them, but he and Danny would prove it. "They think we're lying! You believe us, don't you, Ali?" he begged.

How could I answer that question? I *knew* he was telling the truth. "I don't know, Robert," I answered. "Could it have been some big guy?"

"You think we don't know the difference between a Bigfoot and some asshole out in the woods? That thing squeezed Danny so hard he couldn't breathe. He's got a cracked rib! It lifted him over its head and threw him down! Could some guy do that?"

"Do the reporters believe you?" I had to get off the subject of *me* believing them.

"I don't know," he sighed, with a much calmer tone in his voice. "They act like they do, but Danny says they probably just want a story."

"What about the million dollars?"

He gave me a sinister little laugh the made me cringe. "We've got some ideas about that."

"You're going out there again?" I didn't do a very good job of hiding my shock. I really couldn't believe they'd keep searching for it.

"Damn right! This time we'll get the proof."

"Robert, you can't. You could be really hurt."

"Would that upset you, Ali?" All of a sudden he was sounding like he was flirting with me again. Why did I have to keep dealing with these two dopes?

"I don't want anyone hurt."

"We won't be. Not again."

"What's that mean?"

"I can't tell you, yet. We haven't had time to work it all out."

"Just don't do anything stupid, okay?"

"Don't worry. But I'll call you when we've got the million. Maybe you'd like to help us celebrate."

"Stop it, Robert," I spat out at him. "Just be careful. That thing could kill you."

"So you do believe me," he said with that voice that he thought was sexy. "Oh yeah, we'll be careful. See you at the lodge."

"Robert!" But he'd already hung up. I wanted to tell him to give it up, but those idiots really thought they'd win a million dollars.

Minutes later, Jake rang the doorbell, and I found myself running across the living room to let him in. I threw my arms around him and hugged him as hard as I could. Was I that upset about Robert and Danny? I was upset, but I think most of my reaction was relief that Jake wasn't involved.

"It's okay, Ali. It'll be okay," I heard him saying as he moved us into the house and closed the door behind him.

"It's not okay," I blurted out. "Those two have some kind of plan to win that million dollars, but they wouldn't say what they were going to do."

"Are they sticking to their story?"

"Yeah, but Robert said the police didn't believe them. Jake, was it really a Bigfoot, the loner?" I was talking so fast, I just hoped he could follow what I was saying.

"Yeah, we found the area, and the scent was really clear." Jake was being calm, with a very matter-of-fact attitude.

"They're going to put it in the paper. Will people believe it?"

"People will laugh at it." Jake was saying the words, but didn't sound so convinced himself.

"But a lot of people believe in Bigfoot. Won't they be out looking for one?"

"Maybe, but we can handle it. They've searched for us before, you know," he grinned.

"But now there's two idiots saying one attacked them! You have to stay out of the woods, Jake! You can find somewhere else to hunt, can't you? What if someone wants to capture you, or something?" I was ranting by this time, but I couldn't help it.

"Ah, babe, we'll be okay."

"You don't know that! I couldn't stand it if something happened to you."

"I feel the same way about you. And I love that you're worried about me getting hurt," Jake smiled. "But we've handled this kind of stuff before. We'll take care of it." He put his arms back around me and held me gently.

"What will you do?" I know my voice sounded weak like a little girl, but I was worried. What could they do?

"We'll keep hunting for him."

"Maybe you should leave him alone. What if he comes after you? Or your dad, or Max?"

"Ali, think about it. We can't let him have contact with humans." Jake's voice was so quiet, trying to calm me down. "He's one of us. He's our problem. Dad called some relatives, so there'll be six of us and we'll search in pairs. We'll be okay, and we'll get him."

"Tonight?"

"Yeah. So I won't be able to see you. In fact, I need to get home soon so we can make some plans with Adam and his sons."

"That's who you called? And they'll help you?"

"Adam's dad's cousin and he's got two grown sons, Greg and Pete. Their land is east of ours. They'll help a lot."

Standing there with my arms around his waist, I never wanted to let him go. We were pressed close together, his arms around my shoulders, and I could feel all his chest and ab muscles. I knew how strong and fast he was, but I hated that he'd be going out there to face that horrible loner.

"Take me with you," I whispered, almost begging.

"No way!" He shook his head, and his voice told me that I wouldn't be able to talk him into this one. But I had to try.

"I can help. Maybe I can attract him or something."

"You think we should use you as bait? We'd never let a female out in those woods while a loner's hunting."

"But he's hunting humans."

"He's not really hunting humans, just couldn't resist them. Besides, we'll be human. He'll notice us if he's out there."

"So you'll be as helpless as I would be!" Now I was almost yelling.

"Ali, we won't be helpless," Jake said, using that calming voice again. "We can shift. We can face him as Bigfoot, and it'll be six against one. You have to trust that we know how to do this." He hugged me even tighter. "Do you think Dad or Mom would let me be in danger?"

"Oh, Jake," I mumbled as the tears started again. "I don't know what I think. I'm just so upset and worried."

"I know, sweetheart, but I'll see you tomorrow. You go to work at 11:00, right? I'll pick you up."

"You have to text me as soon as you get done searching tonight. Doesn't matter how late it is. I have to know you're safe."

"I will," Jake smiled. It made me smile back, and that felt so much better than the tears.

"You won't make me wait any longer than you absolutely have to?"

"I won't."

Then he leaned down to kiss me. I squeezed him as hard as I could, not ever wanting to let go. The feel of his arms, his lips, moved through my body. I could smell his warm, masculine scent that made me want to surrender to him every time he touched me. Was I feeling the bond he was so sure about? Or simply lust? No, it was more than that. I cared about *him* and couldn't stand the thought of being without him.

I watched his truck disappear down the lane and suddenly felt very much alone. I wanted to spend my day off with Jake instead of waiting all day to hear from him. I had laundry to do and could do some weeding in the garden, but those chores weren't going to take all day. I still had way too much time for worry.

* * *

The hum of my phone vibrating next to my face woke me at 5:30 the next morning. The night before, I'd put it carefully on my pillow so I'd be sure to hear it. I was half-asleep when Jake called. I'd spent the whole day and evening wondering, worrying, and trying my best to act pleasant in front of the Pattons. I thought I deserved an Academy Award for my performance in front of them.

"Hey," he said quietly. He sounded really tired. "I couldn't stand to just text. Wanted to hear your voice."

"How are you?" I blurted out as I popped up to sit crossed-legged on my bed.

"I'm good. We didn't find anything, though." I could hear his disappointment.

"Nothing?" I realized then how much I'd wanted them to find the loner so it could all be over.

"He wasn't out there, or we would have found him. So we'll go again tonight."

"Again? Maybe he left." I so wanted that to be true, but knew it probably wasn't.

"He might have, but I doubt it. If he thinks he got away with something, he'll stay. This is a good area to hunt. We kinda hope he thinks we won't be able to find him."

"You're sure he knows you're looking? I mean, does he know you're here?"

"He has to. Our scents are all over."

"I didn't think of that."

"I'm gonna' get a few hours sleep and pick you up for work. You sound like you didn't sleep much either."

"Not much. But Mr. Patton could take me, it's no big deal for him to leave work. You didn't sleep at all."

"No way! I need to see you. I want to hold you. Can I pick you up a little early?"

"That'd be great."

"I'll see you about 10:00, okay?"

"Great, get some sleep."

"You, too. Bye, sweetheart."

"Bye."

He was safe. Safe in his own house, in his own bed. It was the fear of him being hurt – I couldn't even let myself consider him being killed – that had kept me up all night. I didn't want him to be the one to face that monster. How could his parents send him out there like that? But, like he said, they wouldn't.

If there was really a danger, his parents would keep him safe. I was sure of that. It was just my own fear that made me so worried. Jake would be fine. They'd get that guy, Robert and Danny would give up, and everything would be fine.

After worrying all night, I realized I was exhausted and had to get some sleep before I went to work. I set my cell alarm for 8:30 to give me plenty of time to get ready before Jake picked me up. I think it only took me about five seconds to fall sound asleep.

Mrs. Patton knocked on my door and woke me up about 7:30. "I'm sorry to wake you, Ali, but I needed to talk to you before I leave for work."

"That's okay," I mumbled in my sleepiness.

"Mr. Jones called and is coming to take you to work this morning. He'll be here about 10:30."

"He doesn't need to. Jake's picking me up at 10:00."

She looked a little irritated. "The point is that he hasn't seen you in a while and wants to talk to you."

"I'll talk to him some other time," I said as pleasantly as I could. I was thinking, *No way. I have to see Jake.*

"Ali," she said with a sterner voice than I'd ever heard, "he's arranged his schedule around yours."

"So has Jake," I practically spat out. I was still sleepy and the idea that they expected me to throw Jake aside to talk to Mr. Jones was starting to make me mad.

"Jake doesn't work. What schedule could he have?"

Mrs. Patton was getting mad, too. I'd never had a fight with the Pattons. Never really argued, but this was worth arguing about. I had to see Jake this morning. I couldn't face working all day without seeing for myself that he was okay.

"I'm leaving at 10:00 with Jake." I wasn't yelling, but the determination in my voice let her know that I wouldn't change my mind.

"Ali, that's not like you." She shook her head, sounding disappointed. "Maybe Jake's influencing you too much."

"You mean a *bad* influence, don't you?"

"You see him every day. Before work, and after work. We have no idea where you are or what you're doing." She hesitated for a second before adding, "Is he manipulating you to do what he wants?"

"You've got to be kidding!" I exploded. She actually thought Jake was manipulating me? "If you think that, you don't know Jake at all."

"No." she shook her head with a worried look. "I don't know Jake. Where's he live, what are his plans for the future? Is he going to school, or getting any kind of career? And you're never here. You just run out and jump in that truck."

She didn't yell, but sounded more serious than I'd ever heard her. I was getting madder and had to force myself to calm down. I couldn't tell her why Jake couldn't go to college. Couldn't tell her about how he was building a cabin for me. And sure couldn't tell her why I needed to see him this morning.

"I'll call Mr. Jones," I said with my voice forcefully calm. "We'll set up another time."

Mrs. Patton sighed. "If you can't talk to me, please tell Mr. Jones about your relationship with Jake. We're worried about you, Ali, and don't want to see you hurt."

"Jake would never hurt me," I said quietly.

She looked down at the floor and seemed to be thinking very carefully about what she wanted to say. "Ali, you have no friends and no real family. I don't know much about you before you came here, but I know you had a lot of friends and were really close to your mother. You can't just erase all that and center your life around one person. No guy can live up to that."

"I'm not doing that," I half mumbled. "I'll call Mr. Jones right now and see if I can go to his office after work."

"How will you get there?" she asked, but sounded like she already knew the answer.

"Jake," I shrugged.

She sighed. "Think about what I said," she said quietly, somewhere between a plea and a command. "Please tell Mr. Jones what you're feeling."

"I ..." I started to say I would but stopped myself from lying to her. I wouldn't tell Mr. Jones what I was feeling about Jake, because I wasn't sure. "I'll talk to him."

"See you this evening," she said. Then she walked over to the bed where I still sat half under the covers and gave me a hug.

Chapter 17

I hurried toward Jake's truck. I could see his attention focused on me through the windshield. He looked tired, yet his eyes were intense. I imagined his worry about the loner was eating away at him.

He never took his eyes off me and, as soon as I hopped up into the passenger seat of the truck, he grabbed me and pulled me into his arms. As his lips devoured mine, I moved my hand to his hair and stroked him, playing with the gentle waves. My other hand rubbed slow circles across his shoulders and upper back. I couldn't get enough of touching him.

He moved his mouth to my neck to nuzzle and nip the skin right under my ear. Both of my hands held his head as my fingers twisted into his hair. I felt more than heard the soft growl that sent a tingling from his lips through my whole body. All the worries in the world disappeared as I was being consumed by Jake.

He pulled away, growling and slightly baring his teeth as he gazed into my eyes. I was mesmerized by that look. A look that I'd seen before out in the woods. Suddenly, he jerked his whole body toward the drivers-side window leaving my arms to fall into my lap. His forehead and hands were pressed hard against the glass.

"What happened?" I whispered, realizing my breaths were short little gasps. All I could think was that I wanted him back in my arms.

He didn't say a word. I watched his back muscles move steadily with his deep breaths and heard another soft growl. It turned into the whining I'd last heard in the forest when he attacked me.

"Jake?" my voice practically begged him to talk to me.

"Did you feel it? Please tell me you felt it," he begged without moving. His voice was deep and rough.

"I ... I felt something. I don't know." What I really felt was confused. I knew he felt the bond, and knew that I was completely ready to surrender to him. Was that desire to bond or arousal as this really hot guy nibbled my neck and held me against his body?

After several seconds of silence, he turned back to the front and put both hands on the steering wheel. Then he turned his head toward me with incredibly sad eyes.

"Ali," he said while he gazed at me. "I almost shifted." I heard the confusion and fear in his voice.

My eyes grew wide and I leaned away from him without meaning to.

"Please don't be scared," he practically whispered as his forehead fell against the steering wheel. "That doesn't just happen," he tried to explain. "I was ready to bond with you like that night in the woods. To bite you and make you mine. Tell me you felt it, too."

Tears rolled down my cheeks, but I didn't do anything to stop them. "When you growled," I stammered. I didn't know how to explain it, but had to find the words. "I could *feel* it. That growl kinda ... moved through me," I whispered.

One corner of his mouth moved into a half smile as he turned back to look at me. "You felt it," he sighed. Then his face lit up into a huge smile as he reached up to wipe a tear from my cheek. "But I know you're not ready. I won't let that happen again, Ali. Not until you're ready. I'm just so tired and missed you, and I need to hunt."

He looked at me with so much love in his eyes. The love and desire were so intense, I almost turned away. But I didn't. I looked back at him and let my gaze tell him how I felt, but still couldn't put it into words. Why couldn't I tell him I loved him? Because part of me wasn't sure I did.

"We'd better go," he said quietly without looking away from me. He leaned forward and brushed my lips with the lightest, softest kiss I could imagine.

We drove without talking most of the way. I didn't think about my feelings for Jake. I just couldn't. Something in me was keeping me from saying that I loved him, but maybe I was starting to feel that love because I wanted to say those words. I wanted to love him. Maybe it was the whole bonding thing. Forever scared me.

I intended telling him about what Mrs. Patton had said, but had too much else on my mind to talk about it. Mrs. Patton probably thought he was interested in sex and nothing else. She'd never understand that he was waiting for me to commit to him for a lifetime.

I had kept my word and called Mr. Jones, but he couldn't see me until tomorrow, my day off. The whole thing could wait until I saw Jake after work. We'd have time to talk and I could make sure he was clear that I knew Mrs. Patton was wrong.

* * *

Jake didn't pick me up after work. He'd called to apologize, and I called Mrs. Patton to come get me. She had to re-arrange some things at work, but Mr. Patton was in Columbus at some meeting, so it had to be her. I don't think she was happy about leaving work, but, at the same time, she had been on my case just that morning about seeing too much of Jake. How could she be mad?

The reason Jake couldn't drive me home from work was bizarre. He said the cops had picked up a guy walking naked along one of the back roads. It was about 4:00 in the morning, the guy ran from them, and put up quite a fight before they finally subdued him. They found the guy's truck about two miles down the road.

I didn't get it at first. "We figure it was the loner," Jake explained. "He probably left his clothes in the truck, and had to shift to find it."

"Couldn't it have been some guy who was crazy or drunk or something?" I asked, sounding as confused as I felt.

Jake's Aunt Jane said he wasn't drunk, but a little confused and out of control like he'd just shifted and still full of Bigfoot hormones. The fact that Jake's aunt was a cop and had given them all the details, amazed me. How amazing that she was right there with all the information they needed. I wondered where else all his relatives worked, but figured that wasn't the time to start asking.

Jake and his dad had gone to the place where the police had towed the guy's truck, and the scent was unmistakable to them. As Jake called me, they were on their way to the spot along the road where the loner had left his truck figuring they could follow his scent to know where he might have been. The whole idea was to get enough information that they'd be able to find out where he'd hunted the night before when they couldn't find him.

I couldn't be upset with Jake for not picking me up. He'd been driving me around every day for weeks, hunting for the loner all night, and barely getting enough sleep. And I knew the loner had to be found. He'd attacked Robert and Danny and could have easily killed them. How long before he did kill someone?

The idea that they planned on killing him, though, still bothered me. Couldn't they just drive him off, threaten him, or something besides killing him? Jake said loners who were so brazen were completely out of control and couldn't be trusted. He said the loner was hunting almost every night, and that meant he was probably more Bigfoot than human anymore.

The guy must not have had any family to help him, and obviously didn't have a female to calm and control him. Jake said he was beyond help, but I could hear the part of him that felt sorry for him. I felt that sadness, too. But, for all that, their only choice would be to kill him.

He'd never be able to live safely anywhere near humans. If they drove him away to another area, he'd just continue until someone was hurt really bad or killed. Sadly, I had to think that's what would have happened to Uncle Max if not for Doug. Could that happen to Jake if I didn't bond with him? I shook my head at myself to get rid of all those thoughts rolling around as I saw Mrs. Patton pulling into the parking lot.

* * *

Jake and Doug spent most of the day following scent trails and discovering that the loner had traveled miles through the whole area. The freshest trail led straight west into Muskingum County.

"So it's not just our land and the park," Doug said, shaking his head.

"He must be hunting every night like we thought," Jake answered. "What're we going to do?"

"Nothing we can do but keep after him. Jane said the police should release him by late afternoon, so he'll be back out hunting right after dark. Let's get home."

By the time they got back to the cabins, it was getting dark. Adam, Greg, and Pete were already there being fed by Max and

Nina. Jake and Doug joined them, eating as they talked through their plans for the night.

They'd search in pairs like they usually did, but spread farther apart to cover more territory. Now that they knew the loner was hunting in at least two counties, they had many square miles of land to cover.

"I'll pair up with Pete," Adam said, glancing at his youngest son. Pete was only fifteen and had only shifted a few times, so he'd have to be watched carefully.

"Then I'll go with Greg," Doug offered. Greg had only been shifting for a couple years and didn't have enough experience to be without an adult. "Max, you take Jake."

"Sounds good," Jake nodded at Max.

"Make sure you have your cell phones. There're a lot of areas without service, but keep them close anyway. Be sure to stay within yelling distance of each other." They all nodded as Doug went over the usual routine. "Let's go."

Jake and Max headed southwest toward the park. Doug and Greg walked north, while Adam and Pete started toward the southeast. They had a huge area to cover, and Doug wasn't sure there were enough of them. If Nathan and his son had been able to join in the search, he would have been much more confident.

"Let's spread out," Max said to Jake, which was their normal procedure. Picking up a fresh scent was more likely if they kept some distance between them.

They'd been searching for hours, and Jake was getting more discouraged as the time wore on. Listening, sniffing, he and Max stayed about fifty yards apart as they moved through the dark forest. They'd caught his faint scent through the whole area, but nothing fresh, nothing that said he'd been there recently. Finally, Max called to him, and they joined together to sit for a few minutes on a log.

"I've been following the stream," Max said. "I'll cross and search that hill above it while you stay on this side for a few miles."

"That'll put us pretty far apart," Jake answered with a concerned look.

"Yeah, but the heavy undergrowth up there would be a great place for him to hide and wait for a deer coming in to drink. I wanna' know if he's been there."

"I could go with you."

"Then we'd miss this side of the stream. You have any cell service?"

"Not out here," Jake shook his head while he pulled out his phone to check.

"If I get a fresh scent, I'll come down behind you, and we can go back up together to follow him."

"Okay," Jake gave in. "If I get a scent, I'll follow at a distance and wait for you. Dad would have a hell of a fit if either of us confronted him alone, so no heroics."

"Jake, man, you know me better than that."

Jake gave him a serious, yet understanding look. "And I know you'd love to get this loner because you feel sorry for him."

"Not sorry enough to let him live," Max said apologetically. "He's too out of control." If he'd been someone looking for a new home, or trying to control his need to shift, Max would love to try to help him. But that wasn't what he was doing. "He's hunting every night. I don't even think a bonded mate could help him at this point."

"Yeah. It's sad, but he's past the point of anyone being able to help him control it."

Max patted Jake on the knee as he got up. "We'll meet within an hour. Be careful."

Jake hated Max's situation and knew that it was really hard for him to hold it together sometimes. He also hated that he could end up just like Max if Ali wouldn't bond with him. Thank God he and Uncle Max had always been close and would be able to help each other if it came to that. If the worst happened, they could at least be sentinels for each other.

Max climbed the hill working his way through the loose rocks and undergrowth. He noticed there was little human scent and realized it was too rough going for most of the casual hikers that used the park.

Finally, Max caught evidence of the loner, but it was old. Probably a week old. He followed the ridge along the top anyway knowing the path back to the stream would be easier farther ahead.

Then he heard the scream. A woman screaming in terror, her sound coming from the other side of the hill, away from the stream. Without a second thought, Max started down the hill, running toward her. What he didn't know was that Jake had heard it, too.

Chapter 18

I didn't expect Jake to call until morning, but couldn't resist hoping that my phone would ring. I'd missed the time we usually spent together and started to realize how much I'd quickly learned to count on him picking me up after work.

Instead of holding and kissing Jake, I spent my time watching TV again with the Pattons. Mrs. Patton wasn't thrilled that I hadn't talked to Mr. Jones, but that really wasn't my fault. He'd had an emergency and cancelled the appointment I made. I'd talk to him eventually.

Climbing into bed about 11:00, I put my phone on the pillow, right next to my head. Sometimes Jake called early enough to wake me up, and I wasn't taking the chance of missing his call.

I wanted them to find that loner and put an end to all the searching every night, but the idea of them killing him still bothered me, even though I pretty much understood that he was beyond hope. Most of the time, I refused to let myself think about it, but it was still there in the back of my head.

About midnight, my phone rang. All the thoughts of the loner flew out of my mind as I answered with a huge smile.

"Hey, Jake," I said without even looking to see who the call was from. I know my voice sounded soft and dreamy.

"Forget Jake. It's Robert," a half-angry voice answered me.

"Robert? Why are you calling so late?"

"I have to ask you a favor."

"A favor?"

"Look, we've got a plan to get that Bigfoot tonight and we need an alibi. We're going to say we were at your house."

"You are not!" I yelled, letting my anger out. The nerve of them. Then I registered what else he'd said. "What do you mean you need an alibi?"

"We have to have proof that we were somewhere else," he started explaining quickly. "There's no way we're strong enough to capture him, so we're going to shoot him."

"No!" This time my voice held more panic than anger. "You can't shoot him!"

"We have to, Ali," Danny said in the background. They must have had me on speaker phone. "It's the only way."

"Are you guys nuts? You'll be arrested for killing an endangered species or something." My mind was whirling. I had to talk them out of this.

"We thought of that," Robert continued. "That's why we're going to say we found the body. That's why we need the alibi, so we can say we left your place late."

"No. I won't do it." My voice was very determined now.

"Then we'll say you're lying because you didn't want anyone to know you were with us," Danny broke in again. "That boyfriend of yours won't hang around long once we tell him you've been hooking up with the two of us."

"You bastards!" I spat out. "No one will believe you, and the cops will know the bullet came from your gun. You won't get away with it."

"Yes, we will!" Danny yelled back. "And we'll get that million bucks. Wait and see."

I knew I was probably wasting my time arguing with them. They were obsessed with that contest. Besides they really had seen Bigfoot. "I don't know why I'm even bothering to talk to you guys. You've been lying about Bigfoot for weeks. You won't find anything to shoot anyway."

"We're not lying!" Danny shouted.

"I thought you believed us, Ali," Robert said more quietly.

"Well, I don't," I answered, trying to sound calm. "I was just playing along with you."

"Then wait and see," Robert continued with a very sinister sound to his voice. "You'll hear from the cops, and you'd better tell them we were at your house until morning. Tell them, or we'll tell that the three of us have been hooking up since we were in school together."

"You wouldn't dare," I started, but they'd already hung up.

I fell back on my pillow, mad as hell, scared to death. What if they actually killed the loner? What if they saw Jake again and shot him?

And what if he believed that I'd been having sex with them? No. Jake would believe me. He had to. The Pattons and Mr. Jones would have to believe me, too. My mind was whirling.

Those idiots were going to ruin everything. Ruin my life and my relationship with Jake. Prove Bigfoot existed and ruin Jake's whole family's life. I was ready to scream.

That's when I knew I needed to get a grip on my thoughts and emotions. Jake wasn't hunting tonight. No one was, except possibly that loner. How bizarre would it be if Robert and Danny shot the loner?

It would solve one problem, but they'd get the proof of Bigfoot's existence, and I couldn't let that happen. I had to call Jake and warn him. His dad would know what to do.

I called over and over again for a half hour, but his phone kept going straight to voicemail. Wherever Jake was, he obviously had no cell service. His dad's phone did the same thing. Each time I called and left a message for one of them to call back, I got more nervous.

The only thing I could think of was to get out there and find Jake, Doug or Max by myself. Stealing Mrs. Patton's car wasn't a good idea on any level, and I'd never be able to explain why I took it, but there was no other choice. I thought about taking her bike, again, but it would take too long. Besides, what if the loner found me on the bike?

After getting dressed, I sneaked down to the kitchen, grabbed the keys off the counter where she always put them, and headed out to the garage. An attached garage was so convenient, but I really wished theirs was stuck out in the back yard. Thankfully, their bedroom was on the opposite side of the house from the garage, but I was still afraid they'd hear me start the car, open the garage door, and drive out.

I got out of the driveway as fast as I could. I didn't know what they'd do if they had heard me. Would they call Mr. Jones, the police, or just wait for me to come back and ground me forever? I was going to be in such huge trouble.

I had no idea where to start searching for Jake, so I simply started in the area I already knew. Over and over, I kept telling myself I was being so stupid, but I couldn't give up. The thought of Jake being out there with those two crazy guys carrying a gun made my heart feel like it was going to stop. Or beat frantically right out of my chest.

As soon as I stopped the car, I realized how much darker the forest was than the other times I'd been there. I gazed at the clouds overhead. I was afraid I wouldn't be able to see a thing once I stepped into the trees.

My only option was the flashlight I knew Mr. Patton kept in the trunk. Besides, maybe the strong light through the trees would make it so Jake would find me. That was much more likely than me finding him.

The forest seemed almost silent. Only a few bugs made their strange creaking sounds, but I kept listening as best I could. I wanted to hear the frantic steps of a deer, or the rustling of raccoons, but it felt like I was the only living thing moving around.

The flashlight was a really good one. As I directed it onto the path, the trees and brush around shone with an eerie glow. I started pointing it into the trees, hoping that Jake or one of his family would see it and come to me as I walked along.

After about an hour, I was loosing my nerve. This really was a stupid idea. I was so alone, tired, and starting to feel like some kind of monster could be hiding behind every tree. All the determination that got me out there was evaporating, and I was starting to think the smartest thing would be to go back to the car and go home.

But I wanted so desperately to see Jake, to warn him. Maybe another half hour. But what if I found one of his relatives I didn't know? How could I explain everything to them? And what if I found Robert or Danny?

I needed to give up and go home. This was too scary, too hopeless. I must have been crazy thinking this was a good idea.

I shone the light around me to try figuring out where I was. Not so easy. Finally deciding that I needed to turn around and follow the same path back, I heard the rustling sound of something moving off to my right.

"Jake?" I called quietly. No one answered.

"It's Ali," I said a little louder.

The sound of movement got louder. Bushes and tree branches moved violently. The huge, dark creature was on me so fast my brain couldn't register what was happening. Within seconds its hands were grasping my waist and I was raised up in the air.

I was above the creature like a baby being held up while its mother smiled into its face. But it wasn't smiling. It growled at me and snarled while my mouth fell open in surprise and shock but, surprisingly, not fear.

Somehow the back of my mind was saying that this was Jake. Jake wouldn't hurt me. He didn't hurt me before, and these growls were his way of saying that he was glad to see me.

I didn't know how, but I'd held on to the flashlight and moved it to shine on his face. The eyes that gazed at me were pale green with gold flecks through them. Not Jake's eyes. Not Doug or Max either.

It took a moment to register, but I suddenly knew this was the loner. The creature started to shake me and bare its teeth like it was ready to bite. All I could do was scream and start beating on its hands and arms. I kept screaming until it dropped me to the ground.

I landed on my butt in the leaves, tried my best to get up, but the Bigfoot got his hands on my shoulders and started shaking me again.

"Let go of me," I screamed, but knew it probably didn't understand.

"No! Bad!" I yelled trying to talk to him the way Doug and Max talked to Jake that night he grabbed me.

He kept shaking me while he growled and gave me another too-close view of his huge, sharp teeth. Then he lifted me again. His grip locked my arms to my sides, so I couldn't hit him anymore, but I kicked as hard as I could.

He kept staring into my eyes and his low growls sounded almost like laughing. So far, he hadn't really hurt me and I got the idea that he was trying to scare me. Well, that was working. I was getting more scared by the minute. How long before this turned into broken bones and bleeding?

"No! Bad! Stop!" I tried again without any results.

I heard the piercing screech from behind me as a deafening roar escaped from another Bigfoot's mouth. Immediately my attacker dropped me to the ground and took a giant step over me to confront whatever was coming at us through the trees.

This new Bigfoot flew down the path and threw itself into the one that had been attacking me. I crawled away to the side as quickly as possible, but kept shining the flashlight at them. I had to know if this was Jake. Had he heard us and come to my rescue?

The eyes were brown, but, in the bright glare of the flashlight, dark. Not Jake's caramel color. Both Doug and Max had brown eyes. Could it be one of them? They'd talked to Jake and got him to let go of me, but these two weren't talking. They were fighting. Hitting, clawing, trying to bite.

Suddenly, a third Bigfoot crashed through the trees. I pointed the flashlight at him as he screeched and panted at the sight of the bloody fight. Then he froze and whined as he squinted through the light and saw me on the ground. Those caramel colored eyes told me it was Jake.

He roared into the night before throwing himself on the Bigfoot that had first attacked me. Now all three of them were rolling around, hitting, raking through fur with their claws, but it was obviously two against one.

Jake and the one that came to my rescue quickly started beating the crap out of the Bigfoot that had grabbed me. Blood was spattering everywhere. I didn't want to look, but I couldn't help it. I kept the flashlight on them so I could see what was going on the whole time. I wanted to believe that I had to make sure Jake wasn't hurt, but the truth was that I just couldn't look away.

Everything was happening so fast, yet it felt like it was going on forever. Finally, one Bigfoot rolled away and left the other two fighting. I realized Jake was still in the fight, but he was definitely winning. The other one crouched next to them, watching.

The one that attacked me was on the ground with Jake beating on him so fast I could hardly keep track of where the blows were landing. Jake was on his knees with one knee on the other one's chest. He extended one huge hand over the Bigfoot's face and stretched his head back. Then Jake roared and plunged his teeth into the throat of the other Bigfoot.

He tore out a huge chunk, sending blood and tissue flying across the forest floor as he shook his head. It was the most horrible thing I'd ever seen. Then it got worse.

Jake ate that chunk of flesh and plunged his teeth into the Bigfoot's shoulder for another bite. Unbelievably, the Bigfoot kept squirming and swinging his arms and legs as he lay there dying, being eaten by Jake.

The other Bigfoot that had left the fight was growling and screaming so loud I wanted to cover my ears, but kept the light shining on Jake instead. Then the one that was either Doug or Max moved back to the fight. He and Jake growled at each other as they both tore chunks out of the one on the ground.

I had been watching as they ate him, but suddenly couldn't watch anymore. I rolled over to my knees and threw up over and over until I thought my whole stomach would come up. I was sweating and breathing like I'd run for miles, but, when the smell of all the blood rose to my nostrils, I heaved again even though nothing was left in my stomach.

Struggling to my feet, I knew I had to get out of there. I ran back down the deer trail as fast as I could, but could still hear the sounds of growling and tearing flesh. Finally, those sounds were behind me as I struggled to find the end of the woods and the parking lot.

It took longer than I wanted it to, but I found it. Shaking all over, I wasn't sure I'd even be able to drive, but I did. Straight out of the park, down the country roads, and into the garage.

The whole trip was like a strange dream that I couldn't exactly remember. There were snatches of things like steering around the curvy roads and stopping at the few stop signs. It was almost like I was driving with my subconscious, which wasn't a good way to drive at all. Thank God the roads were deserted, because I knew I wasn't mentally capable of being a responsible driver.

Chapter 19

I was never so happy to be home at the Pattons, even though the sick feeling of disgust hadn't left me. Jake killed him and ate big parts of him – shared him with the other Bigfoot. I always avoided watching slasher movies because they were so gross. To see that happening right in front of me was so much, much worse.

I knew Jake killed and ate deer, but not people. Jake was the one who told me they were human most of the time. Explained to me how they lived pretty normal lives except for hunting deer every so often. Yeah, and except killing and eating each other.

It was the eating thing that bothered me the most. If he'd shot him, stabbed him, or even broken his neck, I might have been able to handle it. But not the eating. It was barbaric, monstrous, and completely deplorable.

I'd been starting to think that maybe I could bond with him, join him and his family out in the forest to live happily ever after. Maybe I loved him.

Not anymore.

I didn't think I'd ever be able to look at him again, let alone marry him.

When I got to my bedroom, I was horrified with one look in the mirror. Blood and tissue was splattered over my face. My clothes were filthy from rolling around on the forest floor, and my hair looked like a rat's nest, full of leaves and sticks.

I controlled the feeling that I was going to throw up again, stripped down, hid my clothes in the bottom of the hamper for me to wash the next day, and jumped in the shower. I tried to be as quiet as possible and hoped the Pattons didn't hear me showering at three in the morning, but I had to get clean.

Once in my pajamas, I sat on my bed without even hoping that I might sleep. I was still sitting there when I heard the Pattons getting ready for work, and heard the garage door opening. I'd be alone in a few minutes and could wait for Jake to call.

Then came the knock on my door.

"Ali," Mr. Patton said as he stood in the doorway with his wife. "You took the car last night. Where did you go?"

"What?" I answered, trying to think of some bluff, some excuse, anything that would get me out of this. How did they know?

"You left the lights on, the flashlight is on the passenger seat, and the driver's seat is covered with leaves and mud. You've got some explaining to do."

He looked and sounded so calm and matter-of-fact. He expected an answer, but all I could think was the hope that there wasn't blood all over. Somehow, I'd never thought of cleaning up the car.

"I ... I was ..." I was starting to stammer while I tried to put some thoughts together. The best I could come up with was the truth. "I had to go see Jake."

"I knew it," Mrs. Patton sighed. "Jake."

"You don't have to worry about me seeing too much of him, anymore. I'm breaking up with him."

"Did he hurt you, Ali?" Mr. Patton almost shouted. He looked so mad. Madder at Jake for hurting me than at me for taking the car. For some reason that surprised me, but made me feel good that they cared about me.

"No! He'd never hurt me," I blurted out. "I'm just ... it's just over. I'm never going to see him again."

"Are you sure you're okay?" Mrs. Patton asked. They had both moved into the room by this time and stood over me looking as concerned and worried as I'd ever seen them. "You look like you've been crying."

"A little," I admitted. "But I'm okay now."

"We hate to leave you like this," Mr. Patton was saying while I was thinking about whether or not I was ever going to be okay again. "I can call off work if you want."

"Don't do that. It's my day off, so I'll probably sleep all day."

"I hate to leave you like this," Mrs. Patton said while she reached down to hold my hand. "You're sure you're not hurt?"

"I'm sure."

"Call me if there's anything you want."

"I will."

"And we'll talk about the car tonight," Mr. Patton added. He wasn't happy about that part, but I think he felt sorry for me about Jake.

They left for work and I sat staring at the door they closed behind them. I'd said that Jake and I were over without even thinking twice. I cared about him – the human Jake – but I couldn't cope with the way he killed that loner.

I couldn't love a man that was capable of doing what he'd done. No wonder their women didn't go out hunting with them. They were much better off going to work and living normal lives. But I didn't get how they tolerated knowing how vicious their men really were.

Bad enough that he ate deer raw, alive and still bleeding, but a human? That loner might have looked like Bigfoot at the time, but he'd been born human, lived human, and deserved the respect any human would get.

I couldn't get that vision out of my head. I couldn't rationalize what he'd done, or forgive him. Jake and I were done.

Just as I was about to actually fall asleep, the phone rang. This time I looked at the caller ID. It was Jake, and I hesitated before I answered. I really didn't want to talk to him, but easier to tell him now than later.

"Ali, are you okay?" he asked.

"I'm fine," I answered trying to keep my emotions out of my voice.

"What were you doing out there? What the hell were you thinking?"

He was yelling at me? The tone in his voice was just like it was that first night. The night he and his dad told me about shifting when he was being all controlling and telling me what to do.

"How dare you!" I yelled back, louder than him. "I went out there to warn you that Robert and Danny were planning on shooting you. Is that a good enough reason for you?"

"Shoot me?"

"You or any other Bigfoot they found," I half mumbled. I needed to say some things that were going to hurt him and I didn't want to do that.

"Shit! What's with them?" He sounded like he couldn't believe what idiots they were. I'd tried to tell him. "They actually said they were going to shoot one of us?"

"Jake," I whispered as I felt tears rolling down my cheeks. "I need to tell you something. Can ... can you just listen for a minute?"

"Sure, Ali," he practically whispered.

"I ... What I saw tonight ..."

"Yeah, I'm sorry you had to see that."

"Jake," I said with a voice that was begging him to listen. "I can't stand it. I can't be with you knowing that you could do such a thing." By this time, there were waterfalls running down my face.

"What are you saying, Ali?"

Couldn't he just shut up and let me get this out? "I'm breaking up with you, Jake. I can't see you anymore after that."

"No! Let me explain ..."

"You ate another human being!" I practically screamed. Then I kept yelling. "How can you explain that away? I don't think I can even look at you again without seeing the hunks of that guy's body hanging out of your mouth. It splattered so far, I had blood all over me!"

"He was a loner!" Jake's voice wasn't yelling like mine. He sounded desperate. "You've got to understand ..."

"I do understand. If you're telling me he was a monster, then so are you." I choked on my tears as I said that. "Jake," I whispered, "he was just like you."

"Oh, God, Ali ... Please!" I could hear the tears in his voice. It was hard to imagine him crying, and that almost broke my heart.

"I can't, Jake," I sobbed. "I can't ... I can't kiss the lips that I saw tear out that guy's flesh." I began sobbing again and had trouble getting words out of my mouth. "I'm sorry. I'm so sorry. Don't call me again ... Goodbye."

* * *

Jake stood next to his truck and let the phone fall from his hand. He felt frozen, both physically and emotionally. Everything Ali had said flew through his head at hyper-speed and every word hurt. Hurt so bad, he felt like he couldn't go on breathing.

"What happened, Jake?" Max asked as he jumped out of the passenger side of the truck and walked around to Jake. He'd wanted to give him some privacy while he called Ali, but something was wrong. One look at Jake's face told him it was really bad.

They'd both dropped their clothes as they ran toward Ali's screams, willing themselves to shift as they went. Once they were done with the loner, they'd sat, exhausted, until they could shift back to human form. Looking at the shredded body stretched out in front of them, they knew they'd have to hide it well. He'd stayed Bigfoot as he died, and they couldn't let anyone find that body and prove they existed.

Naked, filthy, and covered with the slime from their shifts, Max and Jake rolled aside an old log that had once been a towering oak tree, used sticks to scrape aside dirt and insects, and laid the body into that shallow space. Rolling the log back over to its original spot, they scraped up some of the leaves and sticks to hide the fact that the log had been moved. It would take decades for that log to decay, and the body would decompose along with it.

Finally, they could search for their clothes. All Jake could find were his pants, but knew his shirt would be in shreds. He'd shifted before he could get it off. Max had made it with his clothes intact.

The most important thing to Jake was that his phone was still in his jeans pocket. He needed desperately to call Ali to find out what she'd been doing in the forest, but had to get washed in the stream, dressed, and into an area that had cell reception. They'd finally made it to an area where he could see the bars appear on his phone.

After that call, Jake stared into Max's eyes and seemed to collapse, like every muscle in his body gave up trying to support him. He fell against his uncle and cried, sounding devastated. Max held him and let his imagination pick out all the horrible things that could cause Jake to break down like that. All Max could figure was that someone, someone important, had died.

"Is it Ali, man? Talk to me."

"She left me, Max," Jake mumbled with his head still on Max's shoulder. "She left me."

"Ah, Jake, she's scared. Give her some time," Max said patting Jake's back. "You'll go see her this afternoon and she'll be okay."

"No!" Jake cried looking up at Max. "She hates me, said I'm a monster. And her voice ... her voice, Max. She hates me."

"Let's get home," Max whispered. "Your mom will take care of you."

Max drove while Jake huddled in the passenger seat. He'd stopped crying, but stared blankly out the side window. Max remembered all too well the devastation of losing Lucy, but had no idea what to say to Jake. There was nothing that could be said that would make him feel it less or make him ever be happy again.

When they got to the cabins, Jake walked straight to his room without even acknowledging his mother or father. Max was left to tell them what had happened.

"We got the loner," Max started, but was soon interrupted by Doug's excitement and congratulations. Nina knew there was something else.

"Max," she said quietly, thinking of the blank look on Jake's face. "What happened?"

"Ali was out there." Nina could see the pain in Max's eyes as he spoke. "The loner attacked her, and Jake and I jumped him. She ran, but not until she saw the whole thing. Jake called her when he could ... I didn't hear it all. He says she's left him ... called him a monster ..."

"My poor boy," Nina sighed, sounding like she was about to break down.

"She left him?" Doug was just as upset. "Did he try to explain?"

"I don't know what he said. He wasn't much for talking on the way back."

"I'll go to him," Nina stated as she walked toward his door. Doug and Max watched her walk away, knowing she was the only one who could help him – if anyone could.

Chapter 20

I got off work at 4:00, as usual, but Mr. Patton couldn't come until he got off work at 5:00. It had been weeks since I'd left Jake. Even though I'd stopped crying every minute I was by myself, I still felt alone, isolated.

Last night, I'd finally written another letter to my mother, and it felt good to be talking to her again, but there was also some guilt about not telling her what had been going on in my life. Half way through, though, I made a strange discovery. While trying to explain my thoughts and feelings about breaking up with Jake, I realized I felt the same kind of emptiness I'd had after Mom died.

My grief counselor once told me how we grieve all kinds of things, not just death, but I never thought about grieving the loss of Jake. After all, I'd been the one that broke up with him. I felt that loss, anyway. Empty, so empty.

Waiting for Mr. Patton, I sat on a shaded bench reading on my tablet.

"Ali," a male voice said from beside me.

"Robert," I answered with surprise. "What do you want?"

"We're going out again tonight," he said, almost coldly. "We might need that alibi again."

"I told you I wouldn't do it," I said, already getting angry at him. Angry that they were trying to threaten me into helping them. Angry that they wanted to kill a Bigfoot. Most of all, though, angry and afraid that they'd kill Jake.

"And we told you what we'd do," Danny added with a threatening tone.

"You've been out there night after night for weeks and haven't found a thing. Why don't you give up? Get jobs, for God's sake. Stop being so stupid." I just didn't care anymore about being nice to Robert and Danny. "Maybe I need to go to the police first and tell them what you're planning."

"You wouldn't dare," Robert sneered. "Besides we didn't get anywhere the last time because this shithead," he backhanded Danny's arm, "tripped over a stick and almost broke his ankle. He hasn't been able to walk until now, but we'll get something tonight."

"Keep out of the woods before you trip over a ledge and break your necks."

"Just tell the police we were at your place if they call you," Danny added with rolling eyes. Like he couldn't figure out why I wasn't happy to lie for them.

"Go away," I sneered at them. "I'm not lying for you."

"What happened to the boyfriend?" Danny asked with a grin, looking around the parking lot for his truck. "He dump you already?"

"Shut up. My life is none of your business, so leave me alone." I had to force myself not to hit him, but knew I might not be able to stop myself if they said one more word about Jake.

"Come on, Danny. See you later, Ali," Robert said as he turned to walk away. "Remember what you need to say. If the cops call, just tell them we were together." Danny started to walk away, still laughing at his hilarious statement that Jake had dumped me.

I was fuming as they left and all I could do was stare hatefully at their backs. Part of me wished Jake was around. He'd beat the crap out of them, and they deserved it.

Mr. Patton pulled up a few minutes later and greeted me with a big smile. He and Mrs. Patton were both thrilled about Jake being out of my life, so didn't seem to mind the trip into the park twice a day at all.

What I didn't tell them was that I minded it. I would have much preferred driving myself so I could have the time alone. As it was, I had to pretend that I didn't fell like crap. Pretend that I didn't miss Jake so much that I knew my heart was broken. Pretend that everything was just fine with my crappy life.

"Hey," I said as calmly as I could as we pulled out of the parking lot. "I've been saving my paychecks since I started working and I thought maybe you could help me look for a car." I'd been thinking about it for a couple days and figured I'd ask before he started talking about how I was feeling or mentioning Jake.

"How much have you saved?" he asked.

"I don't know for sure," I answered. "Probably about $500."

"Can't get anything dependable for that," he said, shaking his head.

"Couldn't I borrow the money and make payments?" That's what Mom always did. Why not me?

"Not until you're eighteen."

"Crap, that won't be until school's ready to start. I don't want you to have to drive me to work the rest of the summer."

"We really don't mind, Ali. We really don't, but sometimes it's hard to get away from work when we need to. It would be easier if you had a car, though. Maybe Jane and I could loan you the money."

"Really?" I practically gasped. "You'd do that?"

"I think we could," he said nodding. "It'd save you a lot on interest, and I'd make sure you get something you can rely on."

"That'd be great!"

"We'll talk about it tonight."

I couldn't believe they'd be willing to do that for me. Having my own car would be unbelievable.

For a few minutes as we drove in silence, I felt happier than I had in days. Well, in the weeks since I'd left Jake. But thoughts of him burst back into my mind very quickly, and the idea of having a car was pushed way back out of my consciousness.

I worried about how he was doing, and felt bad that I'd hurt him. He sounded devastated when I said goodbye to him. Mainly, though, I worried about the whole thing of him ending up like his Uncle Max. Alone, unable to control himself, unable to find control from someone he loved. If that happened, it would be my fault.

But we didn't know for sure that Jake and I were meant to bond. He seemed to be sure, but I wasn't. That was the biggest worry in my head. What if he was right? What if we were meant to be together, and now we were both alone? That made me sad enough to feel like crying again, but I made myself control it. I didn't want Mr. Patton to see me crying.

As we parked in the garage, I stepped to the rear door to get my backpack out of the back seat. My eye caught the movement of a silver truck moving slowly down the road past the driveway. *Jake*, I thought.

I knew it was him, and knew he'd been watching me. I'd seen him in the parking lot at work and once, while looking out my bedroom window, saw him parked along the road. He'd texted me a couple times, too, asking if I'd please call him. I didn't. Thankfully, he must not have seen Robert and Danny talking to me. He would have freaked.

I hated that a part of me was glad to catch those glimpses of Jake. Why couldn't we just let each other go?

* * *

Nina tried her best to help Jake, but they all knew it wasn't working. Jake continued feeling tense and edgy no matter how long he spent with his mother's caresses and soft words. The underlying needs of his beast crept closer to the surface each day until he had to give in to the inevitable and hunt again.

Before he met Ali, it'd been easy to wait a week, and even several days beyond that if necessary, but not anymore. He and Max had both hunted the night after they'd killed the loner, which put a strain on Doug. He had to stay up all night to sentinel each one of them, one at a time.

It had been close to three weeks, now, since he'd last seen Ali. Three weeks since she'd told him he was a monster and she couldn't stand to be around him. Three weeks of following her, parking outside her house and the park lodge, longing to hear her voice, hold her and kiss her. And every day, he came closer to being that monster she'd seen.

Jake struggled to fight the pressure of the conflict growing inside him. Bigfoot was pushing himself to the surface, insistent on chasing, catching, and devouring its prey. It was like a deep itch that could only be scratched one way.

More than the drive to shift, though, Jake felt the beast's anger most of the time. He argued over nothing with Dad, Mom, and Uncle Max. He tried to work on his cabin, but got too frustrated. What was the point when he'd never have a mate to live there with him? The constant scowl on his face advertised how he was feeling, and there was nothing any of them could do about it.

Yelling at Max because the toast wasn't dark enough, he stomped out into the forest. Jake needed the peacefulness of nature to calm the resentment that made him shout about nothing, but couldn't find that peace. He stomped around, punched trees, and threw rocks. The anger was consuming him, and he knew he'd need to hunt again that night.

He'd moved to Uncle Max's cabin the week before hoping they could help each other. Things were going pretty well, but Doug still went out with them every time one of them needed to hunt. Adding that to Doug's own feeding schedule meant that Doug was out in the woods almost every night. Jake knew his dad couldn't keep going like that for long.

Leaning against a tree, Jake started thinking that it might be best if he just took off. He'd started to realize that being around him, with his beast so close to the surface, made it harder for everyone. Besides, the two of them and Mom spent every minute worrying about him. Wouldn't it be better to go off alone to deal with his own problems?

He'd be a loner and his life would probably end with a bloody death like the loner he and Max had killed, but why did it matter? At least his parents and Uncle Max could live peacefully. At least they wouldn't have to deal with him anymore.

A tear slid down his cheek at the thought of his mother's face when they had to admit that she couldn't calm him anymore. She'd tried so hard and it had broken her heart, but she wouldn't let Jake see her cry. She'd probably cried against Dad's chest half the night.

He couldn't control his beast, couldn't stop following Ali to and from work, and couldn't stop blowing up at his family over stupid stuff that didn't even matter. He'd ask Max to sentinel him tonight and take off in the morning. That would give him a couple days to get as far away as possible before he had to hunt again.

Jake headed back to the cabin. His mind was made up. He'd pack and take off just before dawn when Max was asleep. Maybe go south through West Virginia and into the Appalachian Moun-tains. Hunting without a sentinel was never a good idea, but it would be easy to avoid humans there. He'd have to get some kind of job and a place to live, but he'd worry about that later.

The hardest part would be leaving Ali. Glimpsing her as she was driving the park roads, walking into work, weeding the garden she'd put in at the Patton's. Every sight of her made him feel a little less lonely. Several days, since she'd gotten her car, he'd walked over as it sat in the lodge parking lot so he could catch her scent. That just made him miss her even more.

Tomorrow, he'd be on his own.

Chapter 21

Mr. Patton had found me an excellent, little Honda CR-V. It was ten years old, but in great shape, a really cool red, and even pretty good on gas. We'd looked for something that I could drive to school and, later, take to college with me.

I'd made my first monthly payment to the Pattons, and knew I'd have to keep working during my senior year, but that was okay. I needed to save as much money as possible for college, anyway, and needed to still have a job while I was in college. I suddenly realized that odds were great I'd be working at some job for the rest of my life. I guess that's what it meant to be an adult.

I'd tried to stop thinking about Jake so much in the last few weeks, but wasn't very successful. Especially since he was still following me around. I saw his truck almost every day in the parking lot when I came out of work, and kept thinking I should walk over and tell him to stop stalking me. But I couldn't do that. I couldn't hurt him anymore than I already had, so I just pretended that I didn't see him.

Leaving work, I looked around like I always did, pretending that I wasn't looking for Jake. I knew his possessiveness and need to protect me was an ingrained part of his Bigfoot side, so couldn't really be mad at him, but his truck was nowhere in sight. My mouth fell open, though, when I got to my car and saw Nina standing next to it.

"Ali," she said quietly.

"Hi," I stammered. I didn't know what to say to her, but in the back of my mind I had this horrible feeling that she wasn't here with good news.

"Jake needs you," she said, but her voice broke. Tears welled up in her eyes.

"What happened?" Now I knew for sure that this was something really bad. Seeing her face, I could feel my own tears starting to fill my eyes.

Nina took a couple deep breaths before getting control of her voice again. "They were hunting last night ..." Her voice broke again with a sob. "Someone shot him."

"Oh, my God!" I gasped.

"They can heal themselves easily with the help of a female, but I can't help him anymore." She shook her head and continued to sob. "Ali, he's dying! He needs you."

"Where? The hospital?"

"At the cabin. He's still shifted. He can't come back until he's healed. Please, Ali, help him."

"Still shifted?" It felt like someone had grabbed my stomach in a big fist and was twisting it. How could I face Bigfoot and try to help him?

"Please, Ali," she begged.

I'd go to him. What else could I do except tell her to let him die? "I'll follow you," I stammered as I unlocked my car door.

We raced along the roads to the cabins that I remembered last seeing with Jake. That had been a wonderful day. This one was shaping up to be horrible. I barely saw the hills and trees, keeping my eyes fixed on Nina's car in front of me. I wouldn't let myself think about Jake because I knew I'd break down and not be able to drive.

We hurried into the cabin and met Doug sitting at the kitchen table. He looked like a wreck.

"Where's Jake?" I had to ask. Now that I was there, I wanted to see him – needed to see him.

"You need to hear what happened," Doug said with no expression. "Have a seat." He reached over to pull a chair out for me and another for Nina.

"What happened?" I asked before I even got completely in the chair.

"Jake and I were sentinels for Max last night. Jake was going to hunt later. I caught the scent of humans and circled around to distract them while Jake watched Max. I heard a shot and ran back to find Max on the ground with two guys leaning over him. That's when Jake came tearing out of the trees screaming. He still had parts of his torn-up shirt clinging to his back, so he must have lost it and shifted really fast. That's a rough way to shift ... hurts like hell."

"Did he attack them?" I practically whispered. I couldn't help asking but really didn't want to hear that Jake had killed Robert and Danny.

"They ran, and he started chasing them, but one of them turned and shot Jake. He took the shotgun blast right in his belly and fell in mid-stride." He was reciting the whole thing like a prepared speech and sounded numb. Like it had nothing to do with his son and his brother.

"We were pretty close to the cave, so I dragged them both there and called Adam and his kids. They helped me carry them back here, but there wasn't much any of us could do.

"He needs a female's strength to heal and shift back to human form. Nina tried," he said, gazing at her with amazing love in his eyes and patting her hand, "but she couldn't help him." He looked at me with such deep sadness, and I could see his eyes begging me to help. "Jake needs you, Ali."

"What about Max? Can anyone help him?" I figured the answer would be no, but had to ask.

"Max died this morning," Doug said with a coldness in his voice that I'd never heard before.

I gasped. Max was dead? Tears ran down my cheeks as I thought that he'd still be alive if the human he loved hadn't left him. I realized that Jake could easily die, too, if I didn't try to help him. Could I do it? Could I give him the strength he needed to survive?

"I'm so sorry," I finally said, wiping the tears from my eyes. "What can I do for Jake? How can I help him?"

Nina took my hand and looked into my eyes. "You'll need to hold him. Stoke his hair and talk to him."

"What should I say?"

"It doesn't really matter. He can't understand much, anyway. Just keep your voice soft and comforting. The most important thing is keeping control of your emotions. He'll feel your calmness and control and use it to heal."

"What if I start to cry again?" I knew my voice sounded like I was ready to break down any minute, but I couldn't help it. I wanted so bad to help Jake.

"He needs to sense your control ... your love."

"But that's just it," I almost yelled, begging them to understand. "I don't know if I love him."

"He loves you," Doug said.

"I know," I said staring down at the table. "I'll try. I'll do everything I can."

Nina stood up, still holding my hand, to lead me down a hallway toward what I assumed was Jake's room. I saw that huge Bigfoot sprawled out across the bed. He was breathing slowly and not moving at all.

"Is he unconscious?" I whispered.

"Yes. He has been since those boys shot him."

"Robert and Danny," I spit out, still staring at Jake's helpless body. "I hate them so much. I swear, if they were here right now, I'd kill them myself."

Nina's head snapped toward me in surprise. I probably should have been embarrassed that I'd said that – and meant it – but I couldn't be. They deserved the death penalty for killing Max and trying to kill Jake, but they'd never get it. No one could ever know what a horrible thing they'd done.

"You need to forget about them and concentrate on helping Jake. Doug and I will be in the kitchen."

Then she left me.

I knew I needed to hold him and stroke his hair. That would have been so easy with the human Jake, but, as Bigfoot, he still scared me. I shook my head to try getting rid of that fear. I'd seen how violent he could be, but knew in my heart that I'd never see that violence directed at me.

Sitting next to him on the bed, I moved his right arm over his chest so I could get closer to him. I could see the dried blood in the hair on his stomach. The blood was all over, but I made myself look away and not think about it.

I squeezed my left arm under his neck and stretched my body out along his so I could hold him. I stared at his face, trying to see my human Jake there, but couldn't. I wished I could have seen his eyes.

Scooting close to press my body against his side, I reached to his face with my right hand, stroked his cheek, and spoke softly. "Jake," I said. "It's me. Ali. Do you know I'm here, Jake? I hope I can help you."

My mind went blank. I didn't know what else to say. All I could think was to tell him what I'd been doing since I'd last seen him.

Nina said it didn't matter what I said since he wouldn't understand, anyway.

"I've just been going to work every day. Not doing much else. The Pattons are helping me buy a car. Yeah, you already know that because you've been following me, haven't you? That's okay, though. I wouldn't admit it to anyone else, but you make me feel safe. I know you'll help me if I have car trouble or anything."

I paused for a minute thinking and continuing to stoke him. "And ... I do miss you. I was happy all the time when I was seeing you every day. It's not that I'm really sad now, but ... yeah, I guess I am sad most of the time.

"I've been writing a lot of letters to Mom. Did I tell you about that? It doesn't matter. I told her all about us. Mainly, I tell her how I feel since we split up. I miss you all the time. Is that love, Jake? I still don't know."

I'd been stroking the side of his head and cheek as I talked. I moved down and felt the hard muscle of his shoulder, arm and chest. My left hand was playing with the hair at the back of his neck. It was all really peaceful and comforting. I continued to rub his chest and gently curl the hair around my fingers.

"I think Mom would tell me to listen to my heart, but I don't know what my heart is saying," I whispered while staring at my hand which was alternately mussing and straightening his hair. "You really scared me, Jake. I wish we could go back to the way we were before that night. I want to feel you holding me and kissing me like you used to, but ... I can't stop seeing you killing that guy.

"Looking at you now, though," I said looking up at his face, "I ... I don't know. It's hard to imagine you being so violent and out of control."

I'd been holding myself up on my left elbow, but it was staring to ache. I scooted down a little and rested my head on Jake's shoulder. It felt so right to lie there, stretched out against him, still stroking his chest and playing with the soft hair on his head.

"I'd ask if you missed me, but I guess the fact that you've been following me around means that you have. I'm sorry. I'm sorry I yelled at you like that on the phone. Maybe I do need to give you a chance to explain. But I don't know if I could ever understand you killing someone like that. It was like you weren't human. Well, that was stupid. You and your dad told me that you aren't really human anymore once you've shifted.

"I think I ignored the Bigfoot thing as much as I could when we were together. I guess I didn't really want to accept how different you are. Do I love you, Jake? If this works, I guess it means that we were meant to be together ... meant to be bonded mates. But do I love you?"

After several minutes of silence, I continued talking about my job, my car, how great the Pattons were for helping me buy it, and how I'd drive it to college next year. Anything. I knew I just had to keep talking about anything so he could hear my voice.

One thing I avoided was any mention of Robert and Danny. I wanted to tell him how they tried to blackmail me, but they just made me so mad. No way could I talk about them and keep my voice steady and calm.

It seemed like I'd been there forever, but the clock said only an hour had passed. How long did I need to stay with him before I knew if it was helping? What if I couldn't help him?

I heard a low growling sound that vibrated through Jake's chest. I felt it against my hand and against my cheek.

"Jake?" I gasped as I moved my head from his shoulder so I could look at his face.

He growled again. A little louder and longer. What did that mean? Was he getting better? Was he gaining consciousness?

"Jake. It's Ali. I came to help you get better. Can you hear me?"

The bedroom door opened. Nina and Doug stood there staring at us. They must have heard his growl, but all I could do was look at them with the question in my eyes. Was it working?

Jake whined and slid his right arm up his chest to rest his huge, hairy hand on top of mine. He pressed our hands into his chest and moaned and whined some more.

"Keep talking, Ali," Nina whispered.

"It's okay, Jake. You're going to be fine. I'll stay right here with you."

Jake's whole body seemed to vibrate, and his face grimaced in what looked like pain. The sounds he made sounded like he was in pain, too. "Does it hurt, Jake? I'm sorry. I don't want you to hurt. Just get better."

Then he started vibrating more. I could feel something wet against my hands as I continued stroking him, and thought immediately of blood. Was he bleeding again? I looked back at Doug and Nina and realized they were smiling.

"He's shifting, Ali," Doug said quietly.

Now I could feel the sticky wetness soaking through my clothes where I was pressed against him. His rich, dark curls seemed to be sinking into his skin. He jerked, shook, groaned, and, the next thing I knew, I was stretched against a human, and completely naked, Jake.

"Ali," he moaned as I finally gazed into those beautiful eyes I'd been longing to see.

I guess I should have been embarrassed to be in bed, pressed against my naked boyfriend with his parents standing over us, but I wasn't. I was just too happy. Happy that he was better. Happy to be with him.

Jake stretched his left arm over us and squeezed me tightly against his side. "I love you," he whispered as he pressed his slimy lips against mine. I kissed him back.

Not a huge passionate kiss, but a kiss that said how happy and relieved we were to be together. It didn't even last very long. Just long enough that I knew, without any doubt, that I couldn't walk away from him again.

"You need some sleep," Doug said as Jake let his arm fall away from me and back to his side. "We'll clean you up when you get some strength back."

Doug pulled the covers up over him while I crawled off the bed. "Don't want you getting too cold," he said quietly.

All the while Jake and I never stopped staring at each other. I didn't want to let go of him. Even though he was completely naked, it wasn't a sexual thing. More of a deep need to be close to him. Maybe I still didn't know what love was, but I knew for sure that I needed him.

Nina leaned down to kiss his forehead and caress his cheek. "You'll be fine now," she said quietly. "We'll see you in a few hours." She turned to me. "Let's go, Ali. His dad will take care of him from here."

I had to tear my eyes away from Jake's, but I followed Nina back towards the kitchen. As soon as we were there, she turned to me with tears in her eyes. "Thank you," she said as she hugged me.

Chapter 22

Doug came back to the kitchen about ten minutes later. "He's asleep," he mumbled as he sat down with us. I expected that he'd be deliriously happy that Jake was getting well, but the look on his face was so serious and miserable. "I told him about Max," he said gazing at Nina.

"Oh," I sighed. That explained his mood. "Did he take it hard?" Nina didn't say anything, but took Doug's hand.

"Yeah, but he wasn't surprised. I think that's why he flew into such a rage and shifted. He knew Max couldn't heal without a female." There was clearly pain in Doug's voice. Pain for Max, and Jake.

"Poor Max," I practically whispered as a tear ran down my cheek again. "Jake will really miss him."

"We all will," Doug answered, nodding.

We sat in silence for a few minutes while I stared at the table. I realized Doug and Nina were gazing at each other. One of those looks that was communicating something, but I wasn't sure what.

"Ali," Nina said quietly. "What about you and Jake? Will you bond with him?"

"I don't know." I was still confused and afraid. Not afraid of Jake, anymore, but still scared of what he was and the lifelong commitment. There was no doubt, though, what Nina and Doug were feeling. They wanted us bonded. They probably couldn't bear the idea that Jake could end up like Max.

"I do know that I need to give him another chance," I continued. "And I need to give myself time to try to understand everything better."

"That's good. And remember that females born in our Family grow up knowing the reality of what our men are. It's hard for human women to accept, but ... just give him a chance."

"Will Jake sleep all night? Will he need me again?" I asked looking at Doug.

"He'll sleep for hours, but I'll need to take him out hunting when he wakes up."

I glanced up at the clock. It was almost nine, and I hadn't called the Pattons. They knew I got off work at four and would be worried. "I'd better go home, then. Will you ask Jake to call me in the morning?"

"Certainly," Nina said with a partial smile. It was the first hint of any happiness I'd seen on her face since she met me in the parking lot at the lodge.

Seeing that smile made me realize that through all the worry about Jake and the grief over Max, I was happy, too. A comfortable happiness that I hadn't felt since I'd sent Jake away.

"Wait!" I said as I stood from the table. "What are you going to do about Robert and Danny? They're so damned determined to win that million dollars ... they'll be out there looking for another Bigfoot. They'll shoot one of you again!" As I spoke my anger at them grew into something close to rage and I practically yelled the last sentence. "Why do they have to be such idiots?" I whined like a little girl.

Doug squinted at me like he was considering something. "I wonder how much it would take to buy them off." Nina raised her eyebrows like that might be a good idea.

"What?" I gasped. "You'd have to tell them Bigfoot is real ... tell them the truth."

"They know Bigfoot's real," Doug said with a shrug. "We wouldn't have to tell them the *truth*. We just need to get them to shut up about us and leave us alone."

"I thought you'd be ready to hunt them down."

"It's tempting," Doug said quietly. "I'll talk to Adam. See if we can come up with something, but it'll have to be soon. We can't let them keep wandering around."

"What about Jake hunting tonight? They'll probably be out there."

"Yeah. Looking for the two bodies they left behind." Doug's voice was so hard, I had no doubt that the idea of killing Robert and Danny was awfully tempting. "But don't worry, Ali," he said seeming to get the thought of vengeance out of his head. "I'll take Jake over to Adam's territory. Robert and Danny stick closer to the park."

"If you say so," I whispered, knowing that I had to trust him. "I'd better get going."

"Ali," Nina said as she stood and took my face in both of her hands. "Jake wouldn't have made it without you. He was getting worse." Her voice broke a little as she said that. "We want you in our Family, but I know that you have to be sure. Come see me or call me anytime. Any questions. Okay?"

"I will," I whispered. She pressed her lips to my forehead and held them there for several seconds. She meant every word she'd said. I could ask her anything, and being part of a family, The Family, was starting to feel like that wasn't such a horrible idea.

* * *

"Wake up, Robert!" Danny yelled as he kicked Robert in the thigh. "Come on, man!"

"Back off ... I'm awake," Robert yelled back.

"It's almost morning. We have to get out there before someone else finds those bodies."

"Are you kidding, shithead? I was waiting for that third Bigfoot to come after us while you were snoring loud enough it was like you were asking him to find us."

"Shut up. Let's just go before someone else finds them."

"Yeah. Since it's your fault we had to leave them," Robert sneered.

"My fault?"

"You could have shot him. I took care of the other two."

"Shot what? The growls coming for us? I never even saw that third one, and you ran as fast as I did."

"I wasn't gonna' face him alone. Let's just go. Get the canvas to wrap them up."

"Yeah, yeah. I've got it."

"Hey, man," Robert finally smiled as they left their campsite, heading back toward the spot where they'd shot two Bigfoot. "This time tomorrow, we'll be millionaires."

"Damn straight!" Danny said with surety.

They searched for an hour, sure of the spot they'd left the Bigfoot bodies, but found nothing. While there were plenty of footprints, they all looked like human hikers. No Bigfoot prints at all. There weren't even stains that were definitely blood on the ground.

"Someone moved them," Robert said, scowling.

"That third one? Dammit!" Danny shouted.

"Don't be stupid! They're animals. Animals don't carry off their dead. And someone took time to clean up. There should be blood all over."

"Than what? Some other shithead ready to claim the million bucks?" Danny said. "Now we're screwed."

"Shut up!" Robert whispered. "Someone's coming."

"Shit!" Danny whispered back with his fear clearly in his voice. "Hide!"

They ducked behind a thicket of trees and brush as they listened to the footsteps coming closer. A flashlight shone on the ground, even though the sun had already risen. It followed the path right where they'd walked from the campsite.

A Bigfoot wouldn't use a flashlight, but they stayed hidden. They didn't want to have to explain to anyone why they were in the woods with shotguns.

The strangers stopped walking, and the flashlight clicked off. "Danny? Robert?" a deep masculine voice called quietly. "We know you're hiding behind the trees. Come on out. We need to talk to you."

Robert and Danny gazed at each other with huge eyes. What was going on? How did this guy know they were there? How did he know their names?

"Come on, guys," the voice continued. "We don't mean you any harm. We need to talk about Bigfoot."

"It's got nothing to do with you," Danny yelled without thinking. Actually, he was thinking of them trying to steal the reward money for proof of Bigfoot. Robert punched his arm and scowled.

"Yes, it does," the voice said calmly. "We're the ones who moved the two you shot."

Robert stepped out pointing the rifle at them. Doug and Adam both held their hands out to their sides slightly, showing they were unarmed. "That's not necessary, guys. We have an offer for you."

"What? Offering to claim the million for us?" Danny asked as he stepped out, also holding his rifle at the strangers.

"Forget the million. We want to make you an offer to get you to leave Bigfoot alone and shut up about what you know."

"Your offer will have to be a million," Robert sneered.

"You think that beer company will give you a million for a dead body?" Adam said. "As soon as Bigfoot's existence is proven, he'll be an endangered species. You'll be fined for killing him ... maybe end up in jail.

"Besides, that company was never going to hand anyone a million dollars. It'd be paid out in forty years and most of it would go to taxes. We're offering you a lump of money. Cash if you want, that no one will know about, so no taxes. How about $100,000? Will that shut you up?"

"What's it to you?"

"We protect them, and the people who run into them. You do realize one of them was ready to kill you last night?" Doug said calmly. "If I hadn't been close, he would have."

Robert and Danny stared at each other, both questioning whether this guy could be believed. "$100,000 apiece," Danny stammered. "Cash."

Robert looked at him like he was nuts. "Shut up, man," he spat out. "You ready to give up 'cause they say they'll give us money?"

"Yeah, I'm ready to give up. Don't you get it? These guys are protecting Bigfoot. That's why we haven't been able to get anywhere. They won't let us get that million," Danny spat out with a hateful glare at the two strangers. "We might as well take their money and forget it."

"He's making sense, Robert," Doug said. "Think about it. If we have to, we'll reveal Bigfoot's existence ourselves. We'll never let you get any money for killing them."

"So, you protect Bigfoot," Robert spat out. "We killed two of them, and you're willing to pay us off and just let us walk away."

"You killed one," Doug said with anger clear in his voice and in his eyes. "The other one is healing. I hope he never finds you wandering around out here. I don't think I'd be able to stop him if that happened. He'll kill both of you."

"Shit!" Danny spit out. "That's it, man! We're done. You wanna' look around for the one who wants to kill us? We need to take their money!" He shouted the last at Robert.

"And all you'll need to do is sign a paper that says you won't come back to the Salt Fork area and won't tell anyone what you know about Bigfoot," Adam said trying to sound reasonable.

"I'm not agreeing to anything until I see the money in front of me," Robert said, shaking his head.

"Then get out of the park for now. We'll meet you back here at 10:00. We'll have the $200,000 with us."

"You'd better show up," Robert threatened without any force in his voice.

"No," Doug said with a forceful tone. "*You'd* better show up. If not, we go to the authorities." He and Adam turned and walked away.

Robert and Danny stared at each other. They didn't know what to say about the shock of running into those two strange men who were offering them more money than they could imagine.

Chapter 23

The Pattons weren't happy, to put it mildly. I expected them to be mad, but it was the looks of disappointment that made me feel horrible. It was almost 10:00, and I hadn't called them or anything to let them know where I was. I hadn't even thought of it. My mind was on Jake.

And here I was, coming home a mess again. The sticky fluid from Jake's shift had dried on my skin and wrinkled work uniform. I held my backpack to my chest to hide what I could, but still had to keep my distance from them and just hope they didn't notice it. I couldn't wait to get into the shower.

"We were worried, Ali," Mrs. Patton said as I opened the front door and spied them both sitting in the living room watching TV and obviously waiting for me.

"I'm sorry," I said sincerely. I really did mean it. I didn't want them worrying about me.

"Jake. Right?" Mr. Patton said without any expression in his voice.

"Yeah. But not what you think." I wanted to make them understand but couldn't think of anything to tell them. I couldn't very well tell them the truth.

"Are you seeing Jake again?"

"Yeah."

"Then it *is* what we think. You took off with Jake without even calling us to let us know you'd be coming home late." Now his anger was seeping out into his voice.

"I didn't take off with Jake," I said, still trying to figure a way to make them understand. "His mom met me at work, and he wanted to see me. I've been at their house."

"Oh, he wanted to see you, so you ran out there to him," Mr. Patton said with a lot of sarcasm.

"His uncle died last night." My voice broke a little when I said that. Not only was it so sad that Max was dead, I was still angry that Robert and Danny had actually killed him. "Jake was really close to Max. He was a really nice man."

"Well, I'm sorry his uncle died, but you still should have called us."

"You're right. I should have called, but I just didn't think of it."

"So you're going to start seeing Jake again?" Mrs. Patton asked. She'd been letting Mr. Patton handle my interrogation, but this was the main thing that worried them.

"Yeah. I'm seeing him tomorrow."

"You know how we feel about that, but I don't see how we can fight it. You'll just sneak around and see him behind our backs, won't you?"

That irritated me. *Hell*, I thought, *it's true, though.* "Yeah, I would," I said with a shrug and a slight frown.

"I'll call Dr. Liston tomorrow to get you an appointment," she said in a very matter-of-fact way.

"Dr. Liston?" I had no idea who that was or why an appointment with a doctor had anything to do with this conversation.

"My gynecologist," she answered. "I think it's about time we talked to her about birth control."

"What? I don't need birth control!" I said with surprise.

"Condoms are good, especially for disease, but why take chances?" She was speaking so calmly, I didn't know what to think of this switch in our conversation.

"We're not having sex," I mumbled, so embarrassed I was sure my cheeks were bright red. The fact that I couldn't look at them probably made them think I was lying.

"That may be," she said sounding like she was sure I was lying, "but we should see Dr. Liston anyway."

"No. I don't want to see her. We're not having sex, so there's no point."

"Ali, there's no reason to be mad or embarrassed. It's obvious where your relationship with Jake is headed, and you should be prepared. It doesn't do any good to start birth control *after* you've had sex."

She had a point. Jake didn't want to have sex until we were bonded, but that could change. We both wanted each other, and could easily give in to our feelings. I didn't even know if he had condoms. Besides, even if we did bond, I didn't want to get pregnant. Having a baby, especially a Bigfoot baby, was way, way down the road.

That made me think of my mom. As much as she loved me, the last thing she'd want is for me to end up like her. Raising a child alone, not able to finish school, and struggling for money my whole life. She'd be having this same conversation with me.

"Can we talk about it tomorrow?" I said quietly. "I'm too tired to think."

"Will you be right home after work?"

"I don't know," I sighed, trying my best to be honest with them.

"I'll make an appointment. It would be good to talk to her even if you decide not to start the pill or anything else. Okay?"

"Yeah. That's okay. Goodnight."

"Goodnight," they both said at the same time.

How embarrassing, how irritating, how incredibly personal that whole discussion was. On top of all that, I was sure they'd be talking to Mr. Jones about Jake and me. Now I'd have to talk about my sex life, or lack of a sex life, with him. Couldn't they just leave me alone?

I blocked it all out of my mind and went to bed after a long, hot shower. Thankfully, I had a clean uniform shirt and extra black slacks. Still, I'd have to hide my dried-slime clothes until I could get them washed. I didn't want Mrs. Patton to face getting them clean.

I slept like a baby. It must have been because I refused to think about anything that was bothering me, which left my brain completely blank. I couldn't even stand thinking about seeing Jake the next day. Everything was just too overwhelming, and I let sleep erase it from my mind.

I got up about 8:00, right after the Pattons left for work, and headed into the shower again, feeling like my hair was still full of Jake's slime. He called about 9:00.

"How can I ever tell you how much that meant to me last night?" he asked without even saying hello.

"You don't have to," I said.

"I felt you there long before I woke up. It was amazing. Like Mom, only so different. It's hard to describe."

"I'm glad it worked. I wasn't sure."

"I was. As soon as I felt you, I started healing."

I didn't know what to say. His words were so sincere, so heartfelt. I found myself speaking from my heart, too. "I could feel our connection. I didn't know if you were getting better, or not, but I felt something."

"I missed you," he sighed.

"Yeah, I missed you, too."

"I wanna' take you to work, but Mom and Dad say I need to stay in bed most of the day. Can I see you after work?"

"The Pattons gave me some grief about seeing you again. They think we're too serious. Maybe it'd be good if you came to pick me up here. You know, like a real date."

"That'd be great. How about 5:30, and we'll go to dinner?"

"Yeah. That's good."

"I'm sorry they gave you a hard time," he sighed.

"It's not your fault."

"They care about you," Jake stated gently. "They don't want you hurt."

"I know."

"Hey, Mom's yelling for me to get back in bed. I'll see you tonight."

"I can't imagine your mom yelling at you," I said with a little laughter in my voice. "See you later."

I pushed the END button and stared at my phone. The whole conversation had been weird, and I wasn't sure how I felt about it. It was intense. It was tender. We didn't let each other get into the serious issues, but there were so many things we needed to talk about.

So many things. Still, the most important thing was how I felt about Jake. It was way obvious that he loved me. The fact that I was able to help him heal himself made it clear that we were meant to be together.

That scared me, but why wouldn't I be afraid? Bonded forever to a man that periodically changed into Bigfoot? A man that needed me to hold that Bigfoot and calm him, stroke him and control him.

Besides, committing to anyone scared me. I'd thought a lot about Mom while I was helping Jake. All those thoughts came back to me as I sat on the edge of my bed, and tears filled my eyes. She was always so good at explaining things to me, and I could almost hear her voice giving me her words of wisdom. I curled up into a little ball on my bed and cried. I missed her so much.

By the time I got up to leave for work, I looked like crap. My eyes were red and puffy. My hair, that had still been wet when Jake called, was a mass of kinks and frizzy curls. A pony tail fixed my hair, but a river full of cold water wouldn't have been enough to fix my eyes.

If I didn't leave for work in the next couple of minutes, I'd never make it. I grabbed a granola bar and a bottle of water for breakfast in the car, and left for work hoping no one would notice I'd been crying. If they did notice, I just hoped they wouldn't mention it.

I put the biggest smile on my face that I could and plunged into helping whoever came up to the desk. Those people were on vacation, enjoying a day at the state park, and deserved to see me looking like life was grand. So I pretended that it was and never let them see all the questions and worry that ate away inside me.

Being there made me think about Robert and Danny. What were they doing? What had they done after shooting Jake and Max? If they walked in here and started bragging about killing two Bigfoot, I'd grab a hunk of firewood from the fireplace and beat the crap out of them. They thought they were so smart, so cool. They were idiots that everyone laughed at. Well, I wasn't laughing anymore. They'd just better not come anywhere near me.

Chapter 24

"They won't show up," Robert sneered. "Those two guys looked like they'd spent the night in a cave, or something."

They'd been sitting on a log for about twenty minutes waiting for the strangers, who were supposed to show up and make them rich.

"They'll show," Danny mumbled, sounding less sure by the minute.

"No friggin' way they've got that kind of money," Robert spit out, standing up to pace back and forth. "I don't know what they were trying to pull, but they were handing us a pile of shit. We'll hear about them claiming the million in a few days. Let's get out of here." He bent to pick up his back pack like he was ready to leave.

"Shut the hell up!" Danny shouted. "I'm not leaving."

Robert sat back down, looking mad as hell, but still not sure enough to leave. They stared through the trees, both hoping those guys would show up with $200,000, but doubting it would happen.

Finally, they heard someone coming toward them.

"Sorry we're late," Doug said. "Can't hurry a lawyer writing up a contract." Doug's eyes were cold, his expression blank. He knew he needed to hold his anger through this meeting and not let these two cause him to react with the violence that was in his heart. The anger that his own Bigfoot wanted to act on.

Robert stared at him. They'd actually had a lawyer? What Robert and Danny didn't know was that Nina's specialty was writing contracts. If it came to it, there was no way it would ever be broken in any court. Robert and Danny would be promising to never reveal anything they knew, and Bigfoot wasn't even mentioned.

"You got the money?" Danny asked with both hope and doubt in his voice.

"Right here," Adam answered. He held out two leather cases that looked like they were meant to hold expensive laptops. Danny's mind flashed to the idea that he'd be able to afford a great laptop, tablet, and any other electronic stuff he wanted.

"Read the contract first," Doug said.

"We don't sign a damn thing until we see the money," Robert said angrily, obviously thinking that they'd sign and get no money at all.

Adam stepped forward and unzipped both cases so the boys could see the bundles of one hundred dollar bills that each contained. Robert and Danny had never seen such a thing.

"Twenty bundles," Adam said. "Each one contains fifty one-hundred dollar bills."

Danny reached up to touch the money, rubbing his finger across one of the bundles to watch the 100's flip by in each corner. He'd never had a hundred dollar bill, let alone this many of them. He'd sign anything to get his hands on that kind of money.

"I gotta' count it," Robert said.

"Read the contract first," Doug answered. "Then you can count before you sign."

They read, understanding about half of it. "What the hell is this?" Robert asked. "I don't know what most of this means."

"That's the way lawyers talk," Doug answered with impatience. "It says you tell no one about anything that went on out here. Not your parents, girlfriends, or future wives and children. You agree to never come near Salt Fork again. Never camp here or wander through the woods. You never track or hunt anything through these or any other woods. If you do any of these things, you pay us double the money we're giving you now. If one of you tells, whether it's next week or fifty years from now, you both pay the penalty of $200, 000 each. You got it?"

"So if this shithead tells some girl to impress her," Robert asks, pointing a thumb at Danny, "I owe you $200,000?"

"Yup. That's what would happen."

"Shut up, asshole," Danny spat at Robert. "I'm the one who said we should do this. I'm not telling anyone. I'm planning on forgetting it ever happened."

"Count the money," Adam interrupted. He knew they'd sign once they touched it. He also knew that it wasn't nearly as much money as they thought it was, and they'd soon spend it all and go back to having nothing. That's when they'd be tempted to tell and might have to be reminded of the contract's terms.

They were scared now, but they'd get over that once the money was gone. That's when they'd need a threat. A threat that would scare them to death. The Family would have to keep an eye on them for a long time.

Robert and Danny each took a case and started counting. Five thousand in each bundle. Twenty bundles. Their eyes grew larger as they went. Danny actually started sweating a little. He was ready to sign anything, agree to anything.

"Okay," Robert said. He was feeling as dumbfounded as Danny. All he could think of was getting his hands on that money.

Doug handed them the contract and a pen. They pressed on the laptop cases and signed without any more questions or comments. Doug checked each one to make sure they'd signed. Done.

"Get out of the park right now. Go home, go to hell for all I care, but get out of here." Doug had had it with them and could barely stand to look at them anymore. They'd killed his brother and almost killed his son. He'd played nice long enough and wasn't able to hide his hatred any longer.

"Chill," Robert said. "We'll get our stuff together and leave to-night."

"Some friends of ours already packed up your camp and put everything in the back of that piece of shit you call a truck," Adam answered. He stepped slightly forward in front of Robert and Danny because he could feel Doug's rage and knew he was about ready to start beating them within an inch of their lives.

"What kind of shit ... you're k-kidding!" Robert stammered.

"Start walking," Adam practically snarled with a clear threat in his voice.

Doug shoved the signed contract in his shirt pocket and had already moved through the trees towards the campsite parking lot. His eyes almost glowed with the anger he'd been hiding during the negotiation, but he couldn't hide it anymore. If he looked at them he might not be able to control it.

Adam nodded his head in the direction Doug had gone indicating that Robert and Danny needed to follow. Adam wasn't trying to hide any of his anger. He wanted those idiots to know they weren't dealing with friends.

Robert and Danny started grumbling about how none of there stuff better be missing or damaged. Like Greg and Pete, Adam's sons, would want any of their shit.

They walked in near silence. When they got to the truck, Robert and Danny saw the two big guys standing next to it and knew they'd have to do exactly what they were told. Still, they made a big show of checking everything while Doug and Adam got more irritated. Finally, they started to get in the truck.

"I'd like to never see either of you again," Doug spat out, "but we'll be watching. When you killed a Bigfoot I'd been watching over for years, my first instinct was to kill you. I was talked out of that. Don't make me wish I'd done it."

Doug glared at them with all the hate he was feeling. Inside, his Bigfoot was struggling to get out to devour these useless humans. He had never felt the need to kill a human, but these two, with their arrogant, smug expressions, were starting to convince him it would be a good idea.

"Doug," Adam said placing a hand on his shoulder. "Let them leave."

Robert started the truck and backed out of the parking space while Doug and Adam watched. Greg and Pete had stood silently, threateningly, along the side of the parking lot, but moved up to join Doug and Adam.

"It's done, Doug," Adam said calmly. "The Family will be watching no matter where they go. They won't be able to turn around without us knowing about it. Let's go."

* * *

The Pattons got home a little after 5:00 like they usually did. I was already changed into my khaki slacks and a leaf-green patterned top. My hair was hopeless after spending all day tied back in a pony tail, so I just brushed it out and put the stretchy tie back on. Jake liked it down, but I couldn't do that unless I washed it again.

"Jake and I are going out to dinner," I said as I joined them in the kitchen.

"Then I guess I'll put one less burger on the grill," Mr. Patton answered.

Both of us spoke quietly. None of us wanted to start some big thing, again. They didn't like the idea of me going out with Jake, but knew that they couldn't stop me.

"He's picking me up any minute," I said.

"What time will you be home?"

"I don't know."

"We've never given you a curfew or anything, but maybe ... why don't you be home by 11:00," he said. Not a question. He was telling me to be home at 11:00.

Mrs. Patton had been cleaning vegetables at the sink. I think they'd talked about the curfew business, and she was comfortable letting him take care of it. Maybe they thought I'd give them an argument.

"Sure. That's fine," I said softly. I didn't like arguments and fights, so whatever time they said would be okay with me.

The doorbell rang. As I headed for the door, I couldn't help wondering what kind of reception the Pattons would give Jake. The easiest thing would have been to duck out the door as I opened it, and take off with him. Avoiding uncomfortable situations never solved them, though.

"Hi," I smiled.

"Hi. Ready to go?" he smiled back.

"Come in the kitchen and say hi to the Pattons," I said. It was somewhere between a statement and a question.

"Do I have to?" he whispered, smiling again as he started walking toward the kitchen.

I didn't need to answer because he was kidding with that question. I knew seeing them would be uncomfortable, but he'd do it.

"Hi, Mr. Patton," Jake said as we walked in. He started to reach out his hand to shake, but stopped once he saw what Mr. Patton was doing. His hands were covered with raw hamburger as he shaped them into patties.

They both gave a half laugh. "Hi, Jake," he said.

"Mrs. Patton," Jake accomplished shaking her hand.

"So where are you two going?" Mrs. Patton asked.

"We haven't decided, yet. Wherever Ali wants to go."

"We'd like her to be home by 11:00," she said as she went back to slicing a potato.

"Sure, no problem." Jake looked like he wanted to say something but didn't know where to start. My stomach was churning a little and I felt like we were on trial somehow.

Jake sighed quietly. "I know you guys think Ali and I are moving too fast. I've told her I think we belong together, but I'm trying really hard not to push her. I'll wait for her as long as I need to. After she graduates, we'll decide where this is going."

"We thought she'd go to college," Mrs. Patton said. She looked like she wasn't happy, but was talking as nice as she could.

"That's good," Jake nodded. "Ali's smart. I wouldn't try to stop her from going."

"But you're not planning on college? You haven't even been looking for a job."

"College isn't for me," Jake answered, looking a little embarrassed. I knew he was as smart as anyone I'd ever met and should go. It was shifting that made it impossible for him. He'd had a hard enough time getting through high school. "One of the mechanics at Dad's dealership is retiring, so I'll be training with him soon."

"You'll be working for your dad?"

"Yeah. I've already done it some, and he wants me to learn all the different parts of the business so I can take over when he's ready to retire."

"That's good," she said, but she sounded doubtful to me.

There was an odd minute of silence as we all stood there. Finally, I couldn't stand it anymore. "We'd better get going, Jake," I said.

"Yeah. Bye," he said as we headed out the kitchen door.

The Pattons said goodbye, I said goodbye, and Jake and I finally got into his truck and started down the driveway. We'd all been so polite. Neither of us said anything to each other as he backed out. I didn't know what to say, and I'm sure Jake felt the same.

Jake pulled over on the side of the road once we were out of sight of the house. "God, Ali. I'm sorry," he said after taking a deep breath.

"For what?"

"It's like they don't trust you anymore, and that's because they don't trust me. I'm really sorry."

"Oh, Jake," I sighed. "You haven't done anything to make them not trust you. It's just that I didn't want to do anything or go anywhere before I met you. They think I'm using you to substitute for my mother. I think Mr. Jones put that idea in their heads. It's not your fault."

"I meant it when I said I wouldn't push you. I'll do anything you say, okay?"

"There is one thing I'd like you to do," I grinned slightly. "Kiss me."

Jake looked surprised. What he didn't know was that the whole time I was soothing his Bigfoot side, staring at the hairy face, I wanted to be kissing his human side. I'd missed him so much.

Without saying a word, Jake scooted over and took my face in his hands. He kissed me so sweetly, so lovingly, I never wanted him to stop. When I heard the subtle vibration of the growl in his throat, it felt so right.

Chapter 25

We had a quick burger and fries at Burger King. We talked about my day at work, Jake's messy sandwich, a new sci-fi movie coming out that Jake wanted to see, and how hot it had been the last several days. Nothing important. Nothing we needed to talk about.

There's no denying that part of our conversation was avoidance, but another part was that we just enjoyed being together without issues or worries. It seemed so long since I'd listened to his voice, or looked into his eyes. So long since we'd been able to laugh and just be together.

Watching him take a huge bite of his double Whopper made me think about the memory I wanted to avoid talking about the most. The vision in my head of Jake devouring chunks of flesh from that loner. It was still there. It still bothered me, and I couldn't understand why he did it.

After dinner, Jake drove us toward the park. He stopped along the road and led us a short way through the trees until we came to a stream tumbling down a steep hill. We sat on a log in silence for a few minutes listening to the water as it gently bubbled over rocks. The sound of it was so relaxing, peaceful.

Jake's arm was around my shoulders, making me feel so close to him. I only wanted to sit there in that peaceful togetherness, but I knew it was the time to ask some hard questions.

"Jake," I started, feeling hesitant, but needing answers. "You said on the phone that night," I was sure he'd know what night I was talking about, "that you wanted to explain. That I didn't understand why you and Max did what you did." I gazed up at him. "I still don't understand."

"I figured that was still bothering you," he said quietly.

"Yeah. It is. But I want to understand how you could do that."

"It's about who we are, Ali. Right now, I'm human. I look human, and, more importantly, I feel and think human. Still, Bigfoot is there deep inside me. He's hidden, subdued, almost like he's in a coma, barely alive. When I shift, the opposite happens. My human self is in that coma. I think like an animal. I'm driven by instinct. I'm really not even conscious of my human side."

"But animals don't devour each other like that."

"Sure they do."

"I mean they don't eat their own kind. A lion eats a gazelle, but not its own kind."

"When a male lion takes over another pride, it kills and partially eats the cubs so the females will be ready to mate sooner. Chimpanzees have been seen eating monkeys and even the infants of other Chimp groups."

"Really?" How disgusting! I'm sure the disgust showed on my face.

"Yeah. And when I'm Bigfoot, I'm an animal," he said quietly like he wasn't sure I wanted to face that fact. "But, you know, there've been human cannibals, too, who ritualistically eat their enemies. It's not easy to think about, but it happens in most predator species, and Bigfoot's a predator."

I stared at him silently for a minute, trying to get my thoughts together. "I think what bothered me the most was that it was you."

"I know," he said with sadness in his eyes. "But it's what I am. I can't imagine not being an animal."

"When I was with you last night, you weren't an animal."

"Yeah, I was," he sighed. "But I hate that you had to see the worst part of it. Killing the loner wasn't about feeding. That was about destroying an enemy who tried to hurt you. Claws and teeth are the only weapons we have, the only thing we know."

"I hadn't thought about it like that."

"But killing like that is rare. Neither of us had ever done that before, and Dad hasn't either. It was all instinct, all we knew how to do."

"It was just so horrible to see, so violent."

"Remember, though, animals aren't always violent. We have our tender moments," he smiled.

I reached up and kissed him.

When our kiss ended, Jake hugged me, pulling me tight against his chest. My face was buried against his neck, and I felt him pull the elastic tie out of my pony tail.

"My hair will look terrible after being in a pony tail all day," I murmured.

"I don't care," he sighed as he moved his face through my hair. I knew he was smelling me. Kinda strange, but I liked it. I liked that my scent was so important and soothing to him.

"Oh, Jake. I ... I was so scared when your mom took me to you last night. Scared I wouldn't be able to help you, and scared of you. You're so big and dangerous looking."

"I'm sorry you were scared. You shouldn't have had to do that until we were bonded."

"But I wanted to. I just didn't know what to do, or if it would help," I was starting to blubber a little, but I needed to get it all out and tell him what I really felt. I took a deep breath. "I knew if it worked it would mean we were meant to bond, and I didn't know if I wanted that. But if it didn't work, you would die! I couldn't stand losing you."

He took my face in his hands, spreading his fingers through my hair on either side of my head. "You saved me," he sighed. The look in his eyes told me how much he meant that and how much he loved me.

I stroked his cheek like my fingers were following the lines of hair on his Bigfoot face, but kept my other arm tight around his waist. It felt so good to be so close to him. "I want to tell you," I started, but hesitated.

"You can tell me anything."

I smiled, knowing that was true. "While I was talking to you and watching your face, I kept getting this vision of me sitting next to Mom's hospital bed, waiting for her to die. That time with her was horrible."

He didn't say a word, but he didn't need to. The expression his face showed clearly how sad he was that I'd gone through that.

"I wanted to leave you," I whispered. "Walk out into the kitchen and tell your mom and dad I couldn't do it. I couldn't stand to watch someone else die. Someone else I-I love."

"Did you say you love me?" Jake practically gasped.

"I've talked to Mom a lot, both in letters and in my head, since she died. Last night, I listened. I could hear her voice inside me, telling me loving you was okay. She told me our love and trust was the most important thing, and we'd overcome the rest. She said we belonged together. You were right, you know. There's plenty of room in my heart for you and Mom."

"Oh, Ali, I love you so much. Say it. Tell me," he whispered.

"I love you, Jake," I whispered, staring into his eyes.

He kissed me. A long, slow, loving kiss that made me gasp when he finally pulled away. "I want to bond with you, marry you, and live our whole lives together. But I know you need to finish school. You need to get your life going before you share it with me. Once you graduate, we'll be together, and that's all that counts."

"I want to bond with you, too. But my life isn't in my own hands until I'm eighteen. The Pattons and Mr. Jones would never let me marry you. They'd want us to wait until after I finish college, but I can't wait that long. I can go to a college close to here. We can live together and I'll commute to school."

"That'll be great. Oh, Ali, I can hardly wait." He buried his face in my hair again and held me even tighter than before. I could hear his subtle growls of happiness and knew I wanted him. Suddenly, Jake stood up from the log, lifting me with him. He held me tight against his chest and kissed me while spinning around until my feet were flying out behind me.

We were both laughing out loud by the time he stopped and put me back down on my feet. We stood there holding each other, listening to the stream babble on its way. I knew without any doubt how much I wanted him.

"Jake," I said hesitantly with my head against his chest. "Mrs. Patton is making me an appointment with her gynecologist. She wants me to go on birth control."

He jerked back to look at me, obviously surprised. "I should have known they'd figure we're having sex," he said.

"Yeah. I'm gonna' go. I figure we're probably headed that way." I said it quietly because I was plain old embarrassed. He'd never even mentioned us having sex, but I had, and I knew he wanted me as much as I wanted him.

"Oh, God, Ali. Yeah," he sighed as he moved his head down to nuzzle my neck. "I've wanted you so bad since that first afternoon at the movies. Every time I've kissed you ..." he practically whispered as I felt his teeth nip my earlobe.

I was melting. His lips and tongue caressed my jaw, moving toward my mouth. As his lips met mine, he was leaning over me, and I could feel every one of his solid muscles straining against my whole body. He growled again as his tongue played with my lips and slid into my mouth. I squeezed him harder to get as close as possible.

Too soon, he pulled away. "Shit, Ali. It's not going to be on the ground or the back of my truck. When I make love to you, it'll be special, some place special, and when we have time to hold each other. I want your first time to be amazing."

"It will be amazing because it'll be with you," I said, rising up on tip-toes to gently kiss him again.

"I want you so much," Jake whispered as he moved back to rubbing his face through my hair.

"I want you, too." I used both hands to stroke and play with his hair. I loved his quiet growl when I did that.

"I need to get you home." His hands went to my shoulders to move me away from him.

"Probably a good idea," I smiled.

We walked back to the truck with our arms around each other. All the way, I couldn't stop thinking about how much I wanted him. I think I'd been pushing those feelings away when I wasn't ready to admit I loved him, but couldn't keep denying them. If we'd had condoms, I think I would have told him the back of his truck would have been just great.

As we got to the truck, he stopped and turned toward me. "There's something else I've gotta' ask you," he said hesitantly.

"What?" I said, having no idea what it might be.

"You know ... Mom can't help me control it anymore," he said, actually looking embarrassed. "Would you consider doing that again?"

"Of course I will," I said. How could he think that I might say no? "When?"

"Tomorrow would be good. I could pick you up again after work, and we could go to my house."

I smiled up at him. "I think I'll enjoy it."

He smiled back with relief. "I know I will."

We drove home talking quietly about nothing important. Holding hands, enjoying each other's company, I could feel his love for me radiating through the truck. It was like another presence with us. His love kept reflecting off me, and my love reflected off him. I couldn't take my eyes off him, but he had to just glance at me while he watched the road.

As he parked in the driveway, he immediately whipped off his seatbelt, scooted over to my side, and crushed me in his arms. His lips were wonderful, and I kissed him back just as passionately as he kissed me.

What had taken me so long to admit I loved him? He'd known all along, but I wouldn't let myself recognize it. Once I said those words to him, it felt so good, so right. The idea of living without him was ludicrous. What a joke, thinking I could send him out of my life and just go on without him.

I remembered so well looking down at his Bigfoot face and letting my mind go blank. That's when I'd heard it. Mom's voice.

Not like she was talking to me from the grave. I heard the words she had said to me about Tommy. Not long before she died, Tommy just quit calling me because he couldn't handle the whole thing of watching me watch Mom die.

"Ali," Mom had said. "Tommy's nice, but he's not the one for you. Wait for the one you love. The one you can't live without. The one who can't live without you. That will be the real thing, and you'll be happy together forever."

That was the love she'd never found, but somehow I had. Jake was the one I couldn't live without, and he couldn't live without me.

We'd be happy as long as we lived, and marrying a Bigfoot meant that would be a really long time.

The next day, he picked me up at the Pattons right after I got off work. We drove out to the cabin talking and laughing, happy being together.

Nina was waiting for us, but quickly sent Jake to the basement. She explained what I needed to do like she had when he was so hurt. I noticed a glimmer in her eyes, and knew that she was sad she couldn't help Jake anymore. She'd probably cry once I'd gone down the basement stairs to him. I understood that. Her son was no longer hers. She was giving him to me.

I was still slightly intimidated when I saw Jake's Bigfoot standing there, waiting for me in the basement, but that only lasted a second. I took his hand and led him to the big, comfy couch. I wrapped my arms around him, stroked his head, and talked to him. Jake growled quietly, whined a little, and even moaned as I played with his hair, moved my hands along his neck and shoulders, and told him how much I loved him.

I stared into those big, pale brown eyes that never changed. Whether gazing at the human Jake or the Bigfoot, I could see his love through those eyes. I held him tighter and caressed the hair from his temple, down along his cheek.

Jake seemed completely relaxed, except for those caramel eyes that gazed into mine and roamed over my face. Looking back at him while I continued to stroke and talk quietly, I began to realize that the distinction between the human Jake and the Bigfoot Jake was blurring.

He was less like two distinct creatures to me anymore. When Jake told me that they didn't consider themselves human, that they were two-natured beings, I was confused, frightened. I got it now.

He was never one without a trace of the other. Neither side could ignore the existence of the other. Neither side could deny the other.

The truth of this was in his eyes that never changed. My view into his heart that constantly let me know how much he loved me. I belonged to him, and he belonged to me. I no longer had even the slightest doubt. I'd be happy with him for the rest of my life.

Chapter 26

Jake and I kept seeing each other every day for the next week. The Pattons and Mr. Jones didn't like it, but what could they do about it? Unfortunately, I found out exactly what Mr. Jones could do.

It was Saturday. I had the day off, and I didn't have any plans with Jake until late afternoon. He had some stuff to take care of at home, and I figured it wouldn't hurt for me to hang out with the Pattons a little. It would be a good day to get some laundry done and weed the garden that was going pretty wild.

"Ali!" Mrs. Patton called. I was on my knees, weeding, and turned to look back toward the house. There was Mr. Jones, standing beside Mrs. Patton and waving at me.

My stomach clenched a little when I saw him. He hadn't shown up unannounced since I'd first moved in with the Pattons, a time when he was still checking them out for Children's Services. This wasn't going to be good.

"Hey, Ali," he said as I stepped up on the back deck. "I thought I'd stop by so we could talk." I hadn't seen him for weeks and knew there was a little accusation behind that simple statement. I hadn't shown up for that last appointment I had with him, so he probably figured I couldn't avoid him this way. He was right. No way out of it now.

"Sure, Mr. Jones," I said, pulling off my gardening gloves.

"Why don't you two use Mike's office," Mrs. Patton said. Mr. Patton walked into the kitchen about then, shook hands with Mr. Jones and they said pleasant hellos. I could tell from the looks on both of their faces that they knew I wouldn't like what Mr. Jones had to say. I wanted to run.

"So, Ali, how are things going?" Mr. Jones started as I sat on the couch in the office, and he pulled over the desk chair so we could be face-to-face. Not going to be a casual chat.

"Good," I answered. "The Pattons are always great."

"Yeah, they are. And they worry about you, almost like you were their real daughter."

I didn't have anything to say about that because I knew it was just his lead-up. The feeling that he was going to tell me something I didn't like kept growing.

"So," he said with a pause like he was picking his words. "Tell me about Jake."

I knew it. He was here to talk about Jake. I wanted to tell him how much I loved Jake and that we were going to spend the rest of our lives together, but knew that would be a huge mistake.

"He's pretty important to me," I stammered. I could have said *Jake's fine, work's great, I'm looking forward to my senior year. See ya' later.* But that would have just been avoiding the inevitable.

"That's what the Pattons said. I'm afraid he's getting too important to you."

"No. No, he's not." I felt like I should be defending Jake, but wasn't sure what to say. My mind had almost gone blank as he spoke because my dread kept growing.

"Ali," Mr. Jones said quietly, looking at me very seriously. "I want you to stop seeing Jake."

"What? Why?"

"The Pattons and I don't think you should be involved with him." I stared at him and I think my mouth had dropped open a little. I thought he'd say I should take things slow, not get too serious too fast. Stop seeing him? Was he really saying this? "Jake's family has had some issues. They're just not the kind of people we think you should be involved with."

The *kind* of people? They were the sweetest, most understanding people I could ever imagine. Well, there was of course the Bigfoot thing, but he couldn't know that. What was he talking about?

"Jake's family is wonderful!" I almost shouted. "What *issues* are you talking about?" I stared at Mr. Jones and knew he had to see the anger in my eyes. It was burning its way right towards him.

"I can't tell you the details, but there have been some, let's say suspicions." He was trying to talk calmly and quietly.

They lived out in those cabins, stayed away from most of the community except when they had to be involved for work, really kept to themselves. Just the kind of stuff that narrow-minded, intolerant people would think was suspicious.

I had told Jake I was sure I loved him, but, at that moment, I really felt the commitment I was ready to make to him and his way of life. I loved him with my whole heart and couldn't imagine being without him for even one day.

My anger, the need to protect Jake from Mr. Jones' stupid suspicions, and my need to defend the man I loved all flared at once. "No!" I said with determination. "I won't stop seeing Jake. There's nothing you can do to keep me away from him."

"Ali," he said with his falsely calm voice. "There are things I can do. The judge will order you to stay away from Jake. I'll get a protection order against him. If he comes anywhere near you, he can be arrested."

"This is crazy," I practically whispered. "Why would you do that?"

"Because I believe it's not safe for you to be around him and his family. If you see him again, I'll go to the judge."

"You can't do that!" I was yelling again.

"I can. And I will."

"Mr. Jones," I whined, flopping back and forth between anger and despair. "What have they done?"

"I can't tell you, Ali. Just know that I don't trust them, and you shouldn't either. I'll check on you tomorrow."

"That's it? You just tell me not to see him, and that's it?"

"Yes. Call him. Tell him you can't see him anymore. I'll talk to you tomorrow."

While speaking those words, he stood and started walking toward the door. My mind was reeling. How could he do that? How could he make a huge proclamation and simply turn to leave? Did he really think I would do what he said?

I wouldn't. I'd call Jake, all right, but I'd be telling him what Mr. Jones said. We'd figure something out. Maybe his dad could talk to Mr. Jones. Maybe his mom could fight Mr. Jones in court. If nothing else, I was more than willing to sneak around and see him behind Mr. Jones' back.

"Mr. Jones," I said just as he got to the door. "I'll be eighteen in a few weeks. There's nothing you can do, then." Surprisingly my voice was calm and even more determined.

"You're still in high school, still a ward of the state, and still under my control. Don't make this harder than it has to be, Ali." With that, he walked out, leaving me alone and baffled. How could he do this?

What happened to that man I thought was so sweet and caring when I first landed in the foster system. That must have been a different Mr. Jones. Nothing like the guy that just demanded I stop seeing Jake and threatened us.

Mr. and Mrs. Patton came in a few minutes later and tried to make me feel better about what Mr. Jones was doing, but I didn't pay much attention to what they said. I let their words float through me while I concentrated on Jake and what we'd have to do to be together.

"It'll be okay, Ali," Mrs. Patton was saying when I finally started to listen again. *No it won't*, I thought without saying it.

"I'm going to my room," I said quietly. The hell with weeding the garden and spending time with the Pattons.

I needed to call Jake. What I wanted to do was tell him to come get me. Better still, I could take my own car and go to him. Both of those choices would cause a lot more problems, though. Mr. Jones had been serious. He'd go to the judge.

* * *

Walter Jones drove back to his office knowing that his meeting with Ali hadn't gone well. He hadn't wanted to threaten her, but that's how it ended up. No matter what, though, he'd do everything he could to keep her away from the Shepherd family.

Thinking of the Shepherd family made Walter think of his sister, Lucy. Like Ali, she'd been young and naive when she met Max Shepherd, and she'd fallen in love almost immediately. Walter had checked out Max's background: no education, having quit school at sixteen, no job except washing cars at his brother's dealership, no prospects for any kind of future.

It was the summer between Lucy's sophomore and junior years of college, but suddenly she was talking about transferring from Ohio State to a school that would be close enough for her to drive to class instead of living in the dorms. She didn't want to be living in Columbus where she couldn't see Max every day. She practically abandoned her friends to spend all her free time with Max.

289

Walter still felt the pain of that last night. He and Lucy had argued, yelling and screaming at each other, about her relationship with Max. Walter wanted her to slow down, think about her own life, and finish her degree at Ohio State. Lucy was ready to marry Max, even though she'd only known him a matter of months and he hadn't officially asked her. She'd run from the fight with Walter directly to Max. Out into that dark, lonely forest.

Campers had heard her screams in the distance. They found her lifeless body wrapped around the trunk of a tree like she'd been thrown there. They tried to resuscitate her, called 911, did everything they could. Nothing could be done, though. Broken bones, internal bleeding, concussion, deep scratches all over her body, that horrible bite to her shoulder.

The coroner couldn't positively identify the animal that had attacked her, but their best guess was a bear. They'd been spotted in central Ohio, and could have easily wandered into the park. The tooth marks weren't clear and couldn't be pinpointed as being from a particular animal.

No matter, though. Walter knew what had killed her. Max. Somehow he'd driven her out of the safety of that cabin and into the dark dangers of the woods surrounding it. What had he done to make her scared enough, or mad enough, to run away from him?

He must have hurt her horribly. Had he hit her or, God forbid, raped her? Or had he cruelly broken her heart? There was no physical evidence, and Walter figured he'd never know exactly why she'd run, but he knew without any doubt that it was Max's fault.

Now he was having the same kind of conversation with another young girl. Ali had fallen under the spell of that Shepherd family just like Lucy. This time, though, Walter had the courts on his side and he'd force Ali to stay away from Jake Shepherd. He wouldn't lose another innocent girl like he'd lost Lucy. No matter what he had to do, he'd keep Ali and Jake apart.

* * *

"Ah, shit, Ali," Jake half-sighed in response to me telling him everything Mr. Jones had said. "Is his name Walter Jones?"

"Yeah. Why?"

"I never thought about it. I should have seen the connection. Walter Jones is Lucy's brother."

"Max's Lucy?" I asked with surprise.

"Yeah. He blamed Max for Lucy's death even though there was no evidence that he'd done anything wrong. But the cops questioned all of us about why Lucy left that night. Walter Jones has always been sure that Max did something that made her run away from him, and I guess he did. That was the night Max told her the truth about us."

"But that doesn't mean Max was responsible for her death. She shouldn't have run like that."

"I know. But he blamed himself, too. She was already upset about fighting with her brother. Max thought, if he'd waited to tell her, she would have been able to accept him. He could never forgive himself for not waiting."

"So now Mr. Jones thinks you're going to do the same thing to me? That hardly makes any sense at all. He acted like your whole family is dangerous."

"He probably thinks we all know what happened with Lucy and we've been protecting Max. God only knows what he thinks is going on out here."

"Talk to your mom and dad, Jake. Maybe your mom knows some legal way we can stop him."

"Yeah, I'll talk to them, but I think our best bet is that you'll be eighteen in a few weeks. He can't do anything once you're eighteen."

"I think I'd have to give up everything from Children's Services. The monthly support, the Pattons, and money for college. I'd be completely on my own."

"You'll never be completely on your own. You'll always have me."

"I love you, Jake. I wish you were here instead of on the phone ... I want to kiss you so bad."

"Me too," he sighed. "I'll talk to Mom. We'll figure something out."

"I guess our date's off for tonight," I whispered. I wanted so much to see him and hold him.

"Yeah. I guess so." He sounded so disappointed. Part of me felt good that he wanted to see me as much as I wanted to see him. "How about if I stop to see you at work tomorrow? What time do you get a break?"

"That's a wonderful idea," I sighed. "My break's about 1:30."

"Then I'll see you tomorrow, but I won't come in. I'll wait for you in my truck. Don't worry, we'll figure something out."

"I know we will. I love you."

"God, I love you, too. Bye, babe."

"Bye."

Chapter 27

I stayed in my room the rest of the night. The Pattons called me for dinner, but there was no way I could go out and sit with them playing nice when I was angrier than I'd ever been. The whole thing with Mr. Jones was their fault. They'd talked to him about Jake.

Mr. Jones had the issue with Lucy and Max, but he didn't know Jake was Max's nephew until the Pattons told him. I hadn't told him Jake's last name, so the Pattons must have. No, I couldn't sit down to dinner with them. I'd rather go hungry.

The next day at work, the morning was going so slow, I thought I was going to scream. I knew time was dragging because I kept thinking about meeting Jake, but that didn't make any difference. Knowing why you feel some way doesn't make you feel different.

Finally! It was 1:25, and I could feel Jake's presence out in the parking lot. Sounds silly that I could feel him, but it seemed like I really could. Maybe it was the bonding that I'd finally accepted, maybe it was simply anticipation and my imagination.

He sent me a text that said he was outside the second floor, in the passenger drop-off area. All I'd need to do was take a few steps to the left and he'd be right there.

Instead of stepping, I ran out to the truck, threw the door open, and jumped into his arms. I hugged him as hard as I could until he pulled back to look into my face. Then he kissed me like I was the only person in the world. So much love in that tender kiss, I thought my heart might explode as I drew that love in and tried to send my love back to him.

"I'd better move the truck," he mumbled against my lips.

I knew we didn't want to take the chance of being seen together but couldn't say I really cared at that moment. All I cared about was being there with Jake's arms around me, but I scooted back to the passenger side, never taking my eyes off him.

He pulled through the passenger pick-up area and turned into a small parking lot at the side of the lodge, continuing until we were parked along the building, out of site of almost anyone who would be around. Then he unhooked his seatbelt and slid over to me.

"I missed you," he whispered into my ear as he nuzzled my cheek and neck.

"I missed you so much," I sighed. His lips on my neck felt unbelievably good, and I never wanted him to stop. But he did.

"What are we going to do?" he asked as he gazed into my eyes.

"I don't know. What did your mom and dad say?"

"Mom says Mr. Jones doesn't have any grounds to legally keep us apart, but Dad thinks he might cause us a lot of grief. He thinks we should go along with him."

"And not see each other?"

"It's only a couple weeks until you're eighteen." I could hear the sadness and doubt in his voice. He didn't like the idea of us not seeing each other, either.

"But what about you? Won't you need me to control you? I want to help you ... what will you do?"

"I'll just hunt more," he said with a gentle shrug like it wouldn't be a big deal. His eyes contradicted his words, though. It wouldn't be easy for him.

I gazed at him for several seconds, not knowing what to say. Then I felt my eyes grow wider as the idea popped into my brain. "Why don't we just run away? We could go anywhere we want." Jake started to shake his head as I spoke. "We'll come back right after my birthday, and no one could do anything to stop us."

"It won't work, Ali," Jake said quietly.

"Why not?" As quiet as he was, my voice was getting louder and almost shrill as details rolled around in my brain. "I have some money saved. If we go to a city, it would take them forever to find us. We'd just lay low for a couple of weeks, and we'd be together!"

"Ali," he sighed. "You're forgetting what I am. Where would I hunt?"

"We'd find someplace. There're all kinds of woods and deer around." It was all making so much sense to me. Seemed like the perfect option.

"Without a sentinel, I'd be a loner out there on someone else's land." His eyes had grown darker, and his voice deeper. He looked so serious. "You know what that could mean."

The pain of the vision appearing in my head had to show on my face. Jake and Max beating, killing and devouring that loner. I stared out the window as I tried to stop thinking about it.

Jake hugged me tighter and I rested my head on his chest. "Shifters can't just take off alone. We can't survive for long without The Family."

I felt tears forming in my eyes. "I'm sorry," I whispered. "I wasn't thinking. I just hate the idea of not being able to see you."

"I know," he said quietly as he stroked my back and I snuggled even tighter against his chest.

"I'm tired of waiting," I practically whispered. "I love you and ... I want to be with you."

"Not until we bond."

"Why not?" I looked up at him with a whine in my voice. "You told me you've had sex with other girls. Why not me? Why do we have to wait?"

"Because you're the one I'm meant to bond with. Those other girls didn't mean anything. With you ... it will mean everything."

"It will mean everything to me, too. I want to be with you forever, so why can't forever start now? Bond with me."

"Bonding's not about sex. It's about taking control ... you taking control over me ... over my Bigfoot side. I told you once that I'd bite you, but you're the one that will offer me your neck and ask me to bond with you. You'll ask me to bite you."

"Then I'm asking. Bite me, Jake. Bond with me ... right now."

"God, Ali," he sighed like it was a prayer. "Change right here and bite through the skin of your neck? And then what? I'd just send you on your way to go back to work and home to the Pattons? Once we're bonded, we're together. I'd never be able to let you live in someone else's house, sleep in their bed every night ... alone. I wouldn't be able to resist coming after you, and it wouldn't be pretty."

"You'd come after me? Or ... your Bigfoot would come after me?"

"We're the same, Ali," he groaned. "Both sides love you and need you. We couldn't survive without you, so we'd do anything to get you back. My human side wouldn't want to do it, but my Bigfoot side wouldn't hesitate to get to you."

"Your mom goes on business trips."

"And it took Dad years to work up to that. He followed her once, and she had to cancel the trip and come back home. He handles it now, but it isn't easy. He goes through hell when she's gone more than a couple days. We have to wait, Ali. It's the safest way. If we're bonded, things could get pretty crazy."

"I hate this," I sighed. "If Mr. Jones would just let us see each other ... but he seemed so damned determined."

We held each other in silence for several minutes. From the look Mr. Jones gave me and the tone of his voice, I didn't think I could change his mind, but I'd have to try. He'd have to listen.

"I hate to say this, Ali, but you have to go back to work."

"Or I could call them and quit," I tried to smile. Probably not very successfully.

"Call me tonight?" Jake asked as he moved me off his chest. He was being so damn reasonable and responsible.

"I'll call," I said quietly, nodding my head.

Jake used his thumb to wipe a tear from my cheek. "I love you, and we'll have the rest of our lives together. It's only a few weeks until you're eighteen, and then they won't be able to stop us."

"Why do those few weeks feel like forever?"

"Because you love me, too," he smiled.

"I sure do."

I held his face with both my hands as I kissed him goodbye. It was a gentle, tender kiss that I hoped showed him that love. He growled quietly as I pulled away.

Without saying another word, I left the truck and walked around the building to go back to work. It was the last thing I wanted to do and I glanced back at Jake several times. He slowly moved the truck so he could watch me all the way through the door.

The afternoon went almost as slowly as the morning had. Instead of waiting to see Jake, though, I was envisioning how horrible the next few weeks would be. Once I was eighteen, though ... No, that battle might get pretty nasty, too.

I'd have to face Mr. Jones and the Pattons and let them know they couldn't tell me what to do anymore. I'd have to stand up as an adult and claim the right to make my own decisions. An adult? Legally, that's what I would be. Emotionally, though, standing up to them made me feel like I was still a little girl.

Mr. Jones would probably get mad and cut off everything I got from Children's Services. The Pattons wouldn't get any more money for letting me live there, so they'd probably kick me out. Maybe I could move in with Jake's parents.

I'd have to find some way to pay for college on my own. As a foster child, I'd have a grant from the government, but I'd probably lose it if I played that independence card and went on my own. I'd definitely have to find a better job to afford four years of college. And my car. I'd have to give it back to the Pattons because I sure wouldn't be able to keep making payments while paying for college. Independence started to sound way over-rated.

I'd been scared before about going off to college alone, but this was even worse. All those thoughts were starting to get me terrified of being on my own, and I had a hard time paying attention to what I was doing at work. Good thing I'd done it enough that most of the jobs were practically automatic.

The day finally ended. I drove straight home from work, getting there before the Pattons. I was sitting on my bed, playing a mindless game on my tablet, and pretty much ignoring a re-run of Cupcake Wars when I heard Mrs. Patton coming up the stairs. I knew it was her because it was steady progress. Mr. Patton always bounced up two steps at a time.

Her knock was gentle. "We're cooking steaks on the grill to-night," she said once I'd told her to come in. "Are you going to join us?"

I didn't want to. I didn't want to talk to them at all, but I'd real-ized that afternoon that they were just doing their job. They were hired to give me a place to live, keep me safe, and report any issues to my social worker. And that's what they did. The big problem was Mr. Jones, not the Pattons.

"Yeah," I answered quietly. "Do you need any help?"

"We can handle it. I'll call you when it's ready."

"Thanks." I wasn't as mad at them as I had been, but still wasn't ready to be too nice.

After dinner, which we ate in near silence, I felt like I desperately needed something to do. I grabbed my gardening gloves and headed out to finish weeding the garden. After all, it was my project. I might as well take care of it.

I picked four tomatoes and two peppers. It felt good to have accomplished something like a productive garden, and I smiled to myself as I carried them into the kitchen. We'd been eating fresh tomatoes for about a week. The Pattons both smiled back as I sat them on the counter, but none of us said anything.

Back out in the yard, I knelt in the grass trying not to think of anything but the weeds that had been sprouting up everywhere. I heard someone coming toward me across the dry grass. August usually got pretty dry, I'd have to remember to water the garden in the morning.

"Ali," Mrs. Patton said as she stopped beside me.

"You want me to cut some herbs?" I asked.

"No. We have plenty." She sat on the grass next to me and reached over to pluck out one of the weeds. "I just wanted to say that we're sorry."

"I know," I said quietly while using the trowel to dig out a stubborn hunk of green that didn't belong in the garden. I knew how sorry they were because the looks on their faces were obvious all during dinner.

"Mike and I want you to know that you'll always be welcome here. Even after you're eighteen."

I finally looked at her. "Thank you. That means a lot."

"I don't think Mr. Jones told you, but we think you should know. He's talking about looking for a different placement for you. Somewhere out of this area."

I felt my mouth fall open a little. That was before the anger boiled up. "He can't do that!"

"Legally, he can, Ali," she said shaking her head. I just kept staring at her with disbelief and the urge to punch something. "We get the feeling that you'll fight him once you're eighteen which means it could end up with you on your own. We don't want that."

"I don't want that either," I said quietly.

Mrs. Patton smiled. "The thing is, though, we don't want to make it too easy for you to turn your back on Children's Services. You'll need their support through college." She sighed. "It's just that we want you to know you're not alone. No matter what, you'll always have a home here."

I reached over and hugged her, feeling like I might start crying. If they let me stay here when Mr. Jones wanted me someplace else, they wouldn't get paid anymore. It'd just be up to them to support me. Then something else dawned on me.

"If you go against Mr. Jones, you won't get any other foster children. You're great at it. I can't let you do that."

"Don't worry about that. They have a hard time placing older kids, so they'll eventually give us someone else. The main thing ..." she said looking very serious. "We don't want you moving in with Jake just because you don't have anywhere else to go."

"We really are serious," I said hesitantly. "You should know we're talking about getting married."

"Oh, Ali," she sighed as her face wrinkled into a worried look. "You're too young for that."

"I know I'm young, but we really are in love." I hadn't said that out loud before, but it felt right. Jake and I were in love.

"What about college?"

"I could go to Muskingum University. I could drive there."

"Muskingum can be pretty expensive."

"I wouldn't be paying to live in the dorms. Or I could go to one of the state school branches."

"I had no idea you'd planned that far ahead."

"We're sure," I shrugged.

Her brows dropped a little as something else popped into her head. "I never did make that appointment with the gynecologist." Somehow her sentence sounded like a question.

"Maybe you should," I said quietly, feeling embarrassed. "We're not having sex. Jake knows I've never been with anyone and we want to wait awhile. But it probably won't be long."

"I'm glad you're waiting. I'll call to make an appointment this afternoon."

"Good. You have my work schedule?"

"Yeah." She smiled again. "Ali, this is the best talk we've ever had. I should probably tell you ... I just found out I'm pregnant."

"Really? That's great. Congratulations!"

"We've wanted a baby for a while. I guess we finally got it right."

We both laughed for a minute and started weeding again. It felt like we were suddenly closer than we'd ever been. I realized they had made a home for me. They'd let me grieve for Mom in my own way, but were always right there when I needed them. I thought I'd grown up a lot since moving in with the Pattons, and they'd helped me do that.

"You'll make a great mother," I said as I dug out another weed.

"I hope so," she said, and smiled.

Chapter 28

The next couple of weeks were grueling and passed so slowly I sometimes thought I might just start screaming.

I only saw Jake for minutes at a time when we met during my work breaks. One day I found him parked next to my car at 4:00 when I left work. He said he'd been there all afternoon because he had to hold me for a few more minutes and couldn't make himself care if someone saw us.

We both knew he needed me to calm him, control him, but we hadn't had that for a while. He was hunting more, but seemed edgy, more agitated. I told him I could sneak out in the middle of the night for us to go to the cave, but he didn't think that was a good idea.

Jake was afraid that the Pattons would find out I'd been gone, and they'd have to tell Mr. Jones. As it was, Mr. Jones called the Pattons every day to see if I'd come right home from work and ask if they had any hint that I'd been seeing Jake.

Mrs. Patton told me that he was still looking for another placement for me but was having trouble finding a place because of my age. They had to place younger kids and ones that had nowhere else to go first, which worked wonderfully for me. I prayed every night that he'd never find a place.

All we could safely do was keep going as we were, with Jake hunting more often and both of us waiting for my birthday.

My eighteenth birthday.

I gazed into Jake's warm eyes as we sat in his truck holding each other. "Today's Wednesday," I said quietly. "A week from today, I'll be eighteen, and no one can stop us from being together."

He sighed deeply. "I've been watching the days on the calendar. Mom says Mr. Jones won't be able to find you a place where you'd only stay for a week. If he tries, she's ready to fight him in court."

"Really? She'd do that?"

He nodded. "She said she'd petition the court not to move you until a judge ruled on it. It'll all take forever, so they won't do anything so close to your birthday. It'd be a waste of the judge's time."

"Then we've made it? We could start seeing each other, and Mr. Jones couldn't do anything?" I asked with a desperate joy in my voice.

"Mom says we shouldn't push it," he answered, shaking his head. "She knows it's getting harder for me, but says Mr. Jones could claim you're in danger and he might get an emergency placement. She says we should still wait."

I know I looked disappointed. "Then we'll have to wait," I sighed. "But it's only a week. What could happen in a week?"

We held each other for as long as we dared. I had to get home from work so the Pattons, and especially Mr. Jones, didn't suspect anything. The whole time, I stroked his hair and face as if he was shifted while whispering how much I loved him. It wasn't like a real calming, but his quiet growls let me know it helped him a little.

* * *

Walter Jones sat in his car watching as Ali climbed out of Jake's truck and pulled away in her own car. The first time he saw Ali run out to meet Jake, he'd been ready to jump out of his car and scream at them for defying him, but knew he couldn't do that. The anger rolled through him until he had to leave to avoid causing a scene right there in the parking lot.

Now he dropped his head into his hands and shivered with fear. He was losing Ali like he'd lost Lucy. The two women had become entwined in his brain. By saving Ali, he could lighten some of the guilt he lived with for losing Lucy.

With their parents gone, Walter had been the only help, the only protection, Lucy had. Instead of keeping her safe, he'd let her fall for a loser like Max Shepherd and let her die. He'd never know for sure what had happened that night, but, for all he knew, Max had killed her himself. There was no way he'd make the same mistakes with Ali.

Walter pulled out of Salt Fork heading for the juvenile judge. He needed to get Ali moved tonight if at all possible. The judge hadn't thought there was enough evidence to require an emergency placement for someone Ali's age, but Walter had to change his mind.

He'd tell the judge that Jake had beaten her if he had to. Say that he suspected drug use. Anything. Anything that would get the judge to move Ali as far away as possible and as soon as possible. Lying to the judge could get Walter fired if the truth came out, but, at that moment, Walter didn't care. He couldn't let himself fail Lucy again.

* * *

After dinner that night, I was in my room playing a computer game and actually doing nothing – except thinking about Jake. The Pattons knocked on my door and came in. From the look on their faces I knew they were coming to my room to talk about something they were pretty uncertain about.

"Ali," Mrs. Patton started, "we shouldn't tell you this, but we ... we just have to."

"What's going on?" I said as I sat up straighter on my bed and crossed my legs, leaning towards them. This did not sound good at all.

"Mr. Jones just called. He found a placement for you in Cleveland."

"You're kidding," I practically gasped. "He's really going to try to move me?"

"He *is* going to move you," Mr. Patton said. "I told him you might refuse to go, and he said he's bringing a police officer first thing in the morning."

"The police? Can he do that?"

"I guess so. If they think there might be trouble, the cops work with Children's Services all the time. And he's even called the lodge and told them you have to change placement and have to quit."

"Oh, my God! You mean I don't have a job anymore?"

"We're so sorry, Ali," Mrs. Patton said as she sat on my bed and took my hand. "We don't want you to go. We think he's wrong to do this, especially since you'll be eighteen so soon. We want you to pack enough for a week and come back here once you're eighteen."

"Are you guys really sure you want to do that? You know Mr. Jones will cut off all my support from Children's Services."

"We know, but you need a home. Bad enough you had to change schools in the middle of your junior year, we can't stand the thought of you moving someplace you've never been and don't know anyone at all. That's just wrong."

"That means so much," I smiled with tears in my eyes. It felt so good that they understood and wanted me to stay with them.

"You're not going to like this, but I have to call Jake. You know his mom's a lawyer. She said if Mr. Jones tried something she'd fight it in court for me. I need to talk to her to see if there's anything we can do so I don't have to leave."

"I think that's a great idea," Mrs. Patton said. "So you've been seeing Jake, haven't you?"

"Yeah. He meets me at work during my breaks. It's only fifteen minutes a day, but at least we get to see each other."

"Then you'd better call. We'll let you talk privately, but come downstairs and let us know what his mother thinks."

Nina didn't have good news. "Ali," she sighed sounding cheerless. "I'll file the paperwork as soon as possible in the morning, but I'm afraid Mr. Jones may come get you early, before the court offices open."

"I didn't think of that," I answered. "The Pattons said he'd be here first thing in the morning." Jake and his dad were talking in the background. They weren't yelling, but I could hear the anger and stress in Jake's voice. "Is Jake upset?"

"Beyond upset," she said quietly, almost whispering. "He's determined to come get you, and I don't know if Doug will be able to talk him out of it."

"Then I'll have to come to him. I'll come tonight."

"That's not a good idea," she continued whispering.

"Jake will lose it if I'm in Cleveland with strangers. He'll show up there, and God only knows what he might do."

"Mr. Jones will know you came to us."

"I don't care. I'd rather hide in the woods for a week than have Jake put himself in danger. I can't take the chance of what might happen."

She sighed with resignation. "I'm glad you understand our men so well. They can't tolerate being separated from their mates."

"I'll tell the Pattons that you'll file the papers, but let them think I'll go with him in the morning. I'll sneak out as soon as they're asleep."

"I wish there was another way," she said. Neither of us liked me lying to the Pattons and running away, but we really didn't have another choice.

"Let me talk to Jake," I said. "I'll tell him."

It goes without saying that Jake was so relieved. I'd heard the anger in his voice as he talked to his dad, but, on the phone, I could hear the stress he was trying to deal with. The idea that I would be in Cleveland with strangers was pushing his control to its limits, but he calmed down easily talking to me. Knowing that we'd be together in a few hours helped a lot, too.

Running away wasn't a good idea, but this wasn't about what Jake and I wanted. It was about what he needed. The beast inside him would compel him to go to any lengths to get me back. Didn't matter that we hadn't actually bonded, yet. The Bigfoot knew that I was the one meant to be with him.

By 11:00 that night when I was sure the Pattons would be asleep, I had a bag packed and was ready to go. They'd been so good to me. I couldn't leave without letting them know I was okay, so I left them a note telling them not to worry. I told them I'd call once I was eighteen, but didn't say anything else. I couldn't leave Mr. Jones any hints about where I was or let him know that the Pattons told me his plans. Of course, he wouldn't need any hints. He'd know where I went.

Driving down the practically deserted country roads toward Jake's house, I suddenly started to think. What was I doing?

Leaving what was safe, I was running into the arms of a man who periodically turned into a monster.

Days short of eighteen, I was committing my life to a man that I barely understood.

I was abandoning dreams of my own future to live a long life controlling a man that couldn't control himself.

Running to a man that wasn't even human. Our children wouldn't be human.

I stopped at the side of the road, clasped the top of the steering wheel, and pressed my forehead against my hands. How could I do this?

More than ever, I wanted to talk to my mother. I started crying from the pain of missing her. She always knew how to help me figure things out. Never one to just tell me what to do, she talked me through problems and led me to solve them for myself. I needed her arm around my shoulders and her soft voice in my head.

"Mom," I begged quietly for her to hear me as tears ran down my cheeks.

Everything in this was about Jake. What he wanted, what he needed. What about me? Could I live out in the woods with his family, with his species? I wasn't one of them. I was a terrified human girl who suddenly had no idea what she was doing.

How could I be part of The Family, surrounded by monsters that some people laughed at while others hunted? Could I comfort him, and watch him turn into a beast that needed to hunt and kill?

In my mind, I could see myself sitting close to that creature stroking his head and softly whispering words he barely understood. I felt his muscular body against mine as he lay dying and I tried to help him heal.

Then I saw his eyes. Those eyes that never changed. Those beautiful eyes that held all his love for me. As human and as Bigfoot, they had seized my heart as I had gazed into them and told him I loved him.

Picturing his eyes, I couldn't walk away from him. Not because of his suffering if I left. Not because he'd never find a mate. Because I loved him. Because my life would be less without him in it.

The life I ran to would be hard. I'd have to face things that I'd never considered before. Certainly my mom had never considered them for me. But I loved Jake with all my heart. And he loved me. That's the thing Mom always wanted me to find.

I wiped the tears from my cheeks and pulled back onto the road. I was still frightened, but knew that I was doing the right thing. I was meant to be with Jake. We were meant to bond and make our lives together.

Chapter 29

Jake ran to my car as I stopped next to his truck. I jumped out and threw my arms around him. How could I have doubted that this was the man I was supposed to spend my life with?

"Ali," Jake's dad said as Jake and I held each other. "Give me your keys. I'm going to hide your car at the dealership."

"Oh," I said. I'd never thought about hiding my car. "Good idea. Here."

"I'll be back as soon as possible, but there won't be any problems until morning."

"Yeah," I sighed. "Mr. Jones will probably come right here looking for me, though."

"Come in the house, Ali," Nina said. "I think we all need to calm down and talk through what we have to do."

I hadn't noticed the other man standing to the side until he started walking to Jake's truck. Nina introduced me to Adam. Big and strong like Jake and Doug, he smiled at me and squeezed my shoulder.

"Don't worry, Ali," he said. "We'll take care of you."

"Thanks," I sighed, smiling up at him.

Here was the first member of The Family that I'd met. Soon I'd be meeting many of them, which felt pretty intimidating. Jake had mentioned Adam and his family several times, though, so he seemed like someone I kind of already knew. Still, it felt bizarre knowing every guy associated with Jake was a shifter.

While Doug and Adam took off to hide my car, Jake and I followed Nina into the cabin. Nina wanted to get me something to eat or drink, but I really didn't want anything. My stomach was already churning, so I settled on water.

"I've been so worried about you," Jake finally said. He'd hardly said anything to me before that. I think he was astonished that our situation had moved so fast and that I was actually there with his family.

I smiled up at him as we sat next to each other on the couch. "I'm glad to be here. No more fifteen-minute breaks from work. We're together now."

"Really? You're not going back to the Pattons?"

"I'm not sure about that," I said with a frown. "But if I do, we can see each other whenever we want. We won't have to hide anymore. The Pattons want me to stay with them even if Mr. Jones cuts me off."

"They told you that?" Nina asked.

"They think he's being unreasonable. They think I'll go to Cleveland for a week, then come back to them. They know I'm happy with them and don't think me seeing Jake is that big of a problem. They know we've been seeing each other during my breaks at work."

"I want you to stay here," Jake said quietly, squeezing my hand. He hadn't let go of me since we'd met in the yard. "I want us to bond."

"Jake," Nina said stroking his hair. "You're too emotional right now to decide when you should bond. I think you should go downstairs and wait for Ali to come to you."

"Will you?" he asked staring into my eyes. He looked so intent and needy.

"I'd love to," I nodded.

Jake smiled and walked away towards the basement without another word.

Nina took his place and sat next to me. "He needs you desperately, Ali. I've never seen him so close to being out of control. I should have asked you before I sent him down there."

"No. That's okay."

"He'll want to bond, but you can't let him."

"I don't think I'm ready, but if he really needs it ..."

"No. Bonding is about domination. He has to be the one that is submissive to you. If he pushes you into it, you'll never have the control over his Bigfoot that you need to have. All of our men are the same," she smiled. "We control the Bigfoot so they can control their human sides. If you let his Bigfoot dominate, he'll be a weaker human."

"Part of me wants to bond with him."

"I know. But they're complicated creatures, and the tie between the human and Bigfoot is hard for us to fully grasp. The human Jake needs to know for sure that you're ready and that it's your decision to bond. But you have to prove your control to his Bigfoot side, you can't give in to what he wants. If you do, his Bigfoot will keep struggling for control over both of you."

"Then I'll control him."

"Be strong. Stand up to him and don't back down."

"Huh," I quietly laughed. "I don't know how strong I can be."

"I do. You've been incredibly strong with Jake, Mr. Jones, and the Pattons. Even the way you've faced your mother's death. When Jake first told me about you, he said you were really young, shy and unsure of yourself. You're not that little girl anymore. You are strong, Ali."

I smiled, but wasn't sure how right she was.

As I walked into the quiet basement, the Bigfoot stood in the center of the room staring at me. Jake's eyes seemed to bore right into my soul. Those eyes communicated how much he wanted to bond, and it would have been very easy to give in to him. If Nina hadn't told me what I needed to do, I might have let him bite me right then and there.

"Sit down," I said with authority, almost meanness in my voice. Jake growled. I was surprised how much he obviously wanted his own way – wanted control.

"Sit," I demanded. Jake stared at me for a few seconds. "Jake. Sit."

He growled quietly again and took a step toward me. His eyes squinted slightly as his lips curled back. The threat in his expression was very clear. He was ready to bite me and complete our bond.

"No," I spat out without moving, even though I really wanted to back away. "Bad."

He continued to glare at me, but something in his expression seemed to soften.

"Sit, Jake. Sit now."

Like a small child who doesn't want to do what he's been told, Jake groaned quietly. Finally, he backed up to the couch and sat down, never taking his eyes off mine.

I sat next to him and reached up to stroke his head. He leaned toward me, growling softly and baring his teeth. He wanted me to give in, to let him bond with me.

Speaking quietly and calmly, I said, "No. You have to behave, Jake. I want to help you."

He growled louder with his mouth moving like he was taking a bite of the air between us. When I didn't flinch or move away from him, he dropped his eyes from mine and leaned into my hand that was still brushing through his hair. "Good," I said. "Good, Jake."

That's when I realized how my heart was thumping. I'd been scared of Jake, which I hated. I loved him, I shouldn't be afraid of him. But I'd stood up to him and made him do what I said. I knew, then, that I could be what he needed to survive in the human world. I could be that control and calming influence he needed.

He whined softly like he was giving in, so I held out my arms and said, "Good. Come."

ake leaned into my arms and rested his big head on my shoulder. With my left hand still stroking his hair, I caressed his face with my right and kept talking to him. With a soft voice, I told him about Mr. Jones and how scared I was that we'd be separated. The words were meaningless to him, but the love in my voice seemed to be getting through to him.

He started stroking my arm as I listened to his breathing and heartbeat slow. His whole body relaxed into my arms as he gladly gave me control over him. I whispered several times, "I love you."

When I left Jake to shift and clean up, Nina looked up from the book she was reading with a question in her eyes.

I smiled at her. "It was like he wanted me to take control. He wanted to do what I told him."

"Good," she sighed with relief. "That's the way it should be. I've been thinking about where you should hide. The simplest thing would be to go to Max's cabin."

"I thought Jake and I would go to the cave. If Mr. Jones brings the police, they'll want to search, won't they?"

"Did the Pattons say he was bringing the police into it?"

"Yeah. He knows I won't want to go."

"I had no idea he was so determined," she shook her head, thinking. "We legally don't have to let them search, but that means he'd try to get a warrant and come back. You're right, the cave would be the safest place for you to go."

Jake came upstairs, having obviously heard what we were talking about. "I'll take Ali there right away," he said. His hair was still wet, and I could see his shirt sticking to his chest in places. Must have been the quickest shower ever without him doing more than brushing close to a towel.

"But you need to be here," Nina said. "If Mr. Jones doesn't see you, he'll think you and Ali ran away together."

"I don't want to leave her there alone, Mom. What if someone else needs to use it?"

"You know that won't happen during the daylight. We'll let Adam know she'll be there, though, just in case."

"I guess you're right," he sighed. He just wanted to be with me, but I understood. I wanted to be with him, too.

The three of us sat in the kitchen and waited until Doug and Adam came back from hiding my car. As we talked, I could see the change in Jake. He was calmer, more his old self. When I'd first gotten there, he was tense and obviously not thinking clearly. Now he was logical and calm while discussing how I was going to hide out for a week. He really had needed me, and, I realized, calming him had also calmed me.

"Nina," Doug called as he came in. Adam was right behind him.

Doug leaned down to kiss Nina, and I noticed that her hand went automatically up to the side of his head to stroke him a couple times. He needed Nina like Jake needed me, and it all seemed so right.

"I think we need to get a couple hours sleep before you head for the cave. Jones won't show up here until at least 8:00 or 9:00, so you can stay here until dawn, anyway," Doug said after a while.

"Good idea," Nina sighed.

"Ali, take my room," Jake said. "I'll hit the couch."

"No. I'll take the couch. I probably won't sleep much anyway."

"Ali, I don't want you in the living room if Mr. Jones shows up to surprise us," Nina said. "Take Jake's room."

So I took Jake's room while Jake claimed the couch and Adam went home. It felt strange at first to crawl into Jake's bed. This was where I stretched out next to him when he needed to heal. Where I discovered how much I really did love him.

I snuggled my face into his pillow and could smell Jake's warm, woodsy scent. Soon, I'd be sharing this bed with him, and we'd hold each other all night and for the rest of our lives.

I fell asleep quickly and slept like I was finally where I belonged.

Chapter 30

Mr. Jones arrived at the Pattons a little after 7:00 a.m. to make sure they hadn't already left for work. If Ali caused any problems, he wanted them there so they were assured everything was legal.

"You didn't bring the police?" Mike asked as he opened the door.

"Ali's always been reasonable. I don't see her causing problems today."

"You should know we told her she could come back to us when she's eighteen," Mike said.

"You can't do that!" Jones practically yelled, his anger and frustration showing clearing. "A foster child can't just choose where there're going to live."

"She's planning on walking away from Children's Services," Jane answered him.

Jones's mouth fell open as he stared at her. "She'll have nothing. You know every penny her mother had went to bury her. Ali'll be destitute. And you sure won't get your money for her."

"We know that," Mike said staying calm. "But she'll find another job and can stay here as long as she wants to."

"You're making a big mistake, here. I'll make sure you never get another foster child."

"We realize that. But we think what you're doing is wrong, and it'll just drive her to Jake and his family even faster. She needs a family. We can't turn our backs on her."

They were all shocked when Jane came back from upstairs and announced that Ali wasn't there. The Pattons hadn't even noticed that her car was gone from the end of the driveway.

"You know damn well she went to Jake!" Jones yelled.

"What are you going to do?" Jane asked.

"I'm going out to that damn cabin to get her," he said with anger and determination as he headed for the front door.

"Please don't make things harder for her," Mrs. Patton said. "Tell her she can come back here. Let her stay with us."

"And see Jake whenever she wants?"

Mr. Jones turned and walked out. No one needed to answer his question.

* * *

I woke to someone touching my shoulder and looked up to see Jake smiling down at me. I couldn't help reaching up to his neck and pulling him down to kiss him. I could feel the subtle, enticing growl as his lips played with mine. The quiet moan, I soon realized, came from me.

Jake reluctantly pulled away and sat on the edge of the bed next to me. His hand never left my face, though, as his thumb stroked my cheek.

"I've thought about kissing you as you woke up for a long time," he sighed. "Although, in that fantasy, I didn't stop at a kiss."

That's when I smiled. "I've had similar thoughts," I said quietly, feeling surprisingly embarrassed. Why should I be embarrassed to tell him that I wanted him? He knew it. I'd told him before.

"Don't tempt me," he smiled back. "It's just barely light, but I have to show you something before we head for the cave. I'll wait for you in the kitchen."

We went together back onto the porch which stretched across the whole front and was about ten feet deep. "I'm gonna' make a porch swing. I just haven't had time."

I squeezed my lips together to keep the sudden tears from sliding down my face. "Mom and I had a porch swing," I whispered.

"I'll get it done right away," he smiled sadly. Opening the front door, he simply said, "Here we are," and stepped aside to let me go in first.

I didn't see a cabin. I saw a home. My home.

To the left was a living room with a huge stone fireplace that went all the way up to the vaulted ceiling. A soft, beige couch and two green and beige, patterned chairs were arranged so the fire would be the center of attention.

On the right, an open kitchen with dark cabinets and stone counters connected to the living room with a big, round dining table. Toward the back, a set of stairs led up to a loft, which covered part of the kitchen, and a hallway that opened toward the back of the cabin.

"Jake, I don't think I can move. You'll have to help me."

He laughed out loud. "Come on, then," he said as he put his hands on my shoulders and started leading me toward the hallway.

We found a half bath first. Nothing exciting, but it was pretty in its simple, earth tone colors. Then we came to another room that was completely empty. It had a doorway that Jake said would eventually be a bathroom.

"This'll be for our first child," Jake said quietly. "But there's plenty of time until he's ready to sleep alone down here. The nursery's upstairs. With us."

I was numb. I knew Jake was building me a cabin, even though I hadn't thought about it, but I suddenly realized he was building much more than that. He was building our future. He was building a place where we would live for many years to come. A place where we would raise a family.

I turned to him and wrapped my arms around his waist, burying my face in his chest. The tears were streaming down. I'd never felt so touched, so unbelievably happy in my life.

"You okay?" he asked as he stroked my back. "I didn't mean to upset you."

"I'm not upset," I mumbled against his shirt. I looked up at him because he needed to hear what I said next. "I'm amazed. Overwhelmed. Ecstatic. You've thought of everything."

"You haven't seen upstairs, yet," he said as his hands slid up to my face and he kissed me.

"Wait," I gasped, breaking away from his kiss. "I can't breathe."

He laughed. "Can you make it up the steps?"

"I think so."

The steps led to the loft which had a simple desk and a loveseat. Jake kept telling me that he didn't want to furnish it too much because he wanted me to decide what other stuff I wanted. He kept talking about pictures, decorations and other furniture that we'd get, but I kept telling him that everything was wonderful.

Then we went down a short hallway into our bedroom. In the center of the room was a beautiful, king-size bed with a dark wooden headboard that stood out against the log walls. Along the far wall, French doors, flanked by big windows, led to a deck with a beautiful view of the forested hills and Salt Fork Lake in the distance. Otherwise the room was empty. No linens on the bed, no rugs, no curtains.

"I didn't know what you might want. There's room for other furniture, and we can do whatever colors you like," Jake mumbled, obviously hoping I'd like my first look at the room where we'd spend our lives loving each other.

I laughed quietly, which gave him a horribly worried expression. That was funny, too.

I hugged him, still giggling quietly. "It's just funny that the only thing you could make a decision about was the bed. It's such a man thing." I looked up into his eyes. "I love that."

He kissed me. A deep, passionate, loving kiss. "You're right. I can't wait until I can love you like I want to," he said as he buried his face in my neck. "Until I can hold you, and make love to you all night. In that bed. It's almost all I can think about."

Jake and I stood there in our future bedroom holding each other for several minutes. Feeling our bodies against each other, stroking each other's backs, wanting to bond and start our lives together. I couldn't stand the waiting much longer, but I couldn't tell him that. I knew he felt the same, and didn't want to put more pressure on him.

"We have to get back," he sighed. "I'll show you the rest next time."

"There's more?"

"Nursery, bathroom up here. And the basement. That's where we'll bond, and it'll be all ours until our son needs you to control him."

"All ours? Our son?"

"Part of the whole territorial thing," he grinned. "My Bigfoot won't share the space I share with my woman ... except with my son."

"I think he'll need to wait until I finish high school," I smiled cautiously. My expression was asking him to please agree with me. I didn't want to spend my senior year pregnant.

"Oh, yeah," he grinned. "Better if he waits 'till you finish college. This is all someday stuff. We'll be together so we don't have to be in any hurry. His room's not even got any furniture."

I punched him lightly in the arm. "Let's go," I said as I turned to walk back downstairs.

Doug and Nina had made a great breakfast of eggs, bacon, toast, and even hash browns. I was strangely uncomfortable sitting there eating with them, but, at first, had trouble understanding why. These were wonderful, loving people that wanted me in their lives. Then I got it.

This was a family. I'd never really had a family. Sure, Mom was the best, but it was different when it was just the two of us. This was a whole family that loved each other and wanted me to be part of them. I felt the huge smile inside me, but kept chewing so it wouldn't show. I didn't know if I could really explain it.

Jake walked me through the woods to the cave. It was farther than I thought, but safer that way. If anyone ever discovered them shifting in the cave, they'd never make the connection with the rest of The Family at the cabins.

It was dark inside until he lit the oil lamps, which gave me the chance to really look around. The only time I'd been there was on the night Jake's Bigfoot had grabbed me, and I wasn't interested in what the cave looked like that night.

It was bigger than I remembered. Along the back wall there were shelves with supplies: extra lanterns, buckets, towels, even extra clothes. A long bench spread out along the left wall, but otherwise it was empty.

"Sorry it isn't more comfortable," Jake said.

"It's fine," I smiled. "My tablet's in my backpack. I'll play a game if I get bored."

"I just hope Jones shows up soon so I can come get you. You have your phone, right?"

"In my pocket," I said, patting my hip.

"There's a close cell tower, so our phones usually work in here, but you shouldn't need it, anyway. Just stay inside," he said before kissing me goodbye.

I hated to see Jake leave. I didn't feel scared or lonely, I just wanted to spend time with him, not hiding in a stupid cave so Mr. Jones wouldn't find me. I wished he'd leave me alone, accept that I could make my own decisions, and go back to the nice, understanding man I'd always thought he was.

Chapter 31

About ten minutes after Jake took off jogging through the woods toward the cabins, I heard footsteps outside. That couldn't be Jake returning already, but maybe Adam was coming to check on me. I got off the bench and took a couple of steps to greet whoever it was, but the last person I ever expected was Mr. Jones.

"How did you find me?" I gasped.

"You two were paying so much attention to each other, it was easy to follow you from the cabin."

"I'm not going with you!" I yelled. This was ridiculous. What gave him the right to do this to me?

"You don't have a choice, Ali," he said trying to stay calm, but I could see the anger rising on his face. "We're going to walk back to my car, and all this foolishness will be over."

"I can't go," I said with as much emphasis as I could muster. "Jake will lose it if I disappear. Why are you doing this? How can you be so mean and hateful to me?"

"I've told you. The Shepherd's are dangerous. You're not safe with them, and Jake is no different than his uncle. I can't leave you in their hands. Listen, I'll call Jake. Tell him you're going with me," Mr. Jones said pulling out his phone and starting to dial.

"Don't! That won't help. Let me call." Maybe I could convince him everything would be okay. Mr. Jones just looked at me and finished dialing.

Jake must have answered on the first ring, because Mr. Jones was talking, trying to explain. I was in a state of numbed shock. I had no idea what Jake might do.

"It's done!" Mr. Jones was yelling into the phone. "There's nothing you can do about it." Then he hung up and looked at me like he'd just proven his point.

"He threatened me!" Mr. Jones spat out with his anger and determination on his face. "They're dangerous and I won't leave you with people like them. You're coming with me."

"Please," I begged, dropping my face into my hands. "Don't do this to me." I had to call Jake. I had to make sure he heard my voice and let it help him control himself.

I pulled my phone from my pocket, but Mr. Jones grabbed my upper arm, stopping me from dialing.

"No!" I shouted, pulling away from him. "I won't leave without talking to Jake. I can't!"

"You can't call him," Mr. Jones said as he clasped my wrist harder and took the phone out of my hand. "I won't let them influence you anymore. Don't you see what they've done to you? How they've brainwashed you?" It was like he'd gone insane. I'd never seen him so angry, so unreasonably determined.

"Then you'll have to carry me," I spat out as I sat on the old bench and clasped my hands onto the seat.

"You think I won't?" he shouted back.

He actually tried to pry my hands off the bench as I struggled to hang on. This whole thing was so unbelievable. He was going to fight me to get me to leave. He obviously didn't know how stubborn I could be because I was determined to fight him back.

"Stop it!" I shouted. "Let me call Jake!"

That's when I heard footsteps racing toward the cave. How could Jake have gotten back here so fast? I had no doubt at all that it was him, but he must have started running as soon as he heard Mr. Jones start talking to him. He sounded close enough that he might have heard me yelling.

Jake flew into the cave breathing like he'd run a marathon. But his face. He had an expression I'd never seen. His mouth twisted into a snarl and his eyes glared at Mr. Jones like he wanted nothing more than to kill him. I imagined it was the same look his Bigfoot had given that loner that night.

"You stay away from her," Mr. Jones said, pointing a finger toward Jake. "I'm taking her where she'll be safe.

"Jake," I said standing up to go to him.

"Stay back, Ali," Mr. Jones said putting his arm out to keep himself between Jake and me.

That was the worst thing he could have done. I saw the sweat beading on Jake's forehead and starting to run down his neck. He hadn't said a word and stood there glaring at Mr. Jones. Then a subtle, whining growl escaped from his lips as his muscles started to clench with pain.

I knew when I saw his shirt dampen with the clear fluid, that it wasn't sweat. Jake was about to shift. Right here, in front of Mr. Jones, he was out of control and shifting. He was so driven to protect me that his Bigfoot had taken over.

I had to do something to stop it. I tried talking to Jake, tried to get to him, but Mr. Jones held me back, which just made everything worse. Thankfully, he wasn't watching Jake, but turned toward me, trying to stop me from going to Jake. Jake's Bigfoot could only see some man trying to take his mate away. I couldn't let Mr. Jones see what Jake really was.

"Let me go to him!" I screamed.

"He's insane. Stay away from him." With that Mr. Jones pushed me back toward the bench.

Mr. Jones was trying to protect me from what he saw as a dangerous, crazy man. What he was really doing was setting himself up to be killed. Jake was starting to shift and his Bigfoot wouldn't hesitate to kill Mr. Jones to protect me.

I had to come up with something to stop this, but had no time to think. All I could do was grab one of the heavy metal buckets the shifters used to wash and swing it with all my might. I hit Mr. Jones right on the back of his head, and he fell to the dirt floor, out cold.

That didn't stop Jake. He was too far into the process to just suddenly stop, so I watched him shift.

It was a magic I could never hope to understand. Some mysterious conjuring of one creature becoming another. I couldn't help but wonder if it was so different from an ugly caterpillar becoming a lovely butterfly. But this didn't happen once in a lifetime. This happened over and over, whenever the creature needed to hunt or needed to protect.

Jake's Bigfoot stood there with his still-damp fur and shreds of his clothes still clinging to him. There was rage and hate in his eyes, but his intended prey was out cold on the floor. His frustration screamed into the cave so loud that it hurt my ears and echoed on and on against the stone walls. He wanted to chase and destroy the man who was threatening his mate.

"Jake," I said, trying to sound as calming and confident as I could. He stared down at Mr. Jones and growled, baring his huge teeth, and ripping the shreds of clothing from his body.

I took a few steps toward him. "Jake! Look at me. It's Ali."

Breathing deeply like he didn't know what to do with his rage, Jake finally looked at me. He growled in my face like he had found another creature he could focus his rage on.

"No. Bad," I said. He continued to glare at me, but I had to get control of him, even though this wasn't the usual situation when he wanted to be calmed and controlled by me.

I reached up to stroke the side of his face, but he pulled away from me. "Stop!" I said as sternly as I could. "Bad!" His gaze softened slightly, and my heart calmed as I saw him responding to my words.

Then I heard the moaning behind me.

Jake's whole concentration zoomed back to Mr. Jones who was obviously waking up from his stupor. I wanted to hit him again, but didn't dare move away from Jake. He'd attack immediately if he didn't have to move through me to get to Mr. Jones.

With my hands on each side of Jake's face, I tried to move his head back to look at me, but he was just too strong. It was like trying to scoot a tree over a couple of inches. Moving my head into his line of sight, I stared at him with my own anger showing. I couldn't find the loving, calming expression that he usually responded to, but anger was better than fear. If he thought I was scared of Mr. Jones, nothing would stop him from attacking.

I heard a shuffling sound, and Jake's head moved to look around me. I moved to capture his gaze again. I didn't dare look away from him, but the scraping against the dirt floor made me picture Mr. Jones trying to crawl backward away from this monster in front of him. That was the smartest move he could make.

Jake leaned forward trying to get around me, with a threatening growl vibrating through him. I shoved back. I plastered my whole body against his and stroked his face as gently as I could. He needed to hear me, respond to me, give in to my control.

"He didn't hurt me," I said quietly. "No danger. Outside. Come outside with me. Outside!"

Finally, Jake was looking at me. Did he have any idea what I said or was he just responding to my tone of voice and my stroking hands?

"Mr. Jones," I said with as much composure as I could, letting Jake think I was still talking to him, "Don't move. Don't say a word. He won't hurt me. He'll follow me if you keep from drawing his attention."

I moved one hand from his face to his head while still pressing against him. "Come. Outside." I tried to put the love I felt for him in my eyes and leaned harder, trying to start him moving backward. He didn't budge.

"Move," I said. "Walk," and I pushed against him again. "Outside."

He took one step back, causing me to sigh with relief. He seemed to like the sigh and whined quietly back to me. "Yes. Good," I said with a smile. "Outside."

Jake let me urge him backward toward the mouth of the cave. We moved together while I still stroked him and continued to tell him he was good.

Once we got through the brush at the mouth of the cave, I kept moving him into the trees. I had to hide him, continue to control him until he could shift back. Of course, once human again, he'd be covered with that goop and naked. But the biggest thing on my mind once he was following my commands was what I could say to Mr. Jones. How could I explain this?

We were in the woods, but still only about fifteen steps from the cave when Jake's gaze left mine. He sniffed the air and growled quietly. Somehow it seemed like a contented growl, not a threat at all.

Doug and Nina walked quickly toward us and stopped in shock when they saw what was going on.

I talked as fast as I could while still keeping my voice calm for Jake and not moving an inch away from him. My adrenaline was flowing, I was scared to death of how all this was going to end, and so relieved to see Jake's parents. But I couldn't let Jake hear any hint of all that in my voice.

"Mr. Jones is in the cave. He tried to take me, and Jake shifted. I knocked Mr. Jones out so he wouldn't see it, but he came to while I was trying to calm Jake. He saw Bigfoot."

"Oh, God," Doug groaned. "You have control?" he asked me.

"Yes."

"I'll go to Jones. Take Jake to the stream off to your left, and get him to shift."

Nina walked toward us as Doug went into the cave. She smiled at Jake. "Good boy," she said, stroking his shoulder. "So good."

Together, we led him to the stream and it didn't take long for him to start shifting back to the human Jake. While he washed in the stream, Nina reached out to hug me.

"You saved us," she said with a sob in her voice. "It's so hard to control them if they're ready to attack, but you did it. You're so strong, Ali. I'm so proud of you." She kissed my forehead. "And so happy that Jake will be with a woman that has such good control over him."

Jake walked back toward us holding a leafy branch in front of his crotch. He looked so silly, I had to laugh at him. "I've never been so humiliated in my life, and you laugh," he sighed.

"Only because I love you so much," I said as I leaned in to kiss his cheek.

"We left the truck in the clearing," Nina said smiling broadly. "The keys are in it. Grab some clothes from the tool chest and come right back."

"Where's Dad? What about Mr. Jones? Ali, I didn't hurt him, did I?" Jake was practically stammering trying to find out what had happened while he was shifted. "Did I hurt you?" He looked so apprehensive, scared to death about what he might have done.

"No. You didn't hurt anyone. You listened to me," I said quickly so he could calm down. More slowly, I sighed, "You wanted to protect me, but you let me calm you."

"Thank, God. Thank you, Ali." Our eyes were locked on each other, and I think we could have stood there forever.

"Get going," Nina interrupted. "I don't know what your Dad is telling Mr. Jones, but we need to get a handle on all this."

Jake glanced at each of us before turning to run toward the truck. I had to bite my lip to control the smile I felt coming on as I watched his pale butt disappear into the trees.

As we walked, Nina told me that Jake had called them as he ran to me. She knew from his voice that he was frantic, so they came as quickly as possible, driving the truck through the underbrush. I told her the whole story of what had happened with Mr. Jones.

When we got back into the cave, Doug and Mr. Jones were sitting on the bench. Mr. Jones was leaning forward with his right arm resting on his knee and his left arm holding a cloth against his head.

"He hit his head pretty hard when he fell," Doug told us with a wink. "He's got a good lump, but he should be fine."

Mr. Jones looked up and got such an expression of relief on his face when he saw me. "Ali," he said coming over to hug me. "I thought that monster was going to kill you. What did you do with him?"

"I just led him away from you," I stammered, not sure what to say.

"I told you," Doug added. "She, Nina and Jake headed him back to his home territory. Jake will come back as soon as he's sure the Bigfoot won't turn back here."

"It really was a Bigfoot?" Mr. Jones asked as he turned back to Doug. "They're real?" He looked at each one of us like he couldn't believe what he was hearing.

"I told you, they're real. But no one can know that. Look, we have to tell you the truth, but you have to swear to keep it to yourself. You can't tell anyone."

The truth? My mind was spinning. Surely Doug couldn't consider telling Mr. Jones the truth. He'd be more determined than ever to get me away from Jake if he knew he shifted into Bigfoot. But I trusted Doug would give Mr. Jones, not the exact truth, but a story that would sound like the truth, yet protect us.

"Not tell anyone?" Mr. Jones said quietly. "I think that thing was going to kill me."

"They have to stay a myth. If everyone knew they were real, they'd be scared to death and hunt them down. But they don't hurt anyone. They don't come after people. He was protecting Ali because he thought you were hurting her."

"How did you stop him?" Mr. Jones asked glancing to me, but Doug answered.

"We're out here to protect them. They know us and understand enough to do what we say. You're just lucky that one knew Ali. She's been working with him, but hasn't met all the others, yet."

"You're training Bigfoot?" Mr. Jones was obviously shocked, gazing at me with fear in his eyes.

"Not training them," I said. "They're not dancing bears."

"They're intelligent enough to know we protect them," Doug thankfully interrupted, because I didn't know what the standard story was. "We lead humans away and keep them in their territory. They've learned a few commands like dogs do, but they'll never be trained or domesticated."

"Why?" Mr. Jones asked. He looked like he couldn't figure any logical reason to do what Doug was talking about.

"We can't tell you everything, but it's vital that they're protected. They're more closely related to us than even chimpanzees, and look what people have done with chimps and other apes. Bigfoot has hidden throughout the world, but can't do that anymore with stuff like the internet. They need our help to survive."

"What's all this got to do with Ali?" he asked.

"I love Jake," I said with determination. "Once I'm eighteen, we're getting married." Mr. Jones's mouth fell open when I said that. "We'll live at our cabin. I'll finish my senior year and go to college from there."

"But, Ali ..." he tried to say.

"No one can say anything to change my mind. Jake and I are meant to be together. I know that's not what you wanted to hear, but I can't hide our plans from you anymore. I love him. And I love what they're doing with Bigfoot. Nothing could make me happier than to live the rest of my life helping them control Bigfoot and keeping them safe."

That's when Jake walked back in. He put his arm around me and kissed my temple. He'd heard every word I'd said.

"We're in love," he shrugged at Mr. Jones.

Mr. Jones stared at me with disbelief for several seconds, before saying, "How can I let you marry him? My job is to protect you."

Nina answered him quietly. "You don't have any other choice, Mr. Jones. If you try to stop Ali from marrying Jake, we'll have to fight you in court. How will it sound when they know you stalked her, tried to kidnap her, and you believe a ridiculous story about us and Bigfoot? We don't want to, but we'd be forced into ruining you. We'd much rather see you wish Ali happiness and keep everything that's happened to yourself."

"You're threatening me?"

"Take it as a threat if you have to. But it *is* what will happen."

"You say you're so sure," Mr. Jones said looking back at me. "That's exactly what Lucy said to me. Have they told you about

After I cleaned up and got dressed, I went out to find Jake sitting there with his mom and dad, talking quietly.

"We'll have breakfast ready by the time you and Jake get back," Nina said as she sipped her coffee.

"You don't have to do that. I'll help," I said.

Nina smiled. "Doug will do most of it." Doug smiled back at her.

"Come on," Jake said grabbing my hand.

I had no idea where we were going, but followed him outside without any hesitation. The rising sun cut through the trees in sharp rays and the evaporating dew smelled fresh and clean. With Jake's arm around my shoulders, and mine around his waist, I felt like we were all alone in the universe. How could I not love being alone with him like that?

I was looking up at his face when he stopped and nodded forward between the trees. I looked where he indicated. A cabin.

Somehow, through everything else that had happened, I'd forgotten about the cabin that he was building for us. The last time I'd seen it, there was just a partially finished foundation. Now, it was a real, finished cabin.

My mouth fell open as I let go of him and walked forward to climb three steps onto the porch. I turned around to look back at him and saw that he hadn't moved an inch. He looked up at me with a question and a little nervousness in his expression.

"It's wonderful," I gasped, answering that unasked question.

"You like it? I can change anything you don't like."

I laughed and ran back to him, throwing my arms around his neck. "How could I not like it? It's perfect."

He held me with my feet swinging off the ground. "You haven't even really seen it yet. Let's go inside."

Chapter 32

Mr. Jones wasn't easy to convince, but Doug and Nina kept talking, answering his questions, and trying to reassure him. Jake and I stood there listening with our arms around each other.

"Who do you work for?" Mr. Jones was asking Doug.

"I can't reveal that," Doug answered, but Mr. Jones wouldn't let it go.

"Is it the government?" he asked. "Does the government know about Bigfoot?"

I lost all my patience with him. None of that was important right now. I needed to know about me. "Mr. Jones," I interrupted. "I think they've told you everything they can. What are you going to do?"

"You mean what am I going to do about you? I don't know."

"Please let me stay with the Pattons until I'm eighteen. I don't want to fight with you anymore, so please don't make me."

"And you want me to let you marry Jake next week when you're not even out of high school? What if you stop going to school or end up pregnant and decide not to go to college?"

"That won't happen," I shook my head.

"Ali's education is too important," Jake added. "We won't have children until after she finishes college."

Mr. Jones laughed. "What about your education? Isn't that important?"

"It's different for me," Jake answered without embarrassment. I was happy to see that. "I work with my hands. I'm starting with Dad's car dealership and I'll take it over when he retires. College isn't the only way to make a good living."

"If you marry him, you'll be out of the system, Ali," he said, looking back at me.

"I know. But I don't need Children's Services anymore. I was glad I got you as a social worker instead of some of the others because you let me be myself. But there're a lot of other kids who need you more than me, now. Isn't the whole point to help me grow up into an adult who can make my own way? I found my way, Mr. Jones. It's with Jake and his Family."

I said the word family with a capital F in my head because that's the way I meant it. I was ready to be a part of The Family and wanted Jake and his parents to hear that. Jake squeezed my shoulder, Doug smiled, and Nina closed her eyes for a second before looking at me with her own small smile.

Mr. Jones sighed. "I can only fight you so long," he said, shaking his head. "I give up. I'll call the Pattons and let them know you're coming back. And, no, I won't mention any of this Bigfoot insanity. Who'd believe me, anyway? But I don't like it, Ali. You're just too young. Please don't rush into marriage like this. Take your time. At least finish high school."

"I'll finish high school and college, but I'll be married to Jake. I know you don't want to hear that, but I can't change how I feel. How we feel."

"The Pattons won't be happy," he added. "And they'll miss you. They've wanted a child for years and have really liked having you there."

"I'll miss them, too, but they don't need me anymore," I smiled. "Jane's pregnant. They'll be very busy soon. Maybe they'll let me babysit once in a while."

"You always did have an argument for all my ideas," he said and actually gave me a grin. Maybe he was starting to realize that I knew what I was doing. Maybe he was just tired of my stubbornness.

* * *

The next week was a whirl.

Jake naturally wanted to bond right away, but Doug and Nina said we had to get married first. Jake wouldn't be able to let me live away from him with the Pattons once we were bonded, and Mr. Jones still wouldn't give his consent for me to marry or move in with Jake until I was eighteen and could do it legally, without his permission. So we waited.

The Pattons gave me a birthday party on Wednesday and invited Jake, Doug and Nina, and Mr. Jones. I think Mr. Jones only came to keep an eye on the Shepherds. He still would have been happier if I wasn't speaking to them. It was really sweet of the Pattons, though, and we had a good time grilling in the back yard.

The Pattons gave me $500 dollars which really floored me. They wanted me to use it for extra stuff I'd need for college. Doug and Nina gave me a really cute outfit, but Nina whispered that there was something else at the cabin for me. She wouldn't tell me what it was. Mr. Jones really surprised me with a $50 dollar bill.

Then Jake walked over to me with a little box and knelt in front of me. "I love you and want us to be bonded together for the rest of our lives. Will you marry me, Ali?"

Then he opened the box so I could see inside. It was the most gorgeous large diamond I'd ever seen. All the time we'd spent talking about bonding and marriage, I'd never thought about an engagement ring. I said yes, hugged him, and felt the tears run down my face onto his shoulder.

On Thursday, Jake and I went to get our marriage license. Once that was done, we were ready.

Friday was a day for Jake and me to get a million things done – separately. Mrs. Patton and I had bought me a new dress for the wedding, a wedding present from them, and I spent some time ironing it and putting it carefully in a zippered dress bag she loaned me.

It wasn't a traditional wedding dress. It was a strapless, form-fitting, pale teal dress that I loved. Mrs. Patton got tears in her eyes when I came out of the dressing room with it on. I laughed, and she started laughing, too.

"What was that about?" I said through the giggles.

"You just look so grown up," she sighed. "I thought my foster daughter was a little girl."

That almost made me cry.

The rest of the day I packed and felt a little sad that I wouldn't be back to that house even though I promised to visit often. The Pattons had given me a home when I desperately needed one, and there was no way I could ever thank them enough. Once I thought about moving in with Jake, though, I found a deep-down joy.

Saturday was our wedding day.

People always say that little girls dream of their future weddings, planning the dress, the place, the honeymoon, and how many hundreds of people will be invited. I never did any of that. Maybe because my mom wasn't married, so never had any stories of her own wedding to tell me.

My wedding, though, was everything I could have wanted, because Jake was waiting for me at his parents' cabin.

Nina asked a judge, who had been a friend for several years, to officiate. The Pattons followed my car out to the isolated cabin, and I got dressed in Nina and Doug's room so Jake wouldn't see me until

I came down the stairs. I left my hair very natural and down around my shoulders because that's the way he liked it.

The look on his face as I walked towards him was priceless. Scared, adoring, dreamy, and numb, all at the same time. My face probably said the same.

We hadn't gone with anything fancy like writing our own vows. Just the basic, but legal, vows that we repeated after the judge. It all went so fast that I had to concentrate because I was afraid I wouldn't remember my wedding if I didn't.

My emotions were all over the place. Finally being with Jake who I loved with all my heart, committing for a lifetime, joining a Family that I knew so little about. All of it combined in a jumble of joy and a little apprehension, but I imagined that's what every woman felt on her wedding day, even if it was a normal, human wedding, which mine wasn't.

Jake's parents, now my in-laws, cooked steaks for us on the grill outside while lobsters boiled in the kitchen. I'd never had lobster before, but holy cow, was it good. We all talked for several hours before the Pattons said they needed to get home. I sent them off with heartfelt hugs, words about how I could never thank them enough, and kisses on each of their cheeks.

Jake and I both kissed Nina and Doug goodnight and walked down the path toward our own cabin.

"So ..." I started saying, nervous as I'm sure I sounded. "What do I need to know about bonding?"

I was still a virgin, but hadn't wanted to be for awhile, and wasn't nervous about what would happen in bed that night. I knew it would hurt at first, but that was okay. I longed to have sex with Jake, my husband.

Bonding had to come first, though.

That scared me.

"You look afraid," Jake said gently as we stood in our own living room.

"Your mom told me what I need to do, but I'm not sure I really know what to expect."

"Then I'll explain on the way to the basement," he answered with a gentle smile.

"Basement? Not the bedroom?"

"The bedroom's for us, but bonding is for my Bigfoot. His space is the basement."

"Oh." What else could I say?

Like Jake had told me, it started like any calming. He stepped into the bathroom to shift while I waited on the couch. When he walked out as Bigfoot, my stomach clenched with fear. I wasn't afraid of him when he came to me for control and calmness. This was different, though.

I held out my arms and welcomed him on the couch as if it was a usual calming session. I stroked him like always, but knew the time had come for something more. If I didn't tell him to bite me and bond, he wouldn't do it. I was the one in control.

I pulled away from him and stood up. He growled softly in com-plaint.

"Come, Jake," I said as I took his big hairy hands into mine. "Come."

My heart was pounding a mile a minute as he took my hands and stood in front of me. He looked confused and a little angry as he continued to growl and whine softly. He wanted me to stay on the couch and calm him.

I turned around to back up against him and swept my hair off my neck. "Bite, Jake. Bond with me," I said quietly, still nervous as hell.

A low growl started deep within him. I felt the vibration as it grew in intensity and volume. Not the screaming, mournful growl I'd heard before in the forest, but a deep, powerful, rumbling growl of desire. I knew it wasn't sexual desire because Bigfoot had no sexual desire. It was the desire to bond, to claim me as his.

Jake put his arms around me like he did that night in the forest. One crossed my chest, one crossed my hips, locking my arms to my body. He stood up to his full height, lifting my feet off the ground while he sniffed my neck and hair.

His lips moved across the top of my back and shoulders. Not kissing, although I guess it could have been considered Bigfoot kisses, but touching me with his lips as he sniffed and whined softly.

"Bond, Jake," I whispered. "Bond with me."

His head pulled back and I heard, and felt, that deep growl again. I couldn't see him, but knew his face was pointed upward as if he was calling into the night sky.

I felt his lips on my neck as he sniffed and whined. His mouth stretched open. Once again, the entire width of my neck was en-closed between his lips and teeth.

Then he bit me.

It hurt.

Nina had warned me that it would hurt, but the intensity still surprised me. After all, this huge monster was biting into my neck. Of course it hurt.

Holding that position for only a couple seconds, Jake soon pulled his teeth out of my flesh and started to lick me. With a wound on each side of my spinal column, his face moved back and forth as he licked those wounds like he was cleaning them.

I knew that what he was doing, what his instinct told him to do, was push his saliva into my wounds. That's what would bond us. His saliva would keep me alive for a century or more. As long as he lived. And it would bond us physically so neither of us would outlive the other by more than a few hours.

It was something in his saliva that changed me, and I could feel the subtle vibration of energy flow through both of us. Like a vampire's saliva made a victim turn into another vampire, I guessed. Maybe this is how the vampire legends started. All I knew was that it felt good. It felt right.

When he was finished, he continued sniffing me. His growls grew weaker, quieter, until the only sound I could hear was his breathing. Still, he never let go of me as he lowered me so I was standing in front of him again.

I felt the fluid excreted by his skin against my back and around my body where his arms held me. I felt the shudder through his muscles as I watched the hair disappear from his arms and he started to shrink down to his still large human size.

"Ali," he gasped. "I'm yours. Yours forever."

"And I'm yours," I said as I turned in his arms to hug a very slimy, very naked Jake. My husband.

"Go shower and I'll be up in a few minutes," he said with a catch in his voice.

"I could stay here and shower with you." My voice sounded almost shy, but I meant it.

A half-laugh burst out of him. "Don't tempt me," he said shaking his head. "I need time to get my human brain back in charge. I'm still a little Bigfoot fuzzy."

"No," I said stroking his muscular chest. "The fuzz is all gone, now."

Jake laughed and scooted me toward the stairs. As I reached my foot to the first step, he pulled me back to him and kissed me. "I love you," he said.

"Me, too," I smiled.

I showered quickly, only half drying my hair, and slipped into my new, soft cream, silky, short nightgown. My new dress was a slimy mess, and I wondered how I would ever explain to the dry cleaner the stuff that was all over it. I'd ask Nina. Then I sat in one of the new chairs that filled the corner of our room, and talked to Mom inside my head.

I told her all about the wedding and bonding with Jake. I told her how happy I was waiting for him to come upstairs. I asked her to watch over us and make me the best wife I could be for such a wonderful man. And I told her I still missed her and always would.

"Hey," Jake said quietly as he came in and walked over to me, taking my hands to pull me into his arms.

"You finished the bedroom," I said after he kissed me senseless.

"Mom and Dad did it. It's your combination birthday and wedding present."

"Nina said there was something else at the cabin, but I had no idea she meant something like this."

"She said it was more important for you to have a nice bedroom rather than have to face furnishing it right away."

"Well, it's beautiful. I never could have made it this nice." I said it was beautiful and meant it, but the truth was that I'd barely looked at it. My mind was too full of thoughts of Jake.

"I'm glad you like it," he smiled.

"I only have one problem," I teased and watched his face drop a little. "You got dressed."

"I didn't want to seem too anxious," he grinned. "But I sure like what you're wearing."

"It's been a long day." I smiled. "Maybe we should get some sleep."

"Not until I make love to you, and show you how much I've wanted you since the first time we met."

I dropped my head to his chest, suddenly embarrassed. Why was I embarrassed? I'd told him how much I wanted him just like he'd told me. I shoved that little bit of shyness aside, and reached up to unbutton his shirt. I couldn't wait to get my hands on those muscles.

Jake made love to me in a way I never could have imagined. He was gentle, slow, and seemed to be concerned only with me. It was a declaration of our love, our need to be together. The experience I'd longed for was everything I hoped it would be. I soon lost count of how many time we both said, "I love you".

We'd be saying it for the rest of our lives.

Chapter 33

School started in another two weeks, and that time was flying by. The first week, Jake and I were alone most days while Doug and Nina worked, and we felt like we were on a honeymoon.

We spent out days walking through the woods, staring at the hills off our balcony, cooking meals together, and making love over and over again. It was glorious, but even the best of times have to eventually end.

Doug thought Jake needed to start working at the dealership, so a week after our wedding, I was left at the cabins alone all day.

Not one to just sit around after straightening and cleaning, I went shopping, visited the Pattons, and cooked dinner for Jake every day. Then I started to feel guilty.

Mr. Jones had taken care of my job at the state park when he called to tell them I had to move away, but that job was only for the summer anyway. I needed to look for something part time that I could do while going to school. I sighed to myself realizing that these slow, peaceful days would soon be ending.

"Why do you need a job?" Jake asked when I told him I was going to make the rounds to shops and fast food restaurants the next day.

"I've got to pay for college somehow," I answered, surprised he hadn't thought of it. "I'll need to keep working then, too."

"You're worried about money?" he smiled.

"Aren't you?" It really surprised me that Jake wasn't worried. We couldn't live on his parent's incomes forever. That wasn't fair.

"But we have plenty of money."

"Your parents have plenty of money, but we don't. Your salary won't pay for college."

"Shit, I never told you." He was smiling even more.

"Told me what?"

"Come here, sweetheart, let me tell you a story," Jake said as he held out his arms for me. I couldn't resist, so I jumped on his lap and stretched my arms around his neck, snuggling against him. He didn't start his story until after we'd kissed.

"We got this land in a government land grant right after we came here from Europe a couple hundred years ago," he said looking right into my eyes. "Years later, we sold a big hunk of it back for the park. We didn't need that much land and with it preserved as a park, we'd still be able to use it. Besides that, we've never really spent a lot of money because we don't buy houses and we don't go on vacations. We've ended up with a boatload in the bank and in investments. That's how Dad bought the dealership. I've had my own investment account since I was born." Then he started smiling again. "We don't need money."

"Are you kidding?"

"How do you think I bought that ring?" he asked as the smile started to grow into a laugh.

"Was it expensive?"

"It's not just a pretty ring ..."

"Gorgeous ring," I interrupted.

"Okay, it's not just a gorgeous ring. It's a very high-quality ring with a big diamond. That and the wedding bands cost close to "$20,000." He shrugged. He shrugged! Like it was no big deal.

I gasped. "I can't wear around "$20,000 on my hand every day. What if I lose it, or get it dirty or something?" I went from staring dumbfounded at Jake to staring at the rings shining there on my finger. I was a little afraid of them.

Jake laughed out loud and pulled me into his arms. "They're insured," he said through the laughter. "It's nice to know you didn't marry me for my money."

"Oh my God, Jake. I had no idea. How much are you talking about?"

"To tell you the truth I'm not exactly sure, but it's millions. I might have built this cabin, but I didn't make all the furniture, the furnace, or granite countertops. I bought them. Out of my ... nope ... out of *our* money. And I bought that truck, too. Dad didn't give it to me. Ali, my dear, you married a rich shifter."

"I figured you built the cabin yourself to save money."

"No. I built it because we're driven to provide for our mates. It had to be done with my own hands."

"That's so sweet." I sighed. "But my Bigfoot's rich? I knew he was handsome, sexy, and the most wonderful man ever, but he's also loaded?"

"Yep," he laughed again. "Oh, and I guess I should tell you that I paid the Pattons for your car loan. They were surprised."

"You paid them? The whole amount?"

"The whole amount. So forget about money. You'll have plenty of time to work when you're done with college. Except for the time you'll take off work to have our babies."

The look he gave me when he said that was unbelievable. So much love in that look. "I know I need to finish school, but I can't wait to have your babies," I sighed as I reached up to kiss him.

* * *

Too soon, it was time for my senior year to start. Part of me didn't want to go because I would miss Jake every day, but the bigger part of me was more than ready to go. I wanted to plunge into that year, make decisions about college, and get on with the rest of my life. Besides, Jake was working, and we'd have each other every evening and every night.

The main office was crowded on that first day with new students getting registered and getting schedules, but I just waited patiently for my turn.

"Hi, Ali. What can I do for you?" the school secretary asked when I finally made it up to her desk. She remembered me from when I enrolled and from all the times I'd come through to see my counselor.

"I need to change my name," I said. She smiled at me, and I realized I'd said those words with a big smile on my face.

"Did the Pattons adopt you?" she asked with a huge smile and expectation on her face. That would have been good news. Everyone knew how great the Pattons were, and not many kids got adopted once they were in high school.

"No," I answered calmly. "I got married a couple weeks ago." She gave me a surprised, concerned look, but that was understandable.

"I'm Ali Shepherd, now," I answered. *And*, I thought to myself, *couldn't be happier.*

Lucy?" He snapped his head back to Doug. "It was a Bigfoot that killed her, wasn't it?"

Doug sighed and dropped his head. "Lucy hadn't met a Bigfoot. She didn't have any idea how to control them. Max tried to explain everything to her, but she got scared and ran out into the woods. The Bigfoot was very young. He didn't intend to kill her, he thought he was playing, but didn't know how to control his strength."

"Playing," Mr. Jones said with disgust. "What did you do with it?"

"He's deep in the forest out west. There're no humans anywhere near him."

"You should have killed him."

"We can't do that."

"And what about your brother, Max? Did he go along to protect that monster?"

"Max loved Lucy," Jake practically shouted.

Doug held out his hand to tell Jake to stay quiet. "If Max had been there when we found them, he would have killed that young one without hesitation. I wouldn't have been able to stop him."

"Then where is he? I haven't seen him since Lucy's funeral."

"Max died awhile ago. Hunting accident. But you need to know that he spent his last years mourning Lucy."

"Fine. Your brother, my sister. All because of a stupid Bigfoot. And you're still protecting them?"

"Any animal is capable of killing," Doug said. "So is any human."

About the Author

    Ellen Fritz is a retired teacher and high school counselor. Over the years of teaching reading and English to students in grades seven through twelve before becoming a counselor, she had the great opportunity to discuss numerous favorite books with students and also took their recommendations for her own reading.

    She finally found herself with the time to give life to the stories that have always been patiently waiting in her head for an audience. "I didn't start writing seriously until I retired and found myself with the time to spend a whole day in front of the computer. The ideas had been in my head for many years but were undeveloped and unexplored. One day, several months after my teaching/counseling career ended, I sat down and started.

Some days, the ideas, dialog, and characters flow from my brain and I can barely type fast enough. Other days, I have to walk away, occupy my mind with something else, and hash through what might happen, what might be said. But both days are valuable.

Tell-Tale Publishing would like to thank you for your purchase. If you would like to read more books by this or another fine TT author, please visit our website:

www.tell-talepublishing.com